CW01501611

Prologue

ZHUANA WAS SADDLING her horse to join the hunt when the steward found her, his face stunned at his own news.

"Your father fell," he said, breathless. "He cracked his skull wide open."

The steward's next words were distant, heard at the bottom of the deepest, darkest hole. For some reason, he was focused on the fact that the chief of the druids had moved the king to one of the grubbiest rooms in the keep, usually set aside for the lowliest guests. But then he fell silent under her stare—the stare of the king's daughter, his only child, his heir.

By the time Zhuana rushed into the ground-floor chamber, her father lay stretched out on his back along the length of a narrow bed. Her footsteps became heavy. Her father's eyes were closed and his breathing came in gasps, each an obvious struggle. She cried out when she saw the bandage around his crown; there was far too much red against the white.

She hurried to his bedside and touched his brow, moving aside hair that was sticky with blood. His dark brown complexion had taken on an ugly pallor. He wasn't an old man, despite the white threads in his beard, but he looked impossibly frail.

"Father, can you hear me? Please, open your eyes." Her vision blurred as she pressed her left hand to her mouth. For a time, she simply stared at the man who had raised her, who had taught her wisdom and was the only family she had. With her free hand, she squeezed his palm, willing him to respond. Miracles were possible. He had always been so strong.

1

Blinking, she lifted her gaze to the man watching her from the other side of the bed. Alric, the chief of the druids, was grim-faced and stood in silence, the only other person in the small chamber. A gaunt man with close-cropped hair, he was clad in the furs that all druids wore. *He's dying!* She screamed at him inside her mind.

But screaming would get her nowhere. Instead, she repeated the druid's lessons to herself. *Stem the flow of blood. Clean the wound. Apply bandages. Warm the body and limbs.* "What else can we do for him?" She heard the ragged emotion in her own voice.

Alric shook his head. "You know I have helped him all I can. His fate is in the Mother's hands. I suggest you say goodbye, Zhuana. Not everyone gets this chance."

"Surely one of your potions—"

"Listen to me." Her teacher's assertive tone was all too familiar. "If there were something that might help, I already would have administered it." His face was hard; she had never seen him so serious. "Time is now moving fast. Your father still breathes, but his heart is slowing. I do not expect him to wake. When he dies—"

"I know enough to know that no one can say for sure—"

"Enough, Zhuana. They will be on their way as we speak—"

"Wait." Hearing something, she put her ear against her father's mouth. At first his words were indistinguishable, the merest hint of whispers. His eyes remained shut, but then she heard a single discernible utterance.

"Survive," her father said softly. She continued to listen, but that was all.

"Father. Father! Can you hear me?" She squeezed his hand again, but wherever he was, it was so deep she couldn't reach him. "He spoke," she said quickly. "Just now."

"Sire? Can you hear me?" Alric peeled back the king's eyelids, before clasping his wrist and then listening to his chest, until he shook his head. His mouth was set in a thin line. "I am sorry, but it doesn't change anything. We have to think about—"

The druid stopped at the sound of loud muffled voices arguing outside the door. The grimy chamber was on the ground floor, with bare stone on one wall, faded wooden panels opposite, and a shuttered and barred window.

The door rattled and crashed open, and a warrior entered the room, a solid, bald man with a zigzag scar on his flat face. Wearing dented armor and a sword in a scabbard, he stopped to stare hard at the king. "Well? Is he dead yet?"

"Show some respect!" Zhuana snapped. "Where is your honor? He is injured but he is still your king."

Alric was also scowling. "The king needs quiet. He hovers between life and death and could do so for several more days. He spoke just a moment ago, and in truth, he may yet recover."

The scar-faced warrior grunted. "Not likely. I've seen my share of dying men." Zhuana felt a chill when he looked at her. He wasn't just registering her presence, he was noting the curved blade she wore at her side. "My vows aren't given to dead men, girl. And I suggest you don't doubt my honor again, or I will teach you something new with that blade."

She narrowed her gaze. "It seems that among other things you also need to listen to your betters. Get out. Now."

He made a show of taking his time, sneering as he turned to Alric. "I want to know the moment he dies. The moment, you hear me? I will be waiting outside."

Alric didn't reply as the man closed the door with a heavy clunk.

Zhuana looked worriedly at Alric. "I know his face. Who is he?"

"He goes by Varden, but his name is unimportant. He will be here on the orders of one of the druadan, and is someone who does not like to announce his master. Your comment about his honor will have rankled."

"But whom is he serving now?"

"You know the druadan. He could be working for Maven Dresk, or someone else altogether." Alric rubbed his jaw, before nodding to himself. "I want you to do something, Zhuana. Go to the door and try to leave. Say whatever you like."

Perplexed, she did as he instructed. She opened the door, and saw not just one man, but five armed warriors standing outside. Two of her father's men were there, but so was the bald, scar-faced warrior, who took a step forward. He didn't stretch out his arms, but he was standing in a manner that wouldn't allow her to make progress.

"Well? It's over? Your father is dead?"

"I need to visit my chambers—"

"Your father is dying and you want to leave?"

Her nostrils flared. "I need to visit my chambers—" she repeated.

"He won't last long. Believe me. I suggest you wait for the end. You don't want to regret it, girl." With his chin, he indicated she return inside.

Her father's two guards stood uncertainly. Noticing her attention, the scar-faced warrior turned. "She should remain with her dying father. You would agree, yes?" When they didn't step forward to support her, she swallowed her fear as she closed the door and returned inside.

Alric raised his eyebrow. "Well?"

"I don't understand. What is happening?"

"Plots, Zhuana. Change is in the air. Maven Dresk and the other druadan will know by now, and will be on their way to the keep. Other men like Varden will be gathering in the city, telling everyone they can that Veldria needs a strong leader. Who among them wants a seventeen-year-old girl as queen? As for me, the last words I heard from your father's lips were to ask for my help—my help with you. Both the druadan and the druids will take my guidance. But if you are dead... what use is my loyalty then?"

Alric stopped when the door opened again, this time just a crack. A different face appeared, one of Alric's druids, a young man also in furs.

"Elder Alric, Maven Dresk has arrived at the keep. Do you still want to know when the other druadan come?"

"I do. Thank you. Now close the door. Quickly." The moment the door closed, Alric returned to Zhuana. "We were discussing the man outside. His instructions will be to hold you here for safekeeping. With your father dying, he thinks you are going nowhere, although he doesn't like your reputation as someone unafraid of a fight."

Zhuana's hand instinctively went to the hilt of her hunting blade. Years with a bow had hardened her fingers and her hands were calloused from sword practice out in the yard. She was lean, with muscles taut from riding and running down deer. "He is right. I am going nowhere. And if he touches me, I will kill him."

"Zhuana!" Alric said sharply. "Use your head. Your father is going to die."

"He spoke just a moment ago—"

"I am the chief of the druids. I know my business."

"You said he may last several days. He may even recover—"

"I lied to buy us time. There is a reason I selected this room rather than another when I saw your father's injury." Alric hurried to the dirty wood-paneled wall and reached out to touch a particular place, pressing a catch to open a panel that swung open wide like a door. "This door leads to a tunnel—"

Despite her surprise, Zhuana shook her head. "No. I will not leave my father."

"What did he say to you just now?"

She hesitated. "Survive."

"Even now, he understands, even if you appear not to."

"No one is going to lay a hand on me."

Alric scowled. "Your stubbornness can be a strength but also a weakness. Bravery must be tempered with wisdom. These are lessons I have tried to teach you. There is a time to fight and a time to flee. It takes courage to know the difference. Open your eyes, Zhuana. There is no valor in staying to fight a hopeless cause, to die when you might endure. Life has many things to teach us, but this is one of the most important."

4

Zhuana fixed her gaze on her father; of all times to leave him, she couldn't abandon him now. She could see his chest rising and falling, although he was more gray than before.

"I know you love your father, and it is to the Mother's Glade that we will bring his body to rest in the ground. At the moment, the wind is shifting—our king is going to fall. But the Mother's Glade is sacred. No one dares spill blood within its circle. Go there now. They will wait to see what will happen next. Some will expect you to call up your loyal followers, of which there are many, to remind them of their oaths, and if necessary, to draw swords and fight for what is yours. Then they will come to understand that your father is gone, but you are still alive. Your father will be buried. You will be crowned. Nobody has to die."

"Surely our enemies have shown their colors, and they will still be alive—"

"If your enemy is indeed Maven Dresk, when some time has passed, make him a member of your council. Lives will be saved by this action. You will show them what you are. A survivor. This is the course of wisdom. Nothing attracts loyalty so much as wisdom. Now go."

Zhuana's muscles were tensed and her jaw was tight. She wanted to fight; anything was better than fleeing.

But Alric wouldn't look away. And deep down, she knew her old teacher was right.

She bent to say a last goodbye to her father. She kissed his forehead, his cheek, and whispered in his ear that she loved him. He gave no visible reaction other than to release a long sighing breath.

"You know the forest. Use your skills and they will never find you."

"But what about you—?"

"I am the chief of the druids. They will never harm me. You know that."

"Thank you for your loyalty—"

"Thank me when you have survived." Heavy footsteps sounded outside. "Now go. Go!"

After one last glance at her father, Zhuana headed to the paneled wall. She squeezed Alric's arm and then entered the passage to make her escape.

Chapter One

AFTER A DARK age came a flourishing, a time of rebirth such as the world had never seen, and at its heart was the great dominion that came to be called the Eternal Empire.

Its official name was the Dymantine Empire, named after Dymantus, the nation that conquered and cajoled, traded and treated its way to supreme status among its neighbors. Size led to ever greater size, until no one could stand in its way, and ever more distant territories joined in the noble effort.

There were even some people – those who rarely left the capital – who said that civilization came to an end outside the empire's border. Many knew otherwise: the diviners, the traveling merchants, and the soldiers fighting distant wars. But all could agree about the empire's scale, its reach, its history and artistic achievements… its role in keeping peace between a multitude of disparate regions, each with a unique culture and way of approaching the world.

After three centuries of growth, people began to call it the Eternal Empire, and everyone knew it would last for another twenty centuries… another thirty.

Forever.

It was then that Emperor Polonius changed the capital's name to Everlast, signifying the empire's commitment to endurance through the ages. There were other great cities, but none could rival Everlast, a city of eleven million inhabitants that felt like the center of the world, and a place that never stopped moving, never stopped growing, and thrived on conflict as much as accord.

In the empire's seventh century, it was high summer in Everlast, with colorful flowers in the parks and gardens, ice clinking in the goblets of the wealthy, and the common folk wiping sweat from their brows, when bells began to peal in unison.

No matter where they were in the city, the bells were perfectly synchronized. Some bells clanged from pointed spires in lofty cathedrals. Others counted the hour from village temples in Everlast's outskirts. Clerks in merchant houses heard the bells and scowled at empty spaces where goods had yet to arrive. Laborers rushed into workshops and slowed in relief, throwing guilty glances at their overseers. In the Great Canal, long barges drifted from their moorings as the peals announced it was time for the vessels to depart.

As clangs bounced from hill to hill, craftsmen and shopkeepers quickened their footsteps as they passed grand facades, the jangling telling them they needed to hurry. Within the decorated buildings, lords and ladies soaked in hot baths, feasted on lavish breakfasts, or groaned in bed and put their arms over their heads, rueing the day they ever tasted wine. It wasn't always easy, keeping up with one's friends.

Approaching Everlast's inner districts, where the streets were narrow and buildings crowded close together, the markets were hives of activity, where hawkers and city folk browsed goods and barely noticed the tolling at all. After all, more bells would sound in just another hour.

In the Corpus District, the collection of buildings that included the University, the Observatory, and half a dozen different temples, the bells signified the start of the workday for a great number of administrators and confessors, clerics and diviners. Souls needed saving. People needed healing. Gateways needed to be traveled.

Reaching Everlast's center, where the Argent Arch stood at one end of Imperial Avenue and faced the Nexus at the other end, the bells coincided with a great number of arrivals, who headed toward the Nexus to attend to important business. A great square edifice, the size of a town, with tall walls and corner towers, the Nexus was home to the Emperor as well as the Marble Court, where the Assembly of Nobles met and argued over the empire's future.

The sound of bells arrived at the Fabric District, where a young woman with copper skin and long auburn hair waited outside the House of Healing.

At first Bethany had been nervous. Now, as she heard the bells announcing the time, the clangs sounded in their own space, making her stomach give jarring little jumps along with them. Whenever someone walked by, her head moved quickly and her eyes focused on the person, before she moved on and searched for the next passerby to come close.

Behind her, the House of Healing's door was closed and the shutters were drawn. A sign near the door announced the House of Healing's name, along with an image of an open hand. The hand was the symbol of the Great Weaver, in her guise as the goddess of health and healing, and by association, the symbol of the clerics who worked inside.

The last bells faded away. As Bethany instead heard the familiar bustle from the nearby market, she paced back and forth in front of the row of closed shutters. The Fabric District wasn't as busy as some of the other quarters in Everlast, but it was busy enough, and in a city with so many people, she kept turning her head one way and then another.

A woman came over, careworn and middle-aged, carrying a small child in her arms. "Are you looking for a cleric? They don't open here on seventh days, but there is another in Night Garden Square."

Bethany shook her head. "I'm meeting someone here."

The baby gurgled. The woman shrugged and bobbed the child up and down as she left. Bethany's eyes continued to dart from person to person, boy to old man, dusty worker to busy trader. She focused on face after face, searching in hope that was always fruitless. Meanwhile, as she walked a short distance and turned on her heel, her thumb traveled over her calloused fingers—an old habit. She rubbed at her eyes. She was tired, as was often the case after working half the night with needle and thread. At the same time, her pacing was getting faster.

White clothing drew her attention. An older man in a pale tunic stood facing a distant market stall. Her breath caught, but then she released a sigh. No, the man at the market was too tall and too thin; he wasn't the man she was waiting for.

Still the minutes kept passing.

Time moved in strange jumps. Another round of pealing bells made her stomach churn, announcing the passage of another hour. Her jaw was sore from clenching. If she had acted on the first set of bells, she would have been early. Now she was definitely out of time.

He had promised to be here – he gave her his word – and he had never failed her before. Where was he? What should she do?

Should she just go? She knew the answer. She had already waited too long. But she was late, and if she went without him she would be on her own. Exposed. Defenseless.

He would come. He had to come.

A dark voice whispered in her mind. Maybe she should just give up. The decision had been taken out of her hands. She should just go to her shop and open it up like any other day.

She lifted her head to look farther down the street and could just make out the sun-bleached awning from her position. It was well past opening hours. As it was, her mother would kill her if she found out she had left the shop closed and customers heading somewhere else.

She could picture the shop's interior: the front counter, the chairs for waiting, the hanging frames draped with clothing. She knew every crack of the uneven paving stones that made up the floor. She heard the cooing doves in her dreams. Every morning, she went there at the same time, a satchel on her shoulder full of needles and scissors and fabric, her mother's finished projects draped over her other shoulder.

Tearing her eyes from her shopfront, she instead looked at her shaking hands, and then bunched them into fists. How many pieces of paper had she issued? How many garments had she carried between the shop and her compound, to the small dormus she lived in with her mother?

She couldn't give up now. No. This was happening. Tomorrow morning she might be back at her shop again, but at least she would have tried. After today, either her life would continue as it was or everything would change forever.

The bells had stopped ringing. Time was slipping away.

She had to make a choice. She couldn't wait forever. She would wait until the count of twenty, and then she would go without him.

If she didn't go, she would lose her opportunity. It would be gone. Taken from her.

This was her chance to become what she had always dreamed of.

A diviner.

She began to count. *One. Two. Three.*

At the same time, even as she counted, she recalled the events of one fateful day.

✦

The celebrations to mark a decade in the reign of Emperor Rigel Regus Livius were unlike anything seen before. Flags crowned every tower of the twelve inner districts. Banners in purple and gold decorated the streets. Placards announced music and revelry, feasting and dancing.

As the day began, it felt like half of the city was heading to Imperial Avenue, the main colonnade that stretched from the broad gates of the Nexus to the Argent Arch, where the people would have an opportunity to witness the greatest spectacle of all. There would be a chance to see the emperor himself, along with his Imperial guardsmen, the strongest of his personal soldiers. Lords and ladies would file past, dressed in their finery, waving and smiling at the onlookers. Finally all eyes would turn toward the arch on its hill, ready to witness a stunning demonstration of Imperial reach.

It was a warm day in spring, with a cloudless blue sky overhead. As increasing numbers of people arrived to take positions on either side of the colonnade, Imperial Avenue itself remained fenced off and empty.

Bethany was ten years old. Her mother had warned her, but she was beginning to feel overwhelmed, not just by being out in central Everlast on her own, but by the sheer number of people. Old and young, rich and poor, stout and skinny, they all gathered together until their numbers became pressing and her chest began to tighten. Still they kept coming, and more people brought more heat, until even her thin clothing felt too heavy.

The little hill she had found early in the day had seemed like a good place, but she had never imagined such a pressing crowd of people. Soon, the taller people around her filled her vision. Her head was tilted back, seeing heads and faces, all facing the same direction, but she couldn't see what they could. She was too surrounded. It was becoming hard to breathe.

She needed to move. But where could she go? Putting her back to Imperial Avenue, she looked one way and then another. All she could see was bigger people and blue sky above them. To begin with, she had to get away from where she was.

Picking a direction, she began to push her way through the crowd, turning sideways when she had to and ignoring the grunts of annoyance. Shuffling past the men and women, she smelled sweat and the occasional whiff of spicy hair oil or a woman's perfume. The array of clothing was beyond anything she had seen before, even in the Fabric District. She pushed past billowing skirts, leather aprons, loose tunics, and tight jerkins. There were other children too, usually held up by their elders or seated on their father's shoulders. In front of her, two fat men shuffled, parting for a moment to open a space between them. For a moment she had a clear view.

And there it was, the solution she had been looking for. High above the crowd stood a gigantic stone statue of a man on a horse, holding a sword to the sky. If she climbed up, she would have an unrivaled view and be free from the press of the crowd.

Her only asset was her size, and so she put her head down to navigate toward the statue. It took time, but as big as the statue was, she was clearly getting closer. But when she was halfway to her destination, the crowd shifted and knocked her to the side. She heard a great roar, but from her position she couldn't make out what was happening.

"Girl." A towering man with curly hair and a kind face bent down and touched her on the shoulder. "The emperor is going past. Do you want me to hold you up so you can see?"

Bethany shook her head; the cheering of the crowd was so loud that talking was pointless. The curly-haired man shrugged and resumed watching the parade, easily looking straight over the tops of the heads in front of him. Bethany returned to making her way past the arms and legs and torsos of all the people trying to get a glimpse.

The emperor wasn't what she had come for. She didn't need to see him. She already knew what he looked like more than well enough.

She slid her way through the city folk, even as they cried and bellowed and she heard the rolling cheers. She occasionally glanced up to keep her path fixed on the statue that she was heading for. But when she was nearly at the statue's pedestal, which appeared as a cube-shaped block made of four tall sloping walls, she heard a woman's excited voice:

"It's happening. The diviners are coming."

It was then that Bethany became desperate.

Moving her head, she searched for someone who might be friendly like the man who had offered to hold her high. But the people were busy, jostling each other for their own view. Even the statue was now missing; a stocky woman was blocking her way. Bethany turned to slide past the woman's wide figure, even as the crowd ebbed and flowed, but she wasn't about to give up. She had come here early and found a good position, before realizing that the number of arrivals made it one of the worst sites she could have picked. She was going to make up for her mistake

The crowd moved again, and there was the statue, visible through a gap between the people .

Even as she pushed through to the statue's pedestal, something was definitely happening from the reaction of the crowd. Her small hands found gaps in between the stones; she pulled herself up, and then her feet found footholds. She kicked her legs and pulled herself higher... grunting and climbing a stretch without stopping. She gasped as her foot slipped, before finding a place again. The top of the pedestal was just above her. She grabbed hold of a horse's stone hoof, gritted her teeth, and pulled herself up, scrabbling to throw her body over the edge, until she was up on top of the stone.

And then she was on her feet, holding onto the statue for support, with her hand on the back of a horse's leg. She faced Imperial Avenue, and when she looked out, her spirits soared as she took in her new view.

The Argent Arch was perfectly revealed, past the sea of people between them. The immense span of marble and granite was wide enough for fifty men to walk abreast, taller than its breadth, and glistened in the sun's rays so that the marble appeared to take on a silver sheen. A paved area surrounded the arch, like a stage that was the focus of all the onlookers. From the hill, a road traveled down and eventually widened to become Imperial Avenue. Watching now, Bethany saw the emperor on horseback, waiting in front of his guardsmen as he gazed up at the void that the arch enclosed.

Angular symbols decorated the arch, carved into the stone, some of them crisp, others worn away until it was clear that some parts were missing. The symbols reminded Bethany that Dymantines didn't build the arch, nor any of the other gateways. The Argent Arch was here when the first Dymantines came from across the sea, more than seven centuries ago. The gateways were different... otherworldly... made by mysterious hands.

Bethany was utterly focused as she watched. At first, she saw nothing. Then something sparked on the arch's surface and a blue line, a flame as thin as thread, coiled around the arch, traveling from one end to the other and back again. She gasped along with the onlookers and guessed this must be what had excited the crowd earlier. A tense, expectant atmosphere now held the crowd in its grip. The stirring began to die down. Everyone seemed to decide that whatever place they had found, it would have to do.

A bright flash appeared inside the Argent Arch, at waist height above the ground, in the center of its two supports. This time, the light didn't dissipate; it grew. The light became a diagonal line, a tear in the air itself. A moment later the tear separated, turning and widening, peeling apart like a slash in the skin of a piece of fruit. Rainbow colors flickered and danced.

The slash became vertical, widening further until the two sides drew apart, creating a rectangular opening, a black void the size of a large doorway. The doorway was slick and shining, like a perfectly dark mirror.

A man stepped out from the doorway.

He wore a gray cloak on his shoulders, along with white trousers and a red tunic decorated in shimmering silver stars: the striking costume of a diviner. Middle-aged, with a pointed beard on his sharp chin, he had a smile for the crowd as he moved until he was no longer under the arch. In one hand, he held a wooden staff capped with a spherical orb. His other hand held a huge, oversized golden chalice.

The black doorway vanished after the diviner emerged, and then he held his chalice high. With theatrical flair, he upended the chalice, turning at the same time so that its contents spilled in an arc over the ground in front of him. The stuff was white and soft, almost like a powder. Bethany was enthralled. She knew what the substance was, but she had never seen it with her own eyes.

"Snow!" the diviner cried in a loud voice for all to hear. "From distant Kargul!"

As the crowd gave a collective gasp, the diviner stepped to the side, just as another crease of light appeared in the area covered by the Argent Arch. The light turned and peeled open, widening to create a black doorway, and this time it was a woman who emerged. The gateway closed, and Bethany saw that she held another chalice, this time made of stone. Whatever was in the bowl, smoke climbed up from it, thick and billowing. Like the previous diviner, she wore a gray cloak and held a tall staff, although in her case, a crescent moon decorated her sky-blue dress. Her actions were just as performative.

"Volcanic rock!" she cried. "From far Ganouda!"

While she spoke, she tossed the contents of the chalice so that glowing black rock scattered over the paved area where she was standing. Each fragment smoked and smoldered while the crowd gave another awestruck exclamation. The diviner bowed and moved away to join her colleague.

Next was another man, holding a glass bowl. He held it up to display the contents rather than spill them. "A blind razor fish, from the deep caves of Talon!"

Another woman followed, stepping from the gateway with a caged bird. The plumage was a garish blend of bright colors, and the bird's trills were so high pitched they carried over the crowd. "A newborn galeon, from the isle of Korandia!"

The display continued, as the diviners demonstrated the breadth of the empire, its diversity of environments, and its role as custodian of the gateways. Bethany saw exotic animals, plants, and foods. Every mineral, every strange creature, and every liquid, had been brought to Everlast's primary gateway straight from the place that each diviner named to the crowd.

Bethany watched stunned.

Nothing was ever the same for her again.

Chapter Two

Ten. Eleven. Twelve.

Bethany stood tensed, poised, even as she searched the street. She should have left when the earlier bells pealed. That would have given her plenty of time.

Where was he?

All she knew was that he wasn't coming.

Was he in trouble? Perhaps he was hurt? He wasn't as young as he had been when they first met. How long ago was that? Nine years? It felt like such a long time ago, and yet at the same time she knew that she had done so little, and was still so far from her goal.

When she met him, she was just ten, and bursting with excitement after what she had seen at the emperor's celebration.

✦

There was often a morning queue at Bethany's shop, and as usual she worked through each customer in turn. As doves cooed in the rafters and several men and women waited patiently, she issued tickets and quoted prices.

After a prim lady left, Bethany finished writing a few notes on her copy of the ticket. The woman's instructions had been detailed, and this was a part of her process, so that her mother would see the notes when she brought the burgundy dress home at the end of the day.

She was absorbed in her task. And so, when she lifted her gaze from the counter to look at her next customer, she was shocked to find herself staring at a diviner.

He was an older man, tall and imposing, and wore a diviner's gray cloak on his shoulders. The rest of his clothing was dark blue, more somber than most diviners, with a trio of silver stars on his breast. He had a long face of dominating features: sharp chin, high cheekbones, sloping nose. A fringe of gray hair encircled the bald circle on top of his head.

"May I help you?" she asked, speaking a little too quickly. Diviners were often addressed by title, but she had never met one in person. "May I help you, Diviner, I meant to say." She bit her tongue; she shouldn't have corrected herself; it was already too late.

Behind the diviner, a cleric in white clothing was next in line, watching and hiding a smile.

"I overheard you talking just now," the diviner said curtly. "Your mother does the stitching, is that correct?"

"It is."

"I have been told she has some skill..." The diviner's mouth twisted; he seemed reluctant. "But this is about more than just a steady hand."

He reached into a bag and then spread a length of black fabric out on the counter. Bethany inspected the material; the fabric had an expensive weave, most likely a kind of sateen. A handful of embroidered white stars decorated the surface, making up part of a constellation; the work was still unfinished.

"The woman working on this banner has worked with us for a long time—long enough to work from memory, however she has just fallen down some stairs." Noticing her reaction, he waved a hand. "She will live, but I now have a problem." He stabbed the banner with his finger. "This must be ready for tomorrow." He stopped speaking, shaking his head to mutter to himself. "How can I even communicate it to you?" He took a breath. "This is the constellation Melita. I need the banner finished, but the stars all have precise positions—"

Bethany was already examining the banner and the finished stars. Touching each in turn, she named them one by one. "Alkana. Parak. Ternika." Her fingers now moved to the empty, unfinished area. "Kalinka. Jaimon. Garam."

The diviner raised an eyebrow. "You know the names?" He harrumphed. "But it is the positions that concern—"

Bethany interrupted. "Alkana is the root star." She pointed and then moved to the next. "Parak is twelve radians from Alkana." Her finger moved again. "Ternika is fourteen radians south and six east. Kalinka is seven radians south." She met the diviner's gaze. "I can do this."

The diviner's frown deepened. "How do you know about the stars?" He cleared his throat. "It does not matter. Your mother is the seamstress. It is best that I explain it to her. Where is she?"

"She works at our dormus. I can't leave the shop to fetch her." She indicated the material. "Diviner, please. I know the stars. I can help my mother get the positions exactly as they should be."

He hesitated but then shook his head. "I am afraid that this is too important, girl. Are you even in academy school? Wait. Of course not. If you were, you would be in class right now. What does your father do?"

The mention of Bethany's father made her hide a scowl. Never think about him, her mother always said. Never want anything from him, and never accept anything if he were to offer it.

"I like the stars," she said, rather than answer the diviner's question about her father. She sounded foolish, even to her own ears. She had to explain so he could understand. "I read about them every day. The knowledge is there, in the Imperial Library, if you look for it." She attempted a smile. "You will just have to trust me." Without waiting for his reply, she began to write out the ticket.

The diviner grabbed her wrist to halt her writing. "You have quite a manner for a girl your age. A diviner's work is not some child's game. The night sky is the domain of the corpus. I suggest you find a more appropriate interest to occupy yourself with."

She tore her hand free. Her cheeks felt hot. "My mother once told me that the stars belong to everyone."

With a scowl, the diviner ripped the ticket from her book. In one swift movement, he squeezed the paper into a ball, and then he let it go. "Your mother was recommended to me, but I believe I will find another seamstress." His nostrils flared. "Pity," he said, as if his decision were her fault.

The diviner turned and left, while Bethany remained behind her counter, glaring at the gray cloak on the tall man's departing back. Her dream was just a tiny sprouting seed, and it was a seed that was already withering. In his life he would learn about things she would never know. He would travel all over the empire, in and out of gateways. He would see incredible sights and come to know strange and unique peoples, traveling a thousand miles in a heartbeat.

She shook herself; there was someone standing in front of her: the cleric in white clothing who was next in line after the diviner. He was an unassuming man with a careworn expression. The creases of his face were smile lines, and she remembered his mirth when she first addressed the diviner. He appeared to be in his late fifties, with bright blue eyes and disheveled, graying hair.

"Good day, young lady," the cleric said. His tone was gentle; after all, he was a healer, working with the sick and injured. "I need this tunic fixed." He gave a rueful smile. "As you can see, I should probably enjoy fewer honey cakes. See? This is where I split it down the side."

With a last glance toward the doorway, she inspected the garment. "How soon do you need it?"

"Next midweek?"

She nodded. "It will be twenty copper rings."

"Yes, yes. That will be fine." He smiled down at her as she wrote up the ticket. "You have an interest in the stars, do you?"

She tore off the paper. "Here is your ticket," she said without replying.

The cleric tilted his head, but he didn't press her further. "Very well. Thank you."

He was a senior cleric, from the gold trim on his collar. As he reached for the ticket, she noticed the shining silver band on his finger. The glistening silver chain around his neck looked even more expensive.

The cleric took the ticket but paused. "There is one thing that puzzles me... How did you gain access to the Imperial Library?"

As she remembered what she had said to the diviner, a gnawing dread sank into her stomach. Her mouth dropped open. She might be about to get into a great deal of trouble.

But strangely, the cleric held out his hands. "Ahh," he soothed. He glanced over his shoulder; no one could hear them. "I am not about to share your secret, young lady. It is an old building, with many ancient passages. And as for the diviner, I doubt he remembers a word you said."

Her brow furrowed, deepening into a scowl. "I haven't been sneaking in. I pay one of the workers to let me borrow the books. I take care of them and I always give them back."

The cleric smiled, and his voice became even softer. "That sounds wonderful. The books should be for everyone, if you ask me."

"You have your ticket, sir." She rapped her fingers on the counter, hoping he would leave.

And he did.

But then, later that day, he came back when she was closing her shop. She was alone, gathering garments together, with early evening light seeping through the windows. This time, as he bumped the door open with his body, he had a stack of books in his arms, high enough to struggle with. He set his stack down on the counter. Pleased with himself, he beamed.

"I always liked the stars too, but it has been a long time since I studied them. These are for you."

She stared at him in surprise. But her mother had always warned her: everything came with a price. "No. Please. Take them back."

"I am not after your money, nor anything else." He regarded her with his warm, slightly amused expression. "A cleric always has too little time for leisure. I work at the House of Healing on Dyer Street," he turned and nodded, "just over there. Are these the kind of books you read? If you like them, I have more."

She couldn't help it; she scanned the pile of books, and then she saw it: *The Diviner's Compendium*. She had read about it but never found it. She wanted it. It was right in front of her. If she took it home, she could be reading it in no time at all.

She hesitated, mouth open and closing. The cleric didn't know her; he didn't even know her name. Books were valuable. She didn't want to owe him a debt. Perhaps she could pay him for just the one book? But how she would do it? She didn't have the money to buy it. His silver ring was worth more than her mother earned in a year.

He noticed her attention. "You're interested in this?" He held out his hand so she could see the silver band. "This is my wedding ring. My wife chose it. And this..." He lifted the chain around his neck to reveal a hanging locket. "This contains a lock of my daughter's hair." He showed her the oval-shaped locket, before letting it fall. "I treasure both items, and so I wear them every day." He smiled. "I even talk out loud, when no one else is around. I find it helps sometimes, to pretend that they are still with me."

The pieces fit; with his messy hair, he didn't seem the type to show off his wealth. And then the rest of what he had said sank in. "I don't understand. What happened to them?"

"The sweating sickness. It struck hard and took them both. I did my best but it wasn't enough. It's been a long time now but I still miss them." He shook his shoulders, as if casting off a weight. "Ho hum. I must be going. I hope you enjoy the books."

The cleric left before she could say anything else.

But their relationship was only beginning.

A week later, she went to the House of Healing on Dyer Street, carrying a bag on her shoulder filled with the books she planned to return. After entering, she glanced around the white-walled interior, looking past the people waiting patiently on benches, until she saw a short-haired woman at a desk, wearing a white smock.

Bethany approached, lugging her bag. "I have something here for the cleric. Sorry... I don't know his name..."

The woman leveled her with a smile. "You must mean Charlton."

Bethany made a sound of surprise; she had just been given someone's first name. "Is that his name?"

The woman's smile grew. "Oh, he's different. Everyone uses his first name."

The door at the back of the room opened, and the gray-haired cleric came out, before stopping in his tracks when he saw her.

"Young lady here looking for you," the woman at the desk said, nodding in Bethany's direction.

"I have your books," Bethany said, hoisting the bag.

The cleric – Charlton – glanced at the bag and then back at her. His blue eyes crinkled with mirth. "Was I not clear, young lady? They were always for you to keep."

For a moment she couldn't speak. "To keep? But why? I don't think I understand."

His smile broadened. "Yes, I think you do."

She stood frozen in place. Something was happening in her chest; her heart was swelling up inside her. It was a warm, but strangely nervous feeling. "You're giving them to me as a gift?"

"Well..." he trailed off, his expression becoming pensive. "I do want something from you." He then smiled again. "Your name."

The people sitting on the benches watched back and forth, evidently enjoying the exchange.

"Oh." She cleared her throat. "Bethany."

"My name is Charlton. Last name Balforth. But everyone calls me Charlton." He paused, and then tilted his head, waiting.

He wanted to know her last name. "Sylvana," she said, even as she knew to expect a reaction.

"Ahh... Bethany Sylvana... I thought you had the look of the Far Reaches. Let me guess. Betani?" He pronounced her name the way her mother said it.

"Mother chose the closest Dymantine name to something from where she... from where we come from."

"Darian?"

"Loriastris."

"Ah yes. That copper skin. The auburn hair. Loriastris." Charlton nodded. "You grew up here, though." He said it as a statement, and she nodded. "You have a lovely name, Bethany Sylvana."

The short-haired woman in white came over and put her hands on her hips. "Charlton..." she said disapprovingly.

"Ah, listen to me. I do tend to talk too much. I have my work to return to. However, Bethany, I usually close up before you. When I am done for the day, I can come and drop some more books off at your shop, if that is all right with you?"

Without waiting for an answer, he bustled off, so that when she replied, she spoke more to herself than to him.

"That would be wonderful," she said softly.

Somehow, miraculously, she appeared to have made a new friend.

✦

Nineteen. Twenty.

Bethany finished counting. It was well past time to go. She was going to have to do this alone.

After one last scan of the street, she put on speed to leave the House of Healing behind. She hurried toward the corner, which she would have to turn to reach the main avenue. But she was moving so fast that she was unable to avoid a collision with an older man dressed in white. The first thing she saw was a startled expression, along with scruffy gray hair and bright blue eyes. He put out his hands to catch her, even as she cried out and skidded to a halt.

"Charlton," she said, panting hard.

Sweat beaded on Charlton's forehead and rust-colored stains tarnished his uniform. He spoke quickly, "I wasn't sure if you would still be here. You do realize the time? I'm sorry. An emergency." He waved a hand. "It doesn't matter. We're late. We have to hurry." He squeezed her hands. "Well, where is she?" He looked around. "Why isn't she here?" His mouth dropped open. "Stars alive, Bethany, please tell me you told your mother?"

"I couldn't..." How could she explain to Charlton that her mother didn't even know about her dream?

"Well, it's already past nine bells. There's no time now." He shook his head. "Oh, Bethany. If you are disappointed, she will not even know that you are upset, let alone why, because you never told her in the first place." He met her gaze, in the disconcertingly kind way he had. "And, my dear... what if you make it through?"

He squeezed her hands again. "It doesn't matter. Whatever you are feeling, let it become energy. Channel it in the right direction." He smiled encouragingly, although her echoing smile was weak. "Excited?"

"Terrified," she said.

"Remember. You create your own opportunities, my dear. Today is no different." He tugged on her hand to get her moving. "Now, quick. We don't have long at all."

Chapter Three

SOUTH IMPERIAL GARDENS was one of Everlast's biggest parks, which on a day when she was already late, wasn't working in Bethany's favor. She and Charlton ran together along the wide path that bordered the park, while farther inside, trails curled like ribbons as they divided the neatly trimmed fields of green grass. Near the manicured gardens, people sat alone or in groups under the shade of the evergreens. Ducks and geese fought each other by the banks of a small pond.

A side access gate was the nearest entrance to their destination: Speaker's Corner, a section of parkland guarded by a tall fence. Bethany rushed up to the gate, but it wasn't just closed, it was locked, with a chain that rattled when she shook it. Through the bars, in the distance, a number of stone benches descended in tiers to a sunken circle, all surrounded by a screen of conifers. She couldn't make out detail, but people were moving about, a great many of them.

Speaker's Corner was so close, and yet the gate was firmly fastened. They were too late; the event had already started.

Shielding his gaze, Charlton spied a figure in a black and white uniform: an official from the corpus, a man with mournful eyes. Charlton called out and waved.

"Hello! Over here!" He kept shouting until the official heard them and stared. Heedless of the attention he drew, Charlton kept bellowing and shaking the gate until, with a scowl, the official finally came over.

"Quick. Open this gate," Charlton said.

"Sorry," the sad-faced man said, although his tone wasn't apologetic at all. "Special event today."

"We are aware of that," Charlton said. He nodded at Bethany. "She is one of the candidates, Bethany Sylvana."

The uniformed official inspected Bethany, and she knew what he was seeing. Plain, simple clothing. Copper skin. Copper hair. His expression was dubious.

"Come on!" Charlton shook the gate again. "Open up!"

The official finally took note of Charlton's gold-trimmed collar; Charlton was a senior cleric, and in the end that was enough to convince him. Taking a key from his belt, he opened the lock and pulled the gate open. "You'd better hurry."

Charlton grabbed Bethany's hand and together they raced inside. Half-walking, half-running, they made their way together toward the hollow where the stone benches were already full of people. A few curious faces turned their way, but the onlookers returned their attention to the long platform at the bottom of the tiers; a spectacle was about to begin, and the crowd had come to watch.

Charlton led Bethany down to the first row, passing several benches on the way. The area at the front appeared to be reserved for family members and a few spaces were still available.

The focus of all attention, the platform, was raised up to waist height, with a short flight of steps in the middle. Built like a stage, it was constructed wide enough to have room for a row of small tables, dozens of them, with each table displaying a large clock on its surface. At the very back, a tower displayed a central clock in clear view of the crowd. The director of proceedings was a stern, white-haired woman in a starry golden dress and gray cloak, standing at a podium where she addressed both crowd and candidates.

The director was in the middle of calling names.

"Kyle Preston," she announced in a loud, clear voice.

A young man with a pinched face and oversized front teeth climbed the stairs to the platform and moved to stand beside one of the clocks. Nearly a third of the clocks had someone in front of them, with all of the candidates around Bethany's age. Bethany and Charlton stood within a milling group in front of the platform, where the other candidates were also waiting.

Bethany tried to slow her breathing. Her face was red from racing to Speaker's Corner and sweat coated her hands and forehead. Had they already called her name? There were no gaps in the clocks that had someone in front of them, so she began to hope that her name had yet to be called. She had to steady herself. There was no use rehearsing—there was simply too much to know.

Her only comfort was that no one could know the names of all the stars in the sky. They would only ask about the major constellations, and about their peculiarities and behaviors.

The planets. The moon. The sun.

Hours. Minutes. Seconds.

Important places in the empire: towns, cities, rivers, lakes, mountains, geological formations, coastal features, seas, islands...

The location of gateways. Distances.

"Carina Mallow," the director called.

An athletic young woman with blonde hair and freckles climbed up the platform and took a place at the next vacant clock. Bethany met a lot of people in the Fabric District, and guessed she might be from the Northern Provinces. As the director continued, however, most of the names and faces appeared to be have their origins in the Inner Territories: Weiland, Sharm, Umber, Turel, Klare, Trent, Greve, and Dymantus itself... Soon, almost all of the clocks had candidates in front of them.

"Xander Cole." Another name from the Inner Territories, possibly Turel or Dymantus. He was a tall young man, well-groomed, with sharp features and the hint of black stubble on his cheeks.

"Bethany Sylvana."

Charlton gave her an encouraging smile. "That's you. Go on. Remember, Bethany: you can do this."

With a final deep breath, Bethany headed up to the platform, focused on the vacant clock next to the handsome young man with black hair. Still feeling the urge to move quickly, she made a little skip as she reached the steps.

Pain flared in her foot. An instant later, she was falling until she lay sprawled face down on the wooden platform, her wrists only catching under her head at the last moment. Rather than laughter, she heard only silence.

Then she saw a pair of expensive-looking leather shoes. The young man, her neighbor, held out a hand. "Are you hurt?"

She took his hand, allowing him to help her to her feet. She straightened, and as she did, her eyes met his.

His eyes were startling: brown in color, flecked with gold. He had paler skin than her copper shade, along with wavier black hair that curled to his collar. He had a sharp chin and wide mouth, currently displayed in a crooked smile. His shoulders were broad, matching his height.

A few moments passed and still she hadn't replied.

"I'm fine," she said quickly, dusting herself off.

"Are you sure?" His expression shifted, from concerned to amused. "People often say they are fine when they are not."

She only nodded as she moved to stand in front of her own clock and tug at her clothing. She glanced again at the young man. The director had given his name: Xander Cole. Standing in front of his own clock, he looked back at her, and the slight smile he returned was still lopsided.

As the director at the podium continued calling names, Bethany had a short time to get accustomed to her surroundings. Looking around, she started. On the other side of her clock, partially hidden from view but just a few feet away, was a man in a chair. The clocks were fashioned so that they had two faces, with twin sets of hands, one looking toward the crowd and the other facing the other way. The man was located where he could watch from the other side, able to judge any movement she made to the hands in front. A sheet of paper lay on a wooden board on the man's lap.

She quickly turned away. She then cast her eyes over the other candidates. It was the same for all of them: each candidate had a man or woman sitting on their clock's other side, waiting patiently, and all of them were diviners.

They had to be assessors. And her assessor's dark eyes were particularly focused on her. While the director called names, she tried not to make contact with the diviner's intense stare. The best thing she could do was ignore him. She tripped. It happened. People fell all the time.

There were few places to look, however, so she decided to study her clock. The device was unremarkable, with two arms, one long, the other short. Inadvertently, she again glanced at the assessor sitting on his chair and watching her. His penetrating eyes bored into her.

No. It couldn't be.

He was a tall man with a visage of sharp angles and a bald head, other than the fringe of gray hair around the base of his crown. Without a cloak, his gray clothing was well-fashioned, with a trio of stars on the breast as the only decoration. She was taken back to her shop, when the diviner had brought her a banner to finish, before spurning her help and instead taking the opportunity to lecture her – a girl not even in academy school – about reading books on the stars.

Her assessor, the man who would be judging her, was the very same diviner.

He wasn't just watching her, his sharp eyes were narrowed. When the director at the podium stopped calling names, and every clock had a young man or woman standing in front of it, the diviner abruptly left his chair. He went over to the white-haired woman at the podium and said something in a low tone. The crowd stirred. He and the director exchanged some words, and then they were both coming over to Bethany's position.

The director addressed Bethany in a voice that wasn't intended to carry. "Your education has come into question."

Charlton was already moving, fearless as he climbed the stairs and came straight over to join them. "What is happening here?" he asked, quietly but firmly.

"You are her sponsor?" the director asked, looking Charlton up and down.

"I am."

"She went to academy school?"

"She did not."

"Then—"

Charlton sternly interrupted. "I am her sponsor and I know the rules. There is no requirement to attend academy school."

"But how could she—?"

"People learn things on their own. It happens all the time—I am a cleric and I should know. She is to be tested just like anyone else. Whether she passes or not, it should be on the merits of her assessment and nothing else."

"She wrote her own submission?"

"Of course she did. Test her now and find out for yourself."

The director glanced at the assessor, and then back to Bethany. "Very well." She gave a crisp nod. "We will proceed as normal."

The director left Charlton with Bethany. More than a few murmurs came from the benches as the cold-faced diviner returned to his place on the chair, and if he was disappointed he didn't show it.

Bethany was left standing with Charlton, and he must have seen the fear in her eyes. The assessment was supposed to be difficult. Having her presence questioned, about whether she was supposed to be here... she wanted nothing more than to flee as fast as she could.

"Lift your chin, Bethany. Look into my eyes. Ignore everyone else. You are trying to become a diviner. Wealthy people do everything they can to get their children where you are now, but they can't exclude you, and I know you belong here. Trust me. You can do this."

Bethany nodded but didn't speak. With a final squeeze of her shoulder, Charlton left to reclaim his position on the benches, and as he gave her a grave nod, she did her best to stand tall. She ignored her assessor, yet he was right there, so close by, sitting behind her clock. How could he be the one she had been assigned?

No. She wasn't going to dwell on him. This was her time. What happened now was up to her. She had come this far, and Charlton was right. She could do this.

"Your attention, please," the director called. "We are now ready to begin." A few people on the benches were talking, and she raised her voice even louder. "Your attention," she repeated. "Thank you. Now. There are twenty places available at the School of Divination, where diviners are trained within the Observatory, in the Corpus District, just a few miles from here. Candidates," she turned her head to address the young men and women, "you have worked hard to get where you are. Requirements are for a sponsor from the corpus – a senior cleric, confessor, or diviner – and a written submission on the three factors you consider most relevant to a gateway's function."

Bethany had read everything she could about the three factors she had chosen. Gateways were always solid in some way: stone circles, tall arches, broad pyramids, and shrine-like temples. They were always aligned to the cardinal points, or to certain stars, or the rising or setting sun at a particular time of year. They were always located somewhere noteworthy, close to a settlement or a harbor or a mine. Whether or not the other candidates picked the same three, her submission had brought her to where she was today.

The director continued, "There are fifty of you, but just twenty places at the school. Most of you will not be gaining entry. The lucky few will enter the school, and even then, most will not complete their studies, which are both onerous and dangerous. Do any of you wish to depart?"

No one did.

"Then let us begin." The director paused to take a breath, and her next words had the sound of a ritual. "Time is everything. It is the great unstoppable force. Time is space and space is time. You cannot travel through the gateways and have others entrust their lives to you without a clear understanding of time."

The director now swept her gaze over the clocks. "You each have a clock and can move the hands as you wish. Your neighbors have a clock as well, and yes, you can look at the person next to you, but you will always be behind if that is your plan, and this examination is done at pace."

Bethany tried in vain to moisten her mouth. She wished she had some water.

"Now, you can obviously adjust your clock to specify a time, such as nine thirty-two. We will not be distinguishing between morning and night, as it will always be self-evident."

The director paused to allow her instructions to sink in.

"In addition to a time, if I ask for a duration, you can use your clock to specify the hours and minutes. For example, if I were to ask you how long until sunset today, the answer as you should know," she glanced at the central clock on the tall tower, "is ten hours and sixteen minutes. In this case you would point to ten, and to sixteen, to indicate this duration."

Bethany focused on her own clock, visualizing herself turning the hands quickly, imagining success.

"Finally, you can use your clock to indicate directions, where due north is twelve, south is six, east is three, and west is nine. One hand might indicate something to the north, another hand something toward the east, or both hands could point in the same direction if only one is asked for. Understood?"

No one spoke up.

"You have heard how the test works. Now for the rules. You each have an assessor watching you. We consider this event to be so important that many busy diviners have devoted their time to be here today." The stern-faced woman indicated the assessors behind the clocks, who were mostly hidden from the onlookers. "For each question you will be given a short period to answer, and then you will be graded, right or wrong. Your time will be brief, and you must remove your hands from your clock the moment the bell chimes."

The director indicated a bell located near her hand.

"Your incorrect answers will be tallied, and when the number reaches two wrong answers, you will be quietly tapped out of the contest. When this happens, you must leave. For you, the day is over. We will continue in this way until there are only twenty of you left. If it is not clear, if you have not removed your hands after the bell chimes, you will be marked wrong. Now. Candidates, prepare yourselves."

There was a shuffle as all of the candidates turned to face their clocks. Bethany moved close enough to reach forward with little effort. She stood poised, heart beating hard, hands ready to deploy at a moment's notice.

"Here is your first question. Using the Argent Arch as the locus, what time is sunset on the next winter solstice?"

Locus meant point of observation. Easy. Bethany moved the two hands on her clock. The assessors wrote down their marks. The bell chimed.

She was surprised at how little time they were given for answers. The director had meant what she said. She tried to ignore the cold-faced assessor on the other side of her clock.

"Using the gateway at Kelway as a locus, what time was sunrise today?"

Harder. Bethany had to know the time of today's sunrise in Everlast, then count the number of ley lines between Everlast and Kelway's gateway, and adjust.

She moved her clock's hands, and had barely removed her fingers when she heard the bell tinkle.

"Using the nearest gateway to Breanne as a locus, what time is sunset today?"

Bethany began with the time of sunset in Everlast, and then shifted to Breanne. But then she remembered: Breanne's nearest gateway was far away at Torvil. She altered her answer, changing the time on her clock. When the bell chimed, she saw that several of the candidates had been tapped out.

"What exact time will the winter solstice occur at the Red Temple of Darsh in Ganouda?"

Bethany moved her clock's hands. A pressure grew between her temples: a headache that merged with her existing tension. More candidates were escorted from the platform.

"What time would you depart the frozen city of Malange if you wanted to arrive at the Hexagon at Sedgeford at the exact moment of the summer solstice?"

When she finished changing her clock, Bethany had a short moment to look around. More than half of the candidates were now gone. If five more people went, she would be successful, and granted a place at the School of Divination. Her own hands began to shake.

"If the moon is directly overhead at midnight, after the passage of a week, what time will it be in the same position?"

More than difficult. Every day, the moon took a number of additional minutes to return to the same position in the sky. Bethany had to multiply the difference by the number of days in the week, and then add that number to the time of midnight.

This time, she only removed her hands from her clock an instant before she heard the bell. The throbbing in her head was timed to her heart beat, and now it was more than painful.

"How many hours and minutes will it take for the planet Memman to cross the sky tonight in Everlast?"

Bethany moved her clock's hands.

"How many hours and minutes will it take for the planet Tosh to cross the sky tonight in Everlast?"

Again she found the answer.

"If you were facing north at midnight tonight, which directions would you look in to see both the moon and the planet Memman?"

Bethany concentrated, and she thought she had the answer. She adjusted her clock, but then realized she had moved the clock's hands based upon the direction she and her clock were facing now, rather than acting as if she were facing due north. Her hands darted forward but then the bell chimed. She bit her lip. Her first wrong answer.

"If you were facing due north, toward the leaf constellation Carlan, which directions would you look in to see the stars Gar and Vespa?"

Bethany worked out the answer and moved her clock's hands. Relief flooded through her; she knew she was right. She had enough time for a quick scan. She became exultant. There were just twenty-one candidates remaining. The bell chimed.

Her eye caught movement. She turned in surprise; the diviner with the sharp features and bald crown was coming up to stand in front of her. He looked down his nose, displaying a sheet of paper in his hand, as he reached out to squeeze her shoulder.

No. Her eyes were wide open with disbelief. She couldn't be out.

Panicked, she threw a glance at the marking sheet he was holding. She saw a row of boxes, and a set of ticks and crosses inside the boxes that had been completed thus far. The system was obvious: a diagonal line for yes, and a second diagonal line against it for no.

One of the boxes was crossed, as expected. She knew she had run out of time.

But so was the question she had just answered. She scanned the clocks. The other candidates' answers were the same as hers. She had answered the question correctly. She even had time to look around.

"What are you doing?" she asked aloud. "I got the answer right."

"Candidate," her assessor said in his crisp, authoritative voice, "you still had your hands on your clock when the bell sounded."

"I did not," she protested.

She heard a few voices from the crowd. A woman called out. "No, she didn't."

"Silence!" the white-haired director of proceedings snapped from her podium. "Next question," she called, "if you were facing south..."

This couldn't be happening. Bethany searched the faces in the crowd, even as the tall diviner took her by the upper arm to lead her away. Charlton's face was white. Most people looked embarrassed for her. They didn't realize what had happened. She knew without doubt that the diviner was wrong.

In the end, there was nothing she could do. She shook herself free. Holding back tears, she descended the platform to ground level. She was barely aware of her surroundings as she left the scene behind.

Chapter Four

SOME SAID THAT on death's imminent approach, a person's story was told in a series of flashing images. Zhuana didn't see any images, but she did reflect on the most impactful periods in her life.

The time when she became queen... that was a period of great change. She never would know what might have happened if she had remained with her dying father – the scar-faced warrior Varden turned up dead in the street – but if there was one thing certain, it was that Alric had saved her life.

The pain and joy of childbirth, that was something that felt as clear as if it had happened yesterday. She had never known she could love someone so small with such intensity.

The brutal death of her husband... As the life left his eyes, and the blood pooled around him, she had experienced an overwhelming agony.

She had known difficult times in her life, and faced many challenges as a ruler, during the eighteen years of her reign.

But nothing like this.

She stood atop Veldria's defensive wall and watched the unnerving number of campfires spread across her vision. The army was big enough to fill the entire ridge in front of her, as well as the slope behind that, and even the mountainous terrain beyond. As the smell of wood smoke reached her nostrils, carried from the forest on the distant ridge, a heavy thud followed the loud crash and crackle of brush. She knew exactly what the crashing trees meant: the invaders were busy making siege ladders, rams, and other weapons of war.

She also knew that if the attack came – when it came – her city's defenses would be overwhelmed.

Why hadn't she had more of a warning? But even if she had known they were coming, what else could she have done?

She should have tried harder with the refugees, despite the fact that with their wild stories, they couldn't agree about anything except that they had to escape where they were. None of them mentioned a conqueror. Instead it was a plague, or having their homes overrun by a horde of people fleeing the south... the most crazed even raved about rampaging black-scaled monsters.

Faced with so many newcomers, she had done what she thought was right. When they begged to be allowed into her city, she had kept her gates closed. With cold words and sharp arrows, she turned the foreigners away.

She understood now that she had been wrong to think the crisis was over. And as a result, everything she knew was going to be destroyed, and everyone she loved was going to die.

Now she had an army of overwhelming size at her gates.

She was the queen, responsible for her people. There had to be something she could do. But as she searched constantly, desperately, with eyes that were never still, there was no movement... nothing at all...

The man she had sent out to make contact should have been back by now.

All of her senses were heightened. She heard her people as they prepared to defend the city... the clatters of swords and armor, the barking of frantic orders, the slap of hurried footsteps on stone, the prayers and rapid breathing. Her snug leather armor felt too constrictive, but when the fighting began, it was what was going to keep her alive. She was keenly aware of the weight of the sword she wore at her side: a single-edged, tapered length of razor-sharp steel. On such a hot night, her long black hair was heavy on the back of her neck, but it was the diamonds woven in her tresses, rather than a crown, that marked her status as queen.

There could only be one reason he hadn't returned. He had tried but he had failed. The next move belonged to her.

As soon as she had the thought, her gaze went straight to her son. Garric had terror in his wide eyes as he fumbled with a shield, trying to strap it to his forearm. He was dark-skinned like her, with wavy hair and the same high cheekbones and fine-boned features.

By the Mother, he was only sixteen... even younger than she had been when her father died.

She left her position to stride through the defenders, passing flaming torches on poles. The battlements stirred as people made way for her, bowing heads as she passed them by.

"Garric," she said. He wasn't as tall as she was, but he soon would be. He turned his head too quickly, so consumed he hadn't even noticed her coming. "Here. Let me help."

She shifted the strap and maneuvered his shield to fix it in place. A few tugs at his leather armor settled it properly around his body, and she also moved his scabbard to place his sword hilt at his right hip. "There."

He looked at her with his father's serious green eyes. The older he became, the more he reminded her of her late husband. He was breathing far too heavily. "What are you going to do?" he asked in a whisper.

She brought her face close to his. "What I have to. I am the queen. I must do what is right for our people."

"You are going to do something. I can tell."

"Whatever happens, you will stay here, and you will be strong, which is your duty, just as I have mine. One day, you will be king. Your actions are always watched and remembered." She remembered her father saying the same words long ago. "Look at our people." She squeezed his arm, forcing him to scan the massed defenders. "We are Veldrians. If they attack, we will make them suffer." She hesitated. "And if I fall, it is you, and our people, who will avenge me."

His expression was painful to watch. "Mother—"

"I am your queen," she said with a frown. She wanted to hug him tight; it might be the last touch they ever had. Instead she cupped the back of his head and spoke into his ear. "No matter what comes, I love you. Remember that. Be strong."

Zhuana couldn't let the people around her see the turmoil written all over her face, so she turned away, straightening as she forced a hard expression. It was difficult enough, steeling herself, and she couldn't allow herself to dwell on what might be in store for her son.

Instead, she took determined steps and returned to her place on the wall, at the same time scanning the battlements until she spied Alric's furs, sunken eyes, and close-cropped graying hair. Her most trusted advisor approached when she beckoned him over.

"My Queen...?"

She lowered her voice. "Maven Dresk has not returned, and I must now think about what to do if he never does."

"Anything I can—"

"I need to know if we have learned anything more about them. Anything at all that might help."

"Of course..." he hesitated. "However, I am afraid I have already shared all that we know. They call themselves the Harna. Their king is Torian Varlish."

"Strange names. But in the Mother's name, where do they come from?"

"All I can tell you is they have come a long way... beyond even a suggestion of our maps." He paused. "This king... what is it you think that he wants?"

She scanned the fires on the ridge. "An army that size needs plunder. It needs food. Whatever their story is, if they wanted to talk, they would have already done so."

He released a breath. "My role is to advise you. I should have seen this coming."

"And how would you have done that?"

"The refugees..."

"We questioned them. I was there too. Something was driving them, but it wasn't—"

A rumbling sound came from the direction of the plain that separated the city from the forested ridge.

Zhuana leaned forward as her mouth tightened. She held her breath, and soon the pounding of rapid horse hooves was unmistakable. She was aware of the people on the battlements exchanging tense glances. The rumble came from just the one horse, growing louder and louder, although nothing could be seen within the darkness outside the city.

She stared hard into the black of night, willing the man she was missing to appear.

Bursting into the light, a horse shot out from the darkness with terrible speed. Heading straight for the city, the animal bared its teeth and gave a spine-tingling scream. Zhuana couldn't prevent a gasp. The horse's back was empty; there was a decorated saddle but no rider. The creature bucked, before racing up to the city and veering hard, until it was running alongside the walls. The horse screamed again, shaking its head, before it panted and slowed, quivering as it snorted. Sweat glistened on the animal's flanks. White foam gathered around its mouth, while its eyes were wild and panicked.

The horse finally stopped a short distance from the main gate, to stand, frightened and shivering. There was no mistaking it: the horse belonged to Maven Dresk, the man she had sent out to make contact with the invaders.

From all quarters came cries and wails of anguish. The druadan had a strong following, and soon the roars of anger and bloodlust began to rise above the rest of the shouts.

Alric must have seen something in her face. "What are you going to do?"

"It is my turn now. If something happens to me, look out for Garric, just as you have done for me. I am going to saddle my horse." It was a struggle not to look at her son. "And I will do what I can to make them leave."

✦

Zhuana reined in.

In front of her, a row of men in armor stood with weapons drawn. In contrast, she was alone. Behind the warriors she was facing, the slope climbed to the tree-lined ridge. The fires were now bright enough to make out the flickering flames.

"I am Zhuana Arianus," she announced. "Queen of Veldria. Where is your king, Torian Varlish?"

For a long time no one moved. Her words felt as if they had been snuffed out like a candle. She spoke in Imperial, the common language between nations, but she didn't even know if these men could understand her.

The moments continued to drag out. She hid her fear and kept her back straight and her face cold. She would wait here forever if need be.

Finally, quiet words were spoken, and one of the Harna turned and left the group. The rest of the warriors remained where they were.

She forced herself to look from fighter to fighter and learn what she could. The Harna had dark eyes, and were skinny, almost skeletal, with sharp chins and hollow cheeks. Their swords were curved and wicked, and they also carried shields, and wore armor of steel and leather.

What was she doing here? Was there really a chance for her to succeed where Maven Dresk had failed? Her palms were damp as she gripped her reins. A strong jerk could turn her horse around, and she could swiftly put on speed the moment she wanted it. If these warriors managed to surround her, however, they could easily hack her into pieces. And if she achieved what she was here to do, she would be placing herself in their power.

Movement made her turn her head. A newcomer appeared from within the trees, a swarthy man on horseback. He was tall and lean, with pockmarked skin, loose clothing under his leather cuirass, and a crimson sash across his torso. Rather than a sword, his right hand gripped a spear, and his horse was even bigger and stronger than her own. She forced herself to stay where she was.

As he approached, the swarthy man maintained a flat, expressionless stare. She returned his gaze as he kept coming, nearer and nearer, until he pulled up close enough to reach out and touch her. He inspected her up and down, seeing her fine armor, the gold on her scabbard and horse's bridle, and the diamonds in her hair. He pointed his spear straight at her.

"You queen?" He asked without preamble, waiting until she nodded. "King Torian Varlish ask you talk." He spoke Imperial but so accented that she struggled with his words.

Whoever this man was, the king had sent him, making him something like an envoy. But what had they done with Maven Dresk?

"We should meet out here—"

"No," the envoy said. He instead turned his gaze toward the ridge. "There. Camp. King Torian Varlish."

Wondering what might be about to happen next, only knowing her own desperation to save her people, Zhuana reluctantly nodded. The invaders had the advantage.

"Very well," she said. "Take me to your king."

Chapter Five

ZHUANA RODE JUSt behind King Torian Varlish's envoy as he led her up the slope, and they traveled in darkness to approach the higher ground where trees speared the night sky. The terrain climbed toward the beginning of the campfires, and they entered the trees at one of the paths that cut through the woods.

Fires were soon all around her, everywhere she looked. She couldn't escape the sensation of being surrounded, and the horse underneath her snorted as he reacted to her apprehension. Men in armor moved about, tending coals, stoking flames. Dark eyes watched her closely, glimmering in the firelight. These men had the same single-edged swords, round shields, and armor of hardened leather. They also had gaunt faces and thin limbs. Not one of them was eating. They were hungry. She could see it in their faces.

Still the envoy kept leading her, uphill and past the first section of forest, to where grasslands stretched out before even thicker woodland. As the vista opened up, her eyes widened at the sheer multitude of fires. Women in billowing dresses traveled through the immense camp. A strange sound split the night: a shrieking baby.

She knew immediately: what she was seeing was more than an army. There was definitely enough of them to overwhelm her city, but at the same time, these people had to be fleeing something, like the others... only a lot more of them.

Their destination was up ahead. The envoy now skirted the grasslands to ride toward a hill where a grand pavilion with fluttering flags looked out over the main host. Flaming torches burned atop poles. Sentries encircled the area, while on the flat hilltop, off to the side, was another cluster of warriors.

She followed the envoy through a gap in the sentries and reined in. The swarthy man with the pockmarked skin climbed off his horse, and she also dismounted.

Then, still scanning the area, she started.

A man sat on the open ground, surrounded by three big Harna with blades drawn and pointed at him. Broad-shouldered and muscular, with a head as bald as a boulder, he had a bent nose he had broken years ago and never set right. He was clad in his leather armor, but his sword was missing and he had a new bruise on the side of his face.

The man was the druadan, Maven Dresk. He returned her surprised stare, catching sight of her just as she saw him.

Her relief swiftly shifted to anger. "What have you done to him?"

The envoy called out to Maven. "You. Tell her."

Maven's voice was rough and coarse, like him. "Apparently my rank does not merit the king's attention. They decided to hold me here to see if you would come. If not, then I must be of little importance."

The envoy frowned at Zhuana. "King waiting." He held out his hand. "Sword."

She bit her lip. She felt naked enough as it was, but whatever happened now, her sword wouldn't get her out of danger. She unbuckled the scabbard and handed it over.

"Now. Come." The envoy indicated the direction of the grand pavilion, making it clear that she should continue.

This time she shook her head. She maintained her hard expression. "No." She nodded toward Maven. "Not while he is under guard. I need my advisor to join me."

The envoy paused, contemplating Maven, and then, without a word, he left Zhuana to head over to the pavilion. He entered, and a few moments passed before he emerged once more. The envoy looked toward Maven's position as he called out something in another language. The three warriors guarding Maven stepped back and raised their blades.

As fearless as ever, Maven straightened and stretched. The druadan cast a dark look over his guards, before he came over to join Zhuana.

"My Queen," he said softly.

"Dan Dresk."

Standing by the pavilion, the envoy now pointedly held the canvas aside, waiting impatiently.

The time had come.

Zhuana held her head high, taking long strides toward the pavilion. With Maven following behind, she paused at the opening. The future of everyone she cared about depended on what happened next.

She ducked her head as she entered.

The air within the pavilion was warm and still, giving it a cloying, claustrophobic feel. On such a hot night, Zhuana would have opened the sides but instead everything was sealed, and the stench of incense burning in a brazier made her want to wave the air away. The brazier's crimson light glowed upon an intricately woven carpet spread out to make a floor, where a single man sat on a flat cushion. From his golden jewelry and the way he watched her and Maven with a predatory stare, he could only be one person.

"I am Torian Varlish, King of the Harna." Torian smiled. "First one of you comes, and now the queen herself. I think I have made an impression." He indicated the cushions in front of him. "Very well. We will talk. Sit."

Zhuana examined the man opposite as she chose a cushion and settled herself. His frame was emaciated, and his eyes were beady, almost feverish. Tattoos decorated one side of his face and traveled in a curling swathe under his chin to disappear under the fabric of his yellow tunic. The incisor teeth of some large predator jutted through each of his earlobes and his black hair was tied back from his head.

He must have had a fondness for strong odors, for around his neck, he wore a pomander on a leather cord, a little cage containing a ball of medicinal herbs and spices. He sipped at a steaming drink, perhaps tea, before placing it on a low table nearby. After he set his drink down, he raised the pomander to his nose for a few moments, inhaling deeply.

Once she was seated, Zhuana tried not to shuffle forward. The cushions were located in positions that felt strange, a little too distant to feel natural.

"You speak Southi?" Torian asked.

Zhuana briefly met Maven's gaze. She had never encountered the name before. "We have our own language, but like you we speak Imperial."

"Imperial?" Torian's brow furrowed; he was speaking an unfamiliar word. "This language is Southi."

His accent was strong, but Zhuana could understand him. In the end, it didn't matter what these people called the language. "I am Zhuana Arianus. Perhaps you have already met Dan Dresk, who sits on my council."

Torian's attention lingered on Maven, but his face gave nothing away. The skinny king returned his attention to Zhuana.

"You are queen here," he said.

"I am the Queen of Veldria," she replied. "You, King Torian Varlish, we do not know of in these parts. Why are you here?"

Torian leaned forward to stare into her eyes. "You know our numbers. We are ready to conquer your city. But you are here, and I offer you a chance to avoid death."

She couldn't reveal her fear. "We have numbers too. And walls that have stood up to stronger forces than yours. What is it that you want?"

"Your city blocks the gap between the mountains. I need safe passage. You must open your gates to allow us through. If you do so, lives will be saved, and our thanks will be to let your people live."

Zhuana fought to hide the sinking feeling weighing down on her. Maven knew it just as she did. There was no way she could give Torian what he wanted.

"Passage to where?" Maven asked.

With another quick glance at Maven, Torian spoke just the one word. "North."

"North?" Zhuana pictured a map of the region. She shook her head. "You can go another way, across the Tang River."

"That big brown river? We tried. We are not swimmers. We are desert people. It is too difficult."

Zhuana knew she had an impossible task: to find an accommodation between Torian's demands and the safety of her people. "We do not know you. We cannot open our gates to so many, even to pass through." She could only see one way for it to work. "We would need a bond." She didn't want to use the word 'hostage', but surely they both knew what she was talking about.

"Bond? What bond?" Torian's lip curled. "You know we can take what we want by force. I ask you again. I demand it. You must open your gates and let us through."

"And I return the same answer," Zhuana said, putting steel into her voice. "If you force us to defend our city, then that is what we will do. Many will die. I suggest you move to another area. We can help you find another route to the other side of the mountains." She paused before deciding to probe. "You must be running from something. It might help if you tell me what it is…"

Torian Varlish shuffled uncomfortably. "Darkness." He wouldn't meet her eyes. "Death."

Zhuana waited, but that was all he said. She was desperate to know more, but her intuition told her that this wasn't the time to push harder. "Perhaps the eastern desert—"

He scowled. "We are already starving. We were a great nation, a great people… And now we are reduced to this. Open your gates. Give us passage north. Or we will take what we want ourselves. We are hungry. You have food."

Sensing his rising irritation, she tried again. "We could take some of your women and children as a bond. We could then escort your men to the border, and then, when it is done, we can let them go."

Torian put his pomander to his nose and inhaled deeply. "You have a child, Queen Zhuana?"

She hesitated, picturing Garric staring from the walls as he prayed for her safe return. "I do."

"I have five wives, four sons, and seven daughters. I love them all dearly. Tell me, would you like to give me your child for safe keeping? Even if it would save your city?" When she didn't reply, his eyes darkened. "I thought that would be your answer."

Zhuana glanced at Maven, but his returning expression gave her nothing. The risk of opening her gates was too great. No amount of gold would be worth it.

"This is a problem we can solve—" she began.

"I agree. Open your gates and let us in."

"You know that I cannot do that. Not without a bond."

"I can give you five men."

Maven shook his head. "It must be five hundred. Women and children."

She shot Maven a warning look. "At the very least."

"No," said Torian. "It would give you too much power over us."

"And opening our gates would give you too much power over us."

Muttering some kind of curse, Torian climbed to his feet. Zhuana reluctantly followed, accompanied by Maven.

"There is nothing more to say. I give you tonight to consider. Tomorrow we will attack. And we all know the outcome. I know it. You know it. We will destroy you. And when we do, we will spill your blood until all of you are dead, every last one of you, before we take everything you have of value. You will be gone. Your names will all be dust."

"Give us a bond—" she tried one last time.

"There will be no bond. Leave now. In the morning we will come."

Breathing heavily, Zhuana left the pavilion. The moments were passing, but she couldn't think of anything to say. Behind her, Maven's face was drawn.

Once more on open ground, she stopped and looked around the hilltop. With the multitude of campfires surrounding her, she scanned the area, her frown becoming deeper.

"Where is my horse?" she asked.

A loud voice called out, and she turned to see Torian's skeletal figure standing framed in the doorway of his pavilion. "Your horse remains here, Zhuana Arianus. It is my horse now. You can consider your options on the long walk back to your city. Remember. I give you until dawn to open your gates. Believe me when I say this. Whether or not your gates are open, in the morning, we will come."

Chapter Six

ON THE JOURNEY back to the city, neither Zhuana nor Maven spoke. Zhuana kept going over and over the same options. Conflict felt inevitable. Her only chance was for Torian to take up her proposal regarding the hostages. Yet she could sense his determination. What was it he was fleeing? Darkness, he had said.

An enemy? Perhaps they could somehow unite against it?

They had left behind the high ground and were crossing the barren field on their way back to the city. In the stretch of darkness, she came to a sudden halt.

Maven stopped also, watching her as she stared toward the campfires along the ridge. "What is it, Queen Zhuana? We need to make plans."

"No," she said. "There is work to be done. But I am not going back to the city. Not yet."

Despite the darkness, she could read Maven's puzzled frown as they faced the direction of Torian's encampment. Maven sat on her council, but they were far from friends. Like her, however, he took his duty to their people seriously, and they would unite to face their common threat. She also knew his talent in matters of war, which was one of the reasons she had sent him to make contact with the enemy.

"I need to know what is driving them." She nodded toward the fires. "I am going back there. I need to find out for myself."

It was some time before he replied, and when he did, his voice was heavy with reluctance. "The risk—"

"I understand the risk."

"But what is it you expect to see?"

"You saw how many of them there are. They abandoned their homeland and traveled all this way, and still they want to keep going. Why? There must be something we can learn." Her voice firmed. "You can return to the city if you like, but this is what I am going to do. I would rather you with me. You have your followers and I have mine. When we agree on a course of action together, we have unity. If we are going to survive this, we can't be pulling in different directions. There is only one question to answer. Are you coming with me or not?"

It took him a little longer, but he could sense her determination. "But you are the queen. If they catch you spying—"

"This forest has kept me safe many times before." She began to walk and spoke over her shoulder. "These are things you do not forget."

This time, she traveled at an angle to the ridge as she re-crossed the plain. She sensed Maven hurrying to catch up with her, and then they were side by side.

Her heart rate picked up tempo. What was driving these people north? Torian Varlish wasn't the first. He might not be the last. She had asked the refugees questions but never truly understood. She wouldn't make the same mistake again.

When they reached a copse of stick-thin trees, she soundlessly put a finger to her lips; from this point they would travel in silence. Together they moved without sound, bodies hunched low to the ground. Creeping forward, they headed toward the camp's edge and farther, to circle around the woods from the other side. Something rustled up ahead and she froze, until a handful of birds flitted across the night sky. Every shifting tree branch or rustle in the bushes made her hold her breath until it was safe to continue.

As they approached a forested clearing, it was Maven who turned and held up his hand. Zhuana crouched, holding herself perfectly still. A moment later, a number of black shadows passed through the trees, man-sized shapes traveling to an unknown destination. She pricked her ears, hearing their murmurs. Together, they waited for some time, before Maven lowered his hand and they continued.

Now within the trees, they forged a careful path, using the screen of bushes to hide them, while also keeping clear of the branches that would snap and crackle if they tried to push straight through.

Sweat trickled down her face and between her breasts.

She and Maven now approached the camp from behind. From high ground, through a gap in the foliage, she again spied the open grassland ahead, and more fires than she had ever seen in one place.

"Maven, wait," she hissed. "Let us see what we can see."

They stood together, soundlessly watching the fires and the moving figures of the people in the immense encampment. She scanned carefully, sweeping the entire area.

What was it she was looking for? What was her plan? Should she try to overhear a conversation? She might not even understand what was being said. Could they take a captive? No... It would be difficult, if not impossible, and carried too much risk of being caught.

Her eyes flicked from place to place. There had to be something, somewhere...

When she saw jagged red spears at her extreme left, she focused her gaze. The blazing fire was different from the others, separated from the camp by a stretch of trees and bushes. With its size and location, it was strange enough to command her attention.

"There." She pointed. "What is that?"

"A fire. A very big one."

She leaned in close to whisper. "I want to see what that is."

Maven hesitated; they would have to work hard to get through to it, but he nodded.

"Remember, this is no deer we are hunting," she murmured into his ear.

After leaving the hillside, the terrain swiftly leveled off. They soon dropped to the ground and crept forward on their elbows, using their knees to push their body along at the same time.

The undergrowth swallowed them up. Distant voices rose and fell, gradually becoming louder. Meanwhile, she heard every scrape and pant that Maven made beside her.

A thorn scraped her cheek. She gently backed her face away from the twig. They kept crawling; she was finding it difficult to know where they were and which way they should travel. But then bright red light flickered through the bushes and they both began to move in a soundless slither; they were almost at their destination. She grabbed Maven and put her finger on her lips, even though he wasn't making a sound. Then she nodded him forward.

They both wriggled their bodies until they were side by side. Together they peered out from the undergrowth.

The fire was even bigger than she had thought when she first saw it. In the middle of a clearing, the raging pyre burned a long way from where she was watching. And yet she could hear a great roar and crackle as it burned logs the size of tree trunks and flames licked each other, competing to reach the sky.

The summer breeze bent the billowing smoke, which was thick and dark. What was she looking at? She tried to understand, even as a putrid, meaty stench reached her nostrils. She sealed her lips. More than anything, she wished she could turn her head and cough.

She caught movement. Her stomach clenched; she now understood why the smoke was so dark. A group of half a dozen coarsely-dressed laborers worked at a pile of corpses, struggling to lift a body by the arms and legs. Once they had their burden in hand, they headed to the fire, swung together, and after a few swings they let go. They moved on to the next body, yanking it from the pile as they worked at a collection of ten or more.

The fire gave a fiery sizzle, drawing her attention. At first she wasn't sure if her senses weren't deceiving her. When the flames reached the body, something came out of it, little sparks like fireflies that crackled and popped, burning up in the heat until they were gone.

As the laborers worked, she noticed something else. The area was under guard, with armed soldiers in a wide circle, watching the laborers every move.

"Look, what is that?" Maven hissed into her ear.

The next corpse was different. The clothes were in tatters, and perhaps it had been a man, but it was hard to say because his face was already blackened—although he had yet to be thrown in the flames. The laborers balked at approaching this body, but a guard barked something and two of the soldiers drew arrows to their ears, forcing their prisoners to continue.

Two prisoners gingerly picked up the body; the black skin extended to the arms. Zhuana watched carefully, taking in everything she could, and then she froze, focused on one detail.

As the corpse traveled toward the pyre, the arm drooped to the side, revealing a hand that was gnarled, with fingers curled like claws. Reflected in the firelight, the skin wasn't just black; it had a diamond pattern and was glossy, like the scales of some reptile.

All of the rumors came back to her, the crazed stories the foreigners had brought to her gates. A mysterious plague... Creatures with shining black scales... She remembered Torian Varlish in his perfumed tent, keeping his distance, holding his pomander to his nose.

She was transfixed, thoughts whirling, even as the pile of corpses grew smaller until the last body was in the fire. The prisoners' work was now finished, and the same guard who had called out before shouted something else. The men in rags went to a series of buckets and scrubbed at their arms with soap and water. After some time, the soldiers closed in, at the same time keeping their distance.

The same guard barked another command. The prisoners stood side by side near the fire and displayed their arms, showing the backs of their hands. One of the other guards moved along the line, inspecting each set of hands, until he came to the last in the row. Even Zhuana could see that this man's fingers were different. His shaking hands looked normal. His fingernails, on the other hand, were perfectly black.

The soldiers immediately called warnings to each other and backed away. Those with bows fitted arrows to their strings; the cowering prisoner was made to move and take several steps away from his fellows.

He stood shaking, pleading. The guards readied their bows. A swift cry saw them draw, aim, and loose. Arrows thunked into the prisoner's torso and he jerked with each strike before collapsing to the ground.

The guards issued more orders. Leaving the arrows where they were, two of the other prisoners picked up their companion's body and carried it over to the fire. They heaved and swung to throw the corpse into the flames. They then headed to the buckets, where once more they scrubbed furiously at their hands and arms.

Zhuana turned to meet Maven's gaze. He didn't often betray much of his inner workings, but his mouth was open and his eyes were wide. She jerked her chin, and he nodded. Soon she was wriggling her frame through the undergrowth to return back the way they had come.

As she worked hard to get herself as far from the camp as she could, soon she was running in a crouch, her back bent. She climbed a slope and then burst into a sprint to reach the open hillside. From her new location, the campfires were little bright dots. She knew she was far enough away to round on Maven and speak without fear of being overheard.

"You saw it," she said quickly. "The darkness. It is already here."

"If I had not seen it with my own eyes, I would never believe it." He turned and spat. "When we get back we need to wash ourselves with lye. And burn these clothes."

"These people... they fled, but they were too late. They are trying to get away from something that is inside themselves. Some terrible sickness..."

"What can we do?"

Zhuana faced the direction of her city. From her high position she could just make out the light of the torches on top of the walls. She now understood the plight of the refugees who were so desperate to get away from the south. Everyone was moving. Entire nations were being uprooted. "They plan to attack in the morning. At the same time, we can't open our gates to them. Not even with a bond. You know it as well as I do."

"No, we cannot. And if they bring this darkness to our people..."

Her mind never stopped working, yet there was only one terrible conclusion to draw. Casting her mind back to all those years ago, she could still picture Alric's face when her father was dying, and she had wanted to stand her ground despite the danger lurking outside.

"There is a time to fight and a time to flee. It takes courage to know the difference. Would you agree, Dan Dresk?"

He didn't reply, but he was listening to her every word.

"There is no valor in staying to fight a hopeless cause, to die when we might endure. I was taught this lesson when I was young."

"What are you saying, Queen Zhuana?" he asked quietly.

"This is going to be difficult. I am going to need your help." Her pain was only just beginning... her pain and that of her people. "Do you know what the last thing my father ever said to me was? He spoke just the one word. Survive."

And that was what she was going to do now.

"We don't have a choice," she said. "It doesn't matter... even if they move on, or if we manage to fight them off. If we don't leave... this darkness will come for us too."

✦

Zhuana climbed the road, traveling on foot like all the people around her, for every horse was burdened with provisions and those too young or old to walk. She led the great exodus from the front, while carts trundled along and the moving column of people left the mountain valley that was home to the city of Veldria. None of them had seen anything like it, not in the most crowded summer feast days or in the celebrations after her coronation. This wasn't just any group of Veldrians; it was everyone, young and old, poor and wealthy, numbering in the tens of thousands. And they would gather even more people from the countryside on their journey.

At first they would be passing through pastures and farmland, and then the sparsely populated regions and neighboring wilds, before heading through lands that none of them had been to before.

Rather than die, they had chosen to live. Even then, however, the choice had been terrible to make. They were abandoning their homeland. They might never return. The Veldrians were now a forlorn, destitute people, trying to find new lands, to travel somewhere they all might be safe.

Zhuana glanced at her son as he trudged along beside her. Garric would never become king in the same way she had become queen, with the druids placing a crown on her head in the glow of Everglade Forest. His green eyes, serious and downcast, mirrored the defeated air of the people around them.

But he was alive.

Now and then, Zhuana turned her head to see what was happening behind her, and she wasn't the only one, although there were many who preferred not to look at all.

Behind them, the city of Veldria was burning.

The black plume rising from the settlement tainted the sky like a tapered thunderstorm. The stench of smoke wasn't just in her nostrils; it burned the back of her throat. Dancing crimson flames caught from building to building, climbed towers, and roared across rooftops. Veldria, her great city, would soon be a shell of what it once was, until time took its toll, and eventually the city became obliterated. Zhuana's eyes were red, but she was the queen, and it was her task, and her burden, to remain strong.

The fire created a barrier between them and the invaders. It gave them time to get away. It meant that no one would occupy Veldria and call the city their own. And one day, if they returned to these lands, they might rebuild anew.

Her people would endure, but what was next?

An image came to her: the scaled skin on the corpse thrown into the fire.

She focused her attention on her son. "Garric?" she instructed. "Show me your hands again. Turn them around. Hold your fingers high."

He did as she asked, and then dropped his hands when she gave him a quick nod. She looked at her own fingernails and at least her hands weren't shaking. The nails were clean and white; she had scrubbed every inch of her body until her skin was red and raw.

On her other side, she heard a throat clear, and turned to see Alric's sunken cheeks and close-cropped hair. "Every druid is checking skin, but we believe that the only ones to make close contact are you and Dan Dresk. I am hopeful that we have made it out before this darkness could reach us and take hold." He looked up ahead, along the road that climbed to the end of the valley. "The question remains, My Queen, how far is far enough? What is our plan? We have food, livestock, weapons, horses... but we cannot travel forever. For how long will our journey continue?"

"As long as it takes to get there." Zhuana reflected upon her conversation with Torian Varlish. He had wanted to go north, and she knew what she would eventually find if she led her people in that direction. The language they had spoken – Imperial – managed to reach the most distant places.

"My Queen... to get where?"

"We have no choice," she said. "This problem is too big for us alone. We need to go where there are libraries of books and people with knowledge. We are going to seek safety in the Eternal Empire."

Chapter Seven

TWO WEEKS HAD passed since Bethany's assessment at Speaker's Corner. The warm, humid summer continued, and now, even in darkness, she tied back the curtains from the window that opened onto her dormus's living area, hoping for a breeze to temper the heat.

While she was at the window, sounds of the city drifted up from below. She was on the fourth level of her compound, but sound always seemed to travel straight up. The high-pitched voices of playing children competed with the warbling music of a flute, while the distant calls of hawkers in the Fabric District's markets reached her ears in the spaces between. She tilted her head back to look up at the night sky, scanning the heavens for the constellations she knew so well. Then she shook her head and returned to her seat at the table.

The dormus was small, but the same could be said for any other dormus in Compound 12C—or any of the matching compounds that dominated Everlast's poorer districts. The living room doubled as a workroom, with a rack full of garments on hangers and dozens of rolls of fabric on shelves, ready to be used. The table was old but sturdy, and its surface tended to be more often covered in fabric than food. A pair of low-slung armchairs sat facing each other in the corner. In the opposite corner, a bench was home to cups, utensils and crockery, as well as an oil burner for cooking. Down the short hallway, past the washroom, a single bedroom contained two matching beds for Bethany and her mother.

After seating herself at the table, Bethany lifted her scissors and cut along the shapes drawn over the fabric. Her role was to prepare the fabric for her mother to then stitch and finish. She could do the basic work, but the pieces that brought in real money, the elaborate dresses, cloaks, and doublets, were something she couldn't yet work on. No matter how hard she tried, she didn't seem to have the ability to reach her mother's level of craftsmanship. Her mother joked that she might know her way around a ball gown in another decade, two at the outside, but it was probably true.

Bethany's mother Maryam was well known for her skill, with a reputation accumulated over years of hard work. Although lately, for some reason while working at the shop, Bethany had been subject to more complaints than usual. She wasn't worried. It was just a run of bad customers, fussy people with too much money and too much time to cause trouble.

As she cut the fabric, the work was mindless enough to allow her thoughts to wander. From long habit, she had positioned herself in view of the stars, but the pinpricks of light that shone against the darkness didn't have the allure they once had. The detailed, intricate, vast realm of knowledge about their positions and behaviors occupied too much space in her memory. It was time to replace the stars with something else.

Hearing footsteps, she looked over as the door to the dormus opened. Her mother entered, carrying something, smiling as she closed the door behind her.

Maryam had the same coloring as Bethany: copper hair, copper skin, brown eyes. She wore dangling earrings, like acorns on metal thread, which she had worn since she was a girl in Loriastris. Maryam was shorter than Bethany, quite small really, but she always had a spring in her step, with the ability to keep moving from dawn until late at night.

A strong, savory odor wafted in along with her mother. Bethany's mouth began to water. Her mother was a talented cook, and knew how to thrust flavor into the blandest vegetables, but more than anything they both loved the street food sold at the market.

"Look what I have, Betani," Maryam said, singing the words as she did a little dance and raised the paper bags. "Flatbreads, covered in butter. From the new stall on Fuller's Lane. I will have to introduce you... he comes from southern Loriastris and makes them just like I remember." With a side-stepping sway of her hips, she slid over to the table where Bethany was cutting the fabric and held up one of the two packets. "This one is a little bigger. Come on. Take it. Leave that. We can wash our hands after."

Bethany set down the scissors and material. Her stomach rumbled, but she didn't take the packet. "I know I'm going to love it, but didn't we say we have to cook at home for a while?"

"Betani, you know we always get through. I can tell when something's wrong. I thought this might cheer you up." Maryam headed over to the pair of low-slung armchairs that filled the other corner of the room. "Come on. Don't let it get cold. Leave the work. There will be time to finish it later. Come sit over here."

Bethany joined her mother as they both sat down. She took the packet; the flatbread was still warm, and she immediately started taking big bites. The texture was crisp in places, chewy and soft in the middle, and the flavor was rich and salty. Food from Loriastris was never light; it was always rich with butter, herbs, and spices. She closed her eyes as she ate. Her mother's flatbreads were always good, but she had to admit that this was even better. The experience of eating it was over far too quickly.

"If I could eat these every day, I would," Maryam said with a sigh of pleasure. "And for once we don't have a pot to clean. Hmm. What's the time?"

"About fifteen minutes past eight," Bethany replied without thinking.

"I will never know how you keep track like that." Maryam looked over at the table where they often sat and worked together. "How is the work going?"

"Well enough."

Maryam watched her carefully. "And it is not the work that is making you sad. Or the shop. Now, what is wrong, my love? I know you love your books. Why have you stopped your reading?"

Bethany didn't meet her mother's eyes. Charlton had always said she should tell her mother about her dream.

But why get her hopes up? Why get her confused? It would have changed their lives. And it wasn't going to happen anyway.

"I have an idea," Maryam said, her eyes twinkling. "There is a young man."

"No, nothing like that."

"Then what?"

"Have you ever wanted something so badly that you can't even say it out loud?"

"Of course. Many times. When you were little, I wanted the best for you, but I was so afraid I couldn't offer it. Now look at the woman you have become." Maryam reached out to squeeze Bethany's hand, and Bethany squeezed her back. "Sometimes we are all afraid to voice our hopes and fears. But I am your mother. You have nothing to fear from me."

Bethany nodded and then ventured a smile. "I think I am just tired."

"Are you sure? It feels like something bigger. Betani, it is good to share your cares." Maryam waited, but Bethany didn't say any more.

Maryam focused on something at the back of the room. "That salt makes me thirsty. Is there water in the jug?" She nodded toward the corner bench.

Bethany turned to face the same direction. Her mother was staring at the clay cooking pot; the water jug was in the washroom, in another place altogether. They were roughly the same color, but looked completely different.

Bethany got up from the armchair. Passing the clay pot, she gave it a quick inspection, before heading to the washroom to find the water jug on the shelf near the basin. She carried the jug back to the living room, where she filled two cups with clear water and gave one to her mother.

Maryam took the cup but appeared confused. "Where did you go just now?"

Bethany frowned. Wasn't it obvious? She turned again toward the jug, which now stood right beside the clay pot. Her mother looked at the two items, but made no reaction, and still appeared to be waiting for Bethany to speak.

A thought crept up, and it made her more than uneasy. She had been getting more complaints at the shop. There had been the plump lady with the crooked sleeve... the old merchant with the coat that wouldn't button up...

The rack of unfinished projects filled half of the room. She headed over to inspect them more carefully.

"Betani?"

Bethany didn't answer. She had been working with her mother for so long that she didn't often pay attention to the work her mother did. She did the preparation work. At the shop, people presented their tickets, paid, took their clothing, and left, and that was the extent of her role. Her mother was the skilled seamstress. Everyone said so, and Bethany knew it too.

But as she lifted up a jerkin and examined the seam, a queasiness settled into her, somewhere inside her stomach. She moved from the tunic to a dress. Then on to a doublet. A pair of trousers.

More than one of the seams was uneven. In places the stitching was sloppy. It was as if someone else had done the work, rather than her mother. This wasn't like her. It wasn't like her at all.

Leaving the racks, Bethany went back to her mother. "Show me your hands."

Puzzled, Maryam held out her hands, and Bethany watched for a moment. No shaking. Her mother's hands were steady. She took them in her own hands, turning them over, checking for sores or signs of swelling. She decided there was no issue with her mother's hands.

"How is your vision?"

"Fine," Maryam said.

"Are you sure?"

"Why, what is it?" Maryam asked too quickly. "Why do you ask?"

Rather than answer, Bethany walked to the corner bench, which wasn't far away. She held up a hand. "How many fingers am I holding up?"

"Don't be foolish, Betani," Maryam grumbled.

"How many?"

"Two."

"It was three," Bethany said.

She returned to crouch in front of her mother and stare into her face. Her mother's eyes looked the same as they always had: brown, soft, loving, gentle.

Maryam harrumphed. "Sometimes when you get to my age you need spectacles. I simply can't afford them at the moment."

"When did you start to notice?"

"I don't know," Maryam said reluctantly. "I thought I was fine. Then, a few weeks ago... I had to stop walking in the street. Everything was blurry. Yesterday I stabbed my own finger and got blood on the piece I was working on. I haven't done that in years."

"A few weeks? That seems fast. Is there anything else?"

When Maryam bit her lip, Bethany's concern became heavier, like a stone sinking through her insides.

"It's nothing," she said.

"Please, tell me."

"I have... well... I have been getting these headaches."

Bethany fought to appear calm. It wouldn't do her mother any good to show her worry. "Headaches..." she said. "How bad are they?"

"Bad enough."

There was only one choice to make. At least she knew where to go. "Tomorrow I'm taking you to the House of Healing on Dyer Street."

"Oh, Betani, it sounds like a lot of trouble—"

"We'll need to get there first thing in the morning. Charlton will make time to see you."

"Betani, no... I told you, there is no real problem. Can't we talk about something else?"

Bethany's lips pressed together; she had already made her decision. She was going to take her mother to Charlton, whether she wanted to go or not.

Chapter Eight

THE SUMMER HEAT gave way to a period of drizzling rain. Bethany was in her shop, collecting everything she needed before she closed up for the day. She bundled up the garments she would take to work on at home, checking each item against her notes, which were now intended for herself, rather than her mother. She was doing a lot of the stitching herself, but she didn't have her mother's nimble fingers, nor her swift, deft movements. It was going to be a long night.

She spent a moment looking at the closed door as the hard rain pattered on the paving stones outside. Charlton had said he might come past, but he must have been caught up with his work.

The bundle went into the oversized garment bag, a satchel made of oilskin to protect it from the rain. She then hoisted the bulky bag, heading to the door, settling the satchel on her hip as she struggled with the door handle until she managed to get it open.

And there he was. Charlton's gray hair was plastered to his scalp. From his appearance, he had been standing where he was, in the rain, without any kind of coat or shelter.

"Charlton?" Bethany stood facing the sodden cleric. "How long have you been there?"

He had never been a good liar. "A little while."

"Why?" She made space for him in the doorway. "Come in, quickly."

Heading back to the bench, she swiftly set down the garment bag. When she turned toward him, Charlton stood squeezing one palm with the other, as if wringing the water from his hands. His white uniform was dripping to the floor, but he didn't appear to care.

He cleared his throat. "About the assessment... I'm sorry, Bethany. I've tried everything I can think of."

"I know that." She didn't take her eyes off his face. "But that's not why you're here."

"No, it is not."

He glanced toward two chairs placed near the doorway in case the queue was long. "Perhaps you should sit down."

Her stomach gave an unsettling jump. "I prefer to stand."

"Very well." He met her eyes. "I visited your mother at home again today. This time I brought someone with me, a friend from the University... someone who knows a lot about these things."

Despite Charlton's ruffled appearance and the anxious cast to his face, he was a senior cleric, and Bethany could only speculate about his understanding of the body and mind. Any friend he brought would have to be knowledgeable indeed.

When she spoke, her voice sounded faint in her own ears. "What is it? Tell me."

"The news is not good. There is no easy way to say this. You were right. Your mother is losing her vision. It is not common, but it is a known condition. And at the rate her sight is failing, you are going to need to think about what to do."

Bethany stood frozen in place.

"But that is not all." Charlton's tone was grim. "The loss of vision could be a sign of worse to come. The eyes and the brain are connected. Her vision appears physically fine, but the headaches and the rate that she is declining indicate a bigger problem."

She still didn't react. It was an effort to even swallow. Charlton was watching. She had to say something. "Your friend... the cleric. How much money do we owe you?"

"Bethany, as I said, she is a friend."

"Thank you." She turned her head away, taking a moment to rub at her eyes. "I have to get this bag home."

"I have probably given you too much information right now." With a wrinkled look of sympathy, Charlton came forward, reaching out to squeeze her shoulder. "Maryam doesn't yet know everything I have told you, although she can probably guess the gravity of her condition. You might want to wait to talk to her about it. You will need to think things through yourself, and find a way to support her as she adjusts. When you are ready, however, if you like I can talk to her with you. Or I can talk to her on my own."

"No. It should be me." She stood staring with eyes unfocused.

"Like I said, it might make things easier if you have a chance to adjust before explaining to her. I will go through a few things with you tomorrow. Bethany... I am sorry."

✦

Bethany couldn't sleep. Distant thunder rumbled and the rain sounded like a waterfall outside the bedroom window. Lying on her back, she looked up with eyes that were wide open, her mind darting around as she stared up at the ceiling. Her mother was asleep in her own bed in the same room, and occasionally Maryam's heavy breathing reached her even above the rain. Her mother was the one she usually turned to for help. What was she going to do? How was she going to tell her?

A strange sound made her frown. Definitely out of place, it was coming from Maryam's direction. She rolled onto her side to quickly face her mother. As she listened intently, the sound came again: something between a moan and a wince. Her mother's body twitched. There could be no doubt. Maryam was whimpering while she slept. She wasn't murmuring or gasping, like someone in the throes of a nightmare. She was making little pained sounds, the way a person might flinch if poked with a sharp stick.

There was nothing Bethany could do right now. Her intuition told her that waking her mother wouldn't do her any good. And so she just lay where she was and watched her mother's suffering. Thunder continued to groan and rain crashed against Everlast's streets. Eventually Maryam settled. But for Bethany, sleep was now impossible. She turned onto her back again and waited for the sun to rise.

She didn't know what they were going to do.

✦

Bethany was up with the dawn; there wasn't much purpose in staying in bed. She gently lifted the lid of her clothing chest, careful to remain quiet as she silently dressed herself. So early in the day, a hint of pale light gave the curtains a faint glow, revealing her mother's sleeping form and the rising and falling of her chest. Maryam's face was smooth; she appeared to be deep in sleep. Blessedly, Bethany didn't hear her any more whimpering.

Ready to depart, Bethany stood and looked down at her mother. What was it Charlton had said? Before talking to her, she should try to work things through herself. All Bethany knew was that she was desperate for some outside air. Her eyes moved to the window; through a gap in the curtains, the sky was gray but the rain was holding off for the moment. Her mother wouldn't be too curious if Bethany said she had gone to the shop early, which would give her some time to think.

After gathering the garment bag, she scribbled a note to explain she was departing early. Leaving the dormus and closing the door behind her, she descended the four flights of stairs to reach the compound's main entrance and soon she was crossing the graveled open area outside.

While she walked the streets, garment bag over her shoulder, the Fabric District was also waking up, with tailors and dressmakers, fullers and dyers, spinsters and weavers all preparing for the day ahead. The rain had made Everlast's streets wet and shining, and the morning sun peeked between the tall buildings, casting long shadows on the paved roads. Men and women set up stalls in the market, or entered communal workshops producing as many garments in a week as Bethany and her mother worked on in a year.

Bethany reached her shop, the key jangling in her hand as she unlocked the door. The door creaked as she opened it wide, but it was much too early for customers.

She set the shoulder bag down on the counter inside. Heading outside again, she closed the door, turning the key in the lock to secure it once more.

Unencumbered, she left the shop behind, eyes straight ahead as she began to walk.

Walking at least felt like she was doing something. People passed her on both sides, but she was barely aware of their faces. Some terrible illness had taken over her mother. Maryam wasn't just going blind; there was some greater problem. She might need medicine, which was always expensive. There was no one to help them. Her mother wasn't originally from Everlast; they had nothing in the way of family to lean on.

It wasn't long before she left the Fabric District behind to approach the West River Bridge. As she crossed its solid span of stone, far below, the Garland River tumbled along fast enough to create little waves that collided with each other. After the recent rain, flotsam drifted under the bridge, leaves and tree branches that gathered in the sluggish areas.

After West Park, a wealthy district where tall fences enclosed the houses and broad trees lined the clean streets, she entered the next quarter, where tall terraced houses, parkland, mighty trees, and paved squares dominated her vision. Soon huge structures beckoned up ahead. She now had a destination in mind, although she didn't know when she had made the decision to come this way.

If the Nexus was the empire's brain, the Corpus was often described as the body. The name lent itself to a quarter in Everlast – the Corpus District – as well as to the body of confessors, clerics, and diviners who studied and explained the nature of the world.

Confessors from the corpus dedicated their lives to the Great Weaver, the architect of the tapestry that was invisible to the eye but connected everything and everyone. Clerics investigated the human form, seeking to shed light upon the mechanisms that enabled a mind to direct speech, blood to invigorate limbs, and the organs to work together in harmony. And diviners were the only people who actually saw the tapestry revealed, using their knowledge of the heavens above and the world below to travel between the gateways.

As Bethany entered the Corpus District, the city was now almost awake, and people walked with purpose. Several temples rose above the lower buildings, some dedicated to the regular cleansing provided by confession, others to the blessing of infants. Young nobles had their weddings at the Temple of Pledges and kept their wills and testaments at the Temple of Records. Imperial Temple held census records and knew better than anyone the size of the empire's population and how many were registered citizens. The Great Cemetery occupied an entire corner of the Corpus District, and in the distance, a group of somber people in black attended a funeral. Uniforms were everywhere: the black of confessors, the white of clerics, the gray of diviners. The conservative coloring clashed with the brighter colors of the men, women, and children with business in the area.

With her destination now clear in her mind, Bethany left behind the huge healing houses that clustered around the University like ducklings around their mother. Rather than the cube-shaped University, she had her eyes on an even more striking location.

Built around a hill, the group of structures grew larger until she had to tilt her head back to take it all in. She was now heading toward the Observatory, where diviners worked at their craft. She raised her gaze to the highest place in the area: the Crystal Dome, a great half-sphere that crowned the hill, displaying sections of thick glass fitted together in a lattice of thin supports and clear crystal panes.

Other parts of the Corpus were Dymantine, but like the Argent Arch, the Crystal Dome was built by the Eidar, the ancients who abandoned the cities and gateways long ago, leaving them for the first Dymantines to find when they came from across the sea.

She came to a halt. There was just a paved square between her and the two huge doors that stood wide open at the Observatory's base. She narrowed her eyes at the open doors, and then gazed once more up at the Crystal Dome.

What she wanted to do was open her mouth and shout up at the Crystal Dome. *I don't want to be part of your school. I never did.*

And yet she knew she would be lying. She did want it. Now her mother was sick. They didn't have any money. She didn't have the skill to do her mother's job.

A droplet stung her cheek.

The sky was now completely gray, with the sun lost somewhere behind the clouds. Another droplet followed. The rain returned, heavier than a drizzle until it was hard enough to bounce off the paving stones. She was wearing a thin cloak and raised the hood up to cover her head. The repetitive drumming of falling rain became louder, mingling with the cries and footsteps as people sped from the area to seek shelter.

Three girls her own age ran together into the Observatory's entrance, but as for her, the sight of the open doors meant nothing. This wasn't a place she was welcome. She had been unfairly dismissed from the examination. There wasn't anything she could say or do. She couldn't succeed where Charlton had failed.

Tugging her cloak tighter, she turned away from the Observatory, to head back the way she had come.

✦

The rain ended as swiftly as it started, and the protection of her thin cloak, combined with summer's heat, meant that by the time Bethany returned to her shop she was nearly dry again. The key was already in her hand as she crossed the road. The streets were relatively empty after another recent bout of rain.

She reached the shop's doorway but something felt strange. She had the sense of being watched, and turned her head towards a pair of sword-carrying soldiers in shining plate armor standing off to the side and talking. From their white cloaks, they were Imperial guardsmen, soldiers who answered directly to the emperor. Guardsmen weren't a rare sight, although it wasn't often they appeared in the Fabric District. She watched them over her shoulder but they weren't angled in her direction. She tried to put them out of her mind.

Above the shop's awning, a pair of doves watched her and cooed. Her garment bag would be just where she had left it. She still had a few minutes before customers would begin to arrive. And today, like yesterday, any promises she gave about the quality of the repairs and alterations would be promises she had to live up to herself. She didn't want to turn down elaborate ball gowns or fancy doublets. They were the jobs that paid well. She also didn't want the shop to develop a reputation for shoddy work. There were no good options available.

Keys in her hand, she reached toward the lock. But a sudden clatter made her stop and frown. The sound of heavy boots was coming from somewhere, growing louder, perhaps even heading toward her.

Her heart began to race. Yes, the footsteps were definitely heading her way. She whirled.

The two Imperial guardsmen stood facing her, close enough to reach out and touch her.

Her eyes shot wide open. They were brawny soldiers, armed with swords, and with the door behind her there was nowhere she could go. White cloaks decorated their shoulders, trimmed with gold. When one of the guardsmen spoke, his tone was low and ominous.

"Bethany Sylvana?" The guardsman didn't wait for an answer. He glanced over his shoulder, checking that no one was close enough to hear. "You are required to come with us."

Chapter Nine

THE SPELL OF RAIN had finally ended. As the sun broke from the clouds, the dripping trees and flowers of the Nexus gardens shed the last drops of water, and the paths of golden brick were soon dry as if the rain had never happened.

Julian Malventus Livius wandered among the trees. His stroll had little purpose; someone watching would have seen a golden-haired, athletic man in his mid-twenties, with frown lines and a downcast turn to his mouth, trying to make it look like he was taking an aimless walk and failing badly. They would have seen Julian, in his fine gold-threaded tunic, white silk leggings, and supple deerskin boots, never straying too far from a certain place. As he hovered, he cast frequent, anxious glances toward the Imperial Palace, where a broad terrace opened onto the extensive gardens he was exploring.

The one thing Julian made sure of, however, was that no one from the terrace could see him. He used flower bushes, statues, and conifers to keep himself hidden from view. There were important men on the terrace. His father was among them. He had told himself he would stay away, but after the rain stopped, here he was.

To pass the time, he took a path that led toward the Cathedral of the Hidden Source, where emperors and empresses were crowned and married by the high confessor. But as the cathedral's tall spire grew, all the sight of the grand entrance did was remind him about his own future... about emperors, crowns, and power.

He turned back and crept up behind a manicured hedge. He peeked through the foliage to watch the terrace, where old men in conservative clothing sat at a long table. More than anyone else, he focused on the man at the table's head, his father, the most powerful man in the world: the emperor, Rigel Regus Livius.

The emperor was speaking with vigor, and to emphasize his points he made a knife with his hand and cut it into his palm again and again.

The emperor was negotiating an agreement. Julian's fate was being decided.

One of the other three men spoke up, raising a finger to challenge the emperor, and Julian's eyes narrowed. The speaker was a tall man in his fifties, with lean limbs, ash-colored hair, and a high, intelligent forehead. Declan Quinn, Lord of Graystone, was the leader of a powerful group of nobles called the Guildsmen. He was also the father of Julian's wife, which made him Julian's father by marriage.

But more than anything else, Declan Quinn was Julian's avowed enemy.

Julian's nostrils flared as he watched through the hedge. Lord Gavin Arturius, the leader of his own group, the Crusaders, appeared to be nodding his agreement to whatever Declan was saying. At least Tristan Benedict of the Wardens was frowning and shaking his head. The emperor, Julian's father, spread his hands in a calming gesture.

Julian could only stand where he was and wait. There was nothing else he could do. Regardless of how hard he had worked, he had to rely on the persuasive powers of his father.

Surely they knew that no one else could take his place? Julian's education had been grueling, as he mastered subject after subject: geography, languages, elocution, debate, logic... He had studied trade, heraldry, war, strategy, and tactics. His body had been battered after decades working at horsemanship, swordsmanship, archery, and wrestling. Knowing he had to be better, stronger, never allowing doubt in others to flourish, he had pushed himself to the highest standard in every endeavor. Even Julian's father hadn't had the same standard of education.

Now his entire future might be taken away from him. Here he was, powerless to intervene, as the decision was made over a cold luncheon and crisp white wine.

The discussion appeared to be reaching an end. Julian's father stood, followed by the three lords, who each displayed a different colored trim on his cloak to indicate the order he led: red for the soldierly Crusaders, black for the land-owning Wardens, blue for the trade-oriented Guildsmen. Ruling the Eternal Empire always meant dealing with the three orders. At the Marble Court, the orders almost always voted as a block. If two of the three orders decided to vote against Julian, there would be nothing his father could do.

The three noblemen moved slowly as they made their departure. Julian remained where he was, jaw tight as he looked on. Final words were exchanged. Then the lords left, and Julian's father continued to stand, watching them depart from his position at the table.

Julian still had to wait a little longer. He should at least stay where he was until the servants had cleared the half-eaten food and dishes from the table.

But as the moments passed, with the three men gone, he couldn't hold back anymore.

He left the hedge to head straight for the terrace. The path neatly divided the lawns of trimmed green grass as he walked with a purposeful stride. Climbing the stairs, he took in the scene on the terrace. Wine goblets decorated the table, haphazard in their placement; the discussion had gone on for a long time. Ice melted in a silver chalice, freshly brought from Kargul by the diviners. Berries, cheeses, nuts, and bread filled platters. The four men had attacked the carcasses of a pair of game birds.

But it was his father who held his attention. Rigel had been a soldier and a general before becoming emperor, and his past was still there in his straight back and the curt, brisk tones he used when speaking. His shoulders were wide, matching his height, and his waist was narrow. However his back was now stooped, giving him a thin look, rather than lean and muscular as he had once been. Neatly combed white hair topped a tall face, with a sharp, hawklike nose.

The emperor was turned toward Julian, regarding him with piercing dark eyes. His mouth was tight, but his face was always a little sour, which generally made him hard to read.

"Well?" Julian asked quickly. "What did they say?"

The emperor held up a hand as a cluster of servants arrived to clear the table. Their work was soon finished, and Rigel then spoke in a thin but commanding voice. "Sit down." He indicated the place beside the table's head, where he was standing. "Julian, do as I say. Sit."

Julian sat, but he was leaning forward, almost perched on the edge of his chair. His father took his own seat, and Julian still couldn't learn anything from his father's expression.

"Tell me. Please. Did they agree?"

The emperor's brow creased in a frown; just a slight one, but it caused Julian's mouth to snap shut. Rigel rapped his fingers on the table in front of him. When he spoke, his tone was surprisingly pensive.

"Julian, I loved your mother, as you know. She always wanted to have many children... but although we rarely understand it, the Great Weaver sometimes has other designs."

Julian remained silent, willing his father to continue, to give him the answer he desperately needed to hear.

"When she died in the birthing chair, I was shocked... the idea had never entered my mind that she might come to harm bringing you into the world. And yet I loved you, and as I grieved, I promised myself that I would make her sacrifice worthwhile. You became all I had, Julian. I promised her that your life would not be an ordinary one."

Rigel looked away, reflecting, and Julian held his breath.

"However I can only do so much. You have had every possible advantage I could give you. And yet your character is your own, and it is not something I can hold myself responsible for. I tried my best. But your father-in-law is a persuasive man as well as a vengeful one. Declan is the leader of the Guildsmen. You must have known they would always vote against your confirmation. I secured the support of the Wardens, and Tristan Benedict and the lords he represents will vote for you..."

Julian's eyes widened. A sinking, sickening sensation was like a heavy stone in his stomach. His vision tunneled in, his father's words sounding like they came from the top of a distant mountain.

"I could not persuade the reds, and the Crusaders will be allowed to vote as they wish, rather than as a block. I have no doubt that after what happened, many will vote against you." Rigel paused, and then stared into Julian's eyes. "I am sorry, Julian. But you will not be confirmed as my heir. When the vote fails, the process will begin to find an alternative successor. They don't think you are fit to be emperor after me. And in all honesty, after the... incident... it is difficult to argue otherwise."

"The incident..." Julian found his voice.

Rigel frowned. "Do not pretend to be dense. You know what I am referring to. The... duel... if you can call it that."

"But there was an inquiry. I was found innocent."

Rigel scowled. "An inquiry that I made sure would find you innocent. I would not have my son declared a murderer." His eyes narrowed. "Dueling has been outlawed for how long? A hundred years? And here you are, at twenty-six years old... You cannot claim to be a child, unlike Bryan Quinn, the only son of a man you could ill afford to turn into an enemy. You should have held off, even for that reason alone."

Julian's face was hot as he spoke in a burst. "What would you have had me do?"

"Temper yourself!"

Julian leaned over his fists, clenched together on the table. "You say you loved your wife. I love mine, and she will always have my support, including when it comes to her family." He could barely speak; he thought he had already explained himself. "Try to put yourself in my position, Father. It was her birthday. Her brother was not invited. But there he was, drunk and saying things I could not let stand. He called her a harlot, to her friends, to her face, and to me, her new husband. Listen to me, Father. Hear what he said…" He enunciated his words carefully. "Bryan Quinn said she had spread her legs for a hundred men – or perhaps two hundred, if she could even remember. How would you react if someone said that about my mother? I did what any man would do. I asked him outside, and I told him to be silent or I would issue a challenge. Was he silent? No. And even when swords were drawn, I sought to give him a flesh wound. The drunken fool staggered right into my blade."

"Before Bryan died at home with his parents weeping over him," Rigel said. "I have heard the story before." He sighed. "There are good reasons why the assembly votes every five years to confirm the successor. All you had to do was remain as you were. Instead you did this to yourself. The assembly will vote against your confirmation. I suggest you go home and explain the situation to your wife."

Julian had tried to prepare himself for both failure and success, but he had to put his hand over his mouth as he swallowed, tasting bile at the back of his throat. This couldn't be happening. What was everyone going to say? His insides churned, like he might empty the contents of his stomach. He had to find somewhere to hide where no one would ever see him.

"Julian, listen to me," Rigel said, lowering his voice. "Control yourself. I did my best. It was hard fought. But you have to see reality. Our empire has lasted for seven centuries. We all have a duty to see that it lasts for another seven more, all the way through to eternity. It is in our name. The Eternal Empire. It is in the name of our capital, this great city, Everlast."

Julian was too old for tears, but he felt his eyes burning anyway. "I have spent my life becoming what an emperor needs to be. Who from the assembly could say the same thing?"

"I know you believe that you have worked hard. But with each new emperor, the empire renews itself. We have had merchants… financiers… architects… philosophers…" The furrows on Rigel's face deepened. "They worry that when I die, someone with a different temperament, or a different set of skills might be needed. Different from the skills and talents that you possess."

"Yes, but that is why I have studied such a range of—"

"Julian, listen to me!" Rigel's aging voice had lost none of its cutting edge. "Stop this. You will not be my successor." He watched Julian's face, making it clear that he had done all he could. "Go to your wife. See what she says. She is a clever woman. No one would argue with that. She will understand."

As Julian stared with eyes unfocused, his head spinning, a steward came up to the table. "The one you asked for is here, Emperor."

Rigel stood. "I must leave you. I have business I need to attend to."

Julian also climbed to his feet. "But Father, you must—"

"I told you, I have done all that I can. You need to prepare yourself. You and your wife. I have worked hard for you. You will not be emperor, but the decision about what comes next must be yours." Rigel turned to the steward, who was waiting patiently. "Very well. Lead the way."

Julian called as his father began to walk away. "Who are you seeing?"

The emperor paused, turning to reply. "Just someone from the city. Nothing that concerns you." He called over his shoulder. "Go, Julian. You need to think about what you plan to do with the rest of your life."

As his father walked away, Julian tried to think of some solution, something his father might have missed, a plan his wife might be able to conjure. He left the table, brow creased and as he headed in a different direction from the one his father had taken.

Gnawing at his lip, he suddenly stopped.

He turned back, changing direction completely. After navigating the hall, he took the fastest path toward his father's personal quarters. Rigel's stately steps meant Julian would be able to get there before him. Julian descended some steps, passed a courtyard and another fountain, and came to a different section. A gilded doorway led to the antechamber inside.

He soon saw a bench, and a girl, obviously from the city, seated upon it.

With copper skin and long auburn hair, she was both pretty and exotic. She wore a brown dress that fitted her well, yet lacked elaborate embroidery or an expensive weave. More than anything, he was surprised at how young she appeared; she didn't look older than twenty.

Julian raised his voice. "You. Tell me your name."

She turned her head toward him and her expression revealed surprise and then fear. Her eyes were soft and brown, wide open as she watched him approach. She may not know who he was, but she could see his clothing and hear his speech.

She climbed to her feet; he was more than a head taller than her. She hesitated. "Bethany." She released her name reluctantly, without offering any family name.

His eyes narrowed. He was a prince; surely she wasn't so dim she couldn't work it out. "Why you?"

"I don't understand."

"Do you really value yourself so low? How much does he pay you?"

Spots of color appeared on the girl's cheeks. She remained silent, however, as Julian stared at her and scowled. His father was the emperor and could have any woman he wanted. Why her? And why not a woman from the Inner Territories, rather than someone with the coloring of the Far Reaches, a region torn by frequent wars with the empire?

His future had been taken away from him, and yet here was his father, leaving him in his time of need, to instead meet this girl from the city.

It didn't matter what she answered... how much his father was paying, nor what it was about her that his father felt drawn to. Rather than challenge her any further, he turned and strode away.

His father was right about one thing. He needed to see his wife.

Chapter Ten

As soon as Julian was gone, Bethany wiped a hand over her face. By all the stars alive, what an encounter to have. She had imagined how it might be, to one day meet him, to speak to him face to face. She could never have guessed he would accost her in the way he had and go on to draw such strong conclusions.

How could she have answered if he had asked, rather than assumed, why she was in the palace? She told herself to be proud of her restraint; it was a good thing she hadn't raised her voice to defend herself. It was better that he didn't know the truth.

Still on her feet, she heard footsteps. Another male figure was approaching, even more richly dressed in white and gold. He still had the same erect way of holding himself, even as he fought the stoop claiming his upper back. He was just as commanding, but he looked old. He was approaching seventy, after all.

Emperor Rigel Regus Livius, Bethany's father, spoke a single word. "Come," he said, beckoning to take her deeper into his personal quarters.

She had no choice other than to follow. Her mother had told her a thousand times never to see him. He was always to be avoided. She should never ask her father for anything.

But he was the emperor. If he sent for her, and his soldiers brought her here, what was she supposed to do?

As she walked through an archway she didn't see any servants. She and her father had complete privacy as they passed through a room filled with hanging flower baskets. Another entrance led to a sitting room, where the furnishings were wooden rather than stone, and divans decorated with plump pillows framed the center. The emperor went to a pair of benches with upturned arms that faced each other across a low table. He settled himself and directed Bethany to the opposite bench.

As Bethany sat, rather than speak immediately, her father inspected her slowly. Meanwhile, she reflected on how he had changed too. It had been six... no seven years since she had last seen him. She always thought he had forgotten about her, but then he would reappear in her life, if only for the briefest moment. The last time she saw him he had wanted to know the common people's view on the endless wars in the Far Reaches. She was young and naive enough to tell him the truth, that people thought the fighting had gone on for long enough. He gave nothing away, and sent her back to her shop. She would never know what influence she had, but soon after, he sent a famous general named Agapon to take charge of the struggle in the east.

"You had an encounter with my son just a moment ago. You were supposed to be waiting in here."

She frowned. "I waited where they told me to wait."

"Yes, I don't expect the mistake was yours. However, if there is a next time, we shall all have to be more careful."

She didn't reply. He was the emperor. It was his choice whether he wanted to see her and how he wanted it done. For her, this was only their third encounter, in the period of a little less than two decades since she had been born.

"Well I suppose what is done is done. My son seems to think you are some girl from the city providing me bed favors."

If he was trying to be humorous, his mouth remained downturned at the corners. He leaned forward, staring into her face.

She made herself meet his gaze. "That was my impression."

"It must have rankled."

"To be honest, I don't expect to have much to do with him."

"True." Rigel's eyes became unfocused, as if he was thinking hard about something. "Bethany... Bethany..." Once more, he looked her over. "Since we last spoke, you have become more of a woman. You are attractive. Different, yes, no one would think you were a Dymantine, despite my contribution to at least half of who you are. But yes, you are comely enough. You have a bright future ahead of you. And that is what we are here to talk about. Your future."

The way he said the last words sent a chill down her spine, and she tried to keep her expression calm, even as she wondered what he wanted.

"Before anything else, however, I have a test for you."

She tensed. "What kind of test?"

Her father ignored her question. "There is a diviner, a woman with yellow hair, originally from Skollard. She was discovered with a group of dissidents." He scowled. "These dissidents were caught in the midst of a plot to kill me. But I was lucky. One of her group, a boy, was caught for another crime and betrayed the group in an attempt to save himself. Do you know what their plan was?"

She knew that an answer wasn't expected.

"The empire is vast, and as emperor, I obviously make use of the gateways. This woman, a diviner, was going to maneuver herself to guide my next travel, and then she planned to leave me in the black tunnel, where only the Weaver would find me." He shook his head. "A terrible fate. Disturbing to say the least."

Bethany had never considered the idea that a diviner might enter a gateway, ready to guide someone to a given destination, but be the only one to emerge at the other end, leaving the other person inside... stranded.

"Now, I have a question for you. What should I do with this diviner? What should be her fate? This is your test, daughter."

She wished she didn't have to do it. "Should she have some kind of trial?"

"Her family is not powerful, Bethany. I am not asking you about process. I want your punishment."

She turned her gaze away from her father's dark eyes. She had to distance herself from her own feelings. Her father was certain of the woman's guilt and so she had to pretend to be too. She needed to be cold... logical. The plot wasn't initiated. But her father thought it was real. Would a few years in prison be suitable? Too little, she decided.

"A decade," she said. "Ten years in prison."

"Ten years," Rigel mused. "Hmm. It is interesting to learn something about how your mind works. Interesting, but also disappointing. You think of justice, yes, but I am expecting loyalty. Not from her, obviously. From you." He leaned forward, and his expression changed, eyebrows coming together in sudden anger. "After ten years, she could still pose a risk. Ten years is enough to maintain ties, to keep her plans alive. There is also the matter of the stories shared by the populace, which are important; stories should never be underestimated."

Bethany couldn't show it, but her mother was right, and had always been right—she wanted nothing to do with the world her father lived in.

Rigel continued, "A threat on my life – treason, no less – should be considered the harshest crime imaginable, with a penalty to make any man's stomach churn. The diviner from Skollard will be dead before the end of the day. Dismembered, taken apart piece by piece. But first, she will watch her children suffer the same fate in front of her. That part is for the stories." He saw her involuntary reaction. "Her children are fully grown adults, Bethany. I am not a savage."

The emperor's thin but cutting voice trailed away, leaving a silence in its wake that was somehow filled with blood and horror. He became reflective again, clearing his throat.

"Again, I am disappointed, Bethany. But I have to hope that you will learn. The empire is plagued by many threats and needs my guiding hand to survive. No risk is acceptable. None. A diviner's life is nothing when compared to the Eternal Empire. Before the empire there was a dark age that continued for a thousand years, two thousand years... it is impossible to say for how long. All we know is that when the first Dymantines came from across the sea, there were only stones to tell the tale. My empire's ruin, and the despair of another dark age, is something to be avoided. Would you agree?"

She nodded. "Of course."

He took a breath, and when he spoke, his tone was a little calmer. "Your world and mine are very different. You have few cares. Whereas I am under constant strain. I need allies everywhere. Do you understand? I have people watching my nobles, people watching the clerics and confessors, people watching the generals and officers, the list goes on."

He changed his tone again, watching her as his voice softened.

"However, I do not have the allies I need among the diviners. This plot could have succeeded. This time, I was lucky. And that is where you come in."

Her eyes widened with confusion.

"When a girl from the Far Reaches is assessed for the School of Divination, it becomes discussed. When the girl fails, and becomes angry, with many in the crowd disputing the result, the rumors grow. I then discover that the girl is you. My own daughter."

"I didn't fail—"

"I believe you," he interrupted.

She tilted her head, waiting for him to continue.

"Let me pose another question," he said. "If I were to help you, and resolve the confusion around your acceptance into the School of Divination, would you help me, your father, in return? Diviners are privy to many things. If my blood were to run true in your veins, and you are strong enough, intelligent enough, to become a diviner, would you be my diviner, even if that fact were known only to you and me?"

Bethany heard her mother's voice. *Never owe him anything.*

"It doesn't matter—" she began.

"Answer me," he snapped.

She hesitated. "They say that becoming a diviner is extremely difficult. If... if I were to somehow make it through, I..." She set her jaw as her voice strengthened. "I would not want to owe my success to anyone. Even to you."

Her father nodded to himself. He changed direction. "How is your mother?"

"As well as ever." A hot sensation grew in her cheeks.

"Please do not lie to me. You do us both a disservice. Regardless of where we are now, your mother and I were once close. Maryam is unwell. And the loss of her vision is just one symptom of a greater disease. I have access to the best clerics in the corpus. The very best, Bethany. They can help her."

She had a sudden image of Charlton standing in the rain, afraid to come in and deliver his news. She again heard the sound of her mother whimpering in her sleep.

"As to your entry to the School of Divination, it is done. The examiners have realized their mistake."

She made a sound of surprise. Charlton had tried everything. "I don't understand."

"I am sure that you do. You were number twenty-one, and now you are number twenty. As I said, it is done."

"But…" she trailed off. "How could that happen?"

"It appears one of the candidates has withdrawn his application. His parents have decided it better that he seek a more… settled life."

She shook her head. What kind of a visit had the young man's family received? "No. I can't accept this."

"You can, and you will. And you will remember that it was I who made this happen for you."

All she could do was shake her head; she didn't know what else to say.

"Diviners help powerful people travel the gateways. As a diviner, you would be of value to me, as my eyes and ears, supporting me from the shadows." Her father paused, once again staring into her eyes. "And as for practical matters, the corpus provides meals and lodgings, for as long as you remain in your studies. Your income would obviously grow substantially, if you were to be successful. Think about your mother. You know she needs more than just prayers, and more than the clerics of the Fabric District can offer. I can see the fear for her in your eyes."

She still didn't trust herself to speak.

"But can you do it? I cannot ensure your success, if you are unable to learn what they have to teach you."

She broke his stare. Her mother. She had to think about her mother. Her mother had warned her never to accept anything from her father. At the same time, his words still rang in her ears. He had access to the best clerics in the corpus…

"How would my mother get treatment?"

"Another matter that is already done. The finest clerics from the University will visit your mother at your dormus tomorrow. If anyone can help her, it is them."

Bethany had no other good options. There was only one choice to make. She would have to go directly against her mother's wishes, even as she sought to help her.

"My mother can't find out. She can never know I agreed to this. She knows that clerics cost money. What should I tell her?"

"Tell her that you prevailed upon the charity of the corpus, and they took pity. Or something else, if you would prefer."

The emperor straightened until he was on his feet, and she followed. For him, their meeting was done. He had accomplished what he had set out to achieve.

"I wish you luck at the School of Divination. Work hard. Now go. The stewards outside will show you the way."

He didn't embrace her, and she didn't know how she would have reacted if he had tried. As she walked away, she glanced back over her shoulder. He was tall, and his wits were as sharp as ever, but he was old. He wouldn't live forever. And his son, Julian, didn't know who she was. She would be free one day... free of any bargain her father thought she had made.

She now faced straight ahead. She would simply have to do her best. Her mother needed help, and by studying, Bethany would be giving her that help. She would have to work hard.

A growing excitement started in her stomach, climbing up her body and welling inside her.

She was going to be a diviner.

Chapter Eleven

JULIAN WAS TOO agitated to sit, and so he paced back and forth. Meanwhile, Samara lounged upon a nearby divan, her eyes on the ornate ceiling while she contemplated.

Clad in a sheer silk dress, gathered around her slender frame with a cord, she displayed her body in hints and suggestions, her creamy light-brown skin almost merging with the beige shade of the fabric. Her dark brown hair unfolded in long tresses, evoking thoughts of both girlishness and elegance. Her eyes were smoky and slightly tilted. While she pondered, she sipped cool white wine from a golden goblet.

"Did you hear me?" As Julian paced, he glared in his wife's direction. "The vote is going to fail. My father said it to my face. I will not be confirmed as his successor. And as soon as they find someone else, there will be no going back. When the time comes... when my father dies... a new emperor will claim the Nexus. Everything will be taken from us. I will no longer be a prince, nor will you be a princess. No one will want to see our faces, and we will spend our lives looking over our shoulders. Men who might have been emperors have a history of dying young."

A slight frown decorated Samara's forehead. She took another sip of her wine. "This was to be expected," she said. When she spoke, her voice was as soft as the silk hugging her body, with the slightest throaty tone.

Julian brought himself to a halt and stood over the young woman who was his wife. Even with the topic as dark as it was, he felt a longing below his belly when he looked at her, the way he always felt when he was with her. Samara's beauty was without parallel. There was grace in everything she did, a femininity beyond any other woman. When she entered a room, all eyes were on her, and even the way she walked was hypnotic, with a sway to her gait and a roll of her hips that on any other woman would have been too bold, even vulgar. But the way she walked, the way she moved; it was all just a part of who she was.

Along with the Imperial Palace, Julian and Samara's villa was located within the Nexus's walled boundary. With its twelve guest rooms, two halls, multiple living areas, fountains, gardens, and private baths, the villa would have been considered a palace in its own right in any other part of the empire. Compared to the Imperial Palace, however, it was just a little house, despite being the residence of the emperor's son.

"Expected?" Julian scowled. "What are you saying?"

Samara continued to inspect the fanciful decorations in the ceiling cornices. "As much as I don't like to mention anything positive about my father, he is nothing short of determined. Bryan was always his favorite. The beloved boy. The future lord of Graystone."

"And now your father is having his vengeance."

"Yes, my love. But there is something you may count on."

"Which is?"

"Me." She gave him a look of strong determination and then returned her gaze to the ceiling. "People always underestimate me. That is what my father did and what he continues to do now. And that is why we will win. To him I was always just a girl who had to be raised until I could be wedded off. My brother was younger but my father was blind to the way he used to taunt me. Just like he did at my birthday banquet. When I struck him to teach him a lesson, I was always the one blamed. And I was the one imprisoned in that convent school. What choice did I have? I escaped. I made something of myself, without help from anyone else. I sold trinkets and bought gold. I sold rubies and bought diamonds. I came to court, here in Everlast. And I met you, my love."

She arched an eyebrow in his direction. "How do you think that made my brother feel? To see me, now a princess, rising above anything he would know as lord of Graystone. I was with you, Julian. It was my birthday feast. And you—you were defending my honor. Unfortunately for us, however, the story they tell doesn't offer the full truth. All they hear is that you, a skilled swordsman, challenged my weakling brother to a duel, and then you ran him through. As I said, this was to be expected."

"Please don't tell me you are happy to lose everything—"

Samara sat up. She set her goblet down on a nearby table, and wriggled so that she was sitting cross-legged and staring into his eyes. Her silk dress shifted as she moved, hiding here, revealing there. She didn't appear to notice. "I didn't say I intend to lose, my love. You are worried you will fail to secure the vote and lose your claim to the crown. Your father tells you that in light of my brother's untimely death, he was unable to secure the support you needed. It then falls upon us to make sure the vote goes the way we want it to. You grew up with a soldier for a father. I grew up with a lawmaker, a man who makes it his business to ensure that votes always go the way he wants them to."

"I have tried, Samara. Without the Reds—"

"Without the Reds, you do not have enough support. I understand the mathematics. You have too few supporters. You have too many opponents."

"Without two of the three orders, we can't win."

"Allow me to correct you." She gave a slight smile to take the sting out of her words. "Our Assembly of Nobles divides itself into three orders. There are the Crusaders, the lords who wear red and give a voice to the empire's military. They are always wanting to ride forth and expand the empire's borders. Then there are the Blacks, the Wardens, landowners who hold onto the past and believe in conserving what we have. And finally there are the Blues, the Guildsmen, who believe in embracing change, in progress. Of the three, who are your strongest opponents?"

"The Blues, of course. Led by your father."

"Correct. However, as I said, on many occasions I have seen my father work to change the outcomes of crucial votes. Like going to war in the Reaches."

Julian snorted. "And look how that ended up."

"The Jaynians rebelled. We had to teach them a lesson." Samara's brow creased just a little. "Now, tell me something else. Is voting at the assembly compulsory?"

"No. Of course not. The nobles are scattered across the empire. For something of this importance, however—"

She held up a hand. "And as a reminder. We know that the Blacks are with you, the Blues are against you, and your father says you have fewer than half the Reds."

Julian nodded.

"As a rule," she continued, "while the Reds enjoy fighting and Blacks like to manage their estates, what is it the Blues are busy doing?"

"They call themselves Guildsmen for a reason. Most are craftsmen and traders. Merchants and the like."

"And with fewer landowners among them, they tend to travel the most. This leads me to my next question. Who is in charge of collecting the empire's taxes?"

"Your father."

"Correct, my father. Lord Declan Quinn of Graystone. The thing is, as he taught me, it is easy to focus on the big power blocks and the heads of the three orders: Tristan Benedict, Gavin Arturius, my father. But voting is a numbers game, and here is what we will do to influence those numbers. We will commence a general tax inspection of goods coming into Everlast—the kind of trading conducted by merchants rather than land owners, who aren't affected at all. What effect will this have? It will keep a lot of Guildsmen busy, and importantly, away from Everlast, making sure they pass inspection."

Julian frowned. "Even if we assume that you can somehow command the empire's tax officials, on the day of the vote the Blues will still come to the city."

"Now, how do most goods come into Everlast?"

"Through the Argent Arch."

"And that is where, on the day of the vote, we will also have officials at this end, inspecting all of the goods entering Everlast through the arch."

"It would be disruptive."

"Terribly," Samara said. "It would slow down everyone: merchants, craftsmen, laborers, farmers... everyone. And that is why we will provide a friendly warning to the people most likely to vote with us. No one wants to be stuck at the gateway. When they hear the warning, they will all make sure to be in the city by at least the day before."

Julian scratched his chin. "Everyone would be trapped at the Argent Arch. But of the people voting, the ones most likely to be caught up will be the Blues."

"Exactly."

"But your father is in charge of the empire's taxes. Not you."

Samara's lips curved in a smile. She put out her hand with the fist closed and dramatically turned it upward, opening her palm to display a ring. Julian's eyes widened. The device on the ring was well known: a spider straddling a star. The signet ring belonged to Samara's father, Lord Declan Quinn of Graystone.

"How did you get that?"

"I keep my eyes and ears open, and when I saw how the vote might be going, I made an unscheduled visit to see my father. I told him I was there to make peace. He barely looked at me, of course, but I know where he keeps his second signet ring, and I was there long enough to get it." Her eyes sparkled as she smiled. "You are looking at the new, temporary, commander of the empire's tax officials. I know how my father issues his orders. On the day of the vote, we will make sure that as many Blues as possible are nowhere near the Marble Court."

Julian's mouth dropped open. He was almost unable to believe her audacity—but he knew his wife. He nodded toward the signet ring. "When your father finds out, he is going to be furious."

She only smiled and shrugged. "But will he admit it in public? Think of the embarrassment."

"But what about the next confirmation vote? The law says another will come in five years. My father is old, but he is not that old."

"Life is a series of crises we must navigate. Let us get through this one first. You are going to be emperor, Julian, with me at your side. All you have to do is reach out and take it."

Samara smiled, reaching up for Julian to take her hands. He came over to squeeze her palms, and her slender fingers squeezed him back. In his mind, he repeated her words. *I am going to be emperor.*

"This is our time," she said. Still holding his hands, she guided him down, until he was sitting on the divan beside her. Their legs were touching, and he was aware of her body heat, like he was a boy again, rather than sharing the space with his wife. "You are going to be emperor, and I will always be your empress."

Moving like a cat, she backed away from him, until she was standing and facing the divan where he sat watching her. She unfastened the material from her body, allowing the garment to fall to the floor. She placed her fingers on his chin, tilting his head as she leaned forward, and he drank in her smell as she came in close and kissed his lips.

Chapter Twelve

KENDRICK CONWAY HATED Everlast. There was no busier city. It was so raucous, so stinking. At least he was only spending time in the Imperial District, one of the quarters nearest the Nexus, where the crowds were thinner and sewers were buried underground. Yet even here, in one of the city's most reputable areas, there was too much noise, and there were definitely too many people.

He scowled as he followed a wide path by the side of the busy road. A hot sun beat down overhead, yet there were few trees to offer shade. Horses and carts trundled past, along with well-dressed men and women on horseback, enough of them that it was miraculous they didn't collide more often. City folk on foot narrowly passed one another, making way without meeting eyes.

The buildings were as crowded as the roads. Terraced villas with intricate stonework framed both sides of the street: the residences of the nobles who frequented the Marble Court. Kendrick was one of their number, a landholder with a sizable estate, but attending the assembly was optional, and he only tended to come for the important votes. This time however, he had been asked to come early. Congestion was expected to grow at the Argent Arch, and the crowds at the city's main gateway were already bad enough as it was.

He became angry every time he came, and it wasn't just the city's frantic pace. Too old or too weak for real battles, some of his fellow nobles took pleasure in a different kind of warfare, where victory depended on rabble-rousing, bribery, and scapegoating. Not him. He knew that pleasant words often covered secret strategies. Every favor came with a price. Politics and more politics. When it came to the Marble Court, he was glad that wherever possible, he had the good sense to stay away. He had his own villa in the city, but that didn't mean he had to use it any more than necessary. As soon as his business was done – as soon as the vote was over – it was back home to Esk for him.

He heard a throat clear, reminding him of his escort walking beside him. The flaxen-haired soldier had greeted him after Kendrick had barely settled in at his villa. With his eager smile and boyish face, he looked far too young to be wearing armor and carrying a sword. And unfortunately, from the way he kept glancing Kendrick's way, he wasn't happy with the silence between them.

"Do you come to Everlast often, Lord Conway?"

"As rarely as I can."

Kendrick was still groggy after his travel. Esk wasn't as far away as some other parts of the empire, but every sense told him that the hour here in Everlast was wrong. The smell of spiced meat was making his stomach churn. Lunch was supposed to still be some time away.

"Your journey was difficult?"

Kendrick replied in a growl. "No. It was the same as it always is." The lad kept watching him, so something more might be needed. "My diviner is skilled. He's been with my family for a long time. I just don't like to travel, that's all."

The flaxen-haired soldier nodded sagely, as if Kendrick had offered wise advice. But as they followed the street, the young man continued to look Kendrick's way; for him, the conversation wasn't over quite yet.

Kendrick wondered what he had been like at the same age, and imagined himself walking beside a swarthy lord with gray in his brown hair, given the honor of showing the older man the way. Kendrick could guess how he looked, with his stubbled cheeks and hard face that had seen too much fighting, his weary dark eyes and the bushy black eyebrows that gave him a fierce glare. Surely anyone would see that glare and know when a man wanted silence? The lad should be off looking for girls, fawning over a pretty lass instead of trying to pry open a dialogue with a grumpy old fighter.

The young man cleared his throat. "Lord Conway?"

When he caught worry in his companion's eyes, Kendrick heard his wife's voice inside his head. Perhaps he was being too harsh on the lad. He might as well get it over with. "Is there something you want to ask me, lad?"

The flaxen-haired soldier summoned his courage. "May I ask you about it? About the siege?"

"No," Kendrick said. The word came out instinctively, before he thought about what he was saying. When his companion's expression became downcast, he immediately regretted it. "I am only jesting." He attempted a dry smile. "Go on. Out with it."

"Is it true that you broke the siege with just twenty men?"

Kendrick tried not to remember, even as he answered. "Twenty-three. There were twenty-three of us."

"What was the hardest part?"

Kendrick stared into the distance. "The hardest part was protecting the diviner. We had to get him inside the castle so he could open the gateway. The enemy knew we needed him. They were the same killers who butchered the other diviner. Never seen such a hail of arrows. We built a wall of shields. Fought hard... with everything we had."

"But you got him into the castle in the end. You saved everyone."

"Aye, lad. We did."

"And you saved the emperor too."

"He wasn't the emperor then. He was a general, but still an important man. Remember, it was years ago."

"But he became the emperor. And he owes you his life."

"If he owes his life to anyone, it is to all the men who died. Not to me, lad."

The young man nodded, but judging from his awestruck expression, he wasn't convinced. Kendrick hoped he had given him enough. At the same time, he felt a simmering anger that he tried to keep inside. If he wanted to talk about a difficult memory, when so many died around him, it should be his own choice.

He raised his gaze, relieved to see a building much larger than the villas they had been passing. The structure was four stories tall, made of thick walls of dark stone, with a tall, spiked iron fence surrounding it. Within the bars, a graveled perimeter was like the killing zone inside a castle's walls. The building looked out of place in the Imperial District, almost like a small fort or keep.

The iron gates were guarded, but Kendrick and his companion didn't slow. The guards gave Kendrick a nod; they knew his face, and both placed hands over their hearts. Kendrick nodded back to them as he followed a short path to a flight of steps that led to the wide open doors.

Kendrick had been here before, many times, and it never changed. He and his escort walked through the entrance beneath a shield on a black flag that was the only sign the building needed. Black gates, black doors, stone walls, black flag. A mood had been set. He was at the headquarters of his order, the group he had effectively been born into, along with his father before him. He was visiting the House of the Wardens, the order also known as the Blacks.

"This way, My Lord."

Kendrick knew the way, but he let the young man lead him inside, up a flight of stairs and down a hallway, until they came to a black door with an iron handle. A knocker jutted from its center, a hammer striking a miniature shield.

Kendrick's escort rapped with the knocker. A moment later, Kendrick heard a muffled voice calling out to enter. Hearing the voice, a warm feeling of anticipation grew in Kendrick's chest. They may not see each other often, but old friends were the best kind of all.

"Thank you," Kendrick said with a nod for the young soldier, who pushed the door open.

"It has been an honor, Lord Conway."

Kendrick entered the room and the door clicked closed behind him. Unable to hide a smile, he peered into a large study with a cold hearth at one end and an oversized desk at the other. A glass-paned window was open to relieve the summer heat. As soon as he saw Kendrick, the man behind the desk leaped out of his chair, bounding over with arms wide open.

"Kendrick!" Tristan cried.

Tristan Benedict, the leader of the Wardens, was a tall, gray-haired, heavy-bellied man, with warm blue eyes, a jowly chin, and smile lines. As was usually the case, his clothing looked expensive, with a shimmering crimson tunic worn over black leather leggings. Even among an order made up of landowners, his estate in Breanne was nothing short of immense, with a grand castle that he and his family called home.

"Tristan." With a wide smile, Kendrick put out his hand, only to see Tristan stop and stare at it in mock astonishment.

"So formal, Kendrick? Look at us, we are old men and so now we have to shake hands? And to think that we shared the same chamber pot for half a year." Tristan opened his arms wide, and gave Kendrick a tight hug strong enough to make Kendrick wince, before they stood back and regarded each other.

"Look at you. You haven't changed a bit," Tristan said.

"We both know that isn't true."

"In all sincerity. Family life is treating you well. You look as strong and hearty as the day we first rode out together." His smile broadened. "A little weathered, perhaps. No doubt Esk's famous winters are not enough to keep you indoors."

"Indoors?" Kendrick pretended to think. "Remind me what that means again?"

Tristan laughed, a big hearty rumble pouring from his chest. "Fairly said. I can picture you riding and hunting but I have to say I find it hard to see you reading by a fire. As for me, I cannot even remember the last time I went hunting. Like I said, you haven't changed a bit. Me, on the other hand." He smiled and patted his belly. "Fine food every day for me. I have too few years left for anything else. You should see what you can get now here in the city." He chuckled, shaking his head. "Remember that time we had to eat horse meat for a month?"

Kendrick snorted. "How could I forget? We ran out of ways to prepare it."

"And you kept burning the pots." Tristan's grin became wider. "Over and over again. Your fingernails were black from scrubbing." He smiled as his eyes became unfocused, before shaking himself after the moment of remembrance. "Ho hum. Time is always marching on, eh? Shall we?"

Tristan indicated the desk. "Us old men do enjoy the comfort of a padded chair."

Kendrick took a seat, while Tristan returned to his place behind the desk, pulling his chair up and leaning forward.

"It is too rare that we see you in Everlast. I mean it, Kendrick. We all wish you would come more often."

"Me? Spend more time in the city?"

Tristan wasn't smiling anymore. "These things are important." He clenched his fist on the table. "You know we could use you at the assembly. If only I could convince you..."

"I would be just another vote."

"We both know that isn't true. Your name is known... Sir Kendrick Conway, the proud knight and savior of Curran Castle. You have more influence than you appear to realize."

Kendrick felt the onset of a familiar restlessness. "Mind if I stand?"

Without waiting for an answer, he left his place to move about the room. Tristan followed him with his eyes as Kendrick inspected the decorations on the wall. Military accolades, earned by Tristan on the battlefield, covered a section, along with Tristan's tournament accomplishments in archery and jousting. Above the hearth, the Imperial banner hung proudly: a crown of gold, set with blood-red stones, against a field of purple. Another wall displayed a second banner, black as night, bearing the shield insignia of their order.

"My tournament victories pale beside yours, I am afraid," Tristan said from his position at the desk. "The best swordsman there ever was. I don't know anyone who would disagree."

Kendrick grunted, returning his attention to Tristan. "We are friends, Tristan—"

"Brothers, Kendrick."

"Brothers," Kendrick nodded, "you know that I feel the same way. I'm sure you also know I'm standing here wondering: how does he plan to convince me? Anthea is my wife, Tristan. Declan is my brother by marriage. I have no choice but to vote with my conscience."

Tristan sighed. "Straight to the point, as always. I am afraid that you are correct. We do need to discuss the confirmation vote. I will say it plainly. I need you to vote with the rest of us."

Kendrick headed closer until he was standing over the desk. "I just explained my position."

"As I said, you have influence, Kendrick. And in this particular case your actions will be watched more than anyone else, with the potential exception of Julian himself."

"I hear the vote is going to go against him," Kendrick said.

"It will."

"And when it does, the process will begin to find another, more suitable successor."

"Correct."

"Then why would I vote to support him? I have to think of my family. I don't need to remind you what happened. Julian murdered the son of my wife's brother—my own nephew. This idea of it being any sort of duel is a farce."

"You are a Warden, Kendrick. A Black. We are the emperor's staunchest allies, and it is important that we be seen to vote along with him, even when it is a lost cause. Perhaps especially when it is a lost cause."

"No," Kendrick spoke in a growl. As close as he and Tristan were, this wasn't the first time they had argued, and it wouldn't be the last. "The rest of you can all vote with the emperor, and I will not think anything of it. But I will not vote to confirm that man as the emperor's heir, not after what he did. Let us just say that his suitability has come into question."

"Think of your family—"

"I am."

Tristan held up a hand. "Listen to me, my old friend," he said softly. "I don't ask you to think of your family lightly. You have been given the honor of hosting the fielding. You, Kendrick. You and your family. At your estate."

Kendrick frowned at the change in topic. "That has nothing to do with this."

Tristan barked a laugh. "It has everything to do with this. How often do we have a fielding? Once every four or five years? Hosting a fielding is not just an honor, it is a sign that you are high in the emperor's esteem, that your *family*," he emphasized the word, "is considered one of the great houses of the empire. Your sons are now of age. You and your wife wanted the fielding so that when they are knighted in ceremony, their names will be remembered. You wanted the fielding so that when your sons compete in the tourneys, they will have the advantage of home ground. Tell me. Troy and Caden—how old are they now?"

"We both know you already know the answer. Troy is twenty-one. Caden nineteen."

"And let us not forget Isabelle."

"Isabelle? She is just twelve. What does she have to do with anything?"

"Ah, my old friend, you may try to fool yourself, but don't forget, I have daughters too. She will grow even more over the next year, and she will be noticed, despite her age. I am sure that when the time comes, you will want her courted by the finest suitors."

"Great Weaver, Tristan. I said she is twelve."

Tristan chuckled, breaking the tension. "One must think ahead—ask your wife. Now, Kendrick, we know what all of this means for your family. The fielding takes place next summer. It will be an important event. I would like it if you could continue to be the host. Please, my old friend. Do not disappoint me."

Tristan was issuing a warning, but as the man who had helped Kendrick get the fielding in the first place, it was his warning to give. He was also close enough to Kendrick to know that Kendrick would do anything for his family.

"And let me be clear, in case there is any confusion... The reason you got the fielding, and not someone else, is because you are a Warden, and because we always – all of us – vote with the emperor. You and I, we are Blacks to the core, and I include you, even if you rarely show up here in the capital. Black is unchanging. There is no argument about its shade. It is always black. When the first Dymantines came from across the sea, what did they find? Ancient buildings. Gateways. The bones of this great city. All abandoned. That is our first and most important lesson. Such a fall must never happen to us. One of the Reds might have been selected for the fielding, but instead it was you. This gives us power over what happens with the new army that we will assemble. For there is another consideration, one that others may not have given much weight to, but one that keeps me awake at night. We are stuck in an endless war with the Jaynians. What if another horde comes to our borders? This fielding is needed for a reason beyond some nobles playing at war. We disbanded the Western Armies, but at the end of the fielding, they must be reformed, ready to defend our empire. I want this fielding to be a success. And that is why it must be you. "

Kendrick blinked. Somehow, Tristan had made it so they were talking about the fielding, rather than the upcoming vote.

"I know there is a generous donation from the assembly," Tristan said. "However the fielding's success is about more than just gold. Do you feel certain your family is up to it?"

Kendrick's eyebrows came together. "You know my wife. Of course we are."

"You will need an immense amount of supplies. Pavilions. Tents. Fences for the jousting. Ranges for the archery. Arenas for sword-fighting and wrestling—"

Kendrick interjected, "Viewing galleries for the high-born. Enclosures for the rest. Latrines. Food and drink stalls. Clerics to tend to the wounded. Confessors to conduct prayers. I am not saying it will be easy, but it is within our capability."

"I am pleased to hear that. And at the knighting ceremony, your sons will become Sir Troy and Sir Caden of Esk. They will compete and win honors, watched by all, and their futures will be assured. When the time comes they will have estates of their own, and grandchildren for you and your wife to visit. Your daughter is young but she will be seen. You don't want a scant choice of suitors. You want the best for Isabelle."

"Enough, Tristan. You have made your point."

"The Wardens are your family too, Kendrick. Many will be watching to see what you do."

"Very well." Kendrick let out a breath. "I will do as you ask. I think my wife will understand, but I am not sure I will be able to say the same thing about her brother. You know it as well as I do, when it comes to Julian, Declan is determined to see him fall."

"Let Declan do as he pleases." Tristan stood up and put out his hand. Kendrick reached out and shook it. "I am glad we can count on you. In fact, there is another vote—"

Kendrick jerked his hand back as if he'd been stung.

Tristan's laughter made his body shake. "I am jesting, Kendrick." Leaving his chair behind, he came around the desk to open his arms. "You should have guessed when I put out my hand. I told you before. Just because we're old men doesn't mean we are no longer brothers."

As Tristan pulled him into an embrace, Kendrick shook his head, but he was smiling. "Just remember. Once this vote is done, it's back home to Esk for me."

"I understand. Just remember what I said. We could use you more often at the assembly."

Chapter Thirteen

BACK OUT ON THE street again, Kendrick's mood was grim. Why had he just agreed to vote in support of Julian, the man who killed his nephew? He knew why. By the stars, it was going to be a big year.

He turned to his flaxen-haired escort. "It's fine, lad. I can find my own way home." When the young man gave him a skeptical look, he attempted a smile. "I've been coming here a long time. It's a big city, but there's a certain logic to it."

"It has been an honor, My Lord."

"When duty calls, you see what you are made of."

Kendrick's words sounded foolish to his own ears, but he felt like he had to say something. He held out his hand and the young man shook it, awe still on his face as he returned to the House of the Wardens.

Meanwhile, something on the other side of the street caught Kendrick's attention. A wiry man with a scraggly gray beard and a lopsided black hat was sitting on a bench and watching him. The man in the hat didn't look away, even as Kendrick frowned, his eyes narrowing until he was pointedly staring back.

Kendrick cursed under his breath. He had been looking forward to heading back to his city villa and enjoying some peace in the comfort of familiar surroundings. But here he was, in Everlast, with an important vote upcoming. Sometimes confrontation couldn't be avoided.

Tension settled onto his shoulders as he looked right and left, waiting for a gap in the passing horses, wagons, and carts, before crossing the street to walk straight up to the man in the black hat.

"I don't appreciate being followed," Kendrick said in a low growl. "I don't remember your name, but I do know who you work for."

"The name is Rowan, My Lord," the man in the black hat said, unperturbed as he climbed to his feet. "My master asked me to see where you went. He thought you might come here, and if that were the case, he bid me to ask that you come to see him. If it pleases you, My Lord."

"He knows where he can find me."

"He isn't far, My Lord. This way. Please."

Rowan indicated, and Kendrick grimaced but finally fell in beside him. He would have to face up to the situation at some point, and it might as well be right away. At least it would be done. He wasn't one to keep his actions hidden. He preferred things out in the open.

As Kendrick followed his companion, they turned from the street onto a wider, busier avenue. The crowds gained force, and Kendrick scowled as he stepped around groups of people who didn't care if everyone else had to go around them. Horses whinnied as they clattered past. Dogs excreted in the street. In the alleyways, piles of refuse buzzed with flies.

Entering a new district, the distant walls of the Nexus came into view as they took an angled path toward Imperial Avenue and glimpsed the Argent Arch, which stood proud and tall on its hill. Turning again, they traveled an avenue where jewelers' shops would have consumed Anthea's attention for hours, before following Long Street, a narrower road that connected to Imperial Avenue. The savory smell of fresh bread made Kendrick look wistfully over his shoulder as he passed a baker's stall.

Rowan led Kendrick straight for a tavern with a wheel-shaped sign proclaiming its name in large letters: *The Cartwheel Tavern*. He climbed the steps and walked inside, as Kendrick followed just behind.

The tavern's interior was dim after the daylight in the streets outside. Wooden tables and benches filled a hall-like space that was now empty after the bustle of earlier hours. The scent of ale permeated the air, along with the more meaty odor of stew.

Kendrick and his companion crossed the tavern's interior, heading to a tall, well-dressed man seated at a corner table. Declan Quinn of Graystone appeared the same as ever, lean enough for his limbs to look thin, with a high forehead and calculating eyes that never stopped working. His ash-colored hair was neatly combed, and he was always clean-shaven. Where Tristan Benedict was the head of the Blacks, Declan was the leader of another order, the Blues, also known as the Guildsmen. And he was a member of Kendrick's family, the brother of Anthea, Kendrick's wife.

Declan spoke without smiling. "Kendrick." He wore black, which he had done ever since the death of his son Bryan. But he had never been a jovial man.

"Declan," Kendrick replied.

"Thank you, Rowan. That will be all," Declan said.

"Very well, My Lord." Rowan bobbed his head at Kendrick. "My Lord." He departed quickly, having completed the task his master set him.

As soon as they were alone, Kendrick scowled. "By all the stars alive, Declan. You had me followed?"

"You know I try to know everything that happens in Everlast, Kendrick. I caught wind that you were in the city and I wanted to find out why. It isn't like you to arrive early for a vote." Declan indicated the seat opposite. "Please. Sit down. Surely we have a few moments to talk."

Kendrick reluctantly sat down at the table. This wasn't going to be easy. He noted the papers Declan had spread out on the surface in front of him. "This is an interesting place to work."

"The owner is a friend, and I like the food." Declan rapped his long fingers on the table. "How is my sister?"

"Anthea is well. And you? How is Meredith..?" Kendrick bit his tongue as he remembered: Bryan's death had cast a dark cloud over Graystone, pulling Declan and Meredith apart rather than together.

"I am sure you have heard from my sister. Meredith spends her days in solitude. As for me, I have my work. I find it makes things easier when I am busy."

"Are you still working on your abbey?" Kendrick changed the subject.

"Graystone Abbey recently occupied much of my time. However there has been no progress at all since the untimely death of my son. I am sure you remember me saying that nothing is more important than preserving knowledge for the empire's eventual fall. Well, it seems that some things are more important after all. Now. Please. I want to know. Why are you here early? Why not come on the day of the vote?"

Kendrick resigned himself to the inevitable. "I was asked to come early."

"By Tristan?"

"Yes."

"And how is my counterpart in the Blacks?"

"Busy."

"As we all are. Well, now that we are here, we may as well get everything into the open." Declan paused, and then fixed Kendrick with his penetrating stare. "We both know why he asked to see you. He was pressuring you to give him your vote."

Kendrick hesitated; here it came. "Which, after serious consideration, I have just agreed to do."

Declan leaned forward, fists bunched together on the table. "After he killed Bryan? Murdered him in cold blood? Julian should be—"

"Declan," Kendrick interrupted. "Tristan says you already have the numbers you need. Julian's confirmation is going to fail."

"Every vote counts, Kendrick. People will see you—"

"People will see me voting with my order. I was selected to host the fielding, Declan. The emperor gave my family the honor. To vote against his son would be too much."

"Anthea—"

"Anthea will understand. Listen. I am sorry. Of course I want Julian gone. And that is what you are going to do. I just can't be seen to be one of the people joining you."

"Can't be seen...?" Declan broke off, glaring hard at Kendrick. "I thought you had courage. And yet here we are. I must have been mistaken."

Kendrick took a long inhale, and then slowly let the breath out. While he had lost a nephew, Declan had lost his son. And Samara was never coming back to her father's arms. In terms of children, Declan and Meredith were effectively now alone.

"As I said, I am sorry. I have never voted against my order and now is not the time to start. If it weren't for the fielding—"

"Burn the fielding."

"If it weren't for the fielding, of course you would have my vote. I am only one of many. They all know what happened, and I know you, Declan. I know how persuasive you can be. Julian will never be emperor. You will see to it. I have complete faith in your ability to get this done."

Declan's face was hard, like stone. "I need you to change your mind."

"I cannot."

"Kendrick—"

Declan stopped when Kendrick stood up. Kendrick had said all he could—he had to vote with his order, and he had to do what was right for his family. As a result, there was no escaping Declan's wrath. The fielding was taking place next summer, less than a year away. In time, his wife's brother would understand.

"I need them to see you vote with the side of justice, Kendrick. That is all I ask."

"And I have to do what is right for my family. Again, I am sorry, Declan. I know you. You will do what must be done."

Chapter Fourteen

FOR BETHANY, CLOSING up her shop was a familiar ritual. First, she gathered the takings and put the coins in a pouch she hid in her dress. She then cleaned, paying particular attention to the area where customers queued. She checked over her notes and made sure they were all in order. She gathered the various projects that had arrived throughout the day and carefully wrapped them in canvas, ensuring not to crush or tear anything delicate.

As darkness settled over the Fabric District, and weariness made her long for home, she hoisted the garment bag, ready to depart. She took one last look over the shop's rear, making sure she hadn't missed anything.

"I would put that back down again, if I were you."

She quickly turned as Charlton entered her shop and then closed the door behind him. He carried a bundle in his hands, gingerly, as if holding something precious.

Bethany set down her shoulder bag. All of a sudden she was wide awake.

"Look," Charlton said. His blue eyes were gentle, but also sparkling, as he displayed the folded garment he was carrying. "You did it, Bethany. You have been accepted. They gave me this..." he met her gaze, "to give to you."

As Charlton handed it out, she took the bundle, focusing all her attention on it. It was a gray garment, in pristine condition, neatly folded and tied with a ribbon. She knew immediately that it was a cloak, and not just any cloak. With shaking hands, she set it down on her bench and untied the ribbon. She then held the cloak up, revealing the hood and inner pockets. The fabric was soft, supple, and expensive. The cloak was even made to her size.

"It is the same as any diviner's cloak. The only rule is that while you are studying, you have to wear gray underneath. If you graduate, then you can wear other colors, and it is customary to take inspiration from the heavens with the designs on your clothing– stars, moons, comets and the like. You must take care of it, and if you don't succeed, then unfortunately it must be returned."

Bethany tore her attention from the cloak. Her conversation with her father was a secret; as far as Charlton was aware, no one had known this was coming. "I don't understand. What happened?"

"I know this comes as a surprise. It was to me. You were number twenty-one. And we both know that you would have made it further." His smile was getting wider as he spoke. "One of the other successful candidates withdrew his application, and so... here we are."

Bethany's insides clenched. Her father had done what he had, without her asking or knowing. But at the same time, she should never have been disqualified. If she could go back, what could she change? It was difficult to understand how she felt.

Could she tell Charlton? No. If she did, she would have to tell him everything, and then he would see her differently. She was doing this not for her father, but for her mother. She would have to do her best with the opportunity she had.

"As they say, the Weaver works in mysterious ways," Charlton said. "You were unlucky to be dismissed at the testing. The Weaver is restoring balance. I am so happy for you, Bethany. You did it. You are going to study at the School of Divination."

She continued to examine the gray cloak, and then Charlton's thoughts obviously went to the same place hers did.

"By the stars, your mother..." he said, staring into her face. "She wouldn't know. Of course not. You didn't know yourself. How has she been? Those clerics... I don't know how you got them to help, but there is no one better at the University."

A diviner's cloak was in Bethany's hands. What was she going to say to her mother? She cleared her throat; Charlton was waiting for her reply. "Her headaches... they've been getting worse. The clerics from the University gave her some medicine. Something called..." She always struggled with the unfamiliar name. "Somnifer... It helps."

"Somnifer?" Charlton made a sound of surprise. "How much have they given you?"

"A small flask." Bethany indicated with her fingers. "She takes a spoonful in the morning and evening. Why?"

"In a few weeks you are going to need more. But somnifer is expensive. Terribly so."

"How expensive?"

"That vial would be worth more than your shop would collect in a month."

"Oh." Her heart sank. "No one told me."

"Listen to me, Bethany. You have this opportunity. They give every student a starting grant. Not much, but it should be enough to get you and your mother through to the end of your studies. You will have to close this shop. I am sorry to be so direct, but that is what is going to happen. I will do what I can, and I can help ensure your mother is cared for. We have people we work with who can help, and I have a particular woman in mind, Dahlia. She is kind, and hard-working, and knows her business. You can count on her, and you can count on me. Becoming a diviner is difficult. You will be too busy to visit often."

Bethany swallowed. The enormity of it all... so much was going to change. She had been touching the cloak, as if its soft feel would comfort her, but she now forced herself to look at the man in front of her, with his round face, covered in disheveled graying hair, his wrinkles and his hopeful blue eyes.

Charlton had done so much for her. He gave her the books; he sponsored her candidacy. Now he was promising to take care of her mother, during a time when, to realize her future, she had to leave behind the woman she cared about more than anyone else.

"Charlton?"

"Yes, my dear?"

How could she thank him? As she remained silent, he stepped forward and his eyes were glistening. He opened his arms, and held her tightly. She hugged him back as hard as she could.

She glanced again at the gray cloak on the counter.

Everything was going to change.

✦

Bethany cleaned up the dormus while her mother sat in one of the old armchairs, staring into her tea. As she worked, Bethany couldn't help but notice the little things being left undone, one by one. Not the things her mother did for them both, but the many contributions Maryam made toward taking care of herself. While Bethany was at the shop, if the water jug was dry, her mother never filled it anymore from the big ewer in the washroom. If Bethany didn't leave food prepared on the table, her mother didn't eat. On hot days, the window stayed closed. On wet days, the shutters were open.

In a frightening space of time, Bethany's mother had gone from small and spry, cheerful and energetic, to frail and fatigued, plagued by powerful headaches. Her long copper hair looked thin and dry. She had lost her love for food, and for her work, and Bethany no longer heard the songs of Loriastris she used to hum. If she did any cutting or stitching, it was only the simplest tasks. She wore the same dangling earrings, which Bethany still thought of as acorns, but the tinkling sound they made as she moved about wasn't audible as often.

As Bethany cleaned and tidied, she reflected on their conversation.

It hadn't gone well.

Bethany hadn't just come home with the cloak of a diviner, she had also picked up her mother's new cane, which was fashioned to be appropriate for her mother's height and weight. She hadn't predicted any repercussions—the cane was ready and the carpenter was impatient to take his final payment, and so she took the opportunity to collect it.

She glanced at the cane now as it leaned against the wall in the corner. It was a length of smooth black ebony, half her mother's height and hooked at one end. Surprisingly thin, it was nonetheless strong.

106

She should have planned things better. She had entered the dormus, garment bag over her shoulder, ebony cane clutched in her hand. Immediately her mother, sitting in the armchair, had squinted at the cane, perplexed, before realizing what it was. Bethany pretended to be enthusiastic as she handed it over, even as her mother's face fell, for she knew what the cane meant. She would need it to walk. And then, she would need it to fumble around in her world of perfect darkness.

And then Bethany's mother noticed the cloak, peeking out the top of the garment bag.

Bethany had to explain it all as if she had been caught unexpectedly, even though she had planned to talk. Her mother already knew about the books, but Charlton's sponsoring of her, the assessment...Bethany told her everything, except for one thing she didn't mention.

Hearing a noise as she tidied, she turned and caught her mother watching her. Maryam was blinking, and then she wiped at her eyes.

"I wish I could see you better. You are such a beautiful girl, Betani." Sounding hoarse, Maryam cleared her throat. "I will never see you clearly again."

Bethany hurried over and pulled the second armchair closer. She sat down and reached out to take her mother's hand. "You know I will come and visit."

"And I will stare at the walls, and imagine your face, rather than see it with my own eyes. As you grow, I won't get to see you change."

"I will always be your daughter. And you will always be my mother. When I was little, you told me stories. You taught me letters and numbers. You fed me and kept me safe. Let me do my part. If I can become a diviner—"

"But you are so young."

"When you were my age you were already following the Imperial army, making money as a seamstress to the soldiers."

"There was a famine. The money was good."

"I know that. I understand."

As Bethany watched her mother's face, her thoughts turned to her father, and how he had occupied such a large role in her mother's life. This was the part Bethany had held back—the part her father played in her admission to the School of Divination.

Silence persisted for a time, as Maryam again stared into her tea.

"Mother... About my father... Would you have come to Everlast, if you hadn't met him?"

"Would I have still come to Everlast?" Maryam's brow furrowed. "Probably, yes. I had heard so much about it from the soldiers whose uniforms I mended. I was already saving to come here and open my own shop when I met him. He was an officer. Much older than me but handsome... Respected. There was a sadness about him that I think I helped him forget. He told me about how his wife died... I might have been the only one he thought he could talk to. Julian was five then, raised by a nursemaid while Rigel stayed with the army. He was always hard-working. Rigel was, I mean."

"And you were married."

She gave a little smile. "After a while we were. Just the two of us and the local elder who married us. We had a sweet little ceremony in the forest, which was plenty enough for me." She glanced at the window, remembering. "And then came the crisis. Emperor Leon was only eighteen when the plague took him. I knew that Rigel was worried... he kept saying there was no clear successor. I told him I was pregnant with you right before they summoned him back home. He said he would come back soon."

"But he never did."

Maryam sighed. "I don't think even he knew what was coming. But then I learned he was going to become the emperor. Everyone was talking about it, of course. I realized he wasn't coming back, and so I decided to travel to Everlast. It was a long journey, but I got here in the end, and when I did I went to the palace and asked to see him. He never came. Someone else did."

Bethany tried to picture her mother, leaving behind the world she knew to travel from the war-torn Far Reaches to the empire's immense, sprawling capital. She had made that arduous journey while pregnant – with her – and holding onto her dream of being reunited with the man she loved.

"They put me in some rooms near the University and had me cared for by the clerics. You were born and I was so happy. And then a man came with some money and a piece of paper. He told me my marriage to

108

Rigel had been annulled. I could take the money as long as I kept my lips sealed. I asked why, of course. I was young and still holding onto dreams of love. They were uncaring enough to tell me the cold truth. Now that he was the emperor, Rigel's supporters would never approve of me. And so it was over. Just like that. After the last time we spoke in Loriastris, I never saw him face to face again."

"He hurt you."

"He did. But it was a long time ago now, my love."

"What was he like, though, in the time that you knew him?"

"We were only together for about a year." Maryam's face softened. "He seemed kind, at least I thought he was, in a part of him that he didn't show to anyone else. With the army, everyone knew I was his, and that was fine with me. It was my idea to get married. That's why I still wear these," she touched one of her earrings, "they say that I am a married woman. And when you were born, Betani, you had two parents who were together, no matter what some confessor's document now says. He already had his son, though. I knew he would never acknowledge you in public."

"I wonder why he never married anyone else?"

"I always thought he would. I suppose it is interesting, but that is all it is. Only Rigel knows how he feels about what happened. He knows how to find us. And like I said, it was a long time ago now."

Bethany squeezed her mother's hand. The weight of harsh reality must have been heavy. And yet her mother had kept going, opening her shop and developing a well-regarded reputation as a seamstress. Not only that, but Maryam had been a wonderful mother to Bethany, generous and kind, thoughtful and understanding.

"I took his money, but that wasn't what I wanted. I wanted him to acknowledge you, and to love you. But he wanted to forget me, and for me to forget him. I'm sure he would have liked me to leave Everlast. But I had to build a future for you, for us, and this was where we had to do it."

Maryam's eyes were unfocused. "I think it scarred him deeply... when his first wife died. The longer I live here in Everlast, the more I learn about him, and he now seems like a different man from the Rigel I knew."

She focused on Bethany. "He saw you again, didn't he, a few years ago?"

"He asked about the wars in the Reaches," Bethany said. "He wanted the mood of the common people."

"I remember. He whisked you to his palace. Asked you questions. Sent you back. Never even asked how you were."

"That's about what I remember."

Maryam let out a long breath, and then focused on the folded gray cloak. "We both know I am going to miss you. More than anything. But I understand... we all have to build a future, in the way that we have available to us. I hope you know how proud I am of you." She shook her head. "The things you have been doing, all on your own... No more secrets, my love. Please?"

"Yes, Mother."

"Tell me something. For you to study to become a diviner... I can barely imagine it." Maryam hesitated. "He wasn't involved, was he?"

"No," Bethany said. It tore her up inside, to lie, but at the same time, she could have passed the assessment on her own, if only they had let her keep going.

"Good. Remember what I have always told you."

"I know."

"It is best if you never ask him for anything. Stay away from their world. It isn't for you or me. I hear stories about people who have spoken out against him and been beaten by his soldiers. The whole time I was with his army, I didn't even understand that they were butchering our people."

"You were young."

"And that son of his, Julian... he is no better. Forget about them. Promise me, Bethany."

"Believe me. I want nothing at all to do with them."

Chapter Fifteen

"I WILL NOW COUNT the votes," the high confessor called, in a powerful voice accustomed to filling large spaces.

Julian leaned forward in his seat. He knew the announcement was coming – of course he did – and yet his heart began to race. He stared hard at High Confessor Roman Valaeric, whose next words would decide his fate. The ancient man's stoop was noticeable, despite the black robe hugging his body, decorated with a pattern of white lines like a weave. As the high confessor sat in a special high-backed chair, he rested his arms on the wooden stand in front of him. After one last sweeping look around the Marble Court, the high confessor bent his head. And then he began to count.

The Marble Court was an immense oval structure, enclosing a long central floor paved with veinous white stone. Tiered seating surrounded the floor, like ripples climbing and spreading from a pebble in a pond. A great arched entrance enabled access at one end, facing the Speaker's Podium at the other, where the high confessor had commenced his counting.

As the current successor, Julian was in a special enclosure of his own, rather than with his father. He was seated but also leaning on the gilded rail, with Samara his only companion. Today might be the last day he would occupy this section.

If so, he would never occupy the highest enclosure of all, where his father was now. He would never be emperor himself.

The high confessor made marks on a piece of paper, lips moving as he counted one voting paper after another. He checked a piece of paper, put it to the side. Made a mark. Moved onto the next piece of paper. Julian's eyes tracked every blink, every mark of the quill pen. The most important votes, the narrowest, were always the quietest during the counting.

The Marble Court was utterly silent.

Julian's gaze was narrowed. Whatever arrangements past emperors had made, it should never have come to this. Of course, the empire was too vast for one man to rule alone. Yes, it was true that if the emperor was the head, the corpus the body, then the nobles were the limbs. But the nobles had too much power... too much ability to block and dither, rather than move the empire forward. The emperor should make the decisions – as head of the empire – and then issue the nobles with their instructions to be followed. Even the succession wasn't decided by the emperor, but instead by a bunch of nobles with strong opinions and opposing views, here at the Marble Court.

Men like Declan Quinn always said that emperors came and went. But the assembly always remained. And it was a sacred principle for the assembly to possess a large degree of independence.

Julian disagreed. He hated the Marble Court. If he could, he would never have to visit this place.

The high confessor continued to count.

Julian had endured confirmation votes before, but never one as uncertain as this. He and Samara had worked hard. They had made plans and put them into action. Samara had ensured that dozens of the Blues led by her father had been unable to make the vote. Because of her, many Guildsmen hadn't even tried to make an appearance, too consumed with explaining the provenance of the goods they traded to the empire's tax officials. Right now, not just nobles, but thousands of other people had been trapped by inspectors at the Argent Arch. It was the worst blockage the gateway had seen in years.

Julian dragged his gaze from the high confessor, to the gallery and the nobles all dressed in their finery. An unusually high number of spaces were empty, but was it enough? Most of the tiers displayed older men in glistening white robes, but he also saw younger lords with oiled hair in the latest fashion. Dotted throughout the assembly he spied the occasional female figure, some clad in diaphanous dresses, others in robes to match their male companions.

The high confessor's voice made Julian's head snap forward.

"The counting is complete," he called. The voting papers made a neat pile in front of him.

Julian reached out to Samara, who sat beside him, and gripped her hand tightly, as she squeezed his palm back. In his peripheral vision, he had an impression of her anxious expression.

"I will now pass the voting papers for verification to the nominated delegates for today's vote." Three nobles came up to the podium, with the chief delegate taking the papers the high confessor handed down.

"Here are my totals," the high confessor said.

As he showed his count to the chief delegate, Julian watched every muscle on every face, eyes flicking between the elderly high confessor and the middle-aged nobleman reading the count. As always, however, there was nothing to be learned. Part of the game of the assembly's votes was to show one's skill at hiding the outcome until the very end.

The high confessor had yet to face forward to address the Marble Court. Instead he kept his eyes on the three delegates, who had retreated to a private area behind the Speaker's Podium to verify the count.

A murmur broke out among the assembled nobles. The tension grew in Julian's jaw, in his shoulders, in the churning of his stomach. Why wasn't the high confessor reading the result? Verification was important, and usually he would let some drama build, but it was unheard of to make everyone wait. The high confessor kept his attention on the three delegates. The vote had to be close indeed.

Julian risked a glance at Samara. Her face was white, the color drained from her olive skin. She was squeezing his hand with the strength of someone drowning.

Blood was roaring in Julian's ears. He was going to be emperor. No. The succession was about to be taken away. Declan Quinn would have his prize. He was going to watch Julian fall, a long, long way. It was all the fault of Samara's fool of a brother. Julian hadn't tried to kill him. Well...

in truth he had wanted to hurt him, and badly. But this... this was too much. Please.

The chief delegate nodded back to the high confessor. Whatever the high confessor had counted, the three delegates agreed with his numbers.

The high confessor cleared his throat and climbed to his feet. He sucked in his chest. He was now going to address the Marble Court and deliver the result.

"The vote to confirm Julian Malventus Regus as heir to the Dymantine Empire..."

Julian held his breath

"Passes. The final tally is 256 for, 255 against, with the tally of absences at 109."

Gasps and more than a few cries filled the air. The murmur became a din, as people swapped opinions about what they had thought was going to happen.

Julian stared at Samara, meeting her wide eyes. He knew that they were both thinking the same thing.

One vote. Julian had won, but he had won by just one vote.

✦

The vote had passed. There was nothing anyone could do but move forward with accepting the outcome.

The day's schedule had been arranged in advance: one sequence of events for a successful confirmation, another for a failure. Everything would now proceed to plan. But for many, the idea of going to plan didn't extend to the vote itself.

Julian now wore a ceremonial robe, with a white diamond pattern and a trim of golden embroidery. The robe's hood hung between his shoulder blades, revealing his shining, golden hair. As he traveled the Marble Court's floor, he was in full view of the gathered assembly, who filled the tiers above, behind, and ahead of him.

Directly in front of Julian was his father. Emperor Rigel Regus took stately steps, and Julian watched each movement so that he could synchronize his own. Where Julian wore white, edged with gold, the emperor's dominating color was stronger: purple with gold on the sleeves and collar. There was another, even starker difference. The Crown of Blood and Gold rested on the emperor's cap of white hair. Made of pure gold, intricate, heavy and beautiful, the crown displayed seventeen immense rubies, including a crimson stone the size of a child's fist, displayed above the rest.

With the vote over, the last to arrive at the Marble Court – the emperor – would now be the first to leave. Julian would walk behind his father, followed in turn by Samara, resplendent in a dress that shone like liquid gold. He risked a quick glance back at her, and she gave him the hint of an encouraging smile. She was as beautiful as ever, the color of her garment contrasting with her light-brown skin and the tresses of her dark hair. When Julian's gaze traveled to the gallery, and to the people clapping, most of the men weren't looking at him, but at his wife.

Julian heard Samara's voice. The sound of clapping filled the Marble Court, a staccato patter that sounded far too listless to Julian's ears but at least meant he and Samara could exchange a few words.

"Keep smiling," she spoke softly from behind him.

She knew him well. He did his best to smooth his expression.

A long way behind Samara, from the Speaker's Podium, High Confessor Roman Valaeric stood with his arms spread wide to bless the procession as it made its way toward the archway and the open air beyond. The clapping continued, as it would the entire way. Now and then, trumpets blasted triumphantly.

Samara's voice reached Julian again. "Smile, Julian. You won."

And yet with just a little change, the flip of a coin, Julian wouldn't now be wearing the robe that hugged his body. The search would have already begun to find a new successor, and he would be hiding away in shame.

He had a victory, but a bitter one. People would tell stories. The stories would spread. Winning the confirmation by just one vote was more than memorable, it would be cemented in people's minds forever.

He scanned the nobles of the assembly. But he wasn't interested in the lords and ladies' appearance, he wanted to gauge their enthusiasm. Everyone was applauding, as was expected of them. However some of the onlookers clapped with gusto, while others put their palms together in a cynical, lackluster fashion.

He couldn't help it. His eyes drifted. And there he was.

Declan Quinn was in the midst of his order, the Blues, with his legs apart and arms crossed. He wasn't even trying to pretend to join his fellows. Declan just stood there and scowled.

Julian knew he couldn't manage a smile, so he kept his face impassive and allowed his rage to show in his eyes. He had given everything. All of the studying, the practice, the testing, the writing, the fighting. If anyone deserved to be emperor, it was him. And yet, he would be haunted forever, by the fact that his confirmation by the assembly was a close call. Far too close for comfort.

Samara murmured again. "You did it, Julian. The empire is going to be yours."

She knew him and how his mind worked. Soon, the procession would pass through the decorated archway at the end of the Marble Court, and Julian focused on the man who stood by the opening.

The giant of a man wore the silver armor and white cloak of an Imperial guardsman. His close-cropped hair was white but he wasn't an old man, and he had smooth pale skin and icy blue-gray eyes. Most striking about him was his prominent jaw and low, sloping forehead. He carried a great sword across his back with the hilt poking above his shoulder. On anyone else the weapon's size would have been impractical, but Veldon Marx was huge, and he was the commander of the Imperial guardsmen.

The guardsmen were Julian's father's soldiers, bound to protect and defend the emperor, to follow his every command. One day, when Julian was emperor, Veldon Marx and his guardsmen would be his.

Samara whispered for his ears alone. "I am going to have two girls join us tonight. To celebrate."

"Celebrate?" he asked bitterly.

"When you are emperor, we will show them. We will show them all. Revenge is sweet, my love."

Julian nodded to Commander Veldon Marx as he passed him by. The massive commander didn't smile, but he nodded back.

And finally, Julian smiled.

Chapter Sixteen

KENDRICK WAITED ON the side of the street, outside the front of his city villa, which was thin and tall, like all of the houses in the area. City folk passed him by, giving a wide berth to the man they saw—a stern-looking lord of some kind, with a warrior's build and long gray-threaded hair.

While he threw impatient glances at his villa's front door, Kendrick scowled.

One vote. Julian won by just one vote.

What had happened? The man was supposed to lose. As most people would have expected, Kendrick and his fellow Wardens had voted to confirm the emperor's son. But the Wardens alone were never enough; Julian's duel had stirred up a lot of strong feelings. Kendrick's vote wasn't supposed to count.

Kendrick knew about the unexpected trouble at the Argent Arch, which had mostly affected the Blues. Rumors were that there had been foul play; after all, who would conduct a series of inspections on the day of an important vote? Many Guildsmen had been absent, meaning that there were fewer to vote against Julian. It had all come down to the one vote.

A vote that belonged to Kendrick.

He had genuinely believed that Declan had the vote secured, or he would have voted the other way, no matter what Tristan said. After Julian killed Bryan Quinn, the man wasn't fit for anything, let alone his position as the future emperor.

And now, as Kendrick waited impatiently, guilt weighed heavily on his shoulders. When he returned home to Esk and saw Anthea, he would have some explaining to do. Tristan had been convincing. He couldn't host the fielding and vote against the emperor's son. But he felt sullied by what had happened. He had truly believed it would go the other way. Everyone had told him as much—even Declan himself.

It was now time to leave Everlast as soon as possible. And no, there was nothing he could say to Declan, his wife's brother would be wherever he was, nursing his hatred, planning his next move. Kendrick would focus on his family. He now had a fielding to plan.

He turned once more toward his villa as the door opened. Old Paxton stood looking around, finally relieved to see Kendrick nearby. Bald and rotund, Paxton's gray diviner's cloak was as tatty as he was. But he was loyal, and had been with Kendrick's family for decades.

"Apologies, My Lord," Paxton said. "This old body doesn't work as well as it once did."

"It happens to us all," Kendrick said. "Come on. Let's go home. Do you think there will be much of a delay at the Argent Arch?"

"This is Everlast, My Lord. The Argent Arch is always busy."

"Then's let's go and get it over with."

It was time to return home to his family. And well past time to wash off the stink of the city.

✦

Later, sweaty and flushed, Julian opened his eyes. He hadn't even realized he had been drifting off.

He heard a brisk, female voice. "Go."

The two naked girls fled the room, leaving Samara and Julian alone in the bedchamber. Samara settled herself back down, placing her head on Julian's chest. He moved his head slightly to kiss her hair. He stroked her unblemished skin.

"I have been thinking," she said softly.

"Hmm?"

"I know it was close. And I know it troubles you, that they will remember. In truth, it troubles me too."

"Do you have to remind me?"

"We need to give them something else to remember. And I know the perfect opportunity. The fielding." Still lying against him, she looked up into his face. "Everyone will be there. The empire is vast, and not everyone follows the votes here in the capital. Most importantly, it is a military occasion, the ordering of an army. You want them to know that you, Julian, will one day be their emperor. It is the perfect time to remind them, and to show them. And it is less than a year away."

Julian frowned as he pondered. As Samara had said, unlike the votes at the assembly, everyone would follow what happened at the fielding. Mercenaries came to fieldings, seeking paid service. Nobles who never attended the Marble Court brought their knights and followers. The emperor, and his designated successor, would accept applause and acclamation from tens of thousands of the empire's fighting men.

"Show them? How?"

"The first day there is always an opening ceremony—"

"I am aware of that. I remember the last—"

"Let me finish, my love. Your father will be presented as emperor, and we will make sure that you are presented as his heir. There will be jousts and other contests, as usual. Then, on the second day the high confessor will conduct the knighting ceremony. Hundreds of the empire's young men will have come of age since the last fielding, having worked hard to be where they are. Their parents will watch with pride, along with great crowds. And then?"

He could guess where she was going. "The oath of fealty."

"The oath of fealty," she repeated firmly. "The lords of the realm will gather along with the newly knighted. Together they will all bend the knee and swear allegiance to the empire and the man who leads it, your father, the Dymantine Emperor. I know my history, and there have been many occasions when the oath has been given to the emperor's delegate. In this case, Julian, that means you. All of those lords we saw today, whether they voted for you or not, would bend the knee while swearing an oath to you. It is a more powerful vision than any vote. And that is what they will remember."

For a moment Julian was lost in the vision of Samara's father, Lord Declan Quinn, bending his knee while swearing his oath of fealty. There was only one problem...

"No," he said. "I understand the idea. And yes, I agree that it would carry more weight than what happened today. Unfortunately, however, my father would never agree to it. He will want to accept the oath himself."

"Why? You are his son."

"He would say it was needlessly divisive. He knows that your father is on a quest to bring me down. What would happen if your father refused to bend the knee? If he asked the Blues to stand tall, rather than give their oath?"

She popped up onto her elbows to look into his eyes. "But don't you see? That is the entire point. We would be forcing your enemies to choose. Either they bend their knee, to you, as the empire's designated successor. Or – by logic if you think it through – they declare themselves against both you and your father."

After a long moment, Julian chuckled. "You have a wicked mind, Samara. But like I said, my father would never agree to it."

"We have almost a year. It is enough time to prepare, and to put a plan together. Don't ask your father yet. We will find a way, my love." She reached up to stroke his cheek with the back of her finger, making his skin tingle. "It is a good plan. When the time comes, at the fielding, believe me, they will all give their oath to you. Any issues with the confirmation will be over. And we will be victorious."

"Believe me. Nothing would give me more pleasure."

She gradually resettled herself, before he heard her voice once more. "Did you see Kendrick Conway at the Marble Court?"

"I saw him."

"It isn't often that he shows his face."

"The Wardens would have summoned him. It was an important vote."

"What do you think of him?"

"Kendrick?" he asked, surprised. He continued to stroke her skin as he pondered. "I know he broke the siege at Curran Castle, but in truth, the few times we've met we haven't had much to say. He rarely opens his mouth unless the conversation turns to horses or the different grades of steel."

A slight smile parted her lips. "From your description, the hero of Curran Castle is an old bore."

He smiled back at her. "And if he is?"

"Do I detect a hint of jealousy, my love? Perhaps you would like to be called a war hero?"

"Jealous? Of Kendrick Conway?"

"He saved your father's life. You know his reputation, and it is decidedly more violent than you would make out."

"No one better with a blade," he intoned. "Or at least that was what they always said. You have to remember, he would have been in his thirties when they last said that about him. What is he now, fifty?"

"Not quite. Late forties, I would guess. He certainly stays lean. Not an ounce of flesh on him that isn't muscle."

He laughed. "You think he is handsome?"

Her own smile broadened. "Well... He is somewhat frightening, with that glare of his..."

"The scowl of a bitter old man, stuck in his glorified past." His smile faded as he shook his head. "Why ask about Kendrick? The man is a proud fool, but I can't see him causing us much trouble." He stifled a yawn. "He even voted with our side, against his own wife's brother."

"The Conways are hosting the fielding. We will need to watch how things unfold, that is all. Even without my father working against us, Anthea Conway is my aunt, and she and I have never seen eye to eye. My father could try to work through her, to do something that affects our position."

"Very well. We will keep an eye on the Conways, just as we will continue to watch your father."

"Good." She snuggled into him, working herself closer into his body. "But for now, let us enjoy this moment. Today, we achieved victory. You are the heir and successor. And one day, I will be your empress."

Samara slid across the bed toward him. Reaching out, she wrapped her arms around his neck, pulling him toward her so that her bare chest was pressed against his.

Julian forgot all about how close the vote had been.

Chapter Seventeen

ZHUANA DREW UP, sawing the reins as she waited for her horse to settle. From her position on high ground, she spent some time assessing the city below her. She was worried, but also skilled at keeping her face as hard as stone. The sound of another horse came up from behind, and Alric reined in beside her.

The druid made his own inspection of the settlement. After their long journey to make it this far, he was even more gaunt and hollow-cheeked, with thinning patches in his close-cropped hair. Summer had passed, and he would now be glad for his furs, just as she was for her pleated leather skirt and thick tunic.

She turned away from the city, to look down the opposite slope. A sea of people filled the broad field, interspersed with wagons and carts, livestock and pack animals. As they fled their homeland, her already sizable group had gathered greater numbers on their way. Her gaze encompassed roughly sixty thousand men, women, and children, all depending on her. She had to find a new home for a vast number of her people.

Thunder rumbled overhead as the sky threatened rain. A cool wind blew across the barren terrain, with only a few gnarled trees to shudder in its wake. Already more than eight weeks had passed, with the terrain changing as the great exodus continued. Jagged peaks encircled the rocky lowlands where the Veldrians now found themselves. They were in mountainous country, passing through lands they knew nothing about.

Fortunately, there was no sign of the black fingernails. Everyone knew what to look for, and all remained vigilant. The druids were key: they kept busy and didn't allow any deviance from their rigorous inspections. Casting her mind back to when Veldria still stood, Zhuana remembered the numerous warnings: a nameless threat, a rising plague, monstrous creatures with shining black scales. This time she was going to heed them.

No matter how far they traveled, the same darkness that came to Veldria would eventually reach her people. With its great knowledge and power, only the Eternal Empire would have a chance of dealing with this threat. She had heard stories about the empire her entire life, and she knew deep down that this darkness was a problem too big for anyone else. She would offer her swords in return for somewhere to call home within the empire's borders. Once she had achieved this first, primary goal, she would work to ensure that no one else would be allowed in, even as the empire's finest minds found ways to combat the darkness that was on its way.

To reach the empire, she had to lead her people north.

And yet this city was now in the way.

As Zhuana faced the settlement below, she was keenly aware that with her she had a powerful force. Her homeland, Veldria, may be gone, but as a people, the Veldrians endured. They may be refugees, forced to abandon their homeland, but at the same time, they were a nation of warriors. Among Veldrians, there was no discrimination between male and female; all were trained since childhood to fight. If the men were bigger and stronger, of course they would be up front, but a woman would be given the same opportunity to prove herself. Some called their horses ponies, but they were nimbler, better trained, and able to run for longer. A Veldrian on horseback, armed with a recurved composite bow, could pepper one opponent after another, while avoiding combat altogether. A warrior on foot, in tough leather armor, armed with shield and sword, could dodge around any armored enemy, finding a weakness before striking home. Under the spell of the druid's firewater, a warrior's fear vanished and wounds felt like minor stings.

Zhuana had a strong force. And given the scale of the city in front of her, this new nation's leaders had every reason to be afraid.

However a fight wasn't what she wanted. She wasn't looking to capture this city and kill the inhabitants before taking over and proclaiming herself queen of her new dominion. She only wanted to get past.

Another rider came up to join her and Alric. By the Mother, Garric was growing fast; soon she wouldn't think of him as anything but a man. He rode comfortably, his lean frame one with his horse, reining in and controlling his mount easily. He was developing into a handsome lad, with his green eyes and fine, sharp features.

"It is bigger than I thought it would be," Garric said, squinting down at the city. "I heard them say it was tiny."

Resting in a valley, the city's broad walls stretched left and right but didn't quite fill the depression between the mountains. Moody gray was the dominant color, the same shade as the nearby peaks, but the conical towers and vaulted spires displayed a hint of grace. A few large structures within the walls might be temples or civic buildings. A road curled down to the city's front gates, with secondary paths traveling along both of the valley's flanks. The black and white specks on the green slopes were livestock: sheep, goats, and cattle.

Alric always spoke to Garric as one would speak to an adult. "Small compared to Veldria, Prince Garric. But big enough to be a problem."

"Can we go around them?"

"Our scouts say it isn't possible," Zhuana said. "We are going to need them to grant us safe passage."

Garric shot her a quick look. No doubt, like her, he was remembering what had happened when Torian Varlish had been in the same position. However Zhuana wanted to think of her past failure as an advantage. Whoever was in charge of this city, she knew how she had felt when she was facing a force strong enough to conquer her homeland.

"Bring our people up," she said. "Let them see our numbers."

Alric must have seen the familiar determination in her face. "My Queen... I hope you are not planning to go down there."

"A show of good faith is necessary for us to start off on the right footing and get us what we need—safe passage through their lands and to the other side of these mountains."

Alric didn't say anything; he merely rested his anxious eyes on her.

"But yes, of course I will be taking an escort."

"I will see it done. The very best of our warriors. For no matter what comes, you are our queen. Not queen of Veldria, for Veldria is gone, but you are still queen of your people."

"Not too many. And be quick." Zhuana watched the stone-walled city. "When I meet with the leaders of that city, this must be handled carefully."

Chapter Eighteen

THE HALL WAS VAST, with a ceiling as high as five men standing on each other's shoulders and a breadth supported by dozens of granite columns. Sound became swallowed within moments of being created, like a candle snuffed between two fingers. The polished floor reflected the light of oversized torches on poles.

Zhuana faced a row of tall stone chairs. Three women and two men frowned down at her—their chairs were side by side on a raised platform, making her feel small, which was obviously the intent. The city, which she had learned was called Grendal, was led by this council of five.

The Grendalese she had seen so far were weathered, hardy people, with wiry frames and coarse, conservative clothing in shades of beige, tan, and brown. The five councilors, however, wore somber black robes and had all shaved their heads, even the women. The effect was to make their age hard to determine, and to lend a cold severity to their expressions. Or perhaps that was just the way they were, and they took their roles seriously enough to never smile. Zhuana sensed that the hook-nosed woman in the middle chair was the overall leader, and had made a point of remembering her name: Elector Drea. However it was Elector Kahn, the swarthy, athletic man beside her who had done most of the talking. As with Torian Varlish, they communicated in broken Imperial.

"We cannot give you what you want," Elector Kahn said in his deep voice. "Find another path."

Zhuana had expected this. "We are running low on supplies and the only other path is too difficult. We cannot take so many across these rocky ranges."

Kahn was unmoved. "That is not our problem."

Another elector, an old woman so pale her skin was nearly translucent, spoke up, "We never asked you to come this way. The decision was yours. If you now find yourselves forced to turn back, then so be it."

"You can keep your city gates closed as we pass," Zhuana said. She hadn't had the same luxury with Torian Varlish, when her own city blocked the valley from wall to wall.

"You could still ravage our farmland," Kahn said.

"I give you my word—"

Kahn shook his head. "You are not known to us. Your word has no value."

"I bring a gift," Zhuana said.

Turning, she nodded to the two strong bearers she had brought with her, who stood beside a wooden chest. Together they groaned as they lifted the chest and carried it to the stone floor near Zhuana's position. The chest made a loud clunk as they set it down, but even that sound became swallowed in the vast hall. One of the big men opened the chest's lid, revealing coins of gold and silver, bracelets, and ivory-hilted blades.

This time, it was the hook-nosed woman in the central chair, Elector Drea, who spoke. "The lives of our people are worth much more than this."

Zhuana's heart sank. She had held out hope. From the moment she entered Grendal, she had kept her eyes open. In this city, metal tools weren't common. The stonework was bare, with little in the way of embellishment or decoration. The Grendalese had some skilled craftsmen, with linen used as fabric, wells with pulleys and chains, and horses pulling wagons. Yet flax wouldn't grow in these mountains, and the spoked construction of the cartwheels used an Imperial design.

To the Grendalese, there was a great deal of wealth in the chest. But still she couldn't sway them.

"You will have to move on," said Elector Kahn, fixing her with a grim stare.

Zhuana didn't want to do it, but she was forced to alter her plan. "We could give you a bond."

"Bond?" asked Elector Drea.

"Hostages." She inwardly prayed that she wouldn't regret what she was offering. "We would be leaving these lands behind as fast as we could travel."

Unlike Torian Varlish, she didn't make a threat but it was there. These people appeared to be farmers rather than warriors. Her people – her army – would butcher them if it came to conflict. If there was one thing she knew, it was that these Grendalese wanted her gone, and fast.

The other electors all turned to watch the hook-nosed woman in the center. Elector Drea was obviously thinking.

"Leave us," Drea said. "We need to talk."

Zhuana turned to her two bearers, who still hovered near the chest. "Close it," she instructed. "Take it back over there and wait." She nodded to indicate the wall by the light-filled archway, leaving them to their work while she walked away from the council of five without bowing; she was a queen in her own right, despite being in the heart of another nation. She left the hall through the archway, passing a pair of guards at attention.

Once she was outside, brisk mountain air brushed against her skin. Despite the hall's size, it had felt oppressive inside. Now, out in the open, she stood on a paved terrace, on the hill the structure crowned, with a view of the surrounding city. The sun would soon set, and mountainous shadows cast broad silhouettes on the streets and houses. Lanterns and candles glowed from the windows, which without exception displayed curtains and shutters rather than glass.

Back in the direction of the hall, two sentries framed the doorway, and both had their eyes on her, clearly curious. What did she look like to them, with her high cheekbones, the diamonds in her black hair, and the leather armor molded to her body? She hadn't set out to be intimidating. She had even left her curved sword behind.

She had already decided that the Grendalese were a gentle people. They had more to fear from her than she did from them. If she had reached a different conclusion, she would never have offered them hostages.

She spied movement; Elector Kahn appeared. Away from the hall, he was about the same height as her, perhaps a little older, and his face was softer in the afternoon light.

"Come," he said.

Without a word, Zhuana followed him back inside. As she entered, her gaze went straight to the bearers by the chest, and although she hadn't expected trouble, she was relieved to see them still standing guard. She returned to her position in front of the five stone chairs, as Elector Kahn resumed his seat.

"We agree to hold a bond," Elector Drea said without preamble. "A hundred of your young boys and girls. Not too old, not too young. Around ten years old. Oh," she stared down at Zhuana and spoke the next condition as if it were an afterthought, "and also your son."

Zhuana's blood ran cold, although she didn't betray any emotion. "He is sixteen."

"This part is not negotiable. These children will need someone to guide them. Your son can be their leader."

"How did you know I have a son?"

"We have been watching you since you were a dozen miles from Grendal."

She frowned, disbelieving. She always had scouts out, keeping watch around the massed collection of her people like sparks darting from a fire. Veldrian rangers knew their business.

"We have all-seeing eyes. Tubes with lenses," Drea said by way of explanation. "Imperial devices that can see things far away. We watched you most closely of all, Queen Zhuana."

Zhuana tried not to scowl. They must have seen her familiarity with Garric, the way she might squeeze his hand or wipe smudges from his face.

"Well?" Drea asked. "What is it to be? Will you trust us, given that you are asking that we trust you?"

She reminded herself: the Grendalese were a soft people. Darkness was coming. She had to continue north.

"Also," Drea said. "We are keeping the gold."

Zhuana's eyes narrowed further. To demand the chest, while she had been thinking about the risk to her son, was suddenly worse than an insult.

"Listen to me," she said. "You want us gone. We want to be gone. But when we go, it will be with our sons and daughters. And with our wealth intact. Let us not make this more complicated than it needs to be."

Again, she left the threat implicit. If they pushed her hard enough, she could attack the city, which for these people was the worst outcome of all. Many Veldrians would die, it was true. But she would win the day.

"Then give us something else," Drea said.

"What?"

"Tell us why you have abandoned your homeland, and where you are going now."

"We are traveling north."

"Why?"

Zhuana tried not to show any hesitation. "A conqueror. Torian Varlish of the Harna. Like many others, we had no choice but to flee."

"And he didn't offer pursuit?"

"We burned our city to the ground. It bought us time." Zhuana heard multiple sharp inward breaths.

It was Kahn who leaned forward. "Should we be worried?"

"We have been traveling for eight weeks. My belief is that your risk is low." Zhuana knew she was lying. The darkness was coming. "Send scouts to the south, if you are concerned."

Drea and Kahn exchanged glances.

"I take it you agree to the bond?" Drea asked.

Could she trust her son's life to these people? It was a terrible decision to make, and so she asked a different question. What would happen to the Grendalese, if something were to happen to her son? Even just the inner query revealed a hint of her vengeful fury. She would lay waste to this city and burn everything to ash.

"A bond," Zhuana said. "A hundred of our children."

"Including your son," Drea said.

"I will trust his life to you. If anything happens to him, you know what will happen next." The look Zhuana gave the council of five was all she had to say to complete her warning.

✦

After two days, Zhuana and her people were nearly through the lands of the Grendalese.

Grendal wasn't a big nation: a walled city in a valley, followed by some towns that diminished in size until they became villages. Tiny hamlets and homesteads decorated the mountainous slopes. Children herded goats and sheep. Farmers mended fences. With summer over and the middle of autumn approaching, villagers worked together in the fields, reaping wheat, harvesting vegetables, plucking fruits and nuts from orchards.

Throughout their journey, the long column of people had followed the same wide road that steadily became thinner and thinner. Locals were curious but kept their distance, as an entire nation made its way past their fences and through their villages. In their wake, they left well-trodden dirt, horse dung, and deep ruts from their cartwheels. Grendalese skirmishers kept pace with them but also avoided contact. Their local escorts eased the way, alerting the locals to their coming.

And then, the journey was over.

Zhuana had passed the last few isolated farms. The road became a path, then a trail, and now it was just a hint of tread left in scrubby grass. On horseback, with Alric beside her, she led her people up a slope that rose out of the valley to head toward a ridge. As her weary horse whinnied, unhappy to find himself with an incline to climb, she was yet to see what lay on the ridge's other side. The afternoon sun shone on her left, telling her she was heading due north.

"Queen Zhuana." The deep voice made her turn, and she saw Elector Kahn pushing his horse into a canter as he rode toward her. For once, he was alone, with his personal escort of soldiers farther down the hill. He pulled up beside her. "I will leave you here." Looking ahead, he pointed toward the ridge's high point. "Beyond is a small lake. It is a good place to camp. Your children will be returned to you before the sun has set."

Kahn regarded Zhuana for a moment with his dark, intelligent eyes. Then he reached out a hand and she took it, clasping his palm.

"Kahn..." Zhuana said.

"Yes?"

Should she warn him? About what was coming? "This conqueror... I would look to your defenses. There is darkness out there."

"We will, and I thank you," he said. Then he dug in his heels, turned his horse, and rode away until he was gone.

Zhuana watched the sun. Nightfall was still hours away. Alric was nearby, looking at her and biting his lip.

"He will be fine," Alric said.

Zhuana kept her emotions hidden. "Come on," she said. "Let us go and find this lake."

✦

Zhuana paced.

She was alone, separate from the great throng of people setting up camp by the shore of the clear blue lake. As she wandered back and forth, she couldn't help but see the camp take shape before her eyes, even though almost all of her attention was on the ridge, where she hoped to see her son and the hundred younger children whose lives she had placed in danger. A group of figures by the lake were familiar; some of her druadan were discussing something, but there was only one thought on her mind.

The sun had nearly set. It had long dropped behind the hills, leaving a glow to indicate its position as it made its way to the edge of the world.

The sky became a glorious painting, washed with gold and pink, purple and dark blue. One star appeared, then another.

Zhuana's lips were pressed together; her hands were clenched into fists. She turned on her heel, realizing that pairs of adults stood near her, also focused on the ridge. These were the parents of the other children. When they weren't fixated on the ridge, they were looking over at her.

She turned again.

And there they were.

She saw a row of little figures appear on the ridge, a wide line of them, running at speed in her direction. She knew the shape of the lean figure with wavy hair in the lead.

"Garric!" she called.

The other parents were running, and remaining in place was one of the hardest things she had ever had to do. Yet she was the queen, and she remained stoically in place as her son raced toward her. He sped down the hill, a broad smile on his face as he charged directly at her. The other parents were already laughing as they hoisted their children in the air.

Zhuana's son was older, however, and she merely gave him a quick embrace, aware of being watched. "Are they all here?"

"All of them," he said. She had emphasized the responsibility he had to take care of the younger children, every last one of them. At the same time, she knew it was largely unnecessary—he was dutiful, and took himself seriously. "All safe and unharmed."

"You have done well," she said. "How were you treated?"

"The food was not the best. But it was no trouble."

Zhuana and Garric turned as one of the fathers called out as he approached. He had a smile on his weathered face.

"My Queen," he said. "I would like to thank Prince Garric, if it causes no problem for you."

"Of course," Zhuana said as he came to a halt in front of her son.

"Prince Garric... my boy says you kept them all strong. My wife and I would like to offer you our thanks. We will not forget what you did, risking your life along with them."

"I will always keep our people safe," Garric said.

The way he said it in a slightly distant, regal manner almost made Zhuana smile; he must have picked up the speech pattern from her. Other parents came to thank her son, making him stand a little taller.

Then Zhuana caught movement; Alric was hurrying toward her. With her son safely returned, she was surprised at the druid's anxious expression. She headed over to take him aside. "What is it?" she asked quietly.

"Queen Zhuana... Maven Dresk is convening a moot," Alric said in a low voice.

"A moot?" She turned, but couldn't see anything past the camp and the people milling about. "That is not within his power."

"I suggest we find out what is happening."

She nodded, about to hurry away when Garric's voice reached her.

"Can I come?"

She hesitated. "Not this time, Garric. Enjoy your moment. Things will not always work out so well."

Chapter Nineteen

ZHUANA WALKED WITH a long stride, forcing Alric to hurry to keep up with her. Her eyes were narrowed, focused on a landmark ahead: a hulking rock by the lake, where a collection of druadan was still gathering. They were a well-dressed group, clad in leather and dyed wool, along with jewelry to mark their status as nobles: a steel ring in the ear for the men, a silver point on the nose for the women. The sky was darkening, but there was enough of an afterglow from sunset to see every face clearly.

The discussion was just beginning. Maven Dresk stood out the front of the assembly, instantly recognizable by his bald head and broken nose, his thick neck and powerful warrior's frame.

"He knows our rules," Zhuana muttered to Alric. "He cannot convene a moot without my lead."

"Apparently it is not a moot." Alric's tone became sarcastic. "It is a supply check."

Maven had yet to see Zhuana. The people he had been waiting for had now arrived, and he called out. "I see you, Dan Henwin. You have been working hard to stretch our supplies of grain. How goes it?"

A space opened around the druadan Henwin, a stocky man in his fifties, with oversized ears and a bushy beard. "We have consumed..."

"Please." Maven beckoned. "Come forward."

Henwin reluctantly left the crowd to head closer to the rock at Maven's back. He cleared his throat and turned to face the group. "We have consumed three quarters of the grain we brought with us." His gruff voice was audible to all.

"How much does that leave us with? Or, I should ask, how long?"

"Another two weeks."

"And then we starve?"

Henwin shrugged. "We run out of grain. But we can hunt. We can forage."

"Thank you, Henwin," Maven said.

At the mention of starving, murmurs broke out among the group of nobles. By now, Zhuana had stopped at the back of the group, but she remained in place, waiting to see where Maven was leading the dialogue. Henwin was one of her allies, and was only speaking the truth as he saw it. Maven, on the other hand... Maven had a purpose. Alric's eyes were on her, but he saw that, for the moment, she was content with watching.

"Dan Taikar." Maven singled out another druadan, a lanky man with a scruffy beard. "You have been scouting the lands ahead. What lies beyond this lake?"

Heads turned, so that everyone was looking at Taikar. Despite his status, he was something of a loner, preferring his own company as he explored what lay beyond the horizon—the man was skilled at what he did.

Taikar nodded toward the north, where the terrain rose to a craggy peak. "I have climbed the peak and seen what I have seen. This is the last clean water we will know for some time. Beyond this region, to the north, is a land of scrubland and swamp. There will not be any hunting for a long time."

Maven put on a worried frown. "It appears our supplies are not just running low, they are running out. It is warm now, but we can all see the leaves on the ground. Autumn is upon us. Soon the trees will be skeletons, and winter will be here." He scanned the crowd as he spoke, and then he spied Zhuana. He must have known she would come. "Ah, Queen Zhuana." He gave a deep bow. "I now give way to you."

Surprised, the people in the crowd turned, bowing heads when they saw her, as multiple voices murmured together:

"My Queen."

"My Queen."

"My Queen."

Maven had set the mood, and now everyone would want to discuss food and water and the difficult journey ahead. The nobles withdrew, parting as they bowed to allow Zhuana to make her way to the front. She stared straight ahead, her chin up and shoulders straight. Soon she was facing the group, with the hulking rock behind her.

She spoke in a loud, clear voice, turning her head as she addressed her nobles, making sure to include them all. "Druadan, we have come a long way, and our journey is not yet done. Tonight is a night to celebrate our success, after I negotiated us safe passage through the lands of the Grendalese. Our children have been returned to us, including my son, Garric, your prince. Enjoy this rest. For it is true, our next passage will be difficult, and we will need to reduce rations." In addition to honesty, they also needed hope. "I spoke to Elector Kahn of Grendal and asked him many questions. After the badlands we will come to a river of clear water and a region of forests filled with game. Working together, supporting each other, we will make it."

"Queen Zhuana, may I ask what else he said? How long until we get through the badlands?" The question was from a tall blonde woman, Dana Klara.

Zhuana locked eyes with Klara. "Perhaps as long as three weeks."

The murmurs began again. Zhuana caught sight of several nobles shaking their heads. Voices began to clamor for attention.

"What about food? If our supplies run out, how will we eat?"

"We could be heading straight into trouble."

"No bread. No water."

"Druadan, listen to me." Zhuana raised her voice, bringing the murmurs to an end. "Our herds are one of the reasons we move so slowly. When we consume our livestock, we will naturally move much faster."

"But then what?" a long-haired warrior whispered to the man next to him. "My men need meat."

The murmurs rose up again. Maven had primed them too well, with all his talk of supplies. What was he trying to accomplish? At first she had thought it an attempt to make her lose face, while he gained standing as he pointed out the weaknesses in her plan to travel north.

But then she understood, with a heavy sinking feeling as she realized what he had planned. And there might be nothing she could do about it.

As if on cue, a deep booming voice called out. "Queen Zhuana... May I speak?"

A space opened up as heads turned toward a huge man a full head taller than Maven. His head was shaved around a topknot, and he had his thumbs hooked in his belt, displaying his bare, muscular arms. His name was Dan Logrin, and he was a childhood friend of Maven Dresk.

"You may," she said. She knew better than to lead her druadan by silencing them.

"I have an idea." Logrin turned toward the ridge that Zhuana's son and all of the other children had come running down. He thrust out an arm to point. "On the other side of that ridge is a farm, and another, and then another. After the farms there is a village. A town. Livestock. Grain. Clothing. Much else, I have no doubt."

Zhuana felt Maven's eyes on her. He didn't reveal much, but she knew him well enough to know when he was pleased.

"Many of our carts carry nothing," Logrin continued. "We should stock up on supplies now, while we can."

"Plunder, you mean, Logrin," a female voice called out.

Logrin sneered. "Call it what you like."

"Our children were treated well," an older druadan said. "We made an agreement, and they stayed true to it."

"And we honored our promise, while we made it through their lands," Logrin replied. He was usually a simplistic speaker; his very words had been put in his mouth by Maven. "The deal is done. We now look ahead, to the future. It is only natural to make new plans."

A chorus of assent greeted his words. Zhuana took note of who was nodding, and the heavy feeling in her stomach grew stronger; they weren't just Maven's supporters. His plan had worked. There was nothing she could do to stop what was about to happen.

"They have soldiers," Dan Henwin said, anxiously rubbing his chin. "We have all seen them shadowing us."

"I have seen their soldiers." Logrin pounded a clenched fist on his chest. "We are Veldrians."

Maven seized his opportunity. "Queen Zhuana... If I may? Dan Logrin speaks good sense."

Zhuana fought to keep her feelings hidden. Should she speak out and say no, as queen, she refused to let this happen? Should she change their course, at great cost to herself, so that in the coming days, they had less food, and cursed her when their children went hungry?

No. As a leader, she couldn't always force her people onto a given path. She also had to adapt. She opened her mouth and raised her voice.

"Here is my view, the view of your queen." Zhuana brought about an instant silence; all eyes were on her. "We are Veldrians. Their fighting men cannot stand against us. Before commencing our next journey, we needed to take stock of our supplies, which is why I asked Dan Dresk to convene this gathering." She nodded at Maven, and he had no choice but to give her a slight nod back. "We need more than we currently have, it is clear for all to see. We could take what we need by force. The question is: should we? Let us ponder that question. These people of Grendal, they took our children, including my son. Why? Because they didn't trust us. If we had taken a wrong step, what would have happened next? They would have killed our children, murdered them, slit their throats and watched them bleed."

She had them now. They were all nodding, faces angry, getting their blood up.

"Why should we embark on this journey without first taking what we need?" she asked. "These people, who put their knives to our children's throats, why should we care for their fates?"

The voices of assent grew louder with every point she made. Meanwhile Maven watched her, his dark eyes calculating.

"When we first came to these lands, and were at the other end of the valley, we saw walls and towers. Fortifications. Large numbers of soldiers. That was when we faced their front. Now that we are turned toward their rear, what do we see, on the other side of that hill?" Zhuana nodded toward the ridge. "A soft underbelly. Plunder. The food we need, there for the taking. There are no walls out here. A few soldiers, but not many. These badlands, that we will soon be traveling—they consider them sufficient protection." She allowed an evil smile to creep up. "But we are already here."

A loud cheer swelled up from the assembled nobles, a cry that would be audible from the immense camp where the rest of the Veldrians were. They would be curious. The news would spread like wildfire.

"Make ready!" Zhuana cried. "At dawn, we strike, and we strike hard."

Another round of cheers was even louder than the last, and the group broke up, leaving Zhuana to watch them leave. When they had dispersed, she turned toward Maven, who knew exactly what he had done. Her mouth opened, but it was Maven who spoke first.

"I thank you for your wisdom, Queen Zhuana." He gave her a deep bow. "We all want what is best for our people. By your leave, I must go and gather my men."

As he strode away, and she watched his back, she muttered for her own ears alone. "The Mother will judge you for this."

✦

Zhuana leaned over the trough. She dunked her head, plunging it deep into the water, making sure to thoroughly wet her hair. Lifting her head up again, she gasped at the cold that made her skin tingle. She rubbed at her face, scrubbing her scalp and hair, before dipping her entire head once more. The water became steadily red.

Something drew her attention, a stinging on her right arm. She still wore her hardened leather armor, and just below the elbow, where a patch of skin was bare before her bracers would protect her forearms, was a thin wound seeping blood. The cut was two inches long, just a light scoring, but the pulse of pain was growing now that she had noticed it.

How did she get it? She had no idea. She had killed four Grendalese soldiers, and as far as she could recall, none of them had made a strike on her.

She pressed the wound, satisfied when barely any blood welled up. After washing the cut with water, she tied a cloth around it. Meanwhile, all around her, she heard the voices of her warriors. Their calls were boisterous, happy, relieved. Triumphant. Tonight they would gorge themselves on their plunder, and congratulate themselves for securing their future.

She was glad to have seen no sign of Elector Kahn. He had left some men behind, but there would be no reason for him to dally rather than head back home to his city.

The surface of the water gradually stilled, and she leaned over the trough to look at her own reflection. She saw fatigue and worry, but she had survived another challenge.

Another face appeared beside her in the water: the boyish wavy-haired visage of her son.

"They were good people," Garric said accusingly.

She turned toward him, keeping her expression smooth. "In the main. There are always good people and bad people. No society is simply good as a whole."

"You know what I mean."

She hesitated, and it was a long time before she replied. "I know," she finally said.

"Why did you do it?"

"I had to."

"You butchered them. Just like everyone else."

A hot feeling came to her cheeks as she scowled at her son. "Garric, as you continue on your journey that will one day see you become king of our people, you will learn many lessons. This one is not complicated. The wolves always prey upon the sheep."

"Torian Varlish was a wolf."

"And we were the sheep. We ran." Littering the ground nearby were the pieces of body armor she had removed to wash herself. She remembered the fighting, the killing. "This time the Grendalese were the sheep. We took what we had to, to survive."

"You did not have to do it."

"Oh?" She raised an eyebrow. "You can see the future, can you? The extra food might save all of our lives. Listen to me, Garric. At all times, you must be thinking of the Veldrians. Not the Grendalese. Not anyone else. If you give the slightest sign that you are valuing another group more than us, on that day you will no longer be king." She returned to the trough, dipping her hands to scrub her fingernails. "It is done. The important thing is that we have the supplies we need."

Garric wasn't finished. "He made you do it, didn't he?"

She didn't answer, instead scrubbing harder. A stubborn crimson ring of dried blood remained on her thumbnail, no matter how hard she cleaned it.

"It was wrong."

Zhuana straightened, rounding on her son. "You do not know what you are talking about. Go to your tent. Now!"

With a heaving chest, Garric stormed away, and Zhuana returned to her scrubbing.

Chapter Twenty

BETHANY STOOD WITH twenty other students, newcomers to the School of Divination. She told herself that she had earned her place, just like the other students. But had she really? She felt like an imposter, neither belonging nor deserving to be where she was.

For a start, she was in a place like nowhere she had been to before. She was standing under the Crystal Dome, the huge half-sphere that crowned the Observatory. A wide blue sky stretched above her, rising from the floor in all directions, so that morning light flooded the vast space. The sections of transparent glass were huge, much bigger than any normal window. The thin white frames didn't look like wood, but also didn't appear to be metal. Mysterious ancient symbols decorated the lattice where the frames made junctions.

Summer was over. Bethany's parting with her mother had felt final, as if she were saying goodbye for the last time. She would be able to visit. But not for several weeks, which was easily the longest time they had both been apart.

Her mother would be cared for. Charlton would be true to his word, and although Dahlia was businesslike, she would keep the dormus clean and help with food, while also assisting Maryam with her medicine.

The old dose of somnifer had gone up. The headaches were growing worse. And if something happened, Bethany would be so close, in the same city, but not where she was needed. It was impossible not to be anxious.

It was Charlton who had walked her to what would be her new home for a time. After traveling through the Corpus District to finally arrive at the Observatory, he hugged her and told her again not to worry about her mother. She wiped her eyes; it had been a struggle not to cry.

After arriving at the Observatory, a servant had surprised her by greeting her by name. Taking her along corridors that branched off from the main hallway, with the floor, walls, and ceiling all made of plain stone, she was given a single room in a row of other rooms. She had her own little bedroom, a desk, and a shelf, separated from a washroom with a small bath, basin, and chamber pot. After a short time to familiarize herself, the same servant had brought her here.

She forcefully brought herself back to the Crystal Dome. Silence hung in the air, creating a tense, expectant atmosphere. The twenty students stood in four rows, with five in each row, assembled like a military formation. Bethany stood with her hands behind her back as her heart sounded loud in her ears.

Ahead and to her right, she recognized a tall student with curling black hair to his collar: Xander, her neighbor at the assessment. She watched him curiously, studying his face in profile. He was about her age, with pale skin, a sharp chin, and a wide mouth. She remembered his eyes, like no other eyes she had seen, deep and brown, with flecks of gold. Seeing him made her think about her fall on the steps. Hopefully he had forgotten.

Interrupting the silence, a murmur came from beside her. "I have to say... they do have a flair for the dramatic."

Bethany turned; the words were directed to her. The young woman looked back with a hint of a smile on her face. She was blonde, and pretty, in a sturdy rather than delicate way, with a dusting of freckles and skin more pale than a typical Dymantine. From the north, most likely. The young woman wore gray trousers and a tunic rather than a dress, but both garments were snug and cut in a jaunty, fashionable manner.

Bethany smiled but kept her mouth sealed. She wanted to reply but everyone else was so silent.

The young blonde woman spoke again. "Are you really from the Far Reaches?"

From the row in front, Xander looked over his shoulder. "Carina. Shh." His eyebrows came together as he frowned, but then when he saw Bethany his expression changed completely.

She thought he might give her the same amused smile he had given her after her fall. Or perhaps a more casual nod of acknowledgement— they had both worked hard at the assessment, and here they were. He had seemed kind, helping her up after her stumble. In that moment, when they met eyes, she had thought that something passed between them.

Instead, he cast her what she could only think of as a venomous glare. He stared directly at her, and then he lifted his chin and faced forward once more.

She stood stunned. Perhaps he thought there had been some mistake, and that she didn't belong here? She couldn't think of anything else to explain his reaction.

The students around her shuffled and straightened when someone entered. From the corridor that led to the dome came an ancient man with a lustrous white beard and bent shoulders. He climbed to the low platform in front of the gathered students, which gave him additional height, and for a moment his back was visible. Unlike the customary plain but plush gray cloak, his cloak bore a symbol: a single, gigantic silver star. Underneath the cloak, his clothing in the same shade shimmered with a thousand tinier stars.

For a time, he regarded them all, while the students watched him back. Bethany didn't need to be told who he was, although his striking costume helped to confirm it. He was High Diviner Azren. His position was the equivalent of the high cleric, or the high confessor. She was looking at the person in charge of all divination in the empire.

"Good morning, students," he said in a thin but audible voice.

"Good morning," they all replied in unison.

"My name is Garl Azren. I once stood where you are," he smiled, "a very long time ago now. You will not be seeing much of me, but I always like to see the new faces, those who may become diviners. I say may, because this is a difficult, challenging, dangerous path that you are now on. You will be tested more than you can imagine." His eyes traveled along the rows of students. He spent time on Bethany, or at least it felt that way to her. "I wish you good luck."

With slow, ponderous movements, the high diviner left the platform. While the students stood in place, the stooped figure with the star on his back grew smaller as he traveled the corridor that connected the Crystal Dome with the rest of the Observatory. Meanwhile a diviner passed him, and stopped to speak a few words before giving a deep bow. The diviner then approached, walking with a brisk stride. Stern-faced and slim, he looked to be in his mid-fifties, with neatly combed black hair, heavy eyebrows, and a short pointed beard on his chin. After reaching the area where the students stood assembled, he climbed up to the platform they were facing.

The diviner inspected the students in front of him. He wore a dark gray vest and trousers, and a gray cloak flowed from his shoulders. "Students, good morning. My name is Diviner Trask."

"Good morning," the students echoed, and Bethany spoke along with them.

"You have had the honor of meeting High Diviner Azren, and as he rightfully said, you are on a challenging path. Before you commence your studies, you must hear my warning. You must not just hear it, you must heed it."

Trask's gaze swept the students as his black eyebrows came together. All of the students were paying close attention, even Carina, the young woman standing beside Bethany.

"You will be tested emotionally. The demands we place upon you will be extreme. This school would rather break you than have the empire's citizens travel with danger. No risk is acceptable, none at all. Our reputation is at stake, and so is the belief that travel through the gateways is safe and effective. We can never have a situation where those who have entrusted their safety to you are subject to harm. If you believe you may not have the resilience, emotionally, to handle this school, then please, leave now. Please."

Trask paused, waiting. Some of the students looked around. Most stared straight ahead.

"You will be tested physically. A diviner's staff is an important tool, it becomes an extension of his or her body. You must wield your staff with skill and precision. The tapestry does not take circumstances or personality into account. Wield your staff wrong, and you will die. You must be strong in your body in order to be strong in your mind. Fatigue will weigh you down. Your stomach will churn from Weaver's Breath. Your vision will be blinded by the stars. This is no place for the weak."

Bethany was holding her breath and forced herself to release it.

"You will be tested mentally. You must have demonstrated a certain aptitude to get to where you are, but this is nothing compared to what you must learn. You must make complex calculations in seconds. You must draw on a wealth of knowledge, immense compendiums, all lodged inside your head." Trask's frown deepened. "Do not take my warning lightly. Now, I ask you again. Does anyone wish to leave?"

No one moved.

"Very well. Moving on, you have until next summer to learn your craft, which, believe me, never feels long enough. For those who make it, at the beginning of next summer you will be assigned a placement where you can continue to learn in the field." He gave a sharp nod. "It is time, then. And time is always of the essence. Please, students, come with me. Front row, follow first, then second row, and so forth."

Trask left the podium and crossed the floor to reach the corridor. The first row dispersed to travel right after him, and then the row in front of Bethany. Some of the students were exchanging glances. A stocky young man grinned with forced jocularity. Xander waited for Carina, which meant that Bethany was just behind them. Xander whispered something in Carina's ear; clearly the two knew each other.

Trask led the twenty students down one stairway, then another, before taking a long passage, and finally coming to a tall set of double doors. The doors were already open, and the group of young men and women emerged through the entrance to find themselves in a vast vaulted space. Bethany tilted her head back. The area was at least five stories high, roofed with timber and stone, and framed by balconies, where green tendrils of plants drooped down from above. An oak tree dominated the area, something strange to be seeing indoors, with broad branches and paving stones going right up to the trunk. On the far side of the space, water tinkled from a central fountain in the shape of a gigantic pair of hands. Stone benches rested under the tree and by the fountain; there were plenty of places to sit. Dozens of horizontal windows in the ceiling let in natural light. The plants draping from the balconies combined with the tree and the sound of flowing water to create a vibrant, pleasant space.

"This is the atrium," Trask said. "It is a general meeting space, somewhere to rest or study or converse when you are not in classes. You will note the wooden board up on the wall, at the end of the atrium, past the fountain. Information you need about your daily routine and meals will be posted there. Please, take a look. There are clocks everywhere." He smiled, softening his stern expression. "This is the School of Divination, after all. Time is everything. Be ready by the fountain in five minutes."

The students nearest the fountain immediately hurried toward the board and the sheets of paper pinned for all to see. In front of Bethany, Xander and Carina went over and she followed. She would have to wait until the others in front were finished before she could take a look.

Bethany caught Carina glancing her way. She wasn't certain, but the fashionably dressed woman appeared to be looking at Bethany's clothing.

"What?" Bethany asked.

"I know all the best tailors. We have to wear gray but if I'm going to wear gray, I might as well wear something comfortable. I can judge everyone here." Carina nodded toward a curly-haired girl. "Wren: premium." She indicated the next girl. "Mudlark: premium." A plump young man was next. "Heron: midrange." She moved on to a skinny girl in a gray tunic. "Crow." She pretended to shudder, and then returned her attention to Bethany. "The only person I can't pick is you."

Bethany considered, but there was only one answer she could give. "Bethany Sylvana."

Carina frowned, confused.

"That's my name." Bethany smiled and shrugged.

"You made it yourself?" Carina put a finger on her lips, inspecting Bethany up and down. She tugged on a sleeve. "Hmm. Not bad..." she trailed off.

Bethany smiled. "But not good either. Believe me, I am the first to know. There is a reason why I am trying to become a diviner."

Carina laughed in a bright burst, causing several of the other students to glance their way. "I wouldn't know how to sew a seam, if I am honest. It is easier to judge than it is to actually make something." She had an infectious smile. "Well then, Bethany Sylvana, I'm Carina. And I'm desperate to know. Are you really from the Far Reaches?"

"Not at all. I'm from Everlast."

"With that coloring..."

"My mother comes from Loriastris. I look like her, but I grew up here in Everlast."

"Ah," Carina said. "In my case I didn't even come here until I was ten. As I keep being reminded, I am from the Northern Provinces, and not a Dymantine at all."

With Carina's coloring, freckles, and pale complexion, Bethany made a guess. She met a lot of people in the Fabric District. "Either Skollard or Kargul...?"

Carina nodded. "Kargul. Good guess."

Bethany recalled her map of the empire. Kargul was far enough north that it was supposed to be permanently cold. She remembered something else. "Didn't the Ice King of Tar—?"

Darkness crossed Carina's face. "The Ice King invaded us. My family had to flee. But even after the empire took Kargul back, it wasn't the same. Our manor was ransacked. They killed all the livestock and stole everything. We sold the estate and came here. I like Everlast, but I miss my horses. And hunting with the dogs. Trout fishing. The evergreens. I'm not really made for city life. You should go to Kargul one day. They call it frozen but it's beautiful and green in the summer."

In front of them, Xander looked back. "And it's beautiful in winter too. If you like ice. Come on Carina. It's our turn. Let's take a look."

"I'm talking to Bethany." Carina frowned at him, before turning back to Bethany. "Xander and I both went to West Park Academy."

Xander turned again. "Bethany..." he said, focusing hard on her. "Ah yes, I remember them calling your name. And I also remember something else..." He rubbed at the dark sheen on his clean-shaven cheeks, pretending to think.

"I fell," she said, returning his stare.

"No, that wasn't it." He tapped his chin. "Ah, yes, I remember now. You didn't make it into the twenty. Instead, it was me... Carina... and my friend Tomek. Do you know what happened? How Tomek isn't here and you are?"

She didn't know what to say. "No."

"Some people spoke to his parents. I don't know who they were, and neither does he. All I know is that between him and his parents, they have now decided he doesn't want to be a diviner after all. It was strange. I know Tomek, or at least I thought I did. How about you, Bethany? How badly does your family want you here?"

"Xander, stop," Carina interrupted. "Bethany had nothing to do with it." She gave Bethany an apologetic look. "I'm sorry. They both dreamed about coming here... Tomek worked really hard to get to the assessment."

Bethany opened her mouth but nothing would come out. *I worked hard too*, she wanted to say. *I could have been in the twenty.* Most of all, she wished she could tell Xander she had played no part in what happened to his friend.

"I'm sorry your friend isn't here," she said quietly.

"Come on," Carina said. "It's our turn. Let's go have a look at the board."

The students in front cleared, enabling first Xander, and then Carina and Bethany to reach the board.

Bethany read the large sheet of pinned paper, which displayed an array of boxes arranged into rows and columns, with each box given a label. Her day was going to be divided between early morning and then morning, followed by mid morning and then a break for lunch. Early afternoon classes led to something different again, and then an evening class, before finally a break for dinner.

Carina spoke to no one in particular. "Have you seen this? They've got us going all day. Look at the names of the classes."

Bethany was glad she wasn't the only one confused. A second sheet displayed the names of their classes as a single list, rather than arranged in a schedule, with only some of them currently allocated to their routine.

Carina read the names from the list aloud: "Meditation. Divination. Logic. Symmetry. Orientation. Catalog. Travel." She paused; the last name sounded ominous. "Delirium."

Bethany took a deep breath. She had given so much to be here. She now had to trust in herself. She was apart from her mother, but she had read the books, and Charlton had faith in her. She had to do everything she could to succeed.

She turned back toward the fountain, seeing that the students were assembling. The five minutes were nearly over.

"Come on," Xander said. "Everything is about to begin."

Chapter Twenty-One

THE GREAT EXODUS continued. Rather than a neat column, the Veldrians were a mass of weary, bedraggled people, with the strong up front and the old and infirm drifting to the rear of the scattered group. Wagons trundled along, pulled by skinny mules. A great number of horses, trained for combat, instead carried people or possessions on their backs. Small children rode in their parent's arms. The last few emaciated sheep and cattle trudged along.

Zhuana marched beside her horse. As the sun drifted toward the horizon and heat began to fall from the day, dried sweat coated her skin. The scrubland and swamp felt like it would go on forever. She was losing track of the days. The vista was always the same: skeletal trees, black marshes, wiry, thorny grass.

She tried to moisten her lips but her tongue felt thick. Everything was being rationed. A number of her people had died, to be buried on the journey. If the badlands went on for much longer, the count of the fallen would grow.

She heard someone approaching and turned. Maven Dresk was heading her way. He came up to join her at the head of the column and rubbed a hand over his deeply tanned scalp. If he wanted to say something, he would.

He cleared his throat, but even then his voice was hoarse. "Queen Zhuana... How long was it that those people of Grendal said this journey would take?"

"It's clear to us both that they lied," she said in her own rasping voice. She wouldn't give him the satisfaction he wanted. "We raided their towns. It was a fair trade."

They had been traveling the badlands for nine weeks. Elector Kahn had told Zhuana that their journey would take just three weeks. But then, the Grendalese always wanted them gone.

She checked back on her son. Garric was helping Alric along, the older druid leaning on him for support. She continued to turn her head, seeing motionless wooden shapes on the scrubby landscape. With their supplies nearly exhausted, carts were being constantly abandoned.

She returned to Maven. "The horses keep trying to drink the swamp water and it's making them sick. Alric thinks we should eat them. He says that otherwise the water will turn their meat bad."

Maven's expression was always difficult to read. "And what answer did you give him, Queen Zhuana?"

"Our horses are our strength. When we get to the empire, strength is what we will need." She stared into his eyes. "If we arrive as a pitiful group of wretches, they will never respect us, and we will never secure our future."

"Once again, I thank you for your wisdom," Maven said. He swept his gaze over the vast number of people, animals, wagons, supplies, and possessions. "We are failing, My Queen."

"We will never fail. We have come this far. These trials will only make us stronger."

He grunted; if he was like her, even the conversation was draining his strength. He remained with her, however, and she found his presence strangely comforting. They may be rivals, but they wanted the same things for their people.

The time passed, and the sun's rays became gentler, more angled to the ground. Zhuana squinted as she spied something up ahead. A row of shaggy shapes filled the horizon; rather than the crisp line of the plain, these shapes were rougher, much more irregular.

She exchanged glances with Maven. The dark orange sun was on her left, and she shielded her eyes until she knew. She was gazing at a row of trees... a forest. She heard a man cry out.

"Those are trees! Come on!"

Another shape appeared, something moving, bobbing up and down as it came from the same direction. The scout was riding hard, and soon a broad smile was clear on the woman's weathered face. The scout reined in, her horse blowing hard and wet patches on its flanks.

"Queen Zhuana," the scout said breathlessly. "There is a forest up ahead. And a river."

"How far?" she asked quickly.

"We will be there before the day is done," she said, her eyes sparkling.

Everyone up front could hear, and cheers began to break out, with the news bouncing from person to person until Zhuana heard bellows and roars, jubilant cries from both men and women.

"Any sign of people?" Maven asked.

"None so far."

"Go," Zhuana said to the scout, nodding toward the mass of people behind her. "I would like you to have the honor of telling everyone what you have seen."

The scout rode off, and Zhuana again felt Maven's eyes on her.

But this time she stared straight ahead.

✦

Horses drank and children swam, squealing in pleasure as they waded and splashed in the shallows. Higher on the banks, fires blazed while men and women prepared for the hunting parties to return. The trees were broad and lush; with emerald leaves glowing in the last of the day's sunlight. It wasn't a huge forest, more of a fringe of trees that followed both sides of the river gully. Even so, a region like this would have deer and wild pigs, rabbits and fat birds.

From her high position on the gully's edge, Zhuana watched for a time. The gorge was big enough for her gaze to take in a great number of her people. They busied themselves, moving about, unaware of her attention.

She decided it was time, and nodded at Alric, who stood beside her. The druid put a horn to his mouth and blew, filling the air with a long, sonorous note.

Everyone stopped what they were doing to see Zhuana on the cliff. They began to gather below the gully's rim, taking in the sight of her, with her skin and hair clean and a supple dress snug on her body.

She drew a deep breath to call out. "My people. This river is called the Byre. We will now rest, and rebuild our strength. We will then follow the river north and west, and eventually we will reach a city, a city by the name of Lexia." She paused and smiled. "Lexia is a border city, within the embrace of the Eternal Empire. From this point forward, we are in lands that appear on Imperial maps. My people, our journey is almost at an end."

The people below cheered, before dispersing and returning to what they had been doing. As Zhuana remained where she was, it was almost like the terrible journey across the badlands had never happened. She smiled, until she heard a voice, and as she turned her head, her smile fell.

"My fears are still with me, Queen Zhuana," Alric said. "We have promised them that this plan will work. After what we have all been through, much depends upon your success." He hesitated and then lowered his voice. "If you fail, they will make you suffer, and the same thing applies to your son."

She spoke in a deadly tone. "No one is hurting my son."

"My Queen... We both know what would happen to him if Maven Dresk were to become king. He couldn't allow a rival. Not one with your father's bloodline."

"Maven Desk, king?" She shook her head. "No. That will never happen." She turned to the north and west, toward the direction they would now be traveling. "When we arrive, we all know what to do. We will hone our weapons and show our numbers. You are right about one thing. We must give them no choice but to reach an agreement."

Chapter Twenty-Two

BETHANY'S EYES WERE closed as she sat cross-legged, hands draped on her knees. She breathed slowly, her chest rising with every inward breath and falling with each exhalation.

Meditation was always the first and last class of the day, and the class that occupied the most time in her weekly routine. And yet, despite so much practice, it wasn't coming to her easily.

She and her fellow students were under the Crystal Dome, and her companions also had their eyes closed. The mood was one of calm. The students didn't make a large group, and the platform was just in front of them, reserving the immense space contained by the dome for other purposes: the Crystal Dome was an important gateway. Bethany wore her short-sleeved gray dress, and the skin of her bare arms felt cold. Her stomach rumbled; it was early in the morning. The physical sensations kept interrupting her attempts at inner tranquility.

Autumn had given way to winter. Bethany hadn't visited her mother for a month, but soon she would be granted a short break for Midwinter Feast. Rather than excitement to go home, however, all she felt was overwhelming worry. The last time she visited, her mother's vision was nearly gone altogether. The headaches were even worse. Her mother now constantly used the black ebony cane. Dahlia's help was invaluable, and yet always Bethany felt guilty. Without the medicine to relieve the pain... She didn't like to think about it.

Let the thoughts come. Observe them. Don't work at them. Focus on the breath.

No matter what she tried, her thoughts were jumbled. She wasn't supposed to try to make sense of them. Her instructor kept telling her that at this early stage she should simply let her thoughts come and go as they wanted. She needed to divide herself into different parts, one of which was a calm observer, separate from her concerns and feelings.

But still the onslaught of worry kept coming. It kept telling her to gain an understanding about what the future might hold. Her mind wanted to dwell, to cast itself forward and try to attain some semblance of control so that she might be at peace. This was what she was supposed to be doing right now: bringing the maelstrom in her mind into a state of calm. Instead, her mind was at war.

She had to hold onto hope that peace would come. She was still early in her studies, and as hard as she found meditation, the other things she was learning were so fascinating she found herself reading late into the night. Her knowledge had progressed; she was pushing herself hard. She remembered when she had stood at the board in the atrium and wondered about the names of the different classes. She now knew what they were.

Meditation, what she was supposed to be doing now, was about learning to remain present rather than lost in planning or retrospection—which was more difficult than it sounded. The techniques learned during meditation helped a diviner achieve focus and calm, to avoid distraction and be aware of more information in the environment.

Divination was the class that always followed meditation in the morning, and simply put, divination meant staff work. At the moment, as Bethany sat cross-legged, she could feel the weight of the pole that lay across her knees. It wasn't a real diviner's staff, with magnetized steel at both ends. Instead it was just a simple length of wood, a practice staff.

And then there were her other classes. In logic she learned about cause and effect. She worked on mental puzzles involving time or the relationships between numbers, people, and objects. Shapes could intersect, join, and subtract. Carina said she hated logic, but Bethany quite enjoyed it.

Symmetry was logic extended to the real life work of a diviner. Bethany studied the effects of an object's weight and size on the tapestry, how to include and exclude objects in her calculations, and how to find the frequency of resonance that the tapestry needed to be tuned to, in order to open and control a gateway.

Orientation was about how to read the tapestry, the lines that connected things together, whether stars or stones. She had to learn a staggering catalog of gateways, settlements, and geographical features, as well as an equally dizzying array of celestial objects in the sky. Everything was connected, but also constantly changing, due to the shifting nature of the seasons or the motions of the heavens. Objects in the sky helped a diviner to navigate, but they didn't stay still, which affected the ability to locate gateways on the land.

Travel was a class Bethany was scheduled to begin in the future, but she knew it covered the principles of what happened once a diviner stepped through a gateway in order to get to the other side.

Finally there was delirium, another class she had yet to start. All she knew was that it was said to be as frightening as it sounded.

A chime broke the silence under the Crystal Dome, telling Bethany that meditation was over. Along with the other students, she climbed to her feet, holding her staff in both hands. Her instructor, Madam Mei, stood on the podium, clutching a staff of her own.

Madam Mei regarded the group for a time. She was wrinkled and wizened, with gray hair she wore cut short, and she projected a quiet, steely confidence. Her voice was always steady, never rising in volume, and she had a stare that the students said felt like she could look right through whomever she leveled it at. As was always the case, she wore a gray robe, belted at the waist.

As the moments passed, for a time Bethany thought Madam Mei was going to say something different from usual. On her way to the Crystal Dome, Bethany had sensed a different atmosphere in the corridors. Groups of diviners spoke tensely in corners, sharing something in hushed tones. Other men and women in gray walked with a hurried stride, carrying expressions that were tense and fearful. Whatever was happening, it mustn't be something Bethany and the other students needed to know about.

"How was meditation?" Madam Mei asked instead. "You should now be able to bring about a state of calm within two or three minutes."

As the other students nodded, Bethany concealed her own despair. She had achieved calm a few times, but today she didn't get there at all; it just felt like there were too many thoughts competing in her mind for attention.

"We now move to divination," Mei said. "Ready yourselves. Staff up."

Mei lifted her staff in both hands so that she held it vertically, and in unison, the students copied the motion. Bethany tried to keep her pole unwavering as she held it tensed, poised, as if she were preparing to strike someone.

Madam Mei then made an incredibly slow movement. The staff moved smoothly, deliberately, so unhurried it appeared unnatural. Mei brought the staff down, turning her body, until the end that had been up was now pointing down.

The movement was measured enough that the students were all able to perform the same action at the same time, creating the impression of being led in an elaborate dance.

Bethany's staff diagonally crossed her body, wobbling a little compared with her teacher's utter precision. Without slowing or pausing, Mei brought her staff to a horizontal position. Bethany copied, doing her best to synchronize her own movements to those of her instructor. Again, Bethany's staff went up. Once more, her pole cut down, slow and measured, like she was bringing down another invisible opponent. The other students appeared to be doing much better than her.

Like meditation, divination was something Bethany found more than difficult, like it was against what her mind and body wanted. Of course it was her lack of skill, but her thoughts and emotions felt like they were demanding to be held onto, to be worked at like a piece of something stuck between her teeth. It was the same with the staff. She didn't want to move so slowly; she wanted to speed up. Her tensed muscles were already aching, and the class had only just begun.

Madam Mei turned around completely, the staff going up and slowly down, and then slicing the air horizontally. Smooth and sedate, she never wavered. She was never anything but calm. Mei breathed while she moved, her inhales and exhales loud enough for Bethany to hear them.

"I want to hear your breathing," Mei said, in between her breaths. "Louder."

Bethany heard the other students' breath whooshing in and out. She tried to do the same thing, but she felt so awkward.

"Better," Mei said.

Then Bethany overextended, lost her balance, and the end of her staff hit the hard floor. The cracking sound it made filled the area under the Crystal Dome. Mei's eyes went to Bethany, but she never stopped moving.

"Your mind must be in the same state it was in during meditation," Mei said. "Find your calm. Focus on your breathing."

Bethany was forced to stop, and then once she had a feel for her instructor's current pose, she resumed. She had been taught what she should do, and when she felt embarrassment or shame, or pressure to do better, she was supposed to put herself into the role of observer. Rather than shove a feeling away, she held onto it, examined it, categorized it, and then it lost its power.

Mei was watching her again, and she was sure that her instructor gave an almost imperceptible nod.

Staff up. Staff down. Step to the side. Smooth. Slow. Unhurried. Turning body, another step, ducking, weaving. Turning body back the other way. Staff horizontal.

Bethany began to lose herself in the strange dance. Perhaps half an hour had passed. Divination class, and this staff work, would continue for another hour.

Ignore the fatigue. Note the pain, hold onto it, then let it go.

She found something akin to calm.

But then the thoughts bubbled up again. She had to get better. She simply had to. Her group had already lost two students, with no doubt more to come. She couldn't allow herself to fail.

Her staff began to dip a little too low, and she struggled not to lose her rhythm when she corrected herself.

Then, even as she regained her balance, she heard an unusual sound.

The atmosphere was always serene in the Crystal Dome, and in the whole Observatory, for that matter. Something was definitely out of place.

The unmistakable clatter of quick, urgent footsteps, was growing louder by the moment.

A middle-aged woman hurried into the vast open space, a gray-cloaked diviner with long brown hair she wore in a braid. Her face was tense as she went directly to the podium where Madam Mei was leading the class.

Mei had already stopped moving. "Students, halt," she said, her voice as even as always.

The diviner with the braid spoke to Madam Mei, whispering something quickly. Mei's face gave nothing away as she nodded. The diviner then left the podium, returning back the way she had come.

"Students," Madam Mei called. "We will break early today. Head to the atrium. You will resume logic classes after the morning recess."

The students exchanged glances, surprised by the change in routine. Bethany turned to Carina beside her, who raised an eyebrow. Past Carina, Xander was also frowning.

Everyone knew to remain silent as they left the Crystal Dome. Yet the murmurs started straight away, until the students were speaking at volume as they followed the corridors and stairways that led to the atrium.

Bethany paused at the top of a stairway to allow Carina and Xander to approach. "What's happening?"

"I'm not sure," Carina said. "Xander?"

Xander shook his head. "I don't know. It feels like something big."

The faces of the other students all combined worry and curiosity. Bethany descended the stairs with Xander and Carina, and soon they were passing through the double doors that led to the atrium.

Several of the students had already claimed benches; others stood under the oak tree or by the fountain shaped like a pair of cupped hands.

A few of the students who had been there a little longer were talking. They appeared animated, and Bethany grabbed at Carina's hand, pulling so that they headed over together.

"...can't be anything good," a stocky student named Gregor was saying.

"What is it?" Bethany asked as she hurried up.

"Lora overheard some of the diviners," Gregor said. "There's something happening at the border."

"What is it?" Carina asked.

"I don't know."

"Which border?" Bethany asked.

"South."

A voice came from behind Bethany, and she turned to see another student, Kyle, a small-framed youth with oversized front teeth. "What does it have to do with us?"

It was Xander who replied. "We're at the Observatory. Whatever happens in the empire, diviners are always the first to know."

"We're not diviners," Kyle said. "We're just students."

"Xander's right," Bethany said. "This school is part of the Observatory. If something important is going on in the empire, they can't keep it hidden from us here."

Xander's gaze rested on her for a moment, but he made no other acknowledgment.

"Students!" called a loud, crisp voice. "Gather please."

All conversation stopped when Diviner Trask entered the atrium. He strode directly to the board at the far wall where notices were put up about their classes and meals, waiting while the students assembled.

His usually neat black hair was a little disheveled but his eyes were as sharp as ever and his pointed beard was crisply trimmed to its narrow point. When a few murmurs came from the back, he brought his eyebrows together until the two young men were silent.

"I have important news. The details are still emerging, but you all deserve to know, and here at the Observatory, it will be impossible for you not to become aware. After all, it is diviners who carry messages from one place to another. It is diviners who bring the empire's armies to where they are needed."

Bethany and Carina exchanged glances. Carina mouthed the single word: *Armies?*

"A foreign army has come to the empire's border, near the city of Lexia. We do not yet know who they are, or what their purpose is, but they are said to be fierce warriors, and there is a very large number of them. Your studies will continue as usual. For the time being, the empire is on guard."

Bethany caught Xander looking her way before she broke contact as Trask as continued.

"Study well. Work hard at your duties. For if there is war, you too may be called upon to serve."

Chapter Twenty-Three

JULIAN RAISED HIS SWORD, one foot forward, the other back, as he moved into a fighting stance. His opponent was new, one of the gladiators from the arena. The gladiator also readied his blade and then they both began to circle. Julian tightly gripped his sword hilt and carefully watched his opponent. It was never wise to make assumptions. The way the gladiator moved his hands and feet was important, but nothing revealed as much as the eyes.

Julian was taller than most men, but the gladiator was a giant who towered over him, with ropy arms and legs like tree trunks. With missing teeth and scars on both cheeks, he was a hard man, who had lived a hard life, and would almost certainly meet a brutal death. He and Julian both used wooden practice swords, but even so, Julian had a helmet covering his head. Julian also wore armor made of interlocking metal plates, while the gladiator wore piecemeal sections of hardened leather. Even in armor, wooden swords could fracture or break a bone.

For Julian, this was a familiar ritual. Three times a week, he stretched his muscles, donned his armor, and faced a new opponent. Some people rested throughout the winter, but he wasn't one of them. He was using the coldest part of the season to improve his skills and prepare for his presentation at the fielding. Most importantly, he was working with Samara to strengthen his alliances with the nobles of the assembly.

His and Samara's plan had solidified. Summer didn't seem so far away now. At the fielding, all of the assembled nobles would bend their knee to him, including Declan Quinn. The vision was clear in his mind. Everyone at the fielding wouldn't see a successor who had barely survived confirmation. Instead they would see Rigel's proud, handsome, educated son. In the span of the empire's history, many heirs had received the oath on the emperor's behalf. When Julian had this second, more public confirmation, he could move forward with confidence, and so could the empire as a whole.

As Julian and the gladiator continued to circle the sandy-floored space within the walled Nexus complex, their short gusts of breath misted in the chill air. Winter had settled its cold fingers on Everlast, and only the conifers in view were still green. The other trees all looked like they were dead, bony frames without flesh or clothing.

The time was right. Julian attacked. His opponent parried and swiftly countered in return. Julian and the gladiator disengaged, to circle each other once more. The towering gladiator hacked down from above. Julian blocked. He darted inside the gladiator's guard to thrust at his torso but the bigger man parried and pushed him back. A flurry of blows between them sounded like a woodcutter felling a tree at furious speed. Julian and the gladiator were both panting hard as Julian lunged to the side. But even as he moved, he realized his mistake when the gladiator guessed where he would be.

A hard smack accompanied a burst of pain as the gladiator's wooden blade smacked against his thigh. He suppressed a cry of pain and kept going. He ducked and rolled, leaping up from a close position to stab toward his opponent's torso. The gladiator sucked in his chest but Julian kept moving. He thrust again into the gladiator's abdomen and experienced a surge of pleasure when his sword struck home.

"Halt!"

Surprised at the sudden shout, Julian backed away and slowly lowered his practice sword. The gladiator also dropped the point of his weapon and looked past Julian's shoulder.

Julian turned to see his father watching.

As Emperor Rigel Regus Livius stood outside the sandy circle, he appeared tall and regal in a pale cloak covering a crisp tunic and trousers in white and gold. His head was bare, despite the chill, displaying his neatly combed snowy hair. Flanking him were two guardsmen, muscular men in shining armor who were almost as big as the gladiator.

Rigel gazed at Julian down the length of his patrician nose. "I do hope you realize that hit to your leg would have disabled you. He won that. Not you."

Julian was still panting hard. He nodded toward his huge scar-faced opponent. "He is one of the best gladiators in the city."

"And yet you must be better."

Julian lifted his sword. "Then watch—"

"Not today," Rigel said briskly. "We have urgent business." He nodded at his two guardsmen, indicating the gladiator. "Take him back to the arena." He addressed the huge man directly. "Never fear. You will still be rewarded as usual." As the guardsmen took the gladiator away, Rigel's expression was grave. "Now, Julian, I have news. What do you know of the Veldrians?"

"Veldrians?" Julian asked, perplexed. "Never heard of them."

"You will soon know a lot more about them. A whole nation of them, an army, just showed up on our southern border."

Julian started. "Have they attacked—?"

Rigel interjected, "They are remaining on the other side of the River Byre—for now. We do not presently know if they intend to remain in place for much longer. It appears we know next to nothing at all, truth be told."

Julian looked into the distance, his heart still racing after his short but frantic fight. Their greatest fears might have been realized. A horde of barbarians had shown up at the border, while all their armies were tied up elsewhere.

But then something else occurred to him.

Other men had made their reputations in the field: his father, Tristan Benedict, commanders like Baden Lynch and Agapon... Even Samara had teased him about Kendrick Conway, the so-called hero of Curran Castle. No one told stories about him. He had never had his own opportunity for greatness. Everyone just thought of him as his father's son—when they weren't connecting him to the death of Bryan Quinn.

He instinctively knew what he had to do. "Call the diviners. I want to go there myself."

Rigel couldn't hide his surprise. "You? I thought to send someone more experienced."

"Don't you see, Father? That is why it should be me. No one has yet seen what I can do."

"Julian, I don't believe—"

"Listen to me, Father, please. I wish I had never met Bryan Quinn, but what happened that night is now in people's minds. When they hear my name, we need them to think about me in a different light." Rigel's hesitation was obvious. "Please."

Rigel took a little longer to consider, but then he shook his head. "No, Julian. This is too important—"

"I am the crown prince. This is my duty. To be your representative. These Veldrians—who else can speak with their leader? Don't you see? It has to be me."

Rigel paused, brow furrowed as he pondered. At last he met Julian's eyes. "As a kind of test, Julian?"

"Yes. As a way to prove myself."

"A test," Rigel repeated. "Very well. Do what you can, but most of all, do nothing rash. At this stage, we need information more than anything else. As soon as you have learned something useful, I want to know about it. Understood?"

"I understand." Julian felt a surge of pleasure and excitement. "Trust me, Father. You won't regret this decision."

✦

Kendrick Conway, Lord of Esk, sat with his family at the glossy rectangular table in the hall at Fernley Manor. Cold was outside and warm hearts were together. A fire crackled in the hearth. Through the clouded paned glass windows, snow covered the conifers and spread like a blanket over the ground. Savory odors wafted from the splendid feast that weighed down the table.

This was how Midwinter Feast should be celebrated. With family. At home.

Kendrick cast an inquiring glance at his wife, Anthea, who sat at his left. His beautiful wife had straight blonde hair and deep, intelligent blue eyes. Tall and slender, she had a love for fine clothing, and on this special night she wore a long-sleeved burgundy dress that complemented her pale complexion. She was a resourceful, religious woman, with a silver spider worn on a necklace she was rarely seen without. The spider was symbolic of the Weaver as the great architect, guiding the fates. And yet the spider perhaps had another meaning, for Anthea was something of an architect herself, skilled at the social maneuvering she undertook on behalf of her family.

Kendrick raised an eyebrow at her, and she smiled as she gave the slightest nod toward their eldest son, her own eyebrow arching as she waited for him to nod in return.

"Troy, I believe it is your turn," Anthea said. "Please. Lead the prayer."

Troy hesitated, but then saw his mother's firm expression and cleared his throat. Kendrick's attention went to his eldest son.

Troy had inherited Kendrick's build, the frame of a natural warrior, but in looks they appeared quite different. He had his mother's fine hair and blue eyes, with flaxen hair a little darker. He was handsome, and at twenty-one, a strong swordsman and rider, with hands on the table calloused from hard work. Whether Kendrick pushed him or not, he would soon be ready to make his own way in the world.

Caden taunted his older brother. "The great warrior ponders. His thoughts begin to take form. But he is hungry and distracted by the food in front of him—"

"Caden, be silent," Kendrick growled.

Troy scowled at his younger brother.

Where Troy had his father's build and mother's coloring, the reverse applied to Caden. Slim but fast and agile, Caden had Kendrick's brown hair and swarthy complexion, and with his mother's intelligence, he was already the more quick-witted of the two brothers. At the same time, given his size, he tended to lose against his older brother when they fought. He had long, delicate fingers and his hair was perfectly combed, without a strand out of place; he groomed himself in the mirror daily, much to his siblings' amusement.

"Just say what Father always says," Isabelle said encouragingly.

Kendrick couldn't help but smile at the youngest member of his family. Isabelle was nearly thirteen, with light brown hair and freckles. She was still young enough to be cheeky but now and then she took on airs and spoke in lofty tones, copying the older women like her mother.

"Enough," Anthea said. "Children, please. Close your eyes. Troy?"

Kendrick reached out to take his wife's hand. On his other side, he also gripped the hand of his eldest son. In turn, Troy held hands with Caden, who held hands with Isabelle, who was beside Anthea as they completed the circle.

As Kendrick closed his eyes, sensing his family through touch, Troy spoke loudly and clearly.

"On this, the year's shortest day, when midwinter sees us leave the year 718 behind and prepare for a new year to come, we thank the Great Weaver for the warp and weft, for the tapestry she has designed for us and continues to expand upon, from now until eternity." It was quite a speech, and Kendrick was proud of his son for not stumbling. "As the threads of our lives grow longer, our Eternal Empire forms the heart of the tapestry, where the threads are thickest. Our empire will endure and grow, even as we remember those who gave their lives in its service, and shine as stars forevermore. We thank the Weaver for the gift of life."

Kendrick repeated, along with Anthea, Caden, and Isabelle. "We thank the Weaver."

As he opened his eyes, Kendrick regarded his family. "Thank you, Troy. And now, in the new year, the year 719, we have a fielding to prepare for. We will need to work hard, and work well together as a family. Troy, Caden... I need to see you working as brothers. Leaning on each other, rather than at odds." He moved on from his sons. "Isabelle, I will want you helping me, and your mother, and your brothers, rather than off hiding and climbing as you always are. Summer will come before we know it. I hope you all appreciate how important this is."

Anthea took up the dialogue, "Your father speaks wisely, children. I hope you understand that the fielding is an honor but also a responsibility. Everyone will be watching us."

Kendrick immediately thought about the bad blood between Julian and Declan. *Everyone will be watching us.*

Anthea was as worried about the situation as he was—probably even more so.

"Now," Kendrick said. He wasn't going to ruin the moment by dwelling on dark thoughts. He smiled at the feast on the table, taking in the roast venison, the black berries, the root vegetables, bone gravy, and wilted sour cabbage. "It's time to enjoy Cook's finest..."

He stood and took the handle of an oversized fork. Usually servants would hover by the table, but this was his tradition, and at Midwinter Feast he enjoyed being the one to carve for his family. He speared the juicy hunk of venison with the long-handled fork and reached for the carving knife at his right hand.

But then he stopped, completely still, as he caught the sound of low but urgent voices. He heard quick, hurried footsteps, and a door opening and closing. The footsteps began to grow louder.

His frown deepened as he turned. Like him, his family had turned away from the feast to instead watch the door to the dining hall. The door opened. Kendrick saw Paxton's bald head and plump figure; his house diviner was wringing his hands.

"Lord Conway... I'm... I'm so sorry to interrupt."

Kendrick couldn't hide his irritation. "Well? What is it?"

"A clarion has sounded. Someone will soon be arriving at the Star Temple."

Troy called out. "Who?"

Isabelle piped up. "Tell them to go away."

"Isabelle!" Anthea admonished.

Caden grinned. "She's just saying what we're all thinking."

Kendrick shot a dark glare at Caden. As he turned back to his family, after a moment, he addressed his sons. "Come on. Both of you. Bring weapons." Anthea's eyes widened with worry. "I am sure it is nothing."

"Can I come too?" Isabelle asked.

"Not you, little one," Kendrick said.

"I'm not that little."

"You're little enough to do as you're told," Kendrick said to Isabelle in a growling voice that seemed to work on everyone but her.

He reluctantly set the carving fork down, even as he knew... To interrupt his Midwinter Feast, something dire must have happened.

✦

Kendrick stood with his gray-cloaked house diviner and his two sons. Together they watched Esk's gateway, known as the Star Temple, and waited to see who was coming.

Winter's darkness enshrouded the area, with pale mist drifting amongst the evergreens surrounding the gateway. A pale moon lit up the clearing, revealing a circular space dominated by the temple of gray stone in the shape of a five-pointed star. Stairs climbed up to the main platform, between two of the star's pointed legs. A large triangle made of stone at the top of the steps was an opening that led to nowhere. Letters in the strange angular style of the Eidar decorated the triangle, along with swirling designs. The Star Temple was one of the empire's smallest gateways, but it was also a privilege for Kendrick to have his own gateway, available for his family's personal use.

The clarion that Paxton had sensed was a courtesy, like knocking on a door. Kendrick had been wondering, but so far he couldn't hazard a guess as to who it might be, and why they would come at this time.

Kendrick, Paxton, and his two sons continued to watch and wait. Behind them, Kendrick also had several of his men-at-arms, soldiers in his service, all wearing brown uniforms displaying the stag insignia of Esk.

Kendrick's hands were becoming cold, forcing him to clasp and blow on them. Who was about to emerge from the area enclosed by the triangular frame? Perhaps something to do with the fielding? Surely it couldn't be supplies. They would have given notice so that he could have his own wagons ready. The Star Temple was a walk-through only gateway, with little space for horses or carts.

Paxton called out, "The gateway is opening, My Lord."

A sizzle sounded from the direction of the triangular frame. A moment later, a bright diagonal line carved the air inside the opening. The line grew longer, even as the light grew brighter, until it forced Kendrick to squint. The slit became an opening, which peeled apart, to form a black upright rectangle inside the stone triangle, with the points of the rectangle touching the apex of the triangle. The doorway was glossy, like a black mirror. As sometimes happened, Kendrick thought he glimpsed stars against the darkness, but they weren't still; they were shifting and darting and swirling.

A diviner stepped out of the opening. She was a white-haired woman, someone he didn't recognize, clutching a wooden staff with a metal-shod base and a shining orb at its summit. After emerging, she put a hand to her head, almost weaving before righting herself. Kendrick kept watching, but there was no one else with her.

The diviner glanced at the gateway and raised her staff into the air, keeping the portal open. Kendrick guessed that she wasn't staying long, which was confirmed when Paxton climbed the steps and she handed him a letter. As soon as the letter was in Paxton's hand, the diviner re-entered the rectangular doorway and the gateway closed behind her.

Paxton headed straight back to Kendrick to hand him the letter. Kendrick felt the attention of both his sons. They all knew the letter's contents had to be important.

Recognizing the seal, Kendrick broke the black wax and read swiftly. As soon as he had finished, he handed the message to Troy, who read it together with Caden. Meanwhile Kendrick stood staring at nothing, as he took in the implications of what he had just read.

To all Wardens:

A barbarian horde has shown up on our southern border, near the city of Lexia. This news is fresh. We have little information to go by. An official summons from the Nexus will go out if necessary but I thought it prudent to update you all immediately.

Be ready for what might come next.

Lord Tristan Benedict, Knight-Captain of the Wardens

"By the stars," Troy said as he finished reading.

"What does it mean?" Caden asked, turning his gaze on Kendrick.

"It means what it says," Kendrick said grimly.

"We could all be called to war," Troy said excitedly.

"Stop that," Kendrick snapped. "If you had any sense, you wouldn't be asking for war. This is serious. Don't you see? We have a fielding, here at Esk, where we will assembling an army. And now there could be war."

Kendrick's sons fell silent. Meanwhile, Kendrick knew the state of the empire's armies. They were all tied up. The empire was in a terrible state of weakness. These barbarians were here, now. But the fielding wasn't scheduled to take place for months.

He couldn't shake off a feeling of doom. What was it all going to mean?

"Come on, boys," he said, unable to hide his troubled tone. "Let's get back to your mother and sister before the food gets cold."

Chapter Twenty-Four

JULIAN STOOD ON a clifftop, wondering what the coming days would bring.

He faced a wide gorge containing the River Byre, the empire's official southern border. There was no wall, but watchtowers stood at regular intervals along the cliff. The river itself was thin, with high banks and sandy expanses along the bottom. The water was shallow, easily forded. There were some defenses, but they were scant.

He held his gaze up high, past the brush and scrub, toward a distant conical hill. The newcomers had already cleared the hill and set up a fortified encampment, with a palisade of logs enclosing an area the size of a large town. He couldn't help shaking his head, awestruck at its sheer scale. The Veldrians had built walls and wooden platforms akin to battlements, with a central tower looming tall.

"As I said," a gravelly voice spoke, "a whole nation of them."

Julian glanced at the uniformed man beside him. Roos Bannon was the commander of Lexia's garrison, a gray-haired, bearded veteran, and an experienced leader. Julian didn't know him well, but from his level-headed manner he gave the impression of a man who would remain steady under pressure.

"And they are clearly settling in to stay," Julian replied.

As he and the commander watched together, Julian still felt light-headed from travel. Only the diviners had to suffer the effects of Weaver's Breath, but he had still crossed thousands of miles in a heartbeat, and his body felt like he had been stretched to an infinite length and squashed to the size of a pinhead. The sun now appeared to be in the wrong place in the sky. It was snowing in Dymantus, but here in the south, the nights were chilly but days remained hot. Even his clothing felt ill-suited to the changed climate—heavy armor along with a thick white cloak and high black boots. Now that he was in the borderlands, at least his sword was a comforting presence, a beautiful double-edged weapon with a jeweled hilt that dangled at his side, together with a dagger on his other hip.

Julian lifted his spyglass, a length of metal tubing with glass lenses at either end. An invention of diviners long ago, it was another reminder that he was the heir and successor to a powerful, advanced empire. These Veldrians were frighteningly numerous, but they were likely just tribesmen wielding clubs and spears.

With the spyglass to his eye, he now inspected the fort. "They are still building, clearly. Nonetheless, they have moved quickly. How long ago did they start?"

"Just over a week, Crown Prince Julian," Bannon said. "Nearly ten days."

"Hmm. Skilled builders. What else do we know? They obviously don't intend to leave. And yet they also have not crossed the border." Julian moved the spyglass slowly, trying to learn more, but the figures he saw were like tiny ants.

"They know they are at the empire's edge, we can be assured of that. They also have numbers to cause concern. All it would take is for the barbarians to cross the Byre and we would be hard-pressed to turn them back."

The city of Lexia lay just a few miles from the section of the river where they were standing. Lexia was a walled settlement, with a garrison and a high-ranking governor, but had little chance of holding firm if the newcomers chose to invade.

After considering a little longer, Julian lowered the spyglass. "Don't call them barbarians or you will get used to it, and so will the men." He spoke matter-of-factly; no one liked to be lectured. "They may not be civilized, but there are a great many of them. We will have to handle this carefully. Any idea of their actual number?"

"We estimate well over fifty thousand. Perhaps even sixty."

Julian let out a breath. "This state of affairs cannot remain. There is water here but not enough food for so many."

"Your Highness?"

Julian turned to see his senior steward, an older man in an elegant uniform, waiting patiently. Past the steward were a number of others, making up the large escort Julian and Bannon had brought with them, here to the empire's border.

"May I ask how long we expect to remain at Lexia?" the steward asked in a deferential tone.

Julian thought for a moment. "As long as it takes to see this through."

The old steward bowed, turning away. "I will arrange quarters."

Julian called out to him. "And also—send for my wife."

He caught a sharp look from Bannon. "Are you sure she—?"

"What are you worried about? If there is trouble, the diviners can take her back to Everlast."

Bannon was unconvinced. "Gateways can fail. Diviners too."

"You don't appear to know my wife," Julian said with a hint of a smile. "She will not be afraid."

"Your choice, Highness."

Julian nodded at the steward, who gave another bow and departed. Lifting his spyglass once more, Julian again tried to see what he could learn about these newcomers. Their arrival had been a surprise, but a good crisis was the mother of opportunity. Whether he delivered an advantageous treaty or a victory on the battlefield, when he solved this problem, the Assembly of Nobles would fall into line, and any questioning about his succession would be forgotten.

"What happened when you made contact?" he asked Bannon, speaking as he scanned with the spyglass.

"We crossed the river and waited, holding an Imperial standard. Before long someone came, and we were surprised to see a lad. Well-dressed, but a lad nonetheless. Asked if I was the emperor." Bannon smiled wryly. "I stated my name and position. He asked me – told me, I should say – to come back with the emperor. I asked if we could bring gifts to their camp. We managed to learn a few things when we delivered them."

Through the circle at the end of the tube, Julian saw people at the top of the tower that speared the sky above the camp on the hill. Even with the spyglass, he couldn't see much of them. He had the impression that they were looking back at him, just as he was seeing them.

"And what did you learn?" Julian asked.

"The Veldrians are ruled by a queen, a woman named Zhuana Arianus."

"Interesting. Did you see her?"

"I haven't, but she watched our envoys from up high when we delivered the gifts. Apparently she is quite beautiful. They also say she is a fighter."

Julian smiled dryly. "In my experience, all women are. What language do they speak?"

"They have their own tongue, but they can manage Imperial well enough."

Lowering the spyglass from the camp, Julian turned toward Bannon.

"See if you can send more gifts, but this time have the envoys bring food to share. With any luck they will get themselves invited to a meal. Build trust. Our encounter must be managed carefully. We need to learn everything we can."

"I will see it done," Bannon said. "They gave us gifts in return. I have them here. Would you like to see?

"Please."

Commander Bannon led Julian past the waiting escort, and over to a beautiful coal-black horse held in place by a young soldier. Placing a hand on the horse's flank, Julian traveled around the animal, examining as he circled. The horse was a male, a gelding, with a glossy coat, powerful frame, and arched neck. His eyes were intelligent as he regarded Julian, giving a soft snort. Julian knew horses, but he didn't know this breed, which was smaller than the chargers favored by the empire's knights. The gelding's muscled frame had the look of an animal that could carry a man for hours.

"This way, Crown Prince Julian."

Bannon next led Julian to a folding table, where a variety of weapons and other objects lay displayed on the surface.

"Sword," Bannon said.

The commander drew a long curved sword from its scabbard, laying the naked blade flat on his hands to present it to Julian. Taking the weapon, hefting its weight and inspecting its length, Julian knew immediately that his assumption about spears and clubs was false in every way. The razor-sharp steel wasn't embellished, but it was as fine as anything made in the empire.

"Shield," said Bannon. "Helmet."

Julian exchanged the sword for the shield, turning it over in his hands, and then the helmet, giving it a proper inspection. He placed each back on the table, as Bannon passed him a bow by the haft.

"And then we have this..."

The full-sized bow was strangely shaped, with ends curved back on themselves, which was something Julian had heard about but never seen before. Its overall design he had seen before: it was a composite bow, made of different pieces of horn, wood, and leather, fitted together and bound. He tested the draw; whoever pulled this bow was strong indeed. He soundlessly handed it back.

"The sword is as good as anything we make," Bannon said. "The bow is better."

"Let us not forget the horse. Small but fast. Agile."

"With the stamina to run all day, I would warrant."

Julian frowned toward the conical hill. "They are sending us a message."

"They are." Bannon paused. "What are your thoughts, Prince Julian? Are you going to meet with their queen?"

"I will, but not just yet. I want to be prepared. Send across the envoys and get them inside the camp. We need all the information we can get. Empower the envoys to offer gold for any gossip, any rumors, anything we can use."

"Very well. I will advise you the moment they return." Bannon hesitated. "One more thing... Prince Julian, what should I tell the governor? People are already fleeing."

"Tell her the crown prince is here," Julian said. "That should tell her enough."

Chapter Twenty-Five

JULIAN WAITED PATIENTLY on the broad, top-floor terrace. He stood with legs apart, a glass of cool white wine in his hand. Over the passing days, he had gradually become used to the temperature here in Lexia, and it no longer felt strange to be warm in the depths of winter. The house where he had taken up residence was tall and narrow, with multiple terraces full of gardens, and was one of the finest manses in the entire city.

Catching movement, he turned to watch Samara walk to the edge of the terrace to take in the view. He followed her gaze and also looked at the same vista, where the terrace opened out onto the town's streets and houses, the copses of trees and the rolling hills. Outside the city, up on a grassy ridge, even Lexia's gateway was visible, where Samara had just arrived from Everlast. The golden rays of sunset lit up the green slope and the circle of tall standing stones.

Her tour complete, Samara headed to where Julian was standing. Her focus went to the goblet in his hand, and then she raised an eyebrow at the steward who stood at attention just outside the terrace's sliding doors. When the uniformed woman didn't react, Samara cleared her throat.

"Fetch me a cup of white wine. And I expect it to be cold...." The steward had frozen, her eyes wide with fright. "Go. Now." The woman fled.

Samara glanced around. "It will do. Who gave you the house?"

"Someone from the Blacks."

"I see..."

Julian followed his wife with his eyes as she returned to pacing around, as if she were checking for dust behind the potted plants or cracks in the stone walls. He knew her, however. He could tell when she was displeased, and had nothing to do with the villa.

Samara was dressed in traveling clothes, which for her meant a crimson tunic and pleated brown skirt. A thick gold necklace adorned her throat, with matching earrings that caught the light when she turned her head. Her dark hair was in additional curls, matching the color of her smoky eyes. As always when he was with her, his attention was drawn to the places where her smooth skin was bare. His wife was irritated, and yet all he wanted was to seize her and take her to their bedchamber. They had spent almost a week apart, which was definitely far too long.

"My Lady," the steward returned, a tray in her hands with a goblet resting on top.

Samara took the goblet, sipped, and finally nodded. "You may leave us. Close the doors as you go."

As the uniformed woman bowed and departed, Julian waited for the clunk of the terrace doors closing. "What is it?"

"This is a bad idea."

For a moment, he thought she had a problem with their lodgings, but there was something deeper at play in her mind.

He frowned. "My father fought in the Far Reaches. When I learned about—"

"This is not a war," she interrupted. "It is a mess. You are not here at the head of an army. All of our armies are busy."

"I—" he began.

"Let me finish. The Armies of the North and East are fighting the Jaynians with Agapon. The Armies of the South are splintered, keeping peace in Lurian, Ganouda, and Kila. As for the Armies of the West, they are disbanded, a bunch of nobles pretending at fighting, and until the fielding there are no plans to put them back together."

"The fielding—"

She interjected. "Meanwhile, the Ice King of Tar is raiding the Northern Provinces and there is nothing we can do about it. If these Veldrians attack, all we can do is rush to the gateway and flee back to Everlast. The rest is inevitable. Lexia will fall, then Bavia, and Gorvia. We will lose the Southern Provinces, at the very least. And everyone will blame you."

He lifted his chin. "I cannot say that I agree with your characterization."

She drew a long breath and released it, and when she spoke again, it was with a completely different tone. "My love," she said in her smooth, throaty voice. Stepping toward him, she took his hands. "We are supposed to be together. You and me, against the world. You, my emperor, and I, your empress."

"Empress?" He pretended to ponder. "I thought Emperor Consort." She raised a mock eyebrow, and he smiled.

"Now is not the time to jest with me," she said, allowing a hint of displeasure to enter her voice . "What I am saying is that you should consult me before doing anything big. And the situation here... this is big." Shaking her head, she paused again, and then moved on. "Have you spoken with this queen?"

"We need information first."

"Good. At least you are using your head." Her eyes developed a familiar pensive look as she stared into the distance. "This information. When you get it, I want to be there."

He hesitated. "Very well."

"We are walking on very thin ice. Danger comes in many forms. You have made a great gamble. When you decided to come, what did your father say?"

"He said it would be a test."

She let out a breath. "Julian... this test... what happens to us if you fail?"

He frowned. "I need to do something to prove myself. I need them to forget about that cursed duel. Surely you can see that?"

"And they will. In time. That is why the fielding—"

"Listen to me. I can do this, Samara. I need your support. Not your doubt."

She met his eyes for a time, thinking. "Very well. I understand that. I do. What is done is done. I am here. And I will help you, in any way that I can."

"That is all I ask," he said stiffly.

She watched him, and the strained silence grew, before her lips curved upward, just a little. "I hear that she is beautiful."

"Who?"

"You know who. The queen. Zhuana."

"I have not heard that."

"Yes, you have."

Knowing better than to talk to his wife about the beauty of other women, he changed the topic. "As far as other preparations go, the diviners are busy bringing soldiers to man the walls here. As you would expect, it is going to take some time."

"How many are available to defend Lexia now?"

"A thousand."

"That is nothing."

"The number grows day by day."

"I am worried, husband."

A soldier interrupted them. "Crown Prince Julian. Princess Samara. The commander sent me with a message. The envoys have just returned."

✦

Julian and Samara followed the soldier to Lexia's town hall, where they traveled a path that skirted the squat building to reach the barracks. The soldier indicated they should enter an annex to the main structure, where double doors opened at the soldier's rapping knock.

Commander Bannon was already seated. He was scratching his salt-and-pepper beard, brow furrowed, apparently deep in thought. Julian saw a pair of young men dressed like scouts, with soft tunics and leather leggings above high boots. As the envoys stood side by side, with their hands clasped together, they were obviously waiting for Julian's arrival.

Julian seated himself beside Bannon, and Samara took her own chair next in the row. Bannon didn't offer a formal greeting, and Julian didn't care; they all had more important things on their mind. Other than a slight tilting of his head, the commander didn't show any sign of surprise at Samara's presence.

"Ready?" Bannon growled. He nodded at the two envoys. "Begin."

The man on the left, a little older despite his clean-shaven face, was first to speak. "As you already know, they call themselves Veldrians. Their land was Veldria, until they abandoned it. They have come a long way."

"Start at the beginning. Why leave their homeland?" Bannon asked.

"A conqueror, so they say. He wanted their lands and gave them an ultimatum. They say they had no choice. Fled and burned their city to the ground. These people are not turning back."

"Why come here?" Julian asked.

This time, it was the younger man who replied. A handsome, square-jawed lad, he had an open, honest face, well-aligned to the task he had been given. "Safety," the young scout said. "Refuge."

Bannon harrumphed. "They want us to give them new lands in the empire, just because they ask? That many people would need an entire province. We can't just give up territory to a horde of barbarians."

"Remember: not barbarians," Julian said. "And as for giving up territory, that barely needs to be stated."

"Do they bring gold?" Samara asked the first envoy to speak.

"Any wealth they possess will be with them, Your Highness. But mainly they have food. Weapons. Tents and clothing."

The younger envoy spoke up. "And a great number of horses."

"Yes," said his older companion, nodding. "And a very large number of horses."

Bannon grunted. "And if we don't let them in, they will force their way in." He glanced at Julian, shaking his head. "What a mess."

Julian carefully avoided looking at Samara. "This queen," he asked, "how does she govern? She must have strong support to uproot her entire nation... to burn their city to the ground. Even with a conqueror at the gates, I would expect that some would rather surrender."

The older envoy replied. "Queen Zhuana is the daughter of the last king, and has reigned for eighteen years. She rules through her druadan, their version of nobles. They are all battle-hardened, as is she."

"Battle-hardened?" Samara raised an eyebrow.

"Go on," Julian said. "Tell us more about her."

"She has a son, Garric." The older envoy addressed Bannon. "You met him, Commander, at the river."

"Him?" Bannon started. He turned to Julian. "A strong lad, lean but fit. Maybe sixteen or seventeen."

"Who is the father?" Samara asked.

The envoy nodded at his younger companion. "Merrin here got one of their women talking…"

"I am not surprised," Samara murmured, low enough that Julian could only just hear her as she looked over the handsome young man.

The young man, Merrin, cleared his throat. "Apparently one of the nobles, Maven Dresk, got into an argument with the queen's husband, a man named Barrix. No one knows exactly what the argument was about, but Maven insulted the queen, called her a…" he hesitated, "a craven dog, yapping at the heels of wolves."

Julian and Samara exchanged glances.

"Go on," Julian said.

"Barrix was a proud warrior and a popular leader. But when he tried to enlist enough support to bring Maven down, his enemy denied the accusation, told everyone he had said nothing of the kind. He only had respect for the queen, he said. It was one man's word against another, and so Barrix had only one option left: he challenged Maven to a duel. One of their customs, apparently. Their mother goddess would decide who was telling the truth in a fight to the death."

"The queen didn't try to stop the duel?" Bannon asked.

Julian spoke up, "How could she? Once it was made public, the insult was a challenge to her rule."

The envoy continued, "It was a bloody fight, but Maven was the victor. Zhuana watched as Maven opened up her husband's chest. Her son watched with her, just a babe in her arms."

Samara put a hand to her mouth. "And this druadan, Maven, still remains a noble?"

"He does, to this very day. Their wise men say their mother goddess spoke, and Maven's word was the truth."

For a time there was silence, as Julian, Samara, and Bannon absorbed the story.

"I will not call them barbarians, but I will think it in my head," Bannon finally said.

"Tell us more about these wise men," Julian said, addressing the older envoy.

"They call them druids. One of them is the queen's closest advisor. As I understand it, they are medicine men, with a knowledge of plants and the like. The Veldrians believe their druids have magical powers. They all believe it."

Bannon snorted. "Like I said. Barbarians."

Samara touched Julian's arm. "In my travels I heard of druids. Sometimes there is truth in stories."

"How about numbers?" Bannon asked. "How many of them are there?"

"We have conferred." The envoy nodded toward his younger companion. "But it is still hard to say. They likely don't know themselves. More than sixty thousand, I would think."

"More importantly, how many of them are fighters?" Julian asked.

"Essentially..." the envoy hesitated. "All of them. Anyone male or female, seventeen or older, is expected to fight when called upon. Mothers with babes carry hunting knives at their hips. Children who can barely walk practice with bows and wooden swords. The boys and girls play games, hiding in bushes or tall grass and doing their best to surprise each other with a sharp stick at the throat. At least, they look like games, but they always have a purpose."

Samara was staring straight at Julian, her eyes now tight with worry.

"Is there anything else we need to know?" Bannon asked.

The older scout glanced at his companion and then shook his head. "Nothing that comes to mind, Sir."

"Very well," Bannon said. "That will be enough for now. Thank you. You may go."

As he pondered, Julian waited until the pair of young men had left, and then rapped his fingers on the table in front of him. He tried not to look at his wife. "I will need to make plans," he said. "Commander, you will soon know what our next steps are to be. In the meantime, keep a close eye on them. If a single person crosses the river, I want to know about it. Watch their camp more closely than you have ever watched anything else."

Chapter Twenty-Six

BETHANY WOULD NOW have to survive her first major test.

Another student had been asked to leave the school early, unable to keep up with the pace in classes, but this test was different, intended to whittle their number down even further. She sat in a waiting area, on one of the wooden chairs provided for the purpose. The room was rectangular, with a door at each end and no furniture other than the row of chairs along each wall. There were few places to rest her eyes, and she avoided staring at the door that Gregor had just left through, just a few minutes earlier. The only other place to look was at Xander, who was directly across from her, the sole other person in the room.

Xander was clearly nervous, staring at the floor, which gave her a chance to distract herself by watching him. He was lean, but too wide in the shoulders to be called lanky; she just thought of him as tall. The wavy black hair that reached his collar had grown in their time at the school. She couldn't deny that he was handsome, with his striking features and infectious smile. The pressure of their studies had taken a toll, however, and it was some time since she had seen the sparkle in his brown, gold-flecked eyes.

He sighed, tensed as he waited, and still he didn't look up, even as the growing silence added to the tension, until she wanted nothing more than to break it.

Whatever problem he might have with her, they were in this situation together.

When she spoke, her voice sounded loud in her own ears. "Do you ever wonder why we are putting ourselves through this?"

He raised his head, frowning as he returned her stare. "Sometimes. Why, do you?"

She hesitated and then smiled. She didn't want to lie; she knew why she was here. "Sometimes." Her smile grew. "But not often."

Unable to help himself, he smiled as well. "Then why did you ask?"

"I thought it might open a conversation." Her smile became a grin. "And here we are." She paused to gather her thoughts. "We have to agree this isn't easy. And we're still closer to the beginning than the end. Why, then? For you, I mean."

"Why am I trying to become a diviner?"

She nodded.

"You go first," he said.

As he leveled his direct attention on her, she knew he was listening to her every word. "I..." she hesitated, "I suppose that this is my dream."

He didn't laugh at her; he simply nodded. "We all have our dreams. And we all had to work hard to get here. I do realize, Bethany, that you must have worked as hard as anyone else."

It wasn't often he said her name. She seized upon her chance, knowing it might not come again. "Xander, I really am sorry about your friend—"

"Stop. Please. It doesn't matter." He paused. "I saw him at Midwinter, did I tell you? When I told him about how much work they have us doing he said he was glad it wasn't him. He might have been saying that for my benefit, but still..."

She hoped that it was true, even as guilt squeezed at her stomach. Her father did it. It wasn't her fault.

Xander spoke again, interrupting her thoughts. "You asked why I want to be a diviner. Did Carina tell you about my family?"

"No." She shook her head. "She only said that you come from a family of traders."

"My father, my mother, my three older brothers, my uncle..." he trailed off. "I know you didn't go to a school like West Park, although you haven't said what school it was. You probably think we're all as wealthy as Carina's family. That might have been true, four or five years ago. But all it takes is one too many failures..."

"What happened?"

"Simply put, my father became ill and Jordan, my oldest brother, made some bad decisions. At the same time, one of my other brothers borrowed some money and gambled it away. He said he only wanted to help, but he made things worse. Much worse."

He looked to the side, his eyes unfocused. "I hope you never find your family broken by debt. I'm here because diviners get paid well, well enough to get my family out of trouble. I'm here because I can do this... and I'm good at it. At least, that's what I keep telling myself."

"You *can* do this," she said.

"I hope so." He continued to look into the distance, pensive. He sighed again but then shook himself. "What about your family?" He ventured a smile. "All I know about you is that you know how to make your own clothes."

She opened her mouth, but she didn't know what to say. He had shared himself with her, and she wanted to do the same thing. But he might have expectations, expectations to share more than she felt comfortable with. How could she explain about her father? She couldn't. Not without revealing her role in what happened to his friend.

As for her own upbringing, she had barely gone to temple school, let alone academy school, before her acceptance at the School of Divination. If it weren't for her mother, and for Charlton, she would never be here. She was just a worker from the Fabric District.

"I..." she began.

The door opened, the same door that Gregor had gone through. Diviner Trask's face appeared; he spied her and beckoned. "Bethany Sylvana. Your time has come."

Bethany's limbs were wooden as she stood up from her chair, wondering about what the test might entail; they hadn't been told anything at all.

"Good luck," Xander whispered.

She followed Diviner Trask from the room and along a hallway. He went to another door and opened it, revealing another stone-walled room beyond.

"Go inside," he said. "You have two minutes."

"Do I—?"

"Go through the door, Bethany. Wait until you are called."

Bethany entered the room, and without another word, Trask closed the door behind her, leaving her alone inside. She was now in another antechamber, similar to the first, in that it had just one door in and another out. However, going by the scene in front of her, her test had clearly begun.

Five broad, circular plates rested on the floor. Evenly spaced and exactly the same size, the plates were made of metal, with each about the size of a small dining table. The plates curved upwards at the edges, not enough to make them bowls, but with enough of a cupping shape to contain their contents.

One plate held a pyramid-shaped pile of yellow sand. The next displayed several blocks of gray stone. A colorful amalgamation of mortar and pebbles rested on the next. Brown dirt filled another plate. The last held chunks of a dark wood.

Bethany's mouth went dry as her heart rate increased. What was she supposed to do?

Two minutes, Trask had said. It was no time at all. She turned from plate to plate. Sand. Bricks. Mortar and pebbles. Dirt. Wood. They were all materials, obviously. How should she use her time?

Her feet didn't move. She stood frozen with indecision. She couldn't fail this test; if she did, she would be out of the School of Divination. Back to the Fabric District, where she would have to find work in someone else's shop. Her mother's medicine would run out. Her headaches would become agonizing.

Her mother's face came to her mind. The visit for Midwinter Feast had been bittersweet. Her mother now couldn't see at all; the blindness had finally come. After fumbling with the food Bethany had picked up from the market, she smiled when Bethany left, but Bethany couldn't escape the feeling that when the door to the dormus closed behind her, her mother would soon be crying.

Why wouldn't someone tell her what she was supposed to do?

The door at the far end of the room opened. Once again, Diviner Trask's stern face and combed black hair appeared. "Your time is up. Come this way."

She passed the plates to reach her teacher, who held the next door open for her. When she walked through, he closed the door behind her, but she was barely aware of the sound it made.

This time, she was in a circular room. The space wasn't vaguely round; it was a perfect cylinder, as if she were inside a huge jar made of stone, and it was immense. Most of the area was in darkness, but she had an impression of space. Only the room's focus, the very center of the cylinder, was well-lit by a handful of torches.

The torches drew Bethany's attention to the raised pedestal they encircled. A path lay in front of her, leading to the pedestal, which was taller than she was. A ladder was set into the pedestal's side.

"Climb," Diviner Trask instructed, "until you are standing on top."

Bethany headed to the ladder and climbed, pulling herself up with an effort. Soon she straightened, taking in her strange position, although she was reluctant to look down. She had enough space beneath her feet to stand and that was all. If she fell, she would likely hurt herself as she hit the hard stone floor.

Meanwhile, Diviner Trask took one of the torches and went to the wall. He traveled around the room's circumference, lighting more torches as he went, until he had created a rim of light. As he returned his torch to its place, for the first time, she could take in the entire area.

There was a huge pyramid-shaped pile, made of sand, thirty or forty feet away.

A low stone wall surrounded her, just inside the room's perimeter, perfectly circular and made of the same gray blocks she had seen in the previous room.

A stone's throw behind her was an arch. Fashioned of mortar and pebbles, the span was twice her height and about the same width.

Next, she saw a mound, made of brown dirt.

And finally, she turned toward a fanciful structure like a temple, built out of dark wood, with solid planking and a peaked roof.

"Time is space, and space is time," Diviner Trask said. "In which direction are you being pulled?" He paused, as if waiting for her, and then spoke again. "Look down."

Down between her feet, on top of the pedestal, was a pointed metal dial, like the hand of a clock. The metal was thin, almost flat to the surface, so that when she nudged it with her foot she barely knew it was there.

"You have five minutes," Trask said.

She quickly scanned, but as with the previous room, there was no clock for her to gauge how the time was passing. Without another word, Trask exited the room, leaving through yet another door.

This time, when the door closed, it made a heavy, final sound.

She was on her own.

And she knew she had to think fast. She had been taught that heavy, bulky masses had an effect on the tapestry. *In which direction are you being pulled?*

Her stomach felt tight and her heart pounded in her ears like she was running. A voice screamed inside her head. *Concentrate!* Instead, all she could do was curse her own lack of intuition.

She had been taking classes in logic. She had spent all this time learning how to think, to apply her mind in novel ways.

The piles in the last room. She had been free to touch, to feel. She understood now; she was supposed to weigh them in her hands. The gray stone might be light, or the dark wood unexpectedly heavy.

She had missed her opportunity. She was going to fail. This was it, the end.

And all the time she berated herself, time was rushing past.

Stop. She could do this. Rather than thrust away thoughts of her mother, she intentionally held on to the memories and worries for the future, again bringing to mind her mother's face. Her mother had worked hard to raise her. All of the reading at night, straining eyes by the light of weak oil lamps, had been for her. Her mother was now blind. Her daughter was no longer a child. She had to prove to her mother that she could handle the responsibility that had been thrust upon her. She had to show everyone that she was worthy of this opportunity. She had to prove it to herself.

After forcing herself to hold onto the thoughts that kept crowding her mind, she was suddenly able to let them drift away. Clarity came to her consciousness. This was the state she had achieved only partially during meditation. Her determination returned.

Logic. How could she use what she had learned, even without weighing the materials in her hands? The low wall of stone bricks surrounded her, a perfect circle within the circle of the room, with her at its focal point. *In which direction are you being pulled?* She knew that the gray stone circle wouldn't pull in any direction; its effect was symmetrical. She could rule it out. It wouldn't send her in any direction but where she already was.

Symmetry. The extension of logic. The dark wood was probably less dense than the other materials, and because it was fashioned into the temple-like structure, it certainly wasn't as heavy or bulky as the huge piles of sand and dirt.

The sand pyramid was diagonally opposite the dirt mound, but the dirt mound was bigger, so if she didn't take anything else into account, the arrow would point that way.

Only the arch remained to skew the direction. The arch was huge, the heaviest of all; it simply had to be to remain standing and support the span above the void beneath it. She wished, however, that she knew just how heavy it was. She couldn't go back into the room and heft a chunk of the mortar and pebble.

She crouched down, shuffling her feet and the dial at the same time until she was facing a direction that took into account the sum of everything she had decided so far. She straightened, and now she was facing somewhere between the arch and the dirt mound, but angled more toward the arch.

The door opened.

"Your time is up," Diviner Trask said as he entered quickly, with long strides. He saw the direction she was facing, but came closer, until he was by her feet, inspecting the arrow's direction. He gave no indication of success or failure. "You may now climb down the ladder."

Trask waited until she was back on the ground, and when she was down, she tried to read his face.

She thought she saw something, perhaps a frown. He stroked the tiny black beard on his chin, which she was learning was something he did when he was irritated.

"Bethany. Come with me."

She followed him from the room, along another corridor, and down a side passage, to a door that didn't look any different from the others. Glancing down the passage, she realized she knew where she was; the atrium wasn't far away.

As he opened the door, she spoke up. "Another challenge?"

"No," he said. "A serious talk."

Trask led her into a room filled with books, stacked on shelves lining every wall except for where a window allowed light from a clear blue sky. He indicated a chair in front of a broad, sturdy desk, and as she took a seat, he settled himself into the thick leather-clad chair on the other side. This wasn't just any room—she was in his personal study.

Her eyes widened as she looked down. Between her and her teacher, on the desk, was a wooden dial lying flat. The arrow had been set in a particular direction. The hand pointed just a couple of notches away from where she had set her own dial, back in the cylindrical room.

But as Trask watched her with his calculating black eyes, she felt a rising dread.

"I will be direct. You have an impressive memory, and you learn well. You have a talent for calculations. Logic comes to you easily, when you are not busy thinking of other things." He rapped his fingers on his desk, and then leaned forward. "However your staff work is the worst I have seen, and what you do not realize is that you have yet to commence delirium, which will test you beyond endurance. You are too easily distracted. You have difficulty setting your mind at ease. You do not have enough focus. Today, you failed to see the opportunity in front of you. We expect better of our diviners."

She tried to brace herself. Here it came; she was going to be dismissed.

"And yet your answer was close, within the allowable range. Perhaps you were lucky. Or perhaps you have a deep intuition that will serve you in the future as you learn the skills you need. Either way, today is a busy day, and it is now time for another student to take the test." He nodded toward the door. "The atrium is on the right as you leave the hallway. You may leave, Bethany. I am sure you have a lot to think about."

"You didn't weigh them?" Carina spluttered. "But how did you know the answer?"

Bethany was uncomfortable, and didn't meet Carina's eyes. "I guessed."

Carina let out a burst of laughter, as both she and Xander shook their heads. Bethany knew she was blushing, and wished she wasn't. She tried to look anywhere else.

The three of them were in the atrium, near the stone benches under the oak tree, given some time to themselves after taking the test. Every time a new student entered, the people already in the area clapped, while their friends hurried over to hug and congratulate them. At the same time, a few faces were known to be missing. They were all wondering how many would be left at the end of the day.

"But Bethany, what did you think you were in that room for?" Carina asked.

Bethany wished she could change the topic. Trask's admonishment was still fresh in her mind. "They didn't say."

"That was the whole point."

"Carina, stop, she's had a tough day," Xander said.

Carina covered her mouth. "He's right. Sorry, Bethany. I'm just relieved you're still with us." She stared into Bethany's eyes. "You were lucky. You realize that don't you? You can't let something like that happen again."

"I know."

Carina tilted her head as if seeing Bethany for the first time. "Is something else wrong? You've been different since Midwinter. Is it your family? The stars know I have my own problems with mine."

Bethany shook her head. "I'm fine."

"But Bethany, the fact is I don't think you are. I know all about Xander and his quest to save the Cole family. With Xander on their side, they will be able to jump from gateway to gateway, buying and selling as they go—"

"I've already told you," Xander said with a frown. "The corpus doesn't allow us to be free agents. I couldn't just go off to work for my family."

"Even so," Carina raised her voice, "we all know why you're doing what you're doing. And you both know about me and my evil step-mother, who doesn't think I deserve to be here." She turned again to Bethany. "You're different, Bethany. You never talk about your parents. To tell the truth, you don't say much at all."

Bethany tried to think of a reply. "Maybe it's just because I don't have much to say."

Carina snorted. "When it comes to family, everyone has something to say."

"Well... I don't have a big family," Bethany said. "It's just my mother and me."

"Your mother from Loriastis," Carina said.

Bethany nodded.

"Where is your father?" Carina asked bluntly.

"My mother raised me on her own. She is... was... a seamstress."

Xander and Carina exchanged glances.

"Was?" Carina asked.

"That's not what I meant. You know I just saw her for Midwinter. She isn't a seamstress anymore. That's what I meant. She just... she lost her vision."

"Your mother is blind?" Xander drew in a sharp breath. "By the stars... Bethany... How... when?"

She found it easier to look away. "It started last summer. It was so fast. She began to get blurred vision. She started to get headaches. We were lucky, though... She was able to see the best clerics from the University. But at the same time, there isn't much they can do for her. The headaches have become bad... it's frightening. She takes medicine, enough that she now spends most of her time sleeping. And the medicine is expensive." Now that she had started, she kept going in a rush. "She has a woman, Dahlia, who looks after her. But I can't see her, not often, and I know I can't leave this school. I have to make this work."

For a time, there was quiet after Bethany's words. Taking a deep breath, she focused on her two companions, seeing Xander watching her with an expression of surprising concern, and Carina's curiosity merged with kindness.

"Bethany..." Carina asked, "you said that you're from West River?"

"From the Fabric District, actually."

"Ah. The other side of the river," Carina said. Bethany was quick to search for judgment, but instead she was surprised to see awe. "How did you get here? What school did you go to? I always assumed it wasn't one of the big ones, but you haven't said."

"I had to work," Bethany said. "A cleric helped me. He gave me books..." Her voice caught a little at the end.

"Wait. You didn't go to academy school?" Xander was stunned.

She shook her head. "I didn't finish temple school either. Not after six or seven."

The silence was complete. Bethany looked away, and then forced herself to once more look at the young man and young woman with her, people she realized she might call her friends.

It was only after some time that Carina spoke firmly. "Bethany, I know you have a lot to worry about, but if any of us is going to get through this school, it should be you."

Bethany stared up at the atrium's high ceiling even as she nodded. She knew what she needed to do.

She had to find her focus.

Chapter Twenty-Seven

JULIAN MALVENTUS LIVIUS, Crown Prince of the Dymantine Empire, stood and waited patiently. He wore his plate armor, his high black boots, and his gold-trimmed white cloak. His golden hair was freshly oiled, shining in the low daylight of late winter. He kept a smooth, calm expression on his face, even as he noticed his pulse increasing. He knew, as did his companions, that something of great importance was about to take place at the River Byre.

With him at the base of the gorge was Commander Roos Bannon. Bearded and gruff, he wore a military dress uniform, without a helmet, and like Julian, he didn't carry a weapon.

There were three others with Julian and Bannon: lords from the assembly, representatives from the three orders. The trio of old men wore white cloaks edged in different colors: red, black, and blue.

Imperial guardsmen also stood in formation. The protective force of the empire's finest soldiers were uniformly tall men, armed with both swords and daggers, dressed in full plate that was burnished and shining for the occasion.

The encounter had been carefully arranged. Julian and his retinue waited near a canvas pavilion erected by the placid flowing waters. The river shifted constantly. The pavilion's location was neither within nor outside the empire, but on the border itself.

Two chairs waited by a table, under the pavilion's sheltering roof.

The Veldrians were already crossing the gorge's floor, and Julian watched as they approached. Queen Zhuana's figure, at the front of her group, was unmistakable. He kept his eyes on her most of all.

Zhuana was nearly as tall as the men with her, and had the darkest skin of her retinue. Her lords – druadan, he reminded himself – had coloring ranging from light brown to olive and even a few paler people. Already, the range of appearance told him something. These newcomers didn't have as many different looks as Julian's guard, drawn from across the vast empire, but the Veldrians were not an insular people; evidently they had long been trading and mingling with others. He reserved the knowledge, along with everything he had learned so far.

Zhuana wore dark brown leather, hardened and formed into armor. Her shoulders were protected, as was her torso, where at her slender waist her armor met a skirt of wide leather strips. There were places where her ebony skin was bare: her biceps, between wrist and elbow; her calves, above her boots, the area below her neck, where she displayed a symbolic sword on a silver necklace, only slightly higher than her breasts.

She had long black hair, tied back from her head in a style like a horse's tail, threaded with diamonds that sparkled when she moved. Her cheekbones were high, fine-featured, like her refined nose and the shape of her ruby-lipped mouth. Julian had been expecting a woman who was striking, but the rumors hadn't been descriptive enough.

Zhuana, the Queen of the Veldrians, was beautiful.

She was also terrifying.

A curved weapon, somewhere between sword and knife, hung in a scabbard from her waist. Her face was stone-cold, like ice. Her eyes were brown and calculating, and matched an expression that gave nothing away.

Zhuana came to a halt. With her were a handful of her advisors, along with a dozen armed warriors who made up her escort. Ignoring the warriors, Julian focused on Zhuana's retinue. Whose opinion mattered to Zhuana the most?

He settled on an older man with sunken cheeks and close-cropped graying hear, remembering that a druid was one of her advisors, and guessing that he must be the man mentioned. Another man of importance was a muscled, athletic warrior with a bald head and a nose that had taken a battering at some time in the past.

"She is armed," Bannon murmured. "That was not the agreement."

Julian's eyes moved to her curved sword, and then he made a decision. "Leave it."

"Are you—?"

"Yes, I am sure."

Julian stepped forward, and Zhuana did too. Together, each watching the other, they went to the pavilion and the nearest chair. At last they both stood behind a chair. Julian put a hand on his heart and nodded his head. Zhuana gave the slightest nod in return.

"Shall we?" Julian indicated the chairs.

"Of course," she replied.

Her voice was like her: stern, commanding. She spoke precisely, and if she were self-conscious of her accent, she didn't show it at all. Her manner of speech, combined with her appearance, made her someone different, which was an unfamiliar feeling. Julian had traveled the empire. But he had never met anyone like her.

He seated himself, studying Zhuana while she took her own seat opposite. When she appeared to be ready, he began.

"Queen Zhuana. I do realize that you asked for my father the emperor, but he is an old man, and rarely journeys outside Everlast. I am Julian Malventus Livius, his son and heir, crown prince of the Dymantine Empire. I speak with the emperor's voice. It is my pleasure to meet with you today."

She didn't reply immediately. As she regarded him, he wondered what she was seeing. Her face certainly didn't give much away. Her eyes reminded him of Samara's: cool, intelligent. A glint in her gaze made him think of a feline.

"Crown Prince Julian Malventus," she said. "It is an honor to meet you. Your gifts were appreciated. I trust that ours were too?"

"Very much," Julian said. Aware of the people nearby, he turned, beckoning to Commander Bannon and the three noblemen with him. "This is Commander Bannon." He introduced Bannon, who gave a stiff bow. "Lord Ravinder of the Knight Wardens." Ravinder, a swarthy, elegant man, bowed in turn. "Lord Manson of the Knight Crusaders." Manson bowed; a typical Red, he was a burly bearded warrior who was always reliving his glory days and known to drink wine with breakfast. "Finally, Lord Harald of the Knight Guildsmen." Harald was ancient, but his wits were sharper than men decades younger. He gave Zhuana a deep bow.

Zhuana inspected each lord as he was introduced. When they bowed, she made no sign of acknowledgement; she was a queen, and it was her due. She spoke when Julian finished, "The Blacks, the Reds, and the Blues."

"You are well-informed."

"Your envoys have shared tales of the empire, but, of course, we have long known of the Eternal Empire's existence. Since coming here, we have also learned what we can."

Spies, Julian knew. His envoys would never have revealed so much.

Now it was Zhuana's turn to beckon. She introduced the hollow-eyed man in furs, whose black stare made Julian feel unsettled. "This is Alric, senior druid." The druid didn't bow, but Julian wasn't about to insist. "Dan Henwin." A stocky older man with big ears and a bushy beard gave a short nod. "Dan Taikar." A lanky, pale-skinned man with a scruffy beard, his nod was even briefer. "Dana Klara." A statuesque woman with her blonde hair in braids simply stared in Julian's direction. "And finally," Zhuana indicated the muscular bald-headed warrior, "this is Dan Dresk."

As soon as he heard the name, Julian couldn't help but appraise the last man, whose first name he knew was Maven. He wasn't as big as some of the nearby guardsmen, or the huge gladiator Julian had sparred with back in the Nexus, but there was little flesh on him that wasn't muscle. From experience, Julian knew that such a solid, powerful frame indicated pent-up strength that could uncoil like a striking snake. Dresk's manner was also confident, unintimidated by anything he saw in the people in front of him.

The man Julian was looking at had killed Zhuana's husband Barrix, the father of her son, Prince Garric. According to the rules of their mother goddess, justice was done and the matter closed. But deep down, what did Zhuana really think? And Maven, did he ever worry that one day his queen would have her vengeance?

As the lords at Julian's back watched the druadan behind Zhuana, there was still a healthy physical distance between them. Introductions were complete. It was time to move the dialogue forward.

"Your people... Where do you come from?"

"South. And east," Zhuana replied. "Our land was called Veldria. Our city carried the same name."

"Was?"

"It is all gone now. We were forced to abandon our lands."

"Forced by what?"

Zhuana raised an eyebrow. "I am sure your envoys told you the stories."

"Please. I want to hear from you."

"A conqueror. Torian Varlish of the Harna. He leads a powerful army. We had no other choice."

Julian frowned. "Should we be worried here?"

She met his gaze. "Yes."

"How big is his army?"

"We saw only part of it. But it was immense."

Julian frowned; he was looking for numbers but now wasn't the time to press; another chance would come. For her enemy to have enough numbers to make her flee, despite the sizable force she commanded... perhaps that said enough.

"We can help you," Zhuana said.

"How?"

"We are a nation of fighters. We are also farmers, craftsmen, and builders. And as you know, we are in need of new lands to call home."

Julian remained silent. Here it came.

"Help us, and we will help you," she said. "When you are attacked – and you will be – we will fight with you."

She left it unsaid, but if this conqueror came, she wanted the empire's protection. If Julian were to ally himself with her, he would naturally be making her enemies his own.

He pretended to ponder, as if he had no previous notion about what she might want. "Our empire is a complex, dynamic place—"

"Your empire is vast."

"—with fertile lands already claimed by the rightful inhabitants of those lands. I understand your request. I am also sure that you understand that what you are asking for is not easy. You are a queen. How would you have felt if newcomers wanted to settle in Veldria?"

Her eyes narrowed; he knew he had struck a nerve. "We don't want to wait."

He decided to test her. "Yes, but you will have to." This time her nostrils flared, but before she said something she might find hard to take back, he spoke up, "We will send some traders to your camp. You can purchase grain, livestock, fruits and vegetables. I will take your proposal to our assembly and we will find a path that satisfies all sides."

"A path that satisfies all sides," she said slowly.

Zhuana stared at Julian with a dark look that gave him a chill. Then she stood up from her chair, giving him no choice but to do the same thing. He tried not to let the tension in the air become revealed in his face. Instead he kept his expression calm, unhurried. Maven Dresk, on the other hand, had a look of open contempt on his face.

Zhuana gathered her nobles, and didn't look back, nor say another word as she left.

Then Julian heard a mutter; the voice belonged to Lord Manson of the Crusaders.

"To expect us to let in a horde of barbarians..."

Maven Dresk stopped walking. For a moment, he stood with his back to Julian's position.

Julian froze. Queen Zhuana turned and raised an eyebrow at Dresk.

Maven turned to face the Imperials. His eyes moved slowly from face to face.

"Big, but slow," he said in a thick, heavy accent. He finished with a sneer.

Maven then resumed walking away with his compatriots. Behind Julian, someone let out a breath. Julian inwardly swore, but waited until the Veldrians were long gone before facing the man behind him.

"You just lost your place here," he said, scowling at Manson.

"Apologies, I thought—"

"I don't want to hear it. Tell Tristan Benedict to send someone else." Julian shook his head. "We can only hope that we are all still talking." He glanced at Bannon. "Send the traders. If they buy, we will know that they are not yet looking for conflict."

✦

Julian lay in bed, staring up at the ceiling. Sweat covered his naked torso. Samara lay snuggled into the crook made between his arm and body. She smelled of lavender and rosewater, along with a deeper, muskier, womanly scent. He absently stroked her bare back and shoulder. Her skin was so creamy, so uniform.

She shifted, propping her head up to look into his eyes. "You must tell me," she said. "Is she as beautiful as they say?" Her full lips curved wickedly. "Just now, were you thinking of her, or me?"

"It is hard to be attracted to a woman you worry might kill you with a sharp blade. She is frightening, truth be told."

"Ah, so she made an impression on you."

He kissed her head and the locks of her dark hair. "Not that kind of impression." He returned to looking up, eyes unfocused, frown lines creasing his forehead.

"What are you thinking about?" Samara asked.

His brow furrowed deeper. "She says they are fleeing a great invasion, and that we should be worried here."

"Do you believe it?"

"There is reason to be skeptical. If she wants an agreement – her swords for our lands – it makes sense to try to frighten us. They may have simply been driven off. Perhaps an invasion was combined with flooding or drought. And yet there is something in her eyes... a shadow."

"She burned her city to the ground. That would make a mark on anyone." Samara rolled over and reached for the goblet on a low table by the bed. She took a sip from her wine, before setting the goblet back down. "What comes next?"

"She bought from our traders. That tells us she is still willing to talk."

Samara returned to her nestling position, her naked frame hugging his body and enclosed by his arm. "Time is on our side, not hers. Every day that passes gives us more men to counter her."

"True."

"But the problem is, she knows it. Her leverage is stronger now than it will be later on."

Imagining the Veldrians pouring across the border, Julian felt a chill.

"We both know we could never agree to her plan," she said. "We would be creating a festering wound inside the empire. No one would vote for it, and rightly so. That leaves us with two options. Either the Veldrians leave, and find new lands somewhere else, or we end up fighting, with the same eventual outcome. The important thing is to control the timing. Now is not a good time. Later is better. You will need to create the impression that progress is being made toward her request."

"Any ideas you have, I am listening."

"Do you remember being tutored in geography?"

"Not one of my strongest subjects," Julian said.

"Really? I quite enjoyed all the learning. Villages. Towns. Cities. Paths. Roads. Trade Routes. Gateways. Rivers. Lakes. Seas. Oceans. Mountain ranges. Mountain passes—"

"—Please, stop."

"Overwhelm her with information. There is a great deal she will be ignorant about. Then, when she grows impatient, bring in some of the lawmakers from the corpus to draw up an agreement. They make an art form of moving slowly. An unexpected late problem. Perhaps she has to visit the Marble Court to make her case. And on it goes."

Julian nodded; as always, Samara's ideas were both clever and sound. "Even so, she will not wait forever."

"That is, unfortunately, true. This is a delicate game we are playing. And the stakes don't get much higher."

Chapter Twenty-Eight

THE FLOOR WAS cold and hard. The sun's rays shining through the crystal lattice felt strong and piercing as they rested bright fingertips on Bethany's closed eyelids and tried to pry them open. The wooden pole that lay across her knees kept reminding her of the staff work to come.

Her thoughts darted from topic to topic. The season was approaching the end of winter. Only fourteen students remained to sit side by side under the Crystal Dome, beginning the day's classes with meditation. Six of their number had now been ejected from the School of Divination and returned home.

And she might soon be joining them.

Her test with the piles of sand and stone had gone badly. She had grasped at her answer intuitively, and still didn't know if she had simply been helped by luck. She had to find her focus. But the more she pushed, the harder it was. She needed to let go.

There had been another test, a written examination asking hundreds of questions about logic and symmetry. At the time, she had thought she might have done well, but now she was worried about the questions she had to read twice. Logic and symmetry were what she was supposed to be good at. If she failed the test, she would definitely be out of the school.

And still she struggled to find any success with meditation.

As she sat cross-legged, her eyes tightly closed, she listened to the sound of her breathing. In an attempt to calm the storm inside her mind, she cast her mind back, to a time before she knew that stars and planets had names and predictable movements.

When she was little, she used to climb up to the rooftop of her compound and stare up at the night sky. The glittering swath of tiny bright lights looked back at her. Against the darkness, they all had subtle variations in their color. Some looked more blue, others perhaps red or yellow or white. There were so many of them, up there forever, able to be seen on any clear night. What was she in comparison?

She remembered the feeling of awe. Compared to the stars, she felt so tiny. The cares of the world meant nothing at all.

That was it. Something slid into place.

Focus on her breathing. In... out. In... out. In... out.

The same heavens would be looking down on Everlast in a hundred years, and she would be gone, and so would be all of her cares and troubles. She was smaller than a speck of sand. She was softer than a droplet of water in the ocean. Like air, there was nothing to her at all.

Like her own breath. The slightest wind. In... out. In... out. In... out.

She heard a chime. She blinked.

The long meditation class was over.

Triumph surged through her, rising up to bring a warm feeling to her face. She had done it. She had found her focus, which strangely meant that she had managed to remain in the present, without being lost in the trials of the past or the hopes and fears of the future. Even as she and the other students straightened and climbed to their feet, the feeling continued to stay with her.

On the platform at the front, Madam Mei stood facing the fourteen students. She had her staff ready, and for the first time, Bethany thought hard about why meditation always flowed directly into divination, the slow dance they performed with their staff in their hands. It must be crucial for a diviner to achieve the correct state of mind before traveling the gateways.

"How was meditation?" Mei asked. She was small in stature, gray-haired and wrinkled like a dried fruit, but as always she radiated calm and power as she stood with her staff poised. "I sense that you are all nearly ready for the next stage. Your real work will soon begin. Perhaps a small taste?"

It occurred to Bethany to worry about what Mei was talking about. Next stage? Real work? She allowed herself to examine her own reaction, studied it, and then let it drift away. Her emotions weren't all that she was. She was able to observe her emotions, and then release them. There was nothing she could do about whatever trial Mei was going to come up with.

Her state of calm remained with her.

"Take your staff and follow me," Madam Mei said.

The instructor raised her staff in a familiar way and brought it down across her shoulder. She turned her body around until she had performed a full circle to face the students once more. Her staff made a slow slice. A diagonal cut. A stabbing blow at an imaginary enemy.

Bethany copied every move. She no longer felt foolish or uncertain. She didn't hesitate. Her breathing was loud and decisive as she lifted her own staff high and then brought it crashing down, but with a movement as slow as an unfurling flower.

As all fourteen students moved in unison, Bethany almost wanted to smile. There was something magical about performing the strange dance as one, with the skill and practice and state of mind to make it seem impossible to shift fourteen young bodies with such precision, especially at the placid rate that they were moving.

"Good. Good," Madam Mei said.

Mei inhaled, turned, exhaled. Her staff performed a complicated spin. Bethany had no difficulty in following. Mei crouched all the way down, cutting the staff across the ground without touching it, just an inch above the hard floor. Bethany's staff made the same movement. She focused on her breathing. She felt good.

"Now, we are going to do something different."

Bethany continued to watch her teacher. Mei never stopped her dance. It remained smooth and very, very slow. But it wasn't quite as slow as before. Bethany shifted her body left, raised her staff, brought it down. She turned halfway around. She spun in a circle. She soon knew for certain: Mei was definitely picking up her pace.

Where before, the audible sounds of breathing were long and soft, like a mother soothing a babe, now Bethany heard whooshing. As Mei increased speed further, Bethany was forced to do the same thing. A hard suck for an inhale. A powerful blow out for an exhale. Staff up. Staff down. Step to the side. Turn. Weave. Thrust.

Mei moved faster still. Bethany moved with her. The moves were familiar, as was the way they flowed from one into the other—without the familiarity, there was no way Bethany could have kept up. She had to forget everything except the dance. Mei picked up speed again.

Now, it wasn't just breathing; the staffs themselves made whirring sounds as they spun from position to position. Bethany's hands were always in the right spot. She had done it slowly, time and time again, which meant that she had been forced to get every detail right, and now that the dance was incredibly fast, she was able to move her limbs and body without needing to think.

Up on the podium, Madam Mei was fighting a dozen unseen enemies. She made grunts and loud cries. Her staff was a blur, moving so fast its distinct shape couldn't be seen. Bethany realized she wasn't watching Mei any longer. She wasn't able to, and perhaps that was part of Mei's intent. She had to rely upon her own body and mind, her experience and training, her clarity of thought.

The experience was like nothing she had felt before. She was uplifted, in unity with the other students, as they all shifted and spun, danced and turned. Joy was the overriding sensation. She didn't want it to stop.

Something broke the mood into terrible pieces.

A loud crack was out of place. A pained cry and a tumble and thump. Gasping, Bethany forced her body to stop moving. Her head whipped round.

One of the students lay on the ground. Bethany's gaze went straight to the blood covering a young man's matted hair. Then she saw Carina's shocked face, as her friend held the staff that had done the damage.

Bethany sat on a bench under the huge oak tree. The atrium was quiet. Students in a variety of gray clothing stood in pairs or alone. Some just looked up at the light coming in from the windows in the roof and the drooping tendrils of the plants on the balconies. Xander leaned against a wall, frowning and staring at the ground.

Even as she watched him, Xander looked past her at something. She turned, following his gaze, as Carina entered the atrium at Diviner Trask's side. Carina was pale and shaken, with strands of her blonde hair loose rather than tied back. Trask's severely combed black hair, combined with his expression, made his face especially stern, and he was running his fingers through the triangular beard on his chin.

"Students, gather," Trask said.

With Carina standing beside him, Trask waited until they were all arrayed nearby. Bethany held her breath. Carina was staring at the ground. Surely she couldn't be leaving? How badly had Gregor been hurt?

"Gregor is injured but he will recover," Trask said. Audible sighs of relief came from all quarters. "His head wound was minor, and he is now being observed by our best clerics, however we do not expect any complications. In another few days, perhaps a little longer, he will be with you in classes once more."

A great weight of relief left Bethany's shoulders. Worrying about being forced out of the school was one thing, but if Carina had injured someone badly – even by accident – she wouldn't be able to live with herself. The tightness didn't leave Bethany completely, however. Carina still wasn't looking up.

Trask continued, "The mistake was not Carina's. I am here to tell you that the error was Madam Mei's. You were not yet ready for what she tried to teach you. Another instructor will take Madam Mei's place. Again, Carina is not at fault. We will have a long break today. Classes will resume in the morning."

Chapter Twenty-Nine

BETHANY TRAVELED THE length of the bookshelf, her eyes flitting across the spines, absorbing the labels and topics as she moved. While many of her classmates had seized the current free time to gather in the atrium or retreat to their rooms, she had chosen the quiet refuge of the Observatory's central library. The library felt like a place that existed outside the flow of time, its few windows admitting little light. The still air carried the familiar scene of aged paper and well-worn leather.

When she came to the books on divination, she slowed and then stopped, searching. Her fingers traveled from spine to spine as she looked for something that would fill the gaps in her knowledge, something new.

Gradually she became aware of someone else in the same section. She tried to ignore the newcomer, but whoever it was came closer, until they were just behind her as she explored the shelf. Trying not to be too obvious, she turned her head.

Xander stood watching, smiling his crooked smile. He didn't say anything; he just waited where he was.

Bethany frowned. "Why are you looking at me like that?"

"They just released the results for the logic and symmetry test," he said, his tone light but teasingly deliberate.

She whipped her whole body toward him, at the same time trying to read his face. "And?"

He shrugged, his brown eyes twinkling. "If you're curious, you'll have to go back to the atrium."

Her expression darkened. "If you know, just tell me."

"And in return...?"

She lifted her chin. "Fine. I just got here, but if I have to go all the way back—"

As she turned, Xander reached out and gently touched her arm. "Bethany, wait. Look, I know it's been a strange day, but Carina's fine. Gregor too. You take everything so seriously—"

"Are you saying this isn't serious, what we're doing?"

"No," he said quickly, shaking his head. "That's not what I mean. No one's saying that." He paused, his tone softening. "Actually, I wanted to ask you for help. Maybe... to find out what books you've been reading lately." His smile returned, slowly widening. "They say no one's ever had a perfect score in the test before. Which is why I think you and I should spend more time together." He grinned. "Not that we aren't friends already."

His words took a moment to sink in. "Perfect score? Are you sure?"

He reached out to squeeze her hands. The contact surprised her, but he held her only briefly before letting go. "Yes, Bethany. That's exactly what I'm saying."

A smile slowly spread across her face. First she had at last had some success with meditation, and now this...

"While we're here... this morning... how did you find it?" he asked, as if reading her mind. "Aside from what happened, I mean."

She tried to find the right word, still smiling as she met his eyes. "Exhilarating."

"I know exactly what you mean." He smiled back at her. "So far we've been busy learning, but eventually we'll be given a real staff. And one day we'll be traveling the gateways."

"If we make it."

"When we make it."

He continued to smile, and Bethany smiled with him, but then the silence between them changed in nature, becoming awkward. He turned to the shelf beside them, slightly pulling out the last book she had touched.

"Resonance of the Tapestry," he spoke the title.

"Urgh." She made a sound of distaste. "Put it away, please."

"With pleasure. I didn't make it past the first ten pages." He opened his mouth, realizing something. "You've read it, haven't you?"

She shrugged, smiling. "I can't say I enjoyed it."

He scanned along the shelves, taking his time, and then raised an eyebrow in her direction. "Which books haven't you read?"

"Of these ones?" She began to touch spines as she walked along the shelf. "This one. This one. This one."

He pulled out another book. "Please don't tell me you've read this one."

"Mass and Density. Translation by Jerome Winter." She gave a little nod.

He shook his head. Meanwhile, she was turned to face him; the last book had reminded her of something.

"Xander?" she asked seriously. "How many times have you seen that a book has been translated?"

He tilted his head at her. "It happens. Why?"

She hesitated, unwilling to reveal her ignorance.

"Whatever it is, you can ask me." He tapped his chin, pretending to think. "The fact is, yes I do enjoy long walks by the river." His eyes twinkled again. "My favorite color is blue. No, I don't yet have a partner for the spring dance."

She couldn't help it; she punched him in the arm. "Stop it. I don't like you making fun of me."

When his grin only grew, she went to hit him again, but he instead caught her hand. His smile fell away. Her eyes went to her hand, held in his. Then he let her go.

"It's good to laugh sometimes. You know I would never make fun of you. I do mean it. You can ask me anything."

She looked into his eyes, uncertain. They were the only two people present. She supposed she was only asking a question. "Translated from what language?"

Xander frowned.

"Have I asked a foolish question?"

"It's fine." He looked like he was choosing his words carefully. "I just forget that you didn't go to academy school. And your mother's from Loriastris. Don't worry. It's natural to want to understand." He glanced one way, and then the other. "Come with me."

Curious, she followed him as he navigated the library, heading to a corridor between the shelves so they could cross the room together. At the back of the immense room, he opened a paneled wooden door, checking on her before heading down some steps.

The area below was dim, lit by a few oil lamps in alcoves. She descended the steps slowly, taking in the sight of another library, smaller than the one above yet filled with dozens of shelves lined up beside each other like soldiers at parade. The ceiling was much lower, but not so low that she felt uncomfortable, making the room feel like a very large cellar. Her eyes moved across the room. This was the kind of place she had always felt drawn to.

Xander clearly knew where he was going, as he led her along a corridor between shelves.

"What is this place?" she asked. "I didn't even know it was here."

"It's called the Vellum Library. They brought us here a few times when I was at West Park."

There were striking maps on the walls, some simple, others rendered in extraordinary detail, with ribbons of curling river and each structure given its own tiled roof and even windows. Looking around as she walked, she took in a series of sketches, seeing strange objects: tools, weapons, things that looked like torture devices. Monoliths clustered in circles, drawn by skilled artists. Castles loomed against stormy skies. Ancient peoples in frightening costumes stared back at her.

"There is a better history section at the Imperial Library." Xander paused to look back at her. "But this is where they have the oldest books. The most important ones."

They were now near the rear of the space and Bethany spied a metal door between two decorated wooden poles. She nodded toward it. "What's on the other side of that door?"

"I asked the same thing. Apparently that's where they keep the oldest books of all."

He glanced at the door, before turning toward her as they both stood beside a bookshelf. Where the bookcases upstairs were tall and widely spaced, the shelves here were more solid and only reached head height. The tomes were bigger, weightier, with more calfskin and parchment, rather than the paper and leather composing most of the books she was familiar with.

"You were asking about why a lot of the books are translated." Xander's penetrating, intelligent eyes met hers. "First, it might help if you tell me what you already know. About our past, I mean. About the gateways."

She furrowed her brow. "I know the first Dymantines came from across the sea. They found the gateways as well as the abandoned cities—Drey, Kelway, Breanne, Myra, Laurel... and Everlast of course."

He nodded. "Keep going."

"There were some tribes—in the Northern Provinces, the Reaches, and in Ganouda. But the Dymantines found many places empty. Abandoned altogether."

"Who then built the cities and the gateways?"

"The Eidar."

Xander nodded again. "Go on."

"People think they fled east, across the Emerald Sea. All we have now are the things they left behind. The first Dymantines used the stone from their houses to build what we have now. Only a few structures remain, mainly the gateways. Parts of the Nexus. And the Corpus District, of course."

"So if the Dymantines didn't build the gateways... if we didn't make them. How did we learn to use them?"

She tilted her head. "I don't know."

Xander went to a book, carefully dislodging the oversized tome from its fellows. He opened the pages slowly, revealing sketches of gateways, one after another. As he reached the Argent Arch, Bethany saw crisper symbols on the arch than those she was used to. Xander's fingertips rested on the huge structure.

"The Dymantines knew that the gateways were special. But no matter how much they tried, they couldn't understand them. But then everything changed."

Xander continued to turn the pages, concentrating as he searched for something. He came to a section where the landscape surrounding the gateways changed, and Bethany saw jungle and bizarre rock formations along with the pyramids and arches.

"After they arrived, the settlers formed nations, eating up the land as the Dymantines occupied the area once held by the Eidar. The different territories fought and squabbled until Dymantus became an empire. The empire spread north and south, and also east. Explorers mapped the Gulf of Shadows and traveled into the Emerald Sea. They discovered the island of Korandia."

Xander swept his hand over the vivid image. Bethany had heard stories about Korandia. It was supposed to be a magical place, wild and mysterious.

"They found people living in Korandia, people still there today. The Korandians are an ancient people, and the Dymantines who met them discovered that their art mimicked the style of the Eidar, and their writing did as well."

Xander turned more pages, until he came to another image of a stepped pyramid, but this time a man faced the pyramid. He wore an elaborate costume, complete with feathers and the spotted skin of a wild cat. As he faced the pyramid, he held a staff dramatically in the air.

"The Dymantines saw something incredible. Some of the Korandians were special, able to travel between the stone temples and pyramids on their island, disappearing at one place and reappearing at another."

Bethany stared wide-eyed at the picture.

"The first diviners were Korandians," Xander said. "The Dymantines gave them prestigious positions, and over time, they shared their skills with others. Adventurous diviners opened up all the gateways we use now, from the Argent Arch to the Temple of Darsh in Ganouda. Much of what the Korandians did was based around ritual, but over time people added to the body of knowledge. Today, divination fits into a system with processes and logic. You know what everyone always says. The empire wouldn't function without use of the gateways."

Bethany tried to absorb everything she had learned. She was so used to the name – the Eternal Empire – that she rarely gave thought to the passage of time. Seven centuries had passed since Dymantus had declared itself an empire. The first Dymantines crossed the sea from the west long before that. And the Eidar...

"How do we know the Korandians aren't the Eidar? Or what's left of them?" she asked.

"When the Dymantines first went to Korandia, a lot of time had passed since the Eidar vanished. Even so, the Korandians remembered the Eidar, and it's from them that we think they went across the sea. We also know that Korandia isn't the only place with gateways. We have gateways scattered across the empire, and beyond our borders as well. They are out there, waiting to be rediscovered, some covered in vines, others buried in sand."

Bethany pictured the book they had discussed upstairs. "People translated books from the Korandians, who learned from the Eidar before they vanished."

"The oldest books are translated, yes."

"What else can the Korandians tell us about the Eidar?"

Rather than reply, Xander returned his book to the shelf and then scanned the spines. Settling on a volume, he took a moment to slide it out, before handing it to her. "This book is all about the Korandians, a rendition of their old myths and legends." He smiled. "I have to warn you. It's quite abstract."

Bethany took the book, which displayed a fanciful creature on the cover, a little man with a bald head except for a tuft on his crown, grinning malevolently while crouching and displaying knobby elbows and knees.

"Xander... Can we use this library whenever we want?"

"Of course. When we're not in classes, anyway. And we both know that isn't much." He nodded toward the stairs leading up to the main library. "Speaking of time away from classes, I'm going to get something to eat." He cocked his head, inquiring.

"You go. I think I'll stay."

"Your choice." He smiled. "Just remember your body needs food sometimes." He must have noticed something in her expression. "What is it?"

She had her mouth open, but closed it again rather than ask her question. It was too obvious. Everyone would have asked it a thousand times.

"Just say it, Bethany, whatever it is."

"How long has it been since the Eidar vanished?"

He didn't laugh at her. "No one knows for sure. Perhaps a thousand years had passed, after they left and the first Dymantines arrived, but that's just a guess, and a lot of people think it could be twice as long, even three times as long. They simply... vanished. And they didn't leave much behind." He smiled again, glancing at the bookshelves. "If you figure it out, let me know. Just don't forget to come up for air."

She watched his back as he left, and then raised her voice to call out, just as he was about to be out of earshot. "Xander?"

He paused. "Yes?"

"Thank you."

Chapter Thirty

THIS TIME, JULIAN and Zhuana were alone as they faced each other across the table, under the shade of the white pavilion. An escort of Imperial soldiers watched Julian, but from a distance. A separate group of Veldrians, on the other side of the gorge, watched their queen.

Julian tried to read Zhuana's face, gauging her desperation, her willingness to go to war to achieve what she wanted. What would it take to get her to take her people and leave? That was the best outcome. What was she more afraid of, the empire's soldiers, like those watching them, or this enemy she was fleeing?

Today, rather than wear her long black hair in the shape of a horse's tail, she displayed it in a fan of long tresses, woven with silver thread. For the first time he realized that her nose was slightly upturned, which suited her high cheekbones. Her face was like the visage of a statue, beautiful but still as stone. As before, she was in fighting garb, and wore her hardened leather armor and skirt of strips. Breaking her gaze, as he searched for somewhere to rest his eyes, from the way she was seated, he could see the smooth dark skin high on her thigh.

"You said you have something for me?" She stared at him with eyes that made him think of a cat about to pounce on its pitiful prey. There was a map of the empire spread on the table between them, but she only had eyes for him.

He cleared his throat. "I do. I have a proposal. Have you heard of the Jaynians? We are fighting them in the Eastern Reaches." He stabbed a finger on the map. "Here."

She still didn't look down at the map. "You want us to destroy your enemies and then we can have their lands," she said in a dry voice.

"It is a fair proposal."

His hope was that she would take it. If the Veldrians helped Agapon defeat the Jaynians, he would solve two problems in a single stroke. Every noble in the assembly would toast his name.

Zhuana shook her head. "We want to be inside the empire, not outside it. Give us a reasonable place to call our own. We will not wait here forever." At last she gazed down at the map. "I saw a map like this as a child. It belonged to my father. It was yellow and faded." Her lips moved as she read the names of places. Realizing she could read Imperial, as well as speak it, Julian filed the information away. "What about here?"

Zhuana was pointing to a place in the north: Kargul.

Julian kept a measured tone; she might know some things, but she didn't know the empire's geography, and he didn't want to embarrass her. "So far away? Could your people handle the cold? In Kargul it's freezing most of the year."

"We are farmers and herders."

"Then I think Kargul is not for you."

"Here?" Zhuana touched a place on the map, also on the far side of the empire. She kept her fingers in place, waiting for him to speak.

Julian shook his head. "Trent. One of the most populous areas. Divided up by counts and barons, dukes... even princes."

"Princes?"

He smiled. "I have an estate there myself." He pretended to ponder. "Hmm. One option... Perhaps... It could be a good one..."

"Where?"

"Here." He placed his finger on a mountain range in the south, not close, but also not far from their present location. "The Kila Mountains."

Zhuana's brow furrowed. "Tell me about it."

"Being in the south, there is a warm climate. No access to the sea, but I don't think that would be a problem for your people."

"Then what is the problem?"

"Eh?"

"You are not giving us these lands unless there is a reason you are willing to give them up."

"There are tribes in the hills," he admitted. She was no fool. "We have never quite been able to root them out."

She shook her head again. "I want another option. If you Imperials, with all your power, cannot get them, then these are not the lands for us. Give it to me. Another option."

Julian rubbed his clean-shaven chin. "I will have to consult—"

She interrupted. "Always with this consulting. My druadan are impatient, and to be clear, so am I. Remember, Crown Prince Julian... Your time is running out."

With a final glance at the map, Zhuana stood up and walked away.

✦

The walled encampment crowning the hill was beginning to take the appearance of something permanent, with a well-trodden road toward the city of Lexia. Wagons and carts traveled back and forth, as the Veldrians traded with the Imperials for the things they needed. Archers dressed in leather kept watch from the makeshift battlements, where they could see all the way to the villas and temples, shops and roads that made up the Imperial border city. To a homeless people, Lexia looked wealthy, fat, more than tempting. If they wanted it, they could take it— this was something that everyone knew.

Zhuana stood on the slope, with her fortified camp at her back, facing the gorge that defined the border. The permanent look of the grassy road made her scowl. The Imperials were getting rich, even as she spent the last of her gold on food for her people. This was no place to settle. She had fresh water but little else.

The darkness was on its way.

With Zhuana were her advisors. Alric stood dressed in his furs, even as spring pushed winter aside. Henwin, the stocky older druadan with big ears and a bushy beard, muttered to himself. Klara, tall and blonde, with a force of loyal followers, watched Zhuana expectantly. Maven, bald and ugly, fingered the hilt of the sword at his side.

Zhuana shook her head. "These offers are not real offers at all. They want us to fight their enemies, to give up our lives, before we can even settle. We know we have them at a time of weakness, but we also know that will not last."

"I have already said this," Maven growled. "The empire will answer only to force." He scowled at Alric, Henwin, and Klara, but to do the same to Zhuana would have been too much. "They are not as strong as you think. They call us barbarians, but I would fight any of these Imperials and win. If we attack, and capture Lexia—"

Zhuana interjected. "Then we turn the whole empire against us. The nobles of their assembly would take immediate notice and do what must be done to drive us away."

"But if we do nothing, Queen Zhuana, then they will drive us away anyway, as soon as they have the power to do it."

Zhuana glanced at Klara and then Henwin, waiting to see if either had any thoughts, but the blonde woman and bearded man remained silent.

"We all understand the risks in front of us," she said. "The time will come when we have no choice but to cross the border and drive north all the way to Everlast. If that time comes, I am not afraid to do what must be done." She had thought hard, and now revealed her decision. She could only hope she wouldn't come to regret it. "For now, we have another way to pressure them. It is time for a show of strength."

"Such as?" Henwin asked gruffly.

"A raid. I will let it be known that I authorized nothing. We are barbarians after all. Unruly and undisciplined."

She didn't even need to say anything; all eyes moved to Maven. The idea of an unauthorized raid would be most plausible if he were the one to do it. And, as they all knew, his followers were the fiercest warriors, the most cold-blooded.

"You will do it?" Zhuana asked him. "One of their smaller villages would be best."

He barely considered the idea before he was nodding. "With pleasure."

Alric's eyes betrayed his worry. "Are we certain that this is the right course of action? It could provoke outright war."

As a druid, neither fighting nor negotiation were part of Alric's domain. He was just voicing the inner fears that they all were hiding.

"We have to apply pressure," Zhuana said. "Time is on their side, not ours. If no one else has any objections?" She met the eyes of each member of her group. "Very well. This council is over." As Henwin and Maven, Klara and Alric left to head up the hill, she called out. "Alric?"

"My Queen?" Alric paused and turned.

"A moment, if you will."

He came back to meet her. "What is it?"

She waited until she could speak freely, but even then she lowered her voice. "My decision is dictated by necessity. I have learned something new. Keep this to yourself." She paused, meeting his gaze.

"Of course, My Queen."

She glanced to the south, toward the badlands. "I sent a small band of scouts, men I trust completely, on a secret quest to see what they could learn. Their task was to travel back the way we came."

Alric couldn't hide his surprise. "When was this?"

"Many weeks ago."

"You sent them back to Veldria? What did they see?"

"They did not make it that far. Only as far as that land we passed through, Grendal." She met his stare directly. "Listen to me carefully. Grendal is gone."

His eyes widened and his mouth dropped open.

"Bodies lie in the street, their fingernails black. Blood flows freely. Crows feast on the corpses. A group of locals was seen moving through a village, burning houses, shooting arrows... slaughtering their own." She swallowed. "They spoke of scaled monsters... once they were people like you and me. They worked together, but like animals."

He finally found his voice. "Why are we keeping this a secret?'"

"We do not want to escape the storm only to bury our dead on the battlefield. Fear leads to poor decisions. When we have a negotiated settlement, then we can tell everyone what is coming. The Imperials may doubt us, but they will send out scouts and see for themselves. Once they know the truth, they will act. It is still our best course of action."

"But what if this darkness finds its way here, while talks are still underway?"

"Now you understand the need for pressure."

They both stood and watched the Imperial side of the border; with watchtowers and pastures, it was cultivated land, so different from the wilderness on their own side.

"We will make this raid and we will see what happens then," she said. "Whether we negotiate something with Prince Julian, or we invade until they capitulate, it has to happen soon."

Chapter Thirty-One

KENDRICK WALKED WITH a long stride. Every midmorning, at the same time, he performed his same tour, asking questions and inspecting the work. Once, this part of his estate was just a wide empty space of grassland, but these fields now had a new purpose, and it was an important one indeed.

He and Anthea had chosen the site carefully. This was one of the most beautiful parts of his estate, and it was also practical, with easy access to the Star Temple by way of a new road. Bright green grass spread out before him, with a distant fringe of evergreens forming a perimeter by a stream that rushed along a stony bed. In front of him, the outlines of arenas, seating galleries, and jousting lists were steadily taking shape. Farther away, entrenched foundations indicated latrines and bathing houses. A flattened area marked with rope would become the main dining hall, which was just one hall of many. More roped areas indicated where the sprawling markets would go.

Tens of thousands of visitors were expected. The Star Temple would be in constant use, even with the gateway reserved for the high-born. When the work was all done, the site in its entirety would rival the scale of a great military encampment.

With spring finally arrived, Kendrick no longer needed to wear his heavy overcoat, but the morning air was cool enough to require thick trousers and a warm woolen vest.

His eyes scanned the field as he walked, his boots crushing spring flowers with each step. Ahead, he spotted his master builder standing by a scaffold, shouting instructions to the team as they hoisted beams into place.

Appraising the new work, worry creased his brow. He no doubt had more than a few new gray hairs.

Everything must be ready.

Given the situation with the Veldrians, the fielding had been brought forward by two months. Everyone, from the builders to the merchants to the members of Kendrick's family, now felt the heightened sense of urgency. A huge number of young recruits, soldiers, aspiring knights, archers, and mercenaries were already being sourced from across the empire. By the end of the fielding, the emperor wanted their new army, the Armies of the West, fully assembled and ready to deploy, with decisions made on officers and separation into companies, brigades, and divisions.

Kendrick stopped. Something was moving, high in the scaffolding, in a different place from where the builders were working. Something that looked like...

"Isabelle!" he called, waving his arms as he put on an extra burst of speed. "Get down from there!"

His daughter was sitting at the highest possible position, with nothing at all to brace her as she watched something in the distance. When she heard his shout, she wobbled and a leg jutted out before she caught herself. For a moment she remained frozen as she regained her balance. Kendrick was now close enough to stare up at her and give her his fiercest glare. She looked back down at him, an impish grin on her freckled face as the breeze tugged at her long, light-brown hair.

"I'm coming!" Isabelle called back, but she didn't move an inch. Instead she was again distracted by whatever it was she had been watching.

"Now!" Kendrick bellowed.

With a resigned sigh, she began to descend the scaffolding, which butted up against a seating gallery tall enough for row upon row of spectators. Kendrick tried to keep his face cold, but every time she shifted her body from one beam to another, hanging from planks and dropping to the level below, he wanted to run forward with his arms out, ready to catch her. She must have noticed how closely he was watching her.

"Watch how fast I can get down!" she called.

She dropped down one level, to grab a beam with both arms and dangle, and then dropped down another. Her hand slipped, but she caught herself to take hold of a crossbeam. She was panting by the time she made it to the ground.

She charged Kendrick at a run, arms wide to wrap around his waist. He thought his face was sufficiently angry, but it seemed to have no effect at all.

"I've told you about climbing," he growled. "One day you'll break a leg. What were you doing up there?"

She grinned at him. "I can climb much higher."

"I'm sure you can. But that doesn't mean you should. I asked you a question."

"Just watching." She shrugged. "From a safe distance."

"Watching what?"

"Troy and Caden. Fighting."

Kendrick's head flicked to the side, in the direction Isabelle had been looking. He began to walk, increasing speed with every stride. Isabelle soon had to run to keep up with him. As he rounded a fence intended to separate the contests from the eating and drinking, loud wooden clacks grew louder, accompanied by grunts and heavy breathing. He headed straight toward another fence up ahead, enclosing a sandy pit reserved for sword fighting, where Troy and Caden were hard at work hacking at each other, both red-faced and angry. It wasn't hard to work out that their fighting had long left the realm of friendly practice.

And yet he slowed as he reached the fence, until he was watching with his hands on the rail. Assessing Troy, and then Caden, he applied his own experience as a swordsman to the two young men, who had both been practicing hard under the instruction of their sword master. They each had a few bad habits: Troy with his stance, Caden with his grip. Troy liked to lead with his shoulder, which Kendrick would have to talk to him about. But his older son was better at keeping his head. In contrast, Caden's eyes were wild with rage; he always had difficulty keeping his temper. Even so, Caden had improved the most. His younger son had grown taller these past months, and almost reached his older, bigger brother's height. Troy had been far ahead but his brother was now closing the gap.

"Aren't you going to stop them?" Isabelle asked.

The two young men circled each other, wooden swords at the ready. Caden's chest was heaving, while Troy's dark blond hair was tousled; he wasn't finding the fight the easy bout he might have expected. His blue eyes were narrowed and his face was grim. Caden's clothes were sandy and Kendrick guessed he had already taken a tumble or two.

The faster of the two, Caden moved into a flurried attack. Troy blocked each consecutive blow, as the wooden blades made a forceful clacking sound each time the two swords met. Caden weaved and Troy stabbed the empty air.

Troy was strong, and when Kendrick took note of how hard his oldest son was willing to strike, he decided it was time to bring the fight to a halt.

He sucked in a breath. "Boys, enough!" he bellowed.

Troy and Caden both shot panicked looks Kendrick's way, neither having realized their father was watching, along with their young sister. Troy lowered his weapon.

Caden didn't.

His face filled with wrath, he smashed his wooden sword onto Troy's wrist. Troy yelped and dropped his weapon. With a snarl, Troy brought up his fists, ready to charge—

"Woah, there!" Kendrick shouted.

He put a boot on the fence and threw himself over. Troy had arrested his motion at Kendrick's cry, and Kendrick hurried over to move the two brothers apart. He stared into Caden's eyes, and then Troy's, waiting until he was satisfied.

"Did you see—?" Troy began, panting.

"How is your wrist?" Kendrick asked.

"Sore."

"Is it broken?"

"No."

"Then stop complaining."

Troy scowled. "It was a cowardly blow."

"That depends on how you look at it," Kendrick said. "You should have withdrawn completely, rather than get distracted. Either that, or kept your guard up."

Caden smirked.

"And you should keep a cool head." This time Kendrick spoke more harshly than he had to Troy. "Anger doesn't make you a better swordsman. In fact, if you don't control it it'll get you killed." He stared grimly into Caden's brown eyes. "Agree or disagree?"

"Agree," Caden muttered.

"That's enough for today. Go on. Get moving." Kendrick herded his two sons across the sandy floor, pushing them along until they had passed through the gate. "Some more timber's just come in by road. Get the planks loaded up and over to the builders." As the two brothers began to walk, he called out.. "Wait. Leave those with me." He held out his hand, until both of his sons had handed him the wooden practice swords.

He then turned his attention on Isabelle, who was walking backward. "You too, freckles. Go and help them. You can be in charge. See if you can stop them from fighting."

"In charge?"

"Really, Father?" Troy asked wearily.

"She's got more sense than the two of you, I would warrant. Go on. Off you go."

As Kendrick's three children headed off together, he spent a moment watching the trio. Caden would cool down and forget he had ever been angry. Troy wouldn't say anything, but he would seethe, and he definitely wouldn't forget.

He ruefully shook his head. He then remembered he had yet to speak with his master builder. But when he turned to face the scaffolding, in a different direction from his three children, he spied the familiar figure of his wife, waving at him, already heading his way.

"Kendrick!"

Anthea wore her straight blonde hair loose, making her appearance both girlish and lovely. As was often the case, she wore a long dress, with her sturdy boots the only nod to the fact that she was striding through a field. Today her dress was long-sleeved to match the cool spring air, snug and tied at the bodice. Its dark green shade was the same color as the conifers nearby.

Fernley Manor was a distant speck behind her, but Anthea and Kendrick were both fit and active, and she had chosen to walk over rather than ride.

"My love," Kendrick said. "You are as beautiful as the flowers of spring."

Anthea raised an eyebrow. "A daisy, or a rose?"

He tried to think of the right answer—behind Anthea were hundreds of yellow flowers, all in his view. "A daisy?"

"Wrong answer," she said, but she met him with a kiss. "Trouble with the children?" She watched their departing figures.

"Boys. Fighting. As usual."

"How goes the work?"

"Steady. But I'm no builder. I have to take Master Colm at his word." He searched her face. "What's worrying you?"

"I've been reviewing the ledger. We're going to need the next tranche of gold if we're going to keep things moving forward."

"I'll send Paxton to Everlast tomorrow."

"Today," she insisted.

"The poor man just came back from Trent. He needs some rest."

She tilted her head. "Very well. Tomorrow."

Together they surveyed the scaffolding, the outline of the dining hall, the empty market section, and then the jousting lists—the long fenced lines where the bouts with horse and lance would draw crowds. For a time they were silent but companionable as they stood together in the middle of the field. In the end, they were facing their children as the trio headed down to the gateway.

"I have no idea why I agreed to this," Kendrick said.

"I think you are actually enjoying it."

"Hah."

"Swords and horses. Your two obsessions."

"No, my obsession is right here." Kendrick leaned in to kiss his wife, enclosing her waist with his arms, and without warning, lifted her up.

"Kendrick!" Anthea looked behind her, in the direction of the builders on the scaffolding, as he set her down. "People might be watching us."

Smiling, he touched her cheek, stroking her hair back from her face, and then glanced again at their three children, who were now tiny figures as they walked together.

"If all goes well, we will soon have two knights on our hands... and as for Isabelle—"

Anthea let out a cry. "By the stars. The dressmaker. I might already be late. I have to go."

She hurried off, and Kendrick called after her. "Nothing too bold. She's too young."

"I know my business, Kendrick Conway, just as you know yours." She was still beautiful, even when she frowned. "Just don't forget the gold."

Chapter Thirty-Two

BETHANY SAT IN a circular gallery, the foremost of three tiers that faced the front of the room. A wooden barrier divided each tier, raised at the perfect height for her to use it as a desk to write on. She leaned forward, her notebook properly placed, a quill pen nearby, ready to write.

The room wasn't huge, but was just right for the dozen students remaining. This was the last class of the day, and as evening approached, long windows brought in rosy light from the gardens outside. The wall that she and the other students faced was smooth and white, enabling her teacher to draw on it.

This class was called travel, and although it had only started recently, it was already one of her favorites. Her instructor was Diviner Aurelia, a tall white-haired woman, both attractive and stern, with a formidable intelligence and a razor-sharp tongue.

Diviner Aurelia paced a short distance, back and forth, which was her habit as she taught. "Thus far we have learned the key stages of travel." She picked a stocky student, Gregor. "First?"

Gregor was quick to answer. "First we have preparation. We review the size of the group and their mass effect. We ensure we know all the key aspects of the departure and destination gateways. We review any celestial changes. We consider any known conditions at our destination."

Diviner Aurelia nodded. "Next?" She now indicated Kyle, a wiry student with prominent front teeth. Carina was of the opinion that Kyle might be struggling to keep up. "Consumption..." He hesitated, long enough for Bethany to worry for him, but then he found his voice. "Consumption is the stage where our mind shifts into an altered state, using the Weaver's Breath."

"Correct," Aurelia said. "You will soon commence delirium class, where you will learn more about Weaver's Breath. After consumption?" Searching the faces in front of her, she selected Carina.

"Then we have location," Carina said in a clear voice. "After preparation and then consumption, this is where we find the right resonance to use our staff to open the gateway."

"Good. And next? Bethany?"

Bethany cleared her throat. "Divination. We open the gateway. We assess that the situation is safe to proceed with travel."

"Correct. And then?" Diviner Aurelia chose a skinny young woman. "Hesta?"

"Travel," Hesta replied. "We enter the gateway and our wards follow. We navigate the path of stars."

"And finally? Xander?"

"Arrival," said Xander. "We leave the path of stars and reconnect with the real world."

"Incorrect," Diviner Aurelia said harshly, and Xander tried to keep his face calm but the startle was there in his eyes. "Oh, you have the correct name of the stage, but never use that word. You do not reconnect, just as you do not disconnect. The tapestry you will navigate is the real world, just as much as this world we find ourselves in now. We diviners are the only ones who get to see it, or at least remember it, but it is real. Understood?"

Xander nodded.

Aurelia's tone softened. "It is true, however, that there is a process of adjustment after arrival. The same applies to your wards, even though they won't have seen what you have. They will be disoriented. It is a time of weakness. If you are expecting conflict, guiding guards or soldiers, you will see the danger first. And your voice is the one that must alert them and shock them into action."

Bethany's breath caught, even as she wrote what she had learned. She hadn't given as much thought to a diviner's skills being applied to warfare as she had to the idea of traveling across the empire.

"Now, something to mention. Those we guide... We call them wards, and I hope it is obvious why. Your wards are under your protection and it is your absolute duty to ensure every ward makes it safe and unharmed to the other side. If you become diviners, you will give your oath, that your first duty is to the safety of your wards. You must never pass judgment or do anything but your best. No matter whom you guide to the next gateway." The teacher paused to let her words sink in. "Any questions?" She saw a raised hand from Kyle. "Yes?"

"When we are navigating the tapestry, how do we make sure our wards stay with us?"

"This will be covered later, but they automatically enter a state of waking sleep. If you were to travel without the Weaver's Breath, you would be in the same state. Your wards are highly suggestible. They will follow where you guide them. Anything else? Yes, Hesta?"

The skinny young woman lowered her hand. "What happens if more than one diviner uses a gateway at the same time?"

"We will also go into more detail as we progress, but in a large space like that under the Crystal Dome, each portal will naturally open near the other. When it comes to smaller gateways, a portal will not open until the one before it has closed. Anyone else?" When there were no more questions, she continued. "Now, today's class is now over, and I have news." Her face became grave, the bearer of grim tidings. "Serious news for you all." She paused, but it wasn't needed; she already had their attention. "Today is an important day. You are to be tested to ensure you are ready for delirium. We have intentionally hidden this from you, and you will later understand the reason why we haven't told you this is coming."

Bethany sat up in her seat. She had been focused, fascinated by everything she was learning. The shock was like a bucket of cold water thrown in her face. By all the stars alive... Not another test.

"If you pass this test, you will soon have your first experience of Weaver's Breath. If not, I have to tell you that your journey at this school is over."

Diviner Aurelia sounded almost apologetic. "Students, I am afraid that this test isn't easy. It must be so. If you had been given the chance to prepare yourselves, it would take away its purpose."

Bethany swallowed.

"You may leave. Assemble in the atrium. We will soon start calling names."

✦

Bethany had never experienced such tension in the atrium before. When people spoke, asking each other if they knew anything, they kept their voices quiet, murmuring as quietly as the water that bubbled in the fountain. Heads were shaking and faces were worried. There wasn't a single person sitting down.

Carina was gnawing at her lip. "What kind of test do you think it will be?"

Bethany shook her head. "I don't think anyone knows."

"Not a written test," Carina said. "We've had no chance to study." She pondered. "Something physical?"

"I suppose it could be staff work..." Bethany said dubiously.

Xander had been staring up at the ceiling high above. "They can't fail all of us." Turning his gaze on Bethany and Carina, he attempted a smile. "Someone has to become a diviner."

"There's only one thing we can be sure of..." Bethany furrowed her brow. "They put a lot of effort into finding our weaknesses."

"You're saying that they want us to be worried?" Carina asked.

"That is exactly what I'm saying."

Xander scratched his jaw. "Diviner Aurelia looked worried. She isn't the type to be overly dramatic."

"You know what? The important thing is that we're not giving up." Carina's expression was determined. "My step-mother would say she was right about me. Whatever it is, we'll all have to just get through it."

"Bethany Sylvana!"

Bethany looked to the side, where Diviner Trask was beckoning.

Bethany entered a room. The space she found herself in was unusual, in that it was on a high floor, with a long skirting barrier along one side, like a balcony rail. However a wall of glass traveled up from the rail to the ceiling, enclosing the area completely.

A diviner sat at a table, watching her as she approached. Clad in a gray tunic and trousers, he had a knife-like chin, high cheekbones, and a sharp nose. Thin hair encircled his crown, which was as bald as a bird's egg.

Bethany's eyes widened. She felt like she had just ingested a huge, heavy stone.

The diviner at the table was the same diviner who had given her the false mark at the assessment at Speaker's Corner. He was the diviner who had challenged her at her shop, when she was just a girl, so many years ago.

If he recognized her, he made no sign of acknowledgment. "Bethany Sylvana," he said. "I am Diviner Gallow."

He remained seated, fixing her with his cold, penetrating gaze. There was a second chair at the table, as well as two books and a sandglass timer on its surface. She assumed that the chair was for her, but she knew not to sit unless instructed to.

"Please," Diviner Gallow said. "Go to the window."

Brow creased, she went slowly to the window, staring through the glass to see nothing but an empty void and vertical stone on the other side. It was only when she looked down that shock wrapped a fist around her heart.

There was her mother, seated by a tree made of stone and a fountain spilling from a cleft in the tree's roots to fill a basin. A low stone wall and a bench enclosed the basin, providing the only place to sit. Bethany's mother, Maryam, remained patiently by the fountain, gazing with unseeing eyes. There was gray in her copper hair. She was always small and wiry, but from Bethany's height, she seemed tiny. She held her black ebony cane, leaning forward, resting on the handle while she waited.

Bethany turned toward Diviner Gallow, who was watching her keenly. "Why is she here?"

"She is here to take you home, assuming you fail this test. Or you can go to her now, and depart of your own accord, should you wish to..." He waited, rapping his fingers on one of the two heavy books on the table in front of him.

"I am staying," she said with a frown.

"Very well. Bethany Sylvana. Here is your test." Gallow indicated the two books. "You will recognize these texts from your catalog studies. This is the Atlas. This is the Cosmolog."

Even as Gallow spoke, a change in the scene outside, below the window, drew her attention. A hook-nosed man in a gray uniform, a steward from the Observatory, stood speaking with her mother. When Maryam replied, there was something about Bethany's mother that wasn't right. Bethany knew her mother. She was trying to hide it, but she was upset.

Bethany nodded toward the view outside. "My mother. What does she know about why she's here?"

Diviner Gallow left his position at the table and walked over to the window to join her. After watching for a moment, he spoke, "A fair question. He is telling her that he knows little at this stage, only that there has been a terrible accident. This is another update. One of our students has been mortally injured, another is merely disfigured." His voice became low and ominous. "He is telling your mother that he does not yet know which of the two students is you."

Bethany cried out. "She thinks I've been hurt?"

"She believes that you may already be dead. The chance is even. The flip of a coin."

"You can't do this—!"

Gallow raised his sharp voice over the top of hers. "Lower your voice right now, Bethany Sylvana, or your test today will be over. You have had problems with your focus. We cannot have diviners who struggle with their focus putting their wards at risk. Now, you have a choice." He returned to the table, resuming his seat, although his cold eyes never left her. "You can go down there and relieve your mother of her burden— which will see you leave this school. Or you can commence your test. Which shall it be?"

The silence dragged out. The steward finished speaking to her mother and left. Maryam sat once more by the fountain. She now had two hands gripping her cane, and was rocking back and forth.

"I will take the fact that you are still here as your answer," Gallow said. "I will now commence your test. Start naming gateways in order from the empire's heart, starting with the Argent Arch." He flipped the sandglass on the table, so that grains swiftly trickled down the narrow neck into the cavity below. "Begin."

Bethany tore her eyes from the window. Sand continued its trickle down the timer. It was going to empty fast. Her heart beat savagely. She didn't have a choice.

"The Argent Arch," she said quickly. "The Portal of Polaris. The Crystal Dome. The Focus. The Stepped Temple of Karth..."

Even as she struggled – not just with the names of the gateways but their proximity to the capital in order – she knew her mother would be frantic. This wasn't fair. The School of Divination was hard, but this was simply cruel. No. She couldn't lose her train of thought.

Gallow suddenly grabbed the sandglass to lie it flat on the table. In effect, he stopped the trickle of grains from one section to another, but could resume the flow at any time.

"Take another look at your mother," Gallow said. Bethany turned, seeing the tension in her mother's face, in her posture. "Do you know how long she has been down there, by that fountain? She has been waiting to hear news about her daughter, her only child, for two hours. Time is wearing away at her. Her mind is hard at work, reminding her of all the students who have lost their lives or their sanity in this training." He smiled as if he had seen a gold coin lying in the street. "Please. Go on. Where you left off."

Focus!

As Gallow returned the timer to its vertical position and sand poured down the hollow, she cleared her dry throat. "The Yellow Pyramid. The Wheel of Klare. The Stone Temple of Var. Kelway House. The Hexagon at Sedgeford. The Star Temple of Esk. Torvil Temple. The Arch of the Pilgrim. The Stone Circle of Graystone..."

She pushed on, retrieving the names, placing the gateways onto the map in her mind, always moving on to the next.

"...The Stepped Temple of Savid. The Pillars of Dust. The Twelve Old Men at Engel. The Colossus. The Shrine of Matoush. The Statues of Malange."

She couldn't stop watching the grains of sand plummeting down the narrow hole in the glass. She was speaking rapidly, so fast she was worried she might mix up her words, even if she had the right answer.

"...The Red Temple of Darsh." As she spoke the name of the final gateway, the most distant from Everlast, she panted with relief. The last few grains tumbled down the sandglass. She had made it.

But congratulations were not forthcoming.

"Now a test from the Cosmolog," Gallow said, nodding to the thicker of the two books. "Name the locator stars in the northern constellations. Backwards. From least to most important." He flipped the sandglass. "Begin."

Bethany gathered her thoughts. "Fensinia. Touris. Milarm..."

Her head was hurting, and she had two fingers on her temple even as she concentrated. Far below, her mother was no longer sitting. Despite her blindness, Maryam was pacing. As she walked, she snapped her ebony cane against the stone wall surrounding the tree-shaped fountain. What was going through her head?

Bethany couldn't allow Gallow to win.

"...Tentorintia. Alappo."

Even as she spoke, someone, another steward, this time a girl, crossed the area where her mother was waiting. The girl obviously didn't intend to stop, but Maryam grabbed her. Whatever the girl said, it enraged Bethany's mother, who raised a fist.

Bethany focused on her breathing. She compartmentalized her mind, separating her emotions from her attendance to the task she had been given. Without all of her practice, she never could have done it.

The last sands rattled around the top half of the timer. She gasped out a flurry of words to reach the end.

Diviner Gallow slumped, evidently disappointed.

He again rapped his fingers on the book, and then he stood up at the table and beckoned. "Come with me."

Gallow headed for a door at the side of the room, opening it to reveal a set of stairs. She warily looked at him and then at the stairway. What was coming next? She had no choice but to follow him, and he remained silent as his footsteps clattered on the steps, down one flight, and then another. He led her through another door, and then they traveled a corridor. Finally Gallow opened another door to reveal a wide, circular space in the open air.

Right in front of Bethany and Gallow, the stone tree towered over the fountain, as water bubbled from its roots, and Bethany's mother stood leaning on her cane, beside the enclosing wall and bench.

Diviner Gallow headed straight over. "Madam Sylvana?"

"Have you found her yet?" Bethany's mother demanded.

"I apologize for the delay. Your daughter was lost somewhere in the library. It took all this time to find her."

"I don't mind the waiting. If she wants to see me I will come, and I will wait all day if I have to. But there was this noise, this horrible screeching. Set my teeth on edge."

"I do apologize. One of our many secret projects, a rather noisy one, I am afraid."

"Perhaps if someone needs to wait, you should have another place where they can do it."

"A worthwhile suggestion," Gallow said.

Bethany stood in silence. She knew her mother wouldn't even know she was present, standing so near. As the truth sank in, it didn't make her recent experience any easier to bear.

"Mother?"

Maryam's head turned quickly. She hurried forward, her arms open, as she and Bethany embraced. "Betani? Oh, it's you. You're here."

Gallow's face remained as cold as ever. "Your time is your own for the next hour." He indicated an arched opening. "Through that arch you will find the gardens. You are free to walk there. After today, you will not be allowed another home visit. Not until you have either graduated or failed in your studies." He clasped his hands in front of his body. "Congratulations, Bethany Sylvana," he said stiffly. Then he turned and walked away.

Bethany watched him go. Fiery anger rose within her.

"Betani?" her mother asked.

Bethany acknowledged her rage. She observed it, understood it, and then it melted away.

"It's so good to see you," she said, holding her mother's hands.

"Is everything all right? He congratulated you. That is a good thing, isn't it?"

"Everything's fine."

"Your voice. You sound a little strained. You can talk to me."

Bethany's eyes welled. Perhaps she didn't want to restore her focus. Perhaps she simply wanted her mother.

Chapter Thirty-Three

JULIAN WAS INCANDESCENT with rage.

He took angry strides as he approached the gateway, the Portal of Polaris, buried in a vaulted chamber deep beneath the Nexus complex. He was dressed in his burnished armor and flanked by four Imperial guardsmen. Even now, about to experience the discomfort of travel, all he could think about was the position he was in. She had betrayed him. That vicious woman, Zhuana Arianus, was a snake.

Torches lit the space, casting flickering tapered shadows. Everything around him was made of stone: the floor, the bare walls, the broad cylindrical columns supporting the ceiling. He passed dozens of the columns as he followed the path to the gateway ahead, where a handful of wide steps led to an upright rectangle, also made of stone, like an oversized empty door frame.

Most gateways were open in some way; after all, their purpose was to allow people, animals, and goods to move through them. The Portal of Polaris was different. The Argent Arch and the Crystal Dome were both famous monuments, but the Nexus's private gateway, while known to all diviners, wasn't publicized, even to the nobles of the assembly. Few outside the corpus even knew it existed.

As Julian approached the gateway, he didn't like the look of the diviner who would be guiding his travel. A weathered old man in brown clothing and a long gray cloak, the diviner was making final preparations, eyes closed and breathing deeply as he gripped his staff and faced the stone frame in front of him.

As the clatter of Julian and his guards' boots echoed throughout the area, the diviner opened his eyes. He frowned at Julian and held out a warding hand.

Julian stopped. The four Imperial guardmen also came to a halt, and the area was now silent without the thunder of boot heels. Julian scowled at the diviner. His anger wasn't helped by the fact that the four soldiers had seen him forced to wait by a fussy diviner completing his rituals.

Finally the diviner raised his staff high. With force, he brought it down. A loud clunk accompanied the slamming of his staff's base on the hard stone floor.

The staff came up again, and then it began to move.

The diviner swung his staff like a swordsman practicing maneuvers. The staff whirled overhead, each slash and stroke faster than the one before it, until a hum in the air was noticeable. As the hum became louder, the diviner gave a harder stroke, as if slicing a man's arm off at the shoulder, along with a sudden cry.

The hair at the back of Julian's neck stood on end. He braced himself. Here it came.

A sound came from the space in front of the diviner, a mixture of a fiery sizzle and the prolonged scratch of tearing fabric.

The gateway opened like a wound, displaying utter darkness within the diagonal gash, but still the diviner wasn't done. He thrust his staff outward and then turned it. The gash lengthened and widened, turning at the same time. He maneuvered his staff again. In moments the diviner was facing a black doorway, polished like a mirrored surface, filling the stone frame around it.

The diviner looked back at Julian and nodded. The old man in the gray cloak then stepped into the darkness, as confident as anyone walking into another room. It was Julian's turn to follow, and he gathered his escort, nodding at the four men, before being the first to climb the steps. He took a single step to take himself into the doorway—

Shift.

—He emerged into a new place, with different air, changed weather, warmer temperature, a foreign view. Disoriented, he put a hand to his head. How long had he been standing where he was? A circle of gray stones surrounded him, hulking monoliths that felt like they were looming over him, ready to topple and crush him under their terrible weight.

He blinked, dazed. It was a struggle not to stagger, and he had traveled a thousand times. Sometimes it was worse; other times it was better. This was definitely one of the worse ones.

He turned toward the old weathered diviner in the gray cloak.

Wait. The diviner's lip was bleeding. *What?* He stared hard at the diviner's mouth.

The bleeding had happened some time ago. The blood was dark and dried. The strange place between gateways... how long had they just spent in there?

"What..." Julian put a hand to his neck, clearing his throat. "What just happened?"

The old diviner tilted his head toward him. "Highness?" His voice was as ancient as he looked. "What is it?"

"Your lip."

The diviner touched his lip, surprised when he touched the dried blood and making a little jerk as he felt some pain. "Oh. Apologies. A bad habit."

"A bad habit? How long were we in there?"

The old diviner hesitated. "Just the usual—"

"What is your name, Diviner?"

"Diviner Masel, Highness."

"Diviner Masel, return immediately to Everlast and report yourself to the corpus."

The diviner's careworn face paled. "Prince Julian—"

"Go. As soon as you are able to. I do not trust you. Tell them what happened. Your superiors will get to the bottom of it."

"I... Very well, Highness."

Julian didn't want to spend any more time in the decrepit diviner's company, and he left the circle of monoliths to meet the wide road that led to the city of Lexia. He rubbed his temples as he walked, but the fog was lifting, and he was beginning to feel human again.

The Stone Circle of Lexia was on a hill, which meant he already had eyes on the border city below. Much farther away, distant but visible on such a clear, bright day, he could make out the fortified camp of the Veldrians.

And there was a familiar figure, smiling as she waited by the road. He hadn't spent much time in Everlast, just long enough to visit his allies and speak with his father, but the sight of his wife was enough to make him forget all about his travel. The pink dress she wore covered her lower half entirely, but was low cut from her shoulders and scalloped at the back, revealing plenty of olive skin. Her hair was fashioned into languid spirals.

"Husband," Samara said, coming forward with arms held wide.

He didn't care about who might be watching as he pulled her in and kissed her. The most beautiful woman in the empire was his. No one would ever take her away from him.

She pushed him back to stare into his face. "I assume you heard the news?"

Seeing the worry in her eyes, his purpose came back in a rush. He inwardly cursed the effects of travel; his wits were still taking time to catch up. He was here to address a critical situation.

"Of course." He cleared his throat. "I came as soon as I heard." He and Samara began to walk toward the town, leaving the guards to follow. "Tell me what you know."

"Raiders. Veldrians. About sixty of them. They crossed the border at night and struck Wist, one of the local villages."

"Wist?" The name meant nothing. "A big village?"

"Big enough. The Veldrians set fire to the houses. Cut down any man or woman who tried to protect home and family. They stole and plundered, but this was worse than theft." She paled, staring into the distance. "They butchered them, Julian."

He made a guess from her distraught expression. "You went there?"

"There were children..." She stopped, putting a hand on her mouth, unable to continue.

He reached out to squeeze her hand. "You shouldn't have gone."

"I had to see for myself."

"What else?"

"Queen Zhuana sent a message, the very next morning. She said she had no knowledge of the raid and was not responsible. She sends her apologies. Her warriors would be disciplined." She met his gaze. "There was no offer of reparations."

Julian turned his head toward the Veldrians' camp on the hill. "The queen knew about the raid. She organized it." The rage that filled him before made his nostrils flare. "We cannot let this stand."

"I understand why she did it, although to murder children..." Samara swallowed; she was also looking in the same direction. "She is telling us that if we do not give her what she wants, and soon, she is going to take it by force."

"Correct."

"But we are not yet ready for conflict..."

"Soon," he agreed, "but not yet."

"Do we then do nothing?"

"No. We are the Eternal Empire. We cannot let them slaughter our people and shrug it off. We must respond in kind. We both know that a price is going to be paid."

✦

Julian sat across from Zhuana, by the sluggish waters of the River Byre, at the same table, but with a different mood in the air. The warmer climate in the south meant that even with the canvas pavilion sheltering them from the sun, it was hot enough to make Julian sweat inside his armor. He allowed his discomfort to show on his face as he stared directly at Zhuana with a blazing fire in his eyes.

"...is unusual for me to lose control of my warriors, but they are restive. There can be no more delays," Zhuana was saying.

He could barely believe her audacity. She sat in front of him—the crown prince and heir to the empire—and told him that the fault was his. People were dead. People the empire was supposed to protect. What good was the empire, what good were its rules and soldiers, if citizens couldn't feel safe within its borders?

Zhuana's face was harder than ever. Her black hair was once more tied behind her head, without a single strand loose. Again, she had brought her wickedly curved sword, carried in a scabbard at her hip. This time, Julian had actually considered asking her to disarm herself, but after some thought, he had simply worn his own sword too. The watching guardsmen on Julian's side looked like they were spoiling for a fight. The Veldrians behind Zhuana stared with icy expressions.

"Restive?" Julian asked incredulously. "They butchered an entire village."

"I have disciplined those who went against my orders."

"Disciplined—?"

"Personally. Now, I have a question of my own. Why will you not give us what we need? You say you must keep returning to Everlast to ask your father permission to offer this or that. Perhaps we should instead be speaking with him."

"We need to talk about the village."

"Enough about the village."

"No." Julian pounded the table with his fist. "Not enough. A price must be paid, or trust between us is gone." He scowled, no longer trying to be calm or polite. He was the tip of the spear, ready to unleash the world's most powerful empire. "I want the heads of sixty of your warriors. We can accept nothing less."

Her eyes widened, but she gave no other reaction. "No. I will not surrender any of my people."

"You are not listening. If you want to keep talking, a price must be paid, for what your people did to mine."

Zhuana's face changed. Her expression was already hard, but slowly she leaned forward. As she prepared to retort, Julian sensed that conflict was close. She would declare war, if he pushed her too hard. He reminded himself that they both wanted a negotiated settlement, rather than war. They simply wanted different results from the settlement. His operation was a delicate one. He needed to let her believe that she still had a chance to get what she wanted in negotiation.

Before she could speak, he leaned forward also, lowering his tone. "You want us to welcome you into our empire. You want us to share everything, lands and citizenship, friends and enemies. Trust must be regained."

He held her gaze, so that for a long time they both stared into each other's eyes. He could see the thoughts in the glint of her irises, as if the lighter flecks there were dancing. She was planning, calculating, deciding...

She broke the stare, to instead turn her gaze toward the direction of her fellow Veldrians. Her brow furrowed.

"I have an idea," she said, returning her attention to him. "I have disciplined my warriors in the way of my people. I consider the price to be paid. However, you say that for you it is a price that must be paid in blood."

"You are correct."

"When opposing wills cannot agree, and the truth cannot be decided, we ask the Mother to decide."

"We worship a different—"

"You want the heads of sixty of our warriors? Then you may take them. I will have sixty of my warriors come here, to this place." She indicated the gorge. "My warriors will be unarmed. Ready for your best. Your finest. To face them and mete out justice."

Seeing Julian's confusion, she continued, "All you must do is take the heads you desire. My warriors will not kneel. They will not surrender. Even unarmed, they will do their best to overpower those trying to kill them. If the Mother believes my men should die, they will die."

At first, Julian was ready to reject her plan, but now, as he considered the idea, he examined her words carefully, looking for a trap. "Sixty of your warriors, unarmed, will face sixty of our best?"

"Yes."

He continued to ponder. Imperial guardsmen were special; when it came to fighting prowess, they were the finest men – and women – in the empire. As the emperor's personal soldiers, the best of them all, they had to prove themselves time and again. Physically they were huge; powerfully muscled, he always felt small beside them. Their skill with weapons was unrivaled; they were promoted only after showing both ability and ferocity. They carried fine swords of folded steel. They wore special armor, designed to look resplendent but also fashioned with interlocking plates to protect them from head to toe.

"Why won't you just give me the sixty heads?"

"Because my druadan would not agree to it. This way it is for the Mother to decide if she should save our warriors."

Was it a ruse? Zhuana was intelligent. It wasn't like her to miscalculate.

He knew what she wanted; it wasn't a mystery: lands inside the empire, Imperial protection from the enemies she was fleeing. Perhaps this was a way for her to save face, now that she had made her point with her raid? He could sense her urgency. Not only were her people vulnerable to this conqueror; the longer they waited, the more time there was for the empire to bring soldiers to the border to drive her away.

She knew he wasn't going to relent—a price must be paid. Trust must be regained, or at least there had to be a show of it.

He could see two options. Either she was using the religious code of her people to provide cover, and give him the price he required. Or she was confident that sixty of her unarmed warriors could defeat sixty armed Imperial guardsmen, clad in full plate armor.

As for him, what was the important thing? He needed to buy time, as well as show the world that her raid had not gone unpunished. Most of all, he couldn't have her declaring war, not until the empire was ready.

What would happen if he refused? If he didn't agree to her challenge she would claim he was a coward... that he had no faith in the empire's finest soldiers. The villagers would never get their justice. If he didn't agree, he would soon run out of time, and she would lead an invasion across the border before he was ready.

If he agreed, he would be risking sixty guardsmen. But he was skilled with a sword, and he had trained against guardsmen. He was confident in their arms and abilities.

Time. That was the important thing. He had an opportunity here to buy the time he needed. There was a way he could use Zhuana's proposal to his advantage...

"Our people will have justice," he finally said. He stood, and Zhuana slowly stood along with him. "However this period is consolation, a holy time in our calendar, when confessors forbid any gladiatorial games. It would be against our religious code to let this take place before this period is over. When consolation has concluded, then this will be decided."

Zhuana let out a low hiss. "How much time?"

"Three weeks."

He waited, holding his breath. He had chosen the duration carefully. A period of months would have been better, but he knew she would never agree to it.

"Very well," she said. "In three weeks the Mother will decide, and we will put this incident behind us."

✦

"Alric!" Zhuana called. She found the druid in his workroom, carefully spooning green powder into a wooden bowl. "I need you. Come."

Startled, he looked up to see her beckoning. It was warm in the druid's workshop, with round iron pots bubbling over controlled fires.

The druid looked particularly skinny without his furs. "I just need to—"

"Now!"

With a sigh, Alric set down his spoon. With one last regretful glance at the bowl, he came over to join her. "That will cost me at least three hours. I will need to repeat the stage—"

"Then that is what you will do," she interjected.

As he followed her from his workshop, she waved at him to hurry. Soon she was striding through the fortified camp, searching while the druid caught up to her. She passed some hunters skinning a deer and children playing a game with sharp sticks. Warriors practiced on each other with wooden swords. Fletchers fashioned arrows. Cooking pots rested on coals, tended by the older men and women.

"Where is Maven Dresk?" she muttered.

"Up in the tower, I believe," Alric replied.

She craned her neck back, heading to an open space so she could gaze up to the very top of the watchtower that thrust up from the very enter of the camp. "Maven Dresk!" she bellowed.

"My Queen."

She whirled and there he was, an amused look on his face. Having heard her shout, a number of people were grinning as they saw Maven standing right next to her.

"Come. We need to speak in privacy."

She led her two companions from the bustling area, heading to the open gates and continuing until they were a reasonable distance from the camp. As they stood on the trail, they inevitably faced the gorge that marked the border.

"I need you both, more than ever before," she said.

"Explain," Maven said.

"The prince is unrelenting. He wants a price to be paid for the raid."

"You told him you had no involvement?" Maven asked.

"Of course I did." She began to pace, thinking. "He wants the heads of sixty of our warriors."

Maven lip curled. "Never—"

"Let me finish. Why did we raid across the border? As a demonstration. Julian insists on blood, and now I see a chance for another demonstration. A powerful one. We are going to pit sixty of our best ravagers against sixty of their guardsmen." She paused, knowing there would be a reaction. "And our ravagers will be unarmed."

"Unarmed?" Maven spluttered. "By all things living—"

"Alric, can you do it?" Zhuana asked. "I need you to go further than you have gone before, to make them braver, faster, stronger... Anything you can do, I want it done."

Where Maven was angry, Alric was pale, his lips pressed together with anxiety. "My Queen, if I could devise a potion for greater strength than those we already use, I would have already done so."

"Use your head. Think outside pure strength. It doesn't matter if the potion eventually kills them. We need them to fight in a fury, to feel no pain, to make every death far more costly than the Imperials ever expected."

Alric tilted his head, considering. "Even if it kills them?"

"This is an opportunity for you to do things you would never normally contemplate. They are going to die anyway. We just need them to fight with spirit."

"Hmm. Very well." He thought for a moment, and then nodded. "I have a few ideas. I will see what I can do."

She turned to Maven. "It is already done. In three weeks, this contest is happening. You are always telling me we are better. What do you always say about the empire? Big, but slow."

Maven shook his head, still disbelieving. "Unarmed?"

"Unarmed."

"I can choose the men?"

"I wouldn't want it any other way." She waited for his reluctant agreement. "Do you both understand? In three weeks, we have to show them what we are capable of. This is a matter of pride. Of honor. And it may very well decide our future."

Chapter Thirty-Four

BETHANY TRAVELED THE long corridor that led to the Crystal Dome. Often she passed members of the corpus using the gateway: confessors in black robes, diviners in gray cloaks, clerics in discussion with crimson stains on their white uniforms. This time, however, close to sunset, she and the other students heading in the same direction had the walkway all to themselves.

Lifting her gaze, she caught sight of the immense dome and its latticed panes glowing with the last of the day's light. The area under the dome was big enough that diviners could come and go without disturbing anything taking place near the platform. Tonight, however, was special, and the gateway's use was discouraged. A long black screen sectioned off the space, so that no matter what happened, whatever the students were doing, their privacy would be assured.

Chairs formed a row between the platform and the black screen. Bethany had tried to come early, but most were already filled. She cast her mind back to her first day, when twenty new students had gathered, standing anxiously as they were given stern warnings. Now, of the original twenty, only eleven students remained. Carina waved her over, already seated beside a chair she had kept vacant at the end of the row. Xander watched soberly from Carina's other side.

No one laughed or smiled. No one talked. Instead, as Bethany crossed the floor, she felt the strange mood settle over her.

They had been told that this would be their most difficult test yet. There were no books to be studied late into the night; after all of their training, they would either be ready or they would fail. It wasn't even an assessment; it was a trial. And they would all be taking it together.

After seating herself beside Carina, Bethany and her fellow students faced their instructor, who stood in front of the platform, gripping his staff in his right hand. The diviner was tall, with a fringe of gray hair surrounding his bald crown.

Tonight, their instructor was Diviner Gallow.

He scowled, impatient as he waited beside a cloth-covered table, despite the fact that none of the students were late. He settled his cold eyes on the last young man to find a place, and then he loudly cleared his throat as his gaze traveled from face to face.

When he reached Bethany, the last person in the row, she fought to keep a calm expression. She could remember the gleam in his eye when he told her that her mother was preparing herself for devastating news, along with his icy tone, and his multiple attempts to distract her.

But she had kept her head then, and she was going to do it now. No matter what was about to happen, she could do this.

Rather than meet his stare, she inspected the staff he was holding. It was a real diviner's staff, and one day she was going to hold a staff just like it. The thin length of polished wood had metal at both ends, with the base a few inches long. The crowning part was different: a round orb, like a balled fist at the end of an arm. She knew from her travel class that both the top and bottom were magnetic, but it was the orb that held her attention. The sphere looked solid, but also intricate, as if it had layers, with fanciful lines decorating its surface.

And then Diviner Gallow began to speak.

"Delirium," he intoned. "A state of restlessness, intoxication, confusion, hallucination. You will be excited. You will be disturbed. You will feel emotions and experience sensations that you cannot describe in words. I will give you a final opportunity to escape tonight's ordeal, although it will obviously mean leaving the School of Divination altogether. No? Then let us begin."

He cleared his throat again. "My name is Diviner Gallow. I will be your instructor for delirium class. Before anything else, however, we must determine that you are ready. This explains tonight's trial."

As he stood beside the table, with the fabric covering it stretching to the ground, the teacher indicated his staff.

"Each staff has a different sequence to prepare it. Yours will be known only to you, and to your superiors here at the Observatory. Listen for the click."

Xander leaned in to whisper something into Carina's ear, although he never had a chance to speak.

"I need perfect silence," Gallow snapped. Xander straightened and swallowed.

The cold-faced teacher waited, and when he was satisfied, he turned the orb a little one way, and then another, and Bethany thought she heard a faint click.

Gallow then removed his hand and dramatically lifted his staff into the air. "As soon as I hear or feel the click, the staff is ready, and I am about to be exposed to the Breath of the Weaver. I now strike the base of the staff on the ground." He brought the staff's metal base down onto the hard floor, using enough force to make a loud thud. "There. It is done. The Weaver's Breath has been released, and after a brief opening, the orb is again sealed. Today, for obvious reasons, my staff is empty: it is used for demonstrations such as this one. Are you with me?"

Bethany nodded, along with several others.

"When you strike the ground, you need some force, but you do not need to inhale deeply, just a normal breath. Be assured, all it takes is the smallest exposure to have the required effect. The staff has a front and a back, and it is the same for the orb. If the staff is facing the correct direction, the breath is projected toward you."

He displayed the staff, walking slowly in front of the students so they could get a closer look. The orb looked like a flower bud yet to unfurl. Bethany could make out nothing of its inner workings.

"You soon grow accustomed to the feel of it, keeping the front facing forward and, importantly, the back toward your face. It should go without saying that you must be mindful of anyone around you. They won't be killed, but... well, the effect is what we are here to learn today."

As Gallow returned to his position beside the table, Bethany glanced at Carina. Her friend was pale, gnawing at her lip, hands twining each other on her lap.

"Yes?" Gallow asked a student, Hesta, who had raised her hand.

"But what is inside the orb?"

"A secret. Known only to a select few. I can tell you that the substance is extremely rare and extremely valuable. When it is exposed to the air, a swift reaction takes place. Yes?"

"The substance... how does it get inside?" Gregor asked.

"You bring your staff here to the Observatory and it is replenished for you. A newly replenished staff can take you on many journeys, however we request that you return to have it renewed at least every month. You have heard this many times, but your staff will always be by your side." Diviner Gallow laid the staff down on the table. "Today, however, is not about the staff, it is about the Weaver's Breath. And so we have prepared something a little simpler."

He crouched down to lift the curtain of cloth and reach for something from under the table. Straightening, he lifted a tray to place it on the table's surface. Small, squat bottles stood in a collection on the tray.

"You will each receive a flask. Listen to me carefully. Do not open your flask until you are told to do so."

Bethany's wiped her palms on her gray dress. She tried not to breathe so quickly. When Gallow wasn't looking, Xander leaned forward to give her and Carina a determined nod. She knew what his nod meant. Only courage would get them through whatever was to come.

Meanwhile, as the last glow of sunset left the sky, and darkness settled over the area, Gallow took the tray and walked to the row of chairs, traveling from person to person until everyone had taken a flask. When he reached her, Bethany took hers carefully. Her brown leather flask had a lid, obviously screwed tightly. She held it gingerly, as if she were holding something both dangerous and delicate.

The perfect black of the night sky above was tempered by the myriad of stars, shining down through the transparent dome. Xander, Carina, Gallow... shadow now softened their faces. There wouldn't be a moon tonight. The timing was probably intentional, although she didn't know what it meant.

"Diviner Gallow?" Hesta asked.

"Yes?"

"Is there a danger in breathing in too much?"

He returned to the table and set down the tray. "I was about to explain, and now seems an appropriate time." Lifting his chin, he addressed the entire group. "There are two main dangers. The first is that there is a threshold that must be met, otherwise the effect is too weak, and you would be at risk of being unable to navigate the tapestry. Pay close attention: this is the greater of the risks. It happens, but only very rarely. Inhale and you will have no problems."

Bethany now had a fast thudding in her chest. *Delirium.* Even the name of the class was frightening.

"The second danger is that you take in significantly more of the Weaver's Breath than the staff is designed to deliver. I have not personally known of this happening. The quantity I have been told would be twenty or thirty times the usual amount. Therefore, Hesta, I would not be concerned with breathing in too much." He paused, examining the group. "Everyone has a flask? Please, hold it up."

Along with everyone else, Bethany held up her flask. The stars gave her just enough light for the eleven outstretched arms to be visible. Her mouth was impossibly dry.

"Your test will now begin. Students! On the count of three, open your flasks. When you do so, hold the lid at least six inches away from your face, and place your nose at the opening. Be ready to close your lids once more, but keep your flask open until I say. One. Two. Three. Open!"

Bethany unscrewed her lid. She put her nose near the opening and smelled a pungent odor, like tar. Sharp and strong, whatever it was hurt the back of her throat.

"Close your flasks once more. Now!"

Bethany put the lid back in place and screwed it closed. Surprising her with his speed, Diviner Gallow strode quickly from chair to chair, collecting all of the flasks. She had never seen him move so fast.

"Everyone, look up at the stars."

Bethany tilted her head back to look up at the night sky, and because she had noticed the stars just a few minutes earlier, she immediately knew that she felt strange. It was as if the number of stars had doubled, and they were both brighter and more colorful than usual.

"It is fast acting," Gallow said. "Be ready."

The stars became brighter and brighter. Her body was rising up, or the heavens were getting closer. A new perception gave her an insight: she could somehow sense that some stars were farther away, others closer. How was that possible?

Her body felt numb. The chair underneath her became soft, like a cushion, and then disappeared altogether. She continued to rise, drawn to the firmament. Wasn't there a lattice somewhere? Where had it gone? Was she now above the dome?

She heard mad laughing. Was it her? She didn't know.

Who was she? Who was her? Was she a person? Are they?

The world around her throbbed and hummed. The humming had a frequency; it resonated like the plucked string of an instrument. The pulsating was one of the most important things in the universe. She longed to rest her fingertips on it, to quiver along with it, to try to change it. She knew she was experiencing the tapestry.

Everything was connected.

Everything and everyone.

✦

"The two who went home, who were they?" Carina asked.

"Lora and Kyle," Xander replied. "Lora said she thought she had gone mad. Kyle believed he had died. They don't want to do this anymore."

Bethany put her hand to her mouth. As she sat on a bench in the atrium, she thought she was going to be sick. Fighting the nausea, she put her fingers to her temples and swallowed.

"Are you all right?" Carina asked from the bench beside her.

She nodded, even as she grimaced.

Xander remained standing. As he spoke, his deep brown eyes were troubled. "I saw all these things... My dead dog."

"Dog?" Carina asked.

"He used to bark a lot. Someone poisoned him."

"That's awful," Bethany whispered.

"I know. But I haven't thought about him in years."

Carina's gaze became unfocused. "I saw all the people who ever lived and ever died floating around, like swirling snow in the air. Then I saw them get smaller and smaller until I could see everything that ever existed, no matter how big, and I was even bigger. It was frightening." She swallowed. "They say it can drive you insane."

"Don't talk like that," Xander said quickly. "Don't even joke about it. That's why we've been training all this time. All the meditation, the testing... We've made it to the last nine students. We can handle this."

"I saw my father," Bethany said in a quiet voice.

Still dazed, she wasn't even sure if she had spoken out loud, but then she became aware of Xander staring at her. Carina had turned to face her.

"I thought your mother raised you on her own?" Carina asked.

"She did."

"Then how did you see your father?"

Bethany opened her mouth and then closed it. With her lips pressed together, she shook her head.

"Did you know your father or didn't you?" Carina demanded. When Bethany didn't reply, Carina scowled. "I thought we trusted each other. The things they put us through... all we have in here is each other."

Bethany stood. "I need to be alone."

"Bethany!" Carina called after her, as Bethany left the atrium to return to her own quarters.

Chapter Thirty-Five

KENDRICK STOOD WITH Paxton, waiting in front of the Star Temple. In springtime, it often rained in the afternoon, but when they left Fernley Manor the day had seemed bright, fresh, and clear. Now, here they were, standing in the drizzle. A clarion had sounded. Someone was coming.

"If this is a merchant trying to sell me something, I am going to have some things to say." Kendrick scowled and then turned toward his old house diviner. "You're a diviner. Do you ever stop someone from doing something foolish, or simply rude?"

"We do as our wards require," Paxton said.

"Hmpf. I remember that time when you refused to take me to Kelway."

"You were drunk. You wanted to take a sword to Sir Kayne."

As water dripped from the hood of his cloak, Kendrick cast his mind back. "I would have cut him in half."

"And that is what I said at the time. You didn't listen, My Lord. It wasn't until I fetched Lady Anthea—"

"Yes, yes. No need to remind me. What was it that fool said again?"

Paxton harrumphed. "It was some time ago, My Lord."

Kendrick stamped his feet impatiently, hands buried inside the pockets of his cloak. At last, he saw a flash of light above the temple's platform, in the area enclosed by the triangular stone frame. The light became a diagonal line, which peeled open and rotated to become a polished rectangular darkness.

A diviner with a staff emerged, a sad-eyed man with unruly brown hair, perhaps a decade younger than Paxton. Right behind him came a tall, long-limbed man with ash-colored hair combed back from his high forehead.

Declan. Of course. Kendrick tried to smooth the irritation from his face as the gateway closed. Declan's diviner walked away from the triangular frame, while Kendrick and Paxton climbed the stairs to greet the two newcomers.

Declan was a little dazed, like everyone emerging from a gateway, with the exception of the diviner who opened it. Kendrick waited until Declan shook himself and finally his eyes gained focus. "Ah, Kendrick," he said, his voice as crisp and dry as ever.

"Declan."

Declan turned to his diviner. "Go with Paxton. He will give you some chambers."

Kendrick rubbed his jaw and hid a glare. Declan's instructions were his way of telling Kendrick that, although he had come without warning, he expected to stay at least the night. The man knew exactly what he was doing.

Kendrick raised his voice, not to be outranked in his own domain. "Paxton, please ask the stewards to find Lord Quinn's diviner some quarters."

Paxton played along. "For how long, Lord Conway?"

"Declan?" Kendrick asked. "For how long?"

"Just the night."

"There you go," Kendrick said. "Just the night. And tell Cook to make an extra place at dinner."

"Thank you, Kendrick," Declan said with a slight smile. "Dinner would be lovely." Feeling the rain, he held out his palm facing upward, and then with a sigh he pulled up the hood of his cloak to cover his head. "It is cooler here than I was expecting. Wetter, too."

"I have never been bothered by a little rain," Kendrick said. As the two diviners went up ahead, he waited for Declan to join him at the bottom of the steps. "We will have to walk to the manor, I am afraid. I didn't bring horses. Bearing in mind, I had no idea you were coming."

"I would have brought my own, but for the little gateway you have here," Declan glanced back at the Star Temple. "My mare would break a leg on those steps. I don't mind walking. I may not be the man you are, but I do look after my health."

They began the journey together, climbing the road to the manor. Kendrick reduced his speed; up ahead, Paxton was a little stiff in his advanced years, slowing the two diviners.

"A brotherly visit... is that your purpose here at Esk?" Kendrick asked.

"A brotherly visit... that among other things. How is my sister?"

"She is well. Busy.

"Hmm." Declan gave Kendrick a familiar calculating look. "Tell me. Have you heard the latest news from the border?"

"The raid on the village?"

Declan waved a hand. "That is old news now. No, I mean the aftermath. The queen professes no part in what happened, but only a fool would believe her. Listen to this... We all know a price must be paid. And so sixty of our guardsmen are to fight the same number of Veldrians, ostensibly the same men who took part in the raid."

"I don't think I understand." Kendrick frowned. "As some kind of trial?"

"It is to be a fight to the death, except the Veldrians are to have no weapons."

Kendrick brow furrowed even deeper. "I suppose the queen can't just execute her own men on Julian's request. No doubt, in her world, who cares about some villagers? But neither can Julian let the raid stand, queen's innocence or not. I have to say, I'm still wondering why the emperor sent him."

Declan scowled. "As well as a murderer, he is also a fool. No one with sense would have staked his reputation on dealing with the situation at the border. The problem for us, however, is that we are the ones who suffer for his mistakes. This situation could explode at any time. Imagine if the queen learned we are reforming the Armies of the West, about the fielding... What do you think she would do then?"

"Is this what you came here to tell me?"

Kendrick and Declan's boots both crunched in the gravel as the broad gates that led to Fernley Manor appeared up ahead, made hazy by the drizzle.

Declan took a moment to reply. "No, it is not." He met Kendrick's gaze, his expression deadly serious. "I came here to remind you of something you should already know."

Kendrick stared straight ahead. Here it came. "Which is?"

"You owe me, Kendrick. After what happened with the vote. It could have all been over, and right now, we might instead be discussing the merits of various successors to the crown. Instead, as you well know, we lost by one vote. And that was after my daughter's meddling. If you had voted with me, against your order, others would have followed, and right now, we would not be facing a future in which that man becomes our emperor."

"I don't know what to say." Kendrick cleared his throat. "No one thought it would go the way it did. And that includes you."

"Perhaps you could start with an apology."

Kendrick stopped in his tracks. They were nearly at the manor's grand entrance, on high ground with a view to the distant fields. The drizzle was coming to an end, leaving a solid gray sky in its aftermath.

"Very well." Kendrick struggled with the words, but he managed to get them out. "I am sorry. Bryan deserved better. I am sure you know why I did what I did, and the pressure we are all under. You obviously want something from me. If it is within my power, I will do it."

Declan's eyes became calculating once more. "Have you given much thought to the fielding?" Kendrick raised an eyebrow; the fielding wouldn't magically organize itself. "I mean in the context of Julian's confirmation. After what happened with the vote, it wouldn't surprise me if he has some plan for the fielding."

"Why would he? The vote went his way."

"As much as it rankles me that his confirmation went ahead, he will be well aware that he doesn't have the majority support of the nobles. His father would know it too. The fielding is an opportunity to build himself up and change the story, while he has the chance to do so."

"Declan, the last thing I want is Julian as our next emperor. As long as it doesn't hurt my family, I will do what I can to help you."

"Meaning—?"

"—The events at the fielding are carefully scheduled. I am the host, and I will make sure that the rules are followed. He has no formal role. Whatever plan—"

"Do you know how he did it? How he won the vote, against all expectations?"

"There was trouble at the Argent Arch—"

"Trouble? Samara stole my signet ring, Kendrick. She signed a number of orders in my name, orders that saw a number of merchants fall foul of the empire's tax officials. I don't need to tell you that the merchants we have in the assembly are disproportionately Blues. Many were so worried about organizing their affairs that they decided to come to the Marble Court at the last moment, on the day of the vote itself. Ah— but what happened on that day? A full inspection of goods coming in and out of the city. Enough to cause the biggest standstill in years."

Kendrick was open-mouthed. "Why didn't you say anything?"

Declan's voice was rising. "Think about what I would be saying, Kendrick. My own daughter visited my home, stole from me – stole my own name – and signed a number of orders that were believable enough that they were actually followed. I lead the Guildsmen. No... I could never reveal the truth. They won, Kendrick. And if they keep playing without rules, without honor, they are going to win the crown. It is your fielding. Let me be clear. I am asking you now. Do not let anyone else take control."

"Very well, Declan. I have told you I will give Julian only the honors I have to. But what about you? What are you going to do?"

As he stood with Kendrick, in view of Fernley Manor, Declan's reply made it clear he had a response prepared. "If Julian had lost the confirmation, we would have begun the process of finding a successor, correct?"

Kendrick nodded warily. "Correct."

"We have five years until the next confirmation vote, but laws can be changed, which is why we have an assembly. If the right successor can be found, after what happened with the vote, I don't believe we would have to wait five years at all."

Kendrick stared into the distance. He had to appreciate Declan's sheer determination. "That makes sense to me, and yes, with broad support, you would probably get the vote passed, but who do you have in mind?"

"I have been busy reviewing the emperor's family line, which led me to something interesting." Declan glanced at the manor, and then back at Kendrick. He looked like he had something important to say. "We all know Rigel had no surviving brothers or sisters. But what do you know of our emperor's years campaigning in the Far Reaches?"

Kendrick could only answer from his own perspective, which was a military one. "Rigel was a general, obviously. Before he defended Curran Castle, he served in Astoria... back then I was in Jaynia. When we met, after we broke the siege, it was the first time we had spoken face to face."

"He asked you to serve under him, didn't he?"

"He did, but the situation was bad in Jaynia—I suppose not much has changed. I wanted to do my part. Rigel went on to Loriastris, if I recall."

"Tell me, Kendrick... Have you ever heard a rumor that Rigel fathered a second child?"

"After Julian?" Kendrick's eyebrows shot up. "No."

Declan shrugged. "It is just a rumor. Unsubstantiated, but—" He broke off. "Ah, Anthea!" he called. "My beautiful sister."

Kendrick turned toward Anthea, who was approaching from the direction of the manor. Blonde and well-groomed, in a sky-blue dress, if she was upset by the lack of time to prepare, she didn't show it. "Declan," she said with a smile, taking her brother's hands as he kissed both her cheeks.

"Uncle Declan!"

Behind Anthea, Caden strode over with a wide smile on his face. He wore riding clothes, and must have come straight from the stables.

"Caden, look at you." Declan embraced Caden before giving him an appraisal. "You are finally as big as your brother." Caden grinned, while Declan squeezed his muscular upper arms.

"Not quite, but nearly," Caden said.

"How is your training? Nearly a knight?"

"I've been busy training with sword and lance. And I'm getting better at riding too. I can show you."

"I would like that very much." Declan looked around. "And where is Troy?"

"Helping the builders," Caden replied.

Declan leaned back to gaze up at the manor's roof. "And Isabelle still loves heights, I see."

Isabelle was up on the roof, sitting back on one of the highest sections, heedless of the slippery surface beneath her.

"Isabelle, get down from there!" Anthea called. "And be careful! It's been raining." She threw Declan an exasperated look. "She probably wanted to see who was coming to the gateway."

"Come on," Caden said. He gave his uncle a playful whack to get him moving. "Come to the stables. You can see my new horse."

Kendrick and Anthea both remained where they were as Caden led Declan toward the stables.

"Did you know he was coming?" Anthea asked.

"Of course not. Apparently he's staying the night. Don't worry, I've asked Paxton to tell the staff."

Anthea searched his face. "My problem is not with giving him a bed, Kendrick. He is my brother. It is the things he has to say that concern me."

Chapter Thirty-Six

"AH, THERE SHE is," Declan said.

Kendrick saw his cook come up the stairs that led to the basement level. A plump woman, with a cap of gray curls, her apron was stained and her arms were dusty with flour.

"Cook, that was superb. I wanted to thank you myself."

"My pleasure, My Lord," she replied. Her eyes moved over to Kendrick, who nodded.

"Thank you, Cook. You may go," Kendrick said.

Cook headed back downstairs, while Declan leaned back in his chair contentedly, his hands resting on his stomach. "You are a lucky man, Kendrick. She really is one of the best."

Troy spoke up. "May I be excused?" He gave Declan an apologetic look. "One of the mares is sick. I need to check on her."

"You may," Kendrick said.

Troy stood, nodding at his uncle before he left. "It is good to see you, Uncle."

As Troy left, Kendrick watched him go. Despite his boyish looks, with his dark blond hair, broad shoulders, and blue eyes, he was carrying himself like a man much older.

Isabelle was the next to wriggle out of her chair. "May I—"

"Yes, love," Anthea said. "You too."

Tossing her long brown hair, she skipped away, happy to be pursuing whatever endeavor she had concocted. Kendrick liked to see her a little childish; there was enough time to be serious later on.

Caden remained where he was, seated beside his uncle. "Uncle Declan, tell us more about what you are doing at Graystone Abbey."

Kendrick and Anthea exchanged glances.

"It's fine, Declan," Anthea said. "I am sure we have all heard enough."

Declan directed a smile at Caden. "It is good to have a curious mind. Graystone Abbey is my great work, Caden, my legacy if you will. These days, Ashton Manor gathers dust, and it is the abbey where I spend much of my time."

Ashton Manor was also where Declan's wife Meredith had secluded herself. Kendrick didn't know much from Anthea, only that Bryan's death had driven a wedge between his parents.

"I wish I could see what you've done," Caden said.

Kendrick was mildly curious, but not enough to travel to Graystone. He had seen the structure before Declan started working on it, and it had the appearance of a place haunted by ghosts.

"Then come and visit. I am sure your parents will let you. It was a fortress before it became an abbey, and so it sits high on a hill, with strong gates and tall ramparts of stone. We have more books than you could easily count. There is no place like it. Effectively, Graystone Abbey is our empire's archive. I am preserving the knowledge the empire will need after the fall."

Caden frowned. "The fall—?"

Anthea placed a quick hand on top of her son's on the table. "That is enough. Caden, off to bed."

"Bed?" Caden asked incredulously. "Mother, I am nineteen years old."

Anthea answered curtly. "I spoke in haste. A mother's children will always remain exactly that in her eyes. What I mean to say is that it is time for you to leave so that the three of us may talk. *Now*, please."

Caden pushed his chair out, scowling as he left without a word.

"Declan—" Anthea began.

"I don't see why—"

"Enough," she interrupted. "You know better than to influence my children."

"I would use the word educate, but we are free to disagree."

Kendrick spoke up, "I know you consider yourself well-read, but even you can't see the future. And as for your so-called archive..." He shook his head. "The empire breaks down, and there you are, in your abbey, ready to come to the rescue."

"No." Declan's tone indicated that Kendrick's words had rankled. "That is not how empires fall. This is not a tale. There can be no easy rescue. Mark my words. Gateways will fail. Barbarians will invade. Crisis after crisis will tear the empire apart. As different leaders claim the Crown of Blood and Gold, the three orders will break down, powerful people taking opposing sides, ripping apart the old alliances. There will be a dark age, like nothing before it. All my archive can do is reduce the length of the dark age, from centuries to decades. Nothing I am doing can stop it altogether."

Kendrick opened his mouth but caught a warding look from his wife.

Declan rapped his fingers on the table. "I do not expect you to understand." He smoothed his expression. "Let us move onto other topics. I hear the emperor is going to make Baden Lynch our new lord marshal, with overall leadership of the reformed Armies of the West."

The news made Kendrick lean forward, eyebrows coming together in a glare. He forgot all about Declan's archive. "Baden Lynch? You can't be serious."

"Do I ever jest about these things?"

"But why him?"

"Think about it, Kendrick. What is his defining characteristic?"

"I can think of several," Kendrick growled. "He throws away the lives of his men. He can win battles, but not wars—"

"He bested you at a fielding, didn't he?"

"That has nothing to do with it. Yes, he beat me once. Over the years, I left him in the dust a dozen times."

Mirth lifted the corners of Declan's mouth. "Go on, then. You were saying?"

"As a leader, you have to judge when to direct your men, rather than lead from the front. That scar on his cheek? He got that in Darian, from an axeman who almost tore off his face. And you know why he always wears a collar buttoned up to his neck? He got that when a Jaynian almost opened his jugular."

"You think he's reckless."

"No," Kendrick said. "His problem is that he thinks the Weaver is watching over him, and every time he survives, it only confirms it in his mind."

"What about what happened in Loriastris? While we are on the subject of Baden Lynch, I would like to hear your version of events."

Kendrick looked down at the table.

"Come, Kendrick," Declan pressed. "We are family. You can share your thoughts with me."

"Another time, Declan. Not with my wife at the table."

Declan waited but finally relented. "Very well. Another time, then. Tell me something else, what order does Lynch belong to?"

Kendrick didn't answer; the question was rhetorical.

"The reason the emperor chose Lynch seems obvious to me. His defining characteristic is that he does not get involved in politics. Whoever is in charge, Lynch will happily follow." He smiled. "Unless, of course, that man is you."

"I plan to be nothing other than a father to my children."

"An admirable aim indeed." Declan smoothly changed the subject. "Troy and Caden are to be knighted at the fielding, are they not?"

Anthea answered, "They are, if the Weaver is kind."

"If there is war, you know they will be going to the front. Perhaps the best way to be there for your sons will be to serve along with them. Just a thought, Kendrick."

Kendrick hid a scowl. Unfortunately Declan might be right. "Well, we have to hope that war is not coming, we have enough of it in the Reaches. For the moment, the fielding keeps us busy enough. It isn't far away. Just six weeks.

Declan wasn't finished. "And another thing to mention about Troy and Caden."

"What about them?" Kendrick asked.

"If there is war, I have some influence among the Guildsmen. As their uncle, it is influence I am willing to wield. Reputations are made on the battlefield."

Anthea spoke up, watching Kendrick, even as she addressed her brother, "And we are grateful for any help you can give us. We may be aligned to the Wardens, but not everyone else is."

"Thank you, Declan," Kendrick said gruffly. "We appreciate the offer. If the time comes, that is."

"We are family," Declan said simply. "We look out for each other."

Kendrick stretched, feeling his muscles groan. The day had been long, and he knew what Declan truly wanted to talk about. "Anthea, did Declan tell you? He thinks Rigel has a secret child."

Declan held up a hand. "Not true. I said there was a rumor." He turned toward his sister. "Is there anything you can tell me?"

"I would not know, even if it were true. We spend little time in the capital."

Declan arched an eyebrow. "I have always believed you to be someone who knows about many things."

She hesitated, casting a quick look at Kendrick. "Very well. I have heard that he had a mistress when he was away campaigning. They were quite close, it is said. That is all I know."

Declan nodded, satisfied with her answer. "He was over there for what, a decade? Long enough to find companionship. This mistress... I am in the process of finding out who she was... Perhaps it is true... perhaps they even had a child."

"Why ask us if you already knew?" Kendrick asked.

"Have you ever known me to be anything but thorough?"

Shaking his head, Kendrick let out an elaborate sigh. "It has been good seeing you, Declan." He stretched again and stood up. "I have an early start tomorrow. Time for bed, if you ask me. I'll leave you two to catch up. Enjoy the rest of your evening."

Chapter Thirty-Seven

IT WAS A WARM DAY, clear and sunny. Everyone gathered at the border wore light clothing, whether it was the tunics and dresses on the Imperial side of the gorge, or the leathers and wool worn by the Veldrians on the clifftop opposite. The onlookers remained on high ground, where they could look down upon the graveled bed below. The River Byre trickled past in a lazy stream, oblivious to the proceedings.

On a flat section of ground, two large groups of warriors stood lined up, ready to face one another.

Many people from above watched Julian as he walked along the row of sixty Imperial guardsmen, and although he didn't carry a sword himself, he wore his armor and a cloak edged with gold. He stood in front of each tall man or woman—four of them were gigantic women—and looked up to meet a set of eyes. They were all varied: brown eyes, black eyes, blue eyes, green eyes. Reaching out to grip a shoulder, he repeated the same words, over and over again.

"Fight well. See justice done." He met the gaze of a grizzled veteran who had to be approaching seven feet tall. He then moved to the next guardsman, a woman as wide as a barrel, with a neck as thick as her head. She gave him a nod as he clasped her upper arm. "Fight well. See justice done." And on it went. "Fight well. See justice done."

All of the guardsmen wore shining silver armor. They were ready to fight; there was no need for scabbards, so they held naked longswords, straight double-edged weapons sharp enough to cut a falling feather. Some carried shields, emblazoned gold and red, like the emperor's crown, with a few flourishes in Imperial purple.

Reaching the last warrior in the line, Julian said his words, receiving a firm nod from the guardsman. He then turned away, and couldn't help noticing Zhuana doing the same thing with her sixty Veldrians. The druid, Alric, traveled along the row with the queen.

He stopped and watched for a moment.

The sixty warriors he was looking at were said to be the fiercest Veldrians fighters. Ravagers, they called them. The Veldrians weren't wearing any armor, as agreed, and wore dark leather vests over long-sleeved woolen tunics. Their leather leggings and soft shoes were strikingly different from the Imperial soldiers they were about to face.

As Zhuana and Alric progressed along the row, the fur-clad druid gave each warrior a long draught from a flask he presented. The act was strangely ceremonial, the druid precisely measuring the amount each person drank. The turn came for a woman with her hair in multiple braids. She wiped her mouth and then put a hand to her temple, weaving a little with her eyes closed. Her queen said something, and the woman nodded. Zhuana and Alric continued. The next man also had to close his eyes immediately after drinking.

Julian frowned. The druid's potion looked like it was going to make the Veldrians sick.

He left the area, returning to the slope that would take him up to the low cliff, where he could watch along with the great number of onlookers. Back in the gorge, Zhuana and Alric also headed to their own high vantage. The Veldrians lined the lip of the gorge, so many they were crowded together.

He remembered what the envoys had said. How many among the Veldrians were fighters? All of them.

The spectators on the Imperial side were just as numerous, however there were more women in colorful dresses and men in fine tunics or working clothes. Julian joined Samara in the place with the best vantage for observing the action below. People allowed a little space around them, but even they were hemmed in on all sides. Spying Bannon, he nodded at the gruff commander.

There were no rules, and so none were announced. The two rows of warriors faced each other on the gravel with about a hundred feet between them. What was going through the minds of the sixty Veldrians, about to be hacked apart by the powerful guardsmen?

The event was ostensibly based on a ritual of the Veldrians' mother goddess, and on the clifftop opposite, a burly Veldrian dressed in skins came forward with a curling bone-colored horn. The man called out something in a booming voice, but from across the gulf of the gorge, Julian only heard something about the mother deciding the fate of the

Veldrians below. The burly man then sucked air into his lungs and gave a loud blast of his horn.

Julian then turned as an Imperial herald in uniform appeared on his side with a silver horn, this time made from metal. The herald called out in a clear, crisp voice:

"These raiders will face Imperial justice today, under the gaze of the Great Weaver." He blew a more strident blast from his smaller horn.

Down below, the guardsmen began to walk forward, swords at the ready. The contest had begun.

The Veldrians burst into action.

From standing positions, they raced directly toward the guardsmen. Julian's eyes widened. By the stars, they were fast. Lithe and sleek as wolves, they darted past the guardsmen without engaging, ducking and weaving until they were on the Imperials' other side.

The guardsmen grunted and slashed. A few charged. The Veldrians kept dodging, making the Imperials lunge and strike at empty air. The ravagers stayed close, diving under sweeping blades, rolling on the ground to shoot back to their feet in different places. In comparison, the guardsmen looked like lumbering beasts.

A bellow came from one of the guardsmen. They restored discipline, dividing quickly into two groups. Each group of warriors in shining armor made a wall, linked together in a row, moving until between them they faced the ravagers. Trotting forward, they began to squeeze the Veldrians in the middle.

Julian saw a spray of blood as a blade collided with a Veldrian. Another fell a moment later. Three were cut down. Four. Five.

Then everything changed.

Snarling, bodies low to the ground, it was the ravagers who shifted into the attack.

Julian blinked. Their speed was inhuman. With the guardsmen in two separate locations, all of the ravagers concentrated their efforts on the same group of armored opponents, the smaller of the two forces. Each guardsman suddenly fought off two or three frenzied attackers at the same time. The huge soldiers stumbled around, trying in vain to throw off the nimbler enemies grappling them. The ravagers pulled their opponents to the ground and wrapped legs tightly around helmets, squeezing hard before performing agile acrobatics.

As a guardsman's neck broke, Julian sensed Samara flinch. Another guardsman went down. Two more. An armored woman on her knees screamed as a ravager lifted her helmet and punched sharp fingers into her eyes.

But again, the initial surprise wore off. The steel plate armor protected the soldiers wearing it, and as the second group of guardsmen entered the fray, blood arced into the air as a guardsman hacked down to tear a ravager's arm from his shoulder. One of the guardsmen was wielding his sword with two hands, and sliced his enemy in half.

Julian heard a loud whisper. "This is better than anything I've seen at the games."

A number of ravagers now held swords. The conflict entered a more grueling phase, as the Imperials showed their skill, blocking, grunting, thrusting, and hacking. Julian made a swift count. He saw perhaps ten guardsmen down. More than a dozen ravagers.

He focused on a bearded soldier whose sword blows were as quick as a striking snake. The guardsman had somehow lost his helmet, and both his face and armor were spattered with blood. He called encouragement to his fellows as he stepped over a body, rushing to a companion's aid as she fought off four enemies at the same time.

The body the guardsman had stepped over was a mangled mess; no one could survive wounds like his.

And yet he climbed to his feet.

The Veldrian was missing an arm at the shoulder. Blood soaked his clothing. His face was coated in the red of his own life force. And yet he picked up a sword from the ground nearby.

Everyone around Julian gasped. The ravager was still bleeding, and yet he moved like he suffered no pain, with no impairment at all. Wielding his sword with one hand, the ravager struck the guardsman from behind. His sword penetrated through the man's armor, directly into his back. The guardsman cried out, turning as his legs collapsed from under him.

More of the downed Veldrians returned to their feet. The guardsmen who weren't already embroiled whirled their heads around in shock. Taking advantage of the surprise, the ravagers came in from behind or attacked Imperials already distracted by an opponent. A guardsman fell with a blade between his shoulder blades. Another Imperial staggered: he had the top half of a ravager wrapped around his legs. The Veldrian's teeth were gritted; he seemed heedless of the fact that the rest of his body was gone.

Julian's mouth was open with shock; the weight of the numbers was shifting. When his guardsmen were gravely wounded, they stayed down. But the Veldrians... the Veldrians got back up again.

The chaotic scene unfolded like a nightmare. All the lunging and tumbling left depressions in the gravel. Fighters on both sides stumbled and often their mistakes were fatal. Blood turned the waters of the River Byre red. Screams of rage and pain accompanied the slashing and hacking, the strangling and punching.

In numbers, the two groups soon looked evenly matched, with about thirty or so warriors on each side. A flurry of blows, some tripping and roaring, and the guardsmen and ravagers both had twenty fighters left. Everyone had a sword who wanted one.

The people around Julian began to call out.

"Kill them!"

"For the empire!"

"Kill! Kill"

The chanting grew in volume: "Kill! Kill!"

Across the void, atop the gorge's other wall, the Veldrians also began to bellow. The volume from the Imperials rose to oppose them, until the two crowds were competing with each other.

Julian swallowed as the carnage below continued. A guardsman lost his sword and his two opponents knocked him over onto his back. The ravagers peeled his armor open and killed him by stabbing again and again.

There were at least eight Veldrians left—eight Veldrians and five guardsmen.

The guardsmen were clearly struggling, weary and outnumbered. A Veldrian with wild eyes leaped up on a soldier's back and used his sword to cut across his opponent's throat. Another guardsman lunged from side to side, trying to catch an enemy, while an unnoticed Veldrian raced up behind him and stabbed him right through his armor.

Six ravagers left. Three guardsmen.

The screams were ragged. Blood clouded the river. Bodies lay half-submerged in the water.

Four ravagers left. Two guardsmen.

The watching Imperials became silent. The Veldrians crowding the clifftop continued shouting.

Three ravagers left. One guardsman.

The last guardsman, a tall man in his fighting prime, had fought beyond all endurance. He had seen his companions fall, and now Julian could only pray to the Great Weaver that the soldier's thread was not yet broken. The guardsman blocked a sword blow. Whirling, he stopped another. The three ravagers all worked at him, like stray dogs on a piece of meat, darting in and out, making the soldier move. A Veldrian with a diagonal wound across his chest charged, taking a sword blow, but wrapping his arms around the bigger man and knocking him over. The guardsman's sword flew away to clatter onto the gravel. With their opponent on his back, the ravagers pulled off his helmet. Julian saw the whites of the soldier's eyes, which were open wide. He was surprisingly youthful, blond and clean-shaven. He convulsed as a blade opened his throat.

The fight was over.

Silence descended upon the area, sudden and heavy, like a blanket thrown over a fire.

The Veldrians' shouting changed as they began to cheer.

The blood drained from Julian's face. This was going to mean his end. He had agreed to pit the empire's finest against a group of unarmed barbarians. And the emperor's soldiers – his personal defenders – lost.

People would be talking about what had happened for years. Decades. Julian's role in what happened would be the biggest of all. He would be mocked. Ridiculed.

He barely gave it a moment's thought. He turned to one of his personal guards.

"Give me your sword," he snapped.

He heard Samara's voice, but it was far away, and he ignored her. "No! Julian..."

"Now!" Julian spat.

The guard swiftly drew his sword from its scabbard, handing it over by the hilt. Julian gripped the weapon with his right hand.

He then walked away from the group of onlookers. He raised the point of the sword above his head, so that all of the people on his side of the gorge could see him.

He sucked in his breath to roar. "Justice will be done!"

He left the crowd and headed to the part of the cliff where a slope descended to the riverbed. As he walked with his chin up and back straight, sword in hand, all eyes were on him. Zhuana was definitely watching. She put out her hands, ending the cries and bellows of her people. An expectant tension settled upon the area as Julian – the empire's crown prince and successor to the throne – approached the three remaining Veldrians.

Bodies littered the area. The destruction was more macabre, more terrible, than the most gruesome battles at the arena. Julian's vision tunneled so that the sprawled-out corpses were blurred in his vision. Of the three remaining Veldrians, one was covered in tattoos and bleeding hard, cut deeply across the torso. The other two were blood-soaked, but only lightly marked, with the oldest warrior bearded while the youngest of the trio had lank long hair and dark, malevolent eyes. All three held swords they had taken from the guardsmen and stood in a row, Julian come near.

"I have come for justice," Julian snarled. Standing on the dried riverbed, he shifted into fighting stance, with one foot forward, the other back, keeping his sword pointed between him and his enemies. "Come on. Let me see what you can do."

The younger warrior with the long hair uncoiled like a spring, leaping forward to send his sword toward Julian's belly. Julian weaved to the side to allow his opponent to overextend, before hacking down from overhead. His blade licked the Veldrian's face, opening up his cheek.

The wound was savage, but the ravager didn't scream; he merely grimaced. Something in the druid's potion was suppressing the pain.

Julian backed away, keeping all three opponents in sight. The older warrior with the beard came in, weaving and dodging from side to side, so fast he made a difficult target. As he delivered a succession of blows, Julian was forced to concentrate, working hard to block them one by one. Coming in from Julian's side, the wounded Veldrian with the tattoos attacked at the same time. Julian timed his blows, ducking and blocking as he moved his feet, and when his opponents got in each other's way he shuffled and swung his sword hard with the force of both arms. His sharp steel ripped through the wounded Veldrian, tearing him all the way through at the shoulder. Not even he would get up from a blow like that.

The younger Veldrian had been circling, and Julian's two remaining enemies tried to flank him, forcing him to face two directions, but he charged straight through them to change position, even as he blocked the next frenzied attack. Once he was clear, a sharp sting flared in his right arm; someone had struck him, but there was no time to check the wound.

The long-haired warrior liked to jump, and the next time he did, Julian guessed where he would be. Julian thrust his blade, and the young man gasped as his blow struck home. Without hesitation, Julian shifted his stance to improve his leverage. With the long-haired Veldrian bent over, Julian brought his sword arcing onto his mid-section, cutting him nearly in half.

He immediately spun to meet an attack from the bearded fighter, the last Veldrian remaining. Julian parried, and then twisted his weapon. As steel scraped against steel, the sword came out of his opponent's hands. The bearded Veldrian stood stunned as Julian brought his sword back. He then thrust hard, using enough force to push the point of his blade through to the other side of his enemy's body. He turned his weapon as he pulled his sword back out again, opening up more of the man's chest. When he removed his sword completely, the last warrior fell down, eyes glazing as he collapsed to the ground.

The fight was over.

Julian stood panting. His vision was still tunneled, and he shook his head to clear it before taking in the entire scene. He had traveled a surprising distance as he fought, although he couldn't really remember running, only fighting and blocking as he avoided a bloody death. His chest continued to heave. He raised his head still higher, looking up to the watching crowd of Veldrians, and then turning toward the onlookers from his own side.

He brought up his right arm to point his sword into the sky. It was only when he looked up that he remembered the wound in his forearm. Blood dripped from his palm, near his wrist. Any deeper and his opponent's blade would have opened an artery.

"Justice is done!" he bellowed.

A powerful roar greeted his cry, as the crowd on the Imperial side cheered.

Chapter Thirty-Eight

BETHANY CLIMBED a steep trail to the top of a lonely mountain. Her calves burned. Sweat poured down her face. The sound of her heavy panting was even louder than the gusting wind. As she rounded a corner leading up to high ground, the late afternoon sun slammed into her. The knapsack on her back felt full of heavy stones, rather than clothing, food, and water. The wooden pole in her hand, a true diviner's staff, had stopped her from stumbling more than once.

She shielded her eyes, squinting up ahead. Then she let out a breath of overwhelming relief. There was no mistaking the sight in front of her. She was nearly at her destination.

She stood catching her breath for a moment. Ahead of her, silhouetted in the approaching sunset, the stepped pyramid glowed like molten gold. Each tier was wider than it was tall, giving the pyramid a broad, hulking shape. A stairway led up to the open summit, where two tall poles speared the sky. The pyramid was oriented to face the setting sun at the summer solstice, if the observer watched from the pair of stone poles at the top.

The gateway's name was the Yellow Pyramid, and although she had studied it in books, she had never seen it with her own eyes. No one had ever managed to figure out why it was here, high up on a mountain, so far from civilization.

She set her jaw. Time was marching onward. With the sun falling toward the horizon, she didn't have long. If she didn't get this right, her long journey, and all of her study... it would all have been for nothing.

She resumed her climb on the steep mountain trail.

The task she had been given allowed her no room for error. She had been walking in the same direction for eight days. Home – the Eternal City, Everlast – was over a hundred miles away. On this, the eighth and final day, she was due back in Everlast before nightfall.

She would soon be opening a gateway, her own, for the very first time. She was alone, with no one to help her or even know if things went wrong. She had to time her travel so that she arrived at the Crystal Dome at exactly sunset—not where she was now, but at her destination. How she accomplished that feat was up to her.

The Yellow Pyramid grew until it was a wide edifice in front of her. She headed straight to the dozens of steps that led up to the pyramid's summit, miniature versions of the slabs that gave the structure its shape. With her staff in hand, she climbed swiftly, and as she gained height, she cast anxious looks at the setting sun. From her vantage, she had an unparalleled view of the landscape of hills and forests, all the way to the distant horizon.

Sweat soaked her clothing. Her panting came hard and fast. Time was passing, and she had yet to reach the summit. She put down her head to climb with more urgency. Her foot nearly slipped from a stone step, making her eyes shoot wide open as she put out her arms to steady herself. The worst thing she could do was fall.

At last, with her legs on fire, she reached the pyramid's summit, where the flat space on top was about fifty paces to a side. She hurried to the very center, where the pair of tall poles created a void between them. From her position at the highest point on the mountain, she could see a vast distance. The sun was straight in front of her, its color shifting to red. Below the glowing orb, the broad plain formed a flat brown horizon.

She bit her lip, frowning at the sun as it descended, like a copper coin falling to the ground below. The sun drifted closer, closer...

"Now," she muttered.

She had reached the pyramid just in time. The sun struck the horizon, and then part of the sun became hidden, as if the edge of the world were eating it a little at a time. As light fell from the day, the golden circle fell until it was half hidden, devoured piece by piece until it was gone completely, the shining part at the top giving a last sparkle before it vanished from view.

Where she was, it was now exactly sunset. The moment it happened, she began to count. "One. Two. Three. Four..."

Where she was and Everlast were two different places. Diviners had to have an understanding of time. Sunset here was six minutes and twenty-four seconds from the time of sunset at her destination. She also had to allow some time for the travel itself.

"One-hundred and one. One-hundred and two…"

Even as she tracked the procession of time, she took a step back to create space, so that the pair of poles was just in front of her. A wind came up, drying the sweat on her skin to make her suddenly cool.

"Two-hundred and eleven. Two-hundred and twelve…"

She gripped the staff tightly. Surely this had to be the most difficult test so far?

"Three-hundred."

She stopped counting out loud, even as she continued to keep track with her ability to keep time inside. It was time to open her gateway. She had to concentrate on what she was doing.

Staff in hand, she stood just in front of the gap between the stone poles as the howling wind tugged her hair in all directions. She could do this. She had to. She knew how far away Everlast was; it had taken her eight days to get here. And yet here she was, at the top of the Yellow Pyramid, about to travel the same distance in no time at all.

Breathing. Focus on the breathing. She looked up at the sky, gathering her senses, taking in everything she could about her environment.

Importantly, departing a strange gateway was easier than arriving at one. The diviners would never have forced her to depart the Crystal Dome and come here to the Yellow Pyramid, a place she had never been to before, if that were not the case. Of all the gateways, the Crystal Dome was the one she knew best. It was where she had her meditation classes and wielded her staff at divination. She had first inhaled the Weaver's Breath under the starry sky, seen through the transparent panes above. As far as her relationship with the tapestry was concerned, the Crystal Dome was home.

Nonetheless, it was important to have a strong sense of the place she was presently in. She took a moment to appreciate the solid weight of the stone pyramid beneath her feet. Below the pyramid, the mountain was another mass that propelled the monument into the sky, bringing it closer to the heavens. The sun, even gone from view, announced its location with a powerful voice. The first stars were starting to appear.

The seconds were passing. She had to act now.

Her mouth was dry. Her chest was heaving so hard that she needed to slow it down. She drew in a deep breath and held it, before releasing it slowly.

She turned the orb that crowned her staff in one direction, and then the other, until she heard a click. Her heart was beating fast as she raised her staff high. She swallowed and then slammed the heavy pole down, striking the stone with the metal at the base of the staff. As she had been taught, she inhaled at the same time.

Something happened inside the staff. She didn't see any change in the decorated orb at the top, but again, she smelled the sharp tang of tar. Harsh and strong, the Breath of the Weaver hurt the back of her throat.

Here it came.

She could go mad. Or she could enter the gateway and vanish, never to be seen again.

No. That wasn't going to happen to her. She was going to be a diviner. This was what she was meant to do.

The world around her started to pulse. There was a rhythm to it, a resonance. The hum came and went. In. Out. In. Out. The vibration grew stronger. Now the pyramid underneath her announced itself. The mountain lifted up and she felt her body rising, as if she were being carried to the top of a tall ocean wave.

She wanted to allow the breath to take over, to delve further into the experience and try to learn about the greatest questions of all. What was the universe? Who put the stars in place? What was the Great Weaver's grand objective?

Instead she took a deep breath and lifted her staff again. It was important to feel the gateway's resonance; it was trying to tell her what she needed to know. The tapestry was like a curtain, blowing on the wind to come nearer and nearer to her position on top of the pyramid. All she had to do was speak to the wind, to touch its pulse, and she would be able to peel the curtain aside.

She began to weave with her staff, slowly at first and then fast. She increased the rhythmic twirling, back and forth, until it was like a display with fire sticks she once saw at the spring fair. The staff touched the tapestry; she was certain. She sensed the staff humming along with the pulsation of the gateway, even as she swept it back and forth, as if she were attacking an elusive opponent.

She gave a hard diagonal slice.

With a resounding, ripping sound, she tore a hole in the air. Bright fiery light made her want to close her eyes, but she forced them to stay open. She made another slice in the same place. The gash grew bigger, and she brought her staff to a halt. With precision now, she took her staff in both hands and cut a shape out of the void in front of her, widening it, until the hole peeled apart and opened up. Her skin never stopped tingling.

She now stood in front of a broad rectangular doorway, a black mirror that glistened like polished steel. For a moment she stood terrified.

And then she took a step through.

Chapter Thirty-Nine

BETHANY WAS IN a strange tunnel, and from her classes she knew its name, although she had never been here before. There was no possibility for her to travel as a learning experience – as another diviner's ward – because she would never remember the things she had seen. And if she were under the spell of the Weaver's Breath, having two alert diviners would make any control impossible. She had to do this herself, in this way.

This place was called the path of stars.

The black tunnel stretched endlessly in both directions. Stars made long darting lines on both sides. She stood with her mouth open and eyes wide. But time was always passing, and part of her was tracking the seconds. She gave a twist of her staff, and the portal closed behind her.

The path of stars was unexpectedly chaotic, dizzying enough to make her blink over and over. The Weaver's Breath was underneath it all, making her alive and excited, agitated and more than a little nauseous. The pulsing continued. She felt like she were being lifted up a few inches, then down again, then up again, down again... Every sense told her she was being shaken, like a doll in the hand of a child.

Her breathing. Focus on her breathing.

Her right hand gripped her staff tightly; it was the staff that would get her where she was going. As her rapid breathing slowed, and her heart calmed along with it, something changed around her—the long lines made by the starlight were shortening, and the stars themselves were becoming sparkling dots. The pinpricks of light still moved, but her confidence grew, and the tension in her shoulders began to ease.

She looked down at her feet. She saw stars below them, but the black void beneath her felt solid.

Time was all that mattered. She had to keep moving. Setting her jaw, staring straight ahead, she began to walk. If she had wards, they would be placid, docile, following her blankly, doing whatever she instructed.

The stars still traveled past her at speed. She was so insignificant. Everything was insignificant. The tapestry was impossibly vast.

Panic made her stop in her tracks. But she had changed. She could use her awe to her advantage. She was tiny enough that her feelings didn't matter; what was her panic compared to the universe?

The panic melted away. A surge of pleasure traveled upwards in her body.

A collection of moving stars drew her attention: the leaf constellation Carlan. After the group in the shape of a leaf, another constellation, Rohann, had the curling appearance of a snake.

She had only just seen them when they were gone. More stars kept drifting past, and then they picked up speed, their darting motion getting faster. The dizziness returned and this time it made her swallow and grimace. She squeezed her eyes shut. The Great Weaver was all. The tapestry was everywhere. Who was she? Where was she? What was happening to her? Was she going to be lost in here forever?

When she opened her eyes again, the stars were again so fast they made long darting lines.

Was this even real? What if, right now, she was standing on top of the Yellow Pyramid, trying to come to an accommodation with the Weaver's Breath she had just inhaled? The sun had set. It would make sense for her to be under the stars.

Perhaps she had failed.

Perhaps she was now insane.

These feelings would go on forever.

She closed her eyes again. Her mother's face came to her. "I believe in you, Betani," she said. "More importantly, I love you."

She drew in a shaking breath. This wasn't going the way it was supposed to.

Another face came to her. She saw Xander, and his face and voice were kind. "You can do this," he said. "You have to."

With her eyes still closed, she sucked in another breath, counting as she did. One. Two. Three. Four. When she let her breath out, she tried to count for twice as long. One. Two. There. Four. Five. Six. Seven. Eight.

With renewed determination, she opened her eyes.

The stars in the tunnel, surrounding her on all sides, were completely still.

She started to walk again, quickly this time, setting a purposeful stride. She made a pulling motion with her staff, toward herself. The stars came forward to meet her. She brought the staff down again, slowing the rate they were moving. There was the leaf constellation again. And a moment later, there was the snake. She swept her staff across the sky, lifting the snake until it was above her head, orientating herself. She then pushed the leaf away, thrusting her staff while she pointed. More familiar constellations appeared. She moved the staff down again. Stop.

The sky viewed from Everlast was something she knew well. At this time of year, at exactly sunset, the five maidens should be... there.

She moved her staff. Stop.

Seeing more familiar stars, the ones she knew best, she steadily arranged them. A yellow star grew larger: her own sun. The sun grew bigger, but for some reason she could look directly at it, and it didn't light up the path of stars. Planets grew from tiny dots to little orbs: Memman, Tosh, and then Kaspar, her own world. A gray sphere came closer: the moon. Her world of swirling clouds, blue oceans, and green and red landscapes grew larger, until it dominated her vision, and then it became bigger still. The sun was now gone, just below the edge of the world.

She had already centered the stars above Everlast. The end of the tunnel, where she was facing, now lined up perfectly with the Crystal Dome. Her destination gateway was calling to her. Time was passing, every sense telling her that she was cutting it close to the planned time of her arrival, potentially much too close. The Weaver's Breath coursed through her, making her stomach churn. She had to get to the Crystal Dome before her time ran out.

She pointed her staff straight ahead, toward the infinite end of the tunnel. She again pulled the orb toward herself. When everything was still, she then lifted her staff in both hands, and with a hard strike, cut it across the darkness. Turning, widening, she soon found herself standing face to face with a tall, rectangular doorway, like a mirror made of shadow.

Was it yet sunset in Everlast?

Now! Quickly! She had to go now!

She took a long step into the portal.

✦

Impact.

Bethany fell forward to sink onto one knee. She kept her eyes closed, face pointed down at the floor, her hair hanging over her face. Her chest convulsed. She gritted her teeth, swallowing until the feeling passed. Her attention went to her left hand, pressed down on the hard stone floor, using the solid surface to ground herself. Her right hand gripped her staff, propping the rest of her body up.

She opened one eye, and then the other. The disorientation was expected, but that didn't make it any easier. Fighting another wave of nausea, she managed not to cough. A burst of pain struck the area between her temples: the spiky onset of a headache that made all other headaches pale in comparison. She stifled a groan. The travel left behind a strange dirty feeling as the Breath of the Weaver began to wear off.

Still on one knee, she raised her head. She was in a large vaulted space, with a platform at one end and an immense transparent dome overhead. Despite being alive, she didn't feel any relief. She was definitely in the Crystal Dome, at the Observatory, in the Corpus District in Everlast. She had come to the right place. But did she pass her test? She tilted her head back to look at the sky above the dome. Vibrant colors streaked the sky, along with dark gray storm clouds and broad swathes of red. With the inclement weather, she had no idea how close she was to sunset.

What was that sound? She heard a clear, soft chiming.

Ding. Some time passed. Four or five seconds. *Ding.*

A white-haired man stood in a distant corner. He wore a diviner's gray cloak and held a small bell and striker. His hand moved. *Ding.*

Someone took hold of Bethany's arm, lifting her until she was standing. A uniformed steward nodded at her, although he said nothing else. He took a moment to look at her, assessing, and then nodded again before walking away. She wanted to ask—how did she go? Was this the right day? It had to be. How close was she to sunset?

A nearby sparkle and shimmer came from the empty air a dozen paces away. A dark-haired girl fell forward, to go through the same experience Bethany had, falling to the floor as she barely kept hold of her staff. As Bethany blinked, paying more attention to her surroundings, she realized that haggard-looking young men and women stood silently in different locations on the floor—the students who had arrived earlier than her.

She heard the bell chime again. *Ding.*

A slender man with a triangular beard – Diviner Trask – stood on the platform at the end of the space. He spent some time taking in the scene, and then he went to speak with the diviner striking the bell. The bell fell silent, and Diviner Trask moved again to the center of the platform.

Trask opened his arms and called out, "Students, congratulations. You are the successful ones. Please, leave the area. You will be tired. There is food and water available in the atrium. You know the rules. Anyone who arrives too long after sunset has failed the test. The ones who arrived early have already departed. You are the fortunate few."

Bethany quickly searched for Xander and Carina, but directly in her vision, the air peeled open as another newcomer arrived. The stocky young man collapsed to the floor, blinking rapidly as he pushed himself from his sprawled out position. The young man – Gregor – coughed and then stared hard at Bethany. The bell had finished striking. He had only just missed the deadline.

"Did I...?" he whispered, and then trailed off. He stifled a sob; he couldn't help noticing her expression of sympathy. As he hung his head, a uniformed steward headed over to help him.

"Come on, Bethany," a skinny young woman, Hesta, beckoned.

Bethany went up to join Hesta, even as she tried to find her friends.

She thought she saw Carina's blonde-haired figure up ahead. And there was Xander, staring straight over his shoulder at her. As relief flooded through her, she and the other successful students left the Crystal Dome, and she made a quick count.

Seven. Only seven.

Hesta addressed her as they walked. "I was on the lucky side of early. You probably don't know, but you arrived right in the middle of the sixty bells. Impressive, Bethany."

Bethany didn't reply, instead hearing her name from up ahead.

"Bethany." Xander had stopped to wait for her.

"Xander."

He smiled weakly. "We did it. Sorry. I'm still a bit... hazy. Where's Carina?"

She opened her mouth to call out to the girl she thought was Carina, but the blonde girl turned, revealing her face in profile. She wasn't Carina. She was Linore.

Hesta spoke, "Carina still hasn't come. Brent and Dray failed too. Too early."

"Still hasn't come...?" Bethany trailed off. "But that means..."

As she realized what Hesta was saying, the knowledge was like a powerful punch in her stomach. *Carina didn't make it. She won't become a diviner.*

"I don't believe you." Xander's tone was angry. "Surely she made it."

"I'm telling you, Xander," Hesta said. She indicated the group. "There are only seven of us. Where is she now?"

Meanwhile, without thinking about what she was doing, Bethany had stopped in her tracks. "Where was Carina going to again? What gateway?"

"Kelway House."

After Bethany's own journey, eight days of hard walking and climbing, she knew all the things that could go wrong. More than anything, she remembered her terror in the path of stars.

"You go on. I'm waiting for her. She might need help. At the very least, she's going to need a friend."

Hesta frowned. "Even if she comes, she failed. She won't be a diviner. We all know that. Aren't you exhausted? I know I am."

Bethany shook her head. "I'm waiting."

Xander had also come to a halt. He met her eyes but he spoke to Hesta. "You go ahead, Hesta. Bethany and I are going to stay."

✦

Bethany and Xander sat on two chairs at the back of the Crystal Dome. Near the platform, at the other end of the cavernous space, a diviner with gray hair and a curly beard stood patiently by the platform, hands behind his back.

Five hours had passed, and there was still no sign of Carina.

Bethany couldn't even guess what trouble her friend had come to. "She could have tripped, hurt her ankle, anything. She might be out there, lost, unable to find her way."

"Kelway House is by the water," Xander said dubiously. "She was planning to take a boat to get there."

"Storms can come unexpectedly. Boats can sink."

"The Pond isn't known for bad weather."

Bethany wanted to ask: then where was she? But there were fears she didn't want to voice. "You're right," she said instead, letting out a breath. "We can't think the worst."

"We can't." Xander stared at the ground. "But I'm worried too." He looked down at his hand, holding it out to her with the palm open, his suggestion obvious but leaving it up to her. She reached out and took his hand, squeezing it gently as he squeezed her back.

"I wish so much she was here," she said in a whisper.

This time Xander didn't reply, and more time passed as they both waited. The Crystal Dome was perfectly silent. The diviner on the chair continued to wait. Bethany's eyelids became heavy. She leaned into Xander and he placed an arm around her. Her head found his shoulder. Her eyes started to drift closed...

Xander spoke up, "Beth..."

As her skin tingled, Bethany's eyes snapped open and she straightened. Xander was already in the process of standing. A black mirror hovered over the middle of the floor, glimmering at the edges, before someone fell out and collapsed. A staff clattered to the hard floor.

The gateway closed. Bethany heard the sound of sobbing.

The young woman was Carina. And her entire body was shaking.

Bethany was already running. She and Xander reached Carina at the same time.

"Carina," Bethany said, kneeling at her side. "Let us help you."

"What day is it?"

Xander was crouched beside her. "What time, you mean?"

"What day?" Carina's voice was piercing; she was almost screaming. "I was in there for days."

Carina sounded strange, different, nothing like herself. Bethany and Xander exchanged frightened glances.

"You're about six hours late," Bethany said.

"No. That isn't true. That place... The tunnel. It was too big. I got lost in there. Round and round."

"Can you stand?" Xander asked.

Carina kept sobbing. "Thinker. Maker. Weaver. Mother. Thinker. Maker. Weaver. Mother." She continued to repeat the same words, over and over. Wincing, she put a hand over her eyes. "Too bright."

Xander looked around. "It's not bright in here."

"Too big," Carina said.

As Bethany tried to soothe her friend, she realized that there were other people nearby. Diviners, a pair of them, both stood watching with grim expressions on their faces.

"Step back," she heard a stern female voice. "Let us take her."

"I want to help her," Bethany insisted.

"With what she is going through, you cannot help her," said the other diviner, the bearded man.

"Then let me go with her."

The first diviner, a woman with long black hair, gave Bethany's arm a tight squeeze, almost a pinch. "Step away, both of you," she instructed, and Bethany reluctantly moved back. "She needs darkness. No stimulation at all. This is not the first time we have seen this. We will be lucky if we can save her mind."

The pair of diviners got Carina to her feet. Bethany and Xander watched in horror. Carina was still mumbling, barely walking in a straight line, as the diviners both led her away.

Chapter Forty

AS HE SAT IN a comfortable chair, Julian turned his hand over, inspecting the scar connecting his thumb to his wrist. By the stars, he had been lucky. Just a little deeper...

The clerics had told him to look for redness or swelling, but the empire's best healers had done their work well, and he couldn't see any sign of infection. After a few weeks, the sutures holding the wound closed had been removed. Now he was just left with a thin purple line. He had been told it would turn white over time, and if he was lucky, the scar would fade altogether.

It was good to be back in Everlast, far from what passed for civilization at the southern border. A warm spiced tea rested on the side table beside his chair. He had just finished reading his letters, and the pile of correspondence formed a tidy pile on a different table. The day ahead would be busy, visiting his allies, speaking with his spies about the actions of his enemies. But it was good to be home.

He heard movement as Samara entered the villa. She had cut her curling hair a little shorter, and he liked the new look on her. Even walking toward him, holding a scroll, with a frown on her face and a pensive look in her eyes, she moved with hips swaying, making his mind turn to other things.

Later. He had work to do. That would come later.

"Another letter," Samara said, holding up the scroll. "From her. She trusts that you are recovered and ready to come to a final settlement."

"She must wait." He grinned wickedly, holding up his hand. "As you can see, I am still confined, with healers by my bedside."

"Look at you." Her tone was exasperated, but he knew she wasn't truly angry. "Proud of yourself, aren't you? You fool. You crazed, brave, terrifying fool."

"It worked though, didn't it? Imagine if we had let them win. Instead, I am a hero. And my injury has bought us all the time we need. The fielding is just weeks away. Already the empire is mobilizing. The sleeping giant is waking, and when he roars, he is going to be loud indeed."

Samara held up Zhuana's message. "You don't want to read it yourself?"

"Not particularly. I will instead look forward to driving her from our border and destroying her people completely."

She set the scroll down with his other letters. Coming over, she reached out and picked up his hand, turning it over to inspect the wound. "No infection. You were lucky."

"The Weaver protected me." He gave a dry smile. "And it appears that their mother goddess did too."

Her finger traveled along his scar. "I was terrified when you went out there," she said in her soft, throaty voice. "There is truth in the stories about these druids and the potions they make. The way they kept fighting... it was unnatural. At first, I thought they had found a way to conjure life back into the dead."

"We learned a hard lesson," he said, reluctant to admit the truth. His spirits swiftly lifted. "But more than anything, people will remember how it finished, with the crown prince striking them down until they were no more. I went to the border to change the way people think about me. And that is exactly what I did."

"These potions... How long does the effect last, I wonder? Was it wearing off, by the time you—?"

He snatched his hand away. "It was my skill that won the day. You do realize how long I have trained—?"

"Shh," she soothed and then smiled. "I was there, remember? I saw how you fought. Like a lion." He calmed, and she pulled over another chair to sit beside him, dragging it close so he could smell her spicy, floral scent. "What worries me, however, is not the stories about how you restored the empire's honor." Her expression was serious. "Julian... what if the Veldrians are even more of a threat than we originally thought?"

He cast his mind back, remembering, and a shadow crossed his face. But then he shook himself. "They have yet to face our knights, charging with lances. We are slow to rise, but once we move to the attack, nothing in this world can stop us."

She nodded, with the familiar thoughtful look in her eyes. Then she changed the subject. "How is your father?"

"The clerics say it is just a minor case of congestion."

"I will make a prayer for him the next time I visit the cathedral." She hesitated. "Speaking of your father, the fielding will soon be upon us. The time is approaching to speak with him about the oath of fealty. Not yet, my love. But soon."

Julian scowled, his good mood evaporating. He had thought his father would be proud of what he had accomplished at the border. The Veldrians were still there, it was true. But they had also not invaded. He had worked hard to delay them for as long as he had, and everyone but his father had been filled with praise and admiration after he risked his life for the empire's pride.

"In truth, I am not sure if the right time will come. I told you. He always accepts the oath himself. If I ask that I take his place, I know what his answer will be."

"Do not worry, my love. Have patience. The right time will come. Meanwhile, I have arranged a fitting with the tailor. Following that, another session with the jeweler. At the fielding, you will be presented to the most powerful nobles in the realm, but also, most importantly, to the reformed Armies of the West. They will see you as the emperor-in-waiting. This is an important moment for you—potentially the most important in your life. Everything is going to be perfect."

Zhuana peered through the bushes. She lay flat on her stomach with Alric beside her. Together, they stared into the barren wasteland they had crossed after leaving the land of Grendal.

"Be ready," Zhuana said. "Keep watching." A moment later, she spoke again, "This is it. Here they come."

Alric watched carefully, but his eyes weren't as sharp as hers. A dry, dusty wind blew across the brown rocks and gnarled trees. They had traveled a great distance from her border camp, but now that they were here, all of a sudden, the border didn't feel so far away.

Alric made a low sound, and she knew he could finally see it: a dark speck, getting bigger. Then another. Silhouetted against the blue sky, more shapes appeared. Soon the nearer ones became larger, even as more figures appeared behind them.

The closest shapes took form. Despite having an idea about what he would see, Alric sucked in a sharp inward breath. There was now a growing number of black, human-like figures. They had a strange way of walking, a sideways saunter. The only word that came close was slinking.

Sensing Alric's eyes on her, she turned her head to meet his gaze.

"I told you," she said grimly.

Alric returned his attention to the black figures. "They were once people. I can scarcely believe it. Look at them now."

Some of the creatures were still clothed, wearing rags that might have once been tunics or skins or leathers. Several, however, had lost their clothing completely. None of them had hair. Their bodies were sleek and reptilian, covered in diamond skin. The smaller ones might be female, but then again, they might not be.

Zhuana focused on the nearest, even as it came closer to her position. The creature had red eyes with vertical black pupils. Its nose was snubbed to its face, with two holes for nostrils and a thin-lipped mouth. The creature's mouth was open as it panted, revealing sharp, pointed teeth. A grubby, torn, loincloth covered the area below its sleek belly. Its skin was patterned, and its fingernails were entirely black and hooked like claws.

Another of the approaching creatures was much smaller, half the size of those around it. Zhuana felt both sadness and anger come over her. The thing had once been a child.

Her mouth was tight as she turned back to Alric. "Have you seen enough?" She had to work to hide her fear. When Alric nodded, she sucked in a breath and called out in a powerful voice. "Ready... Take aim!" She paused. "Loose!"

Arrows flew from the screen of forest, peppering the nearest scaled creatures until they collapsed down dead. The archers then left the trees, bows in hand with arrows fitted, wary as they advanced. Spreading out, they approached the rest of the stragglers, and began to loose their arrows at will. One creature collapsed. Another. Soon all of the creatures were down.

"Our scouts will keep watching," Zhuana said. "These are just the first to find their way across the badlands, and we will continue to search for more. But eventually, we both know that a great number of these creatures will come. They may not reach the border for months, but it is going to happen. This time, though, we will not be taken by surprise. That has happened once before and never again."

"People are going to find out," Alric said.

She nodded. "They are." She paused. "Come on. Let us return to the border. We have important decisions to make."

✦

Zhuana met Commander Bannon on the wide trail that connected her fortified camp to the nearest crossing of the River Byre, and onward to the town of Lexia.

The gray-haired, bearded soldier gave her a bow, before handing her a message.

She took the scroll, unfurling it to scan the contents. It wasn't long, and she read it quickly.

My regrets... wounds still plague me...

She furled the scroll back again and stared hard into the commander's eyes. "Do you know what this says?"

"No," Bannon replied in his gravelly voice. "But I do know that the crown prince has yet to recover—"

She cut him off, although she was wise enough not to reveal her thinking. If there was one thing she hated, it was anyone wasting her time. "We will continue to wish for his recovery."

"As we all do." The commander of Lexia's garrison bowed again, before turning and departing. As he mounted his horse, Alric came up to stand beside her, and they watched him ride away together.

Zhuana spoke without looking at the druid. "We both know what is coming. I also do not trust them. There is something brewing, I can sense it. We must hasten our preparations for war."

"The other druids and I have spoken. As things stand, we cannot provide enough firewater for a lengthy campaign."

She frowned; it wasn't the news she wanted. "What is it you need? Manpower? I can have every man and woman—"

"We need two of the prime ingredients. If we buy any more from the empire's traders, I fear they will grow suspicious."

She thought hard, eyes narrowed until she made her decision. "Do it anyway. The suspicions are there, no matter what we do now. Whatever you need, Alric. Just ask, and I will have every hand working to help you."

"My Queen." The druid bowed.

"Alric?" She was speaking to herself, as much as to him. "I think we both know where this is leading. We must sharpen our swords, fashion our arrows, muster our horses, and ready our armor. We must put a battle plan together, to take their towns and cities, one by one." She wasn't a rash person. She knew exactly what she was contemplating. "The time for war will soon be upon us."

Chapter Forty-One

BETHANY WALKED THE corridors of the School of Divination, heading for her next class. When the hallway crossed another corridor, she spied a familiar distant figure, a gray-clad diviner with a triangular face, neat black hair, and a pointed beard on his chin.

"Diviner Trask!"

She hurried to meet him, calling after him again. Trask glanced over his shoulder and saw her approaching. There was a time when she had been intimated by her teachers, and Trask was the highest ranked. But she wasn't going to wait.

"Ah, Bethany. I have it in my schedule to come and see you at the end of classes."

"I want to see her... Carina..."

His expression changed, becoming surprisingly compassionate. "That is why I was planning to talk to you. I don't have long to speak now, unfortunately." He hesitated. "The fact is, Bethany, there is not going to be an opportunity for you to see her."

"I need to—"

"The decision was made. She is gone, Bethany."

"Gone? Gone where?"

"Back home, with her family. It is regretful that you could not say goodbye, but we have to think of her best interests in a case like this."

Bethany felt her chest tighten painfully. "But... How is she?"

"Physically, she is fine. Mentally... she will need a great deal of time to recover. If, that is, recovery is even possible."

The simple statement made her throat catch, but she wouldn't cry in front of her teacher. "Can she... can she talk? Or write? Perhaps I could get a message to her?"

"At this stage, she needs to think as little as possible about this place. For her own good, it is best that she forgets all about you. I am sorry." He sighed. "I must go. Try to put this from your mind, as difficult as it is."

With a final look of sympathy, Trask continued along the corridor, but Bethany remained where she was.

She and the other students had been warned, time and time again. How many times had their instructors mentioned the potential for danger? And yet... even then, she had never believed that their training might result in something so terrible.

She wiped her eyes, and as her emotions changed, her eyebrows came together as she glared in Trask's direction. Something didn't feel right. What was it? What was it inside of her that made her feel so angry?

She had an idea about what it might be.

✦

"Bethany."

Hearing her name, she lifted her head to see Xander standing over the table. She hadn't been aware of him approaching, let alone watching what she was doing as he stood right over her.

She was in the Observatory's basement library, the special one he had shown her, with books spread out on the table in front of her. Lines of text and drawings of gateways filled her vision. Xander rested his eyes on the books, and then returned his attention to her.

"Bethany, listen to me. We both know that there is nothing you can do to help her. And there is certainly nothing in these books. Do you know the time? Do you realize how late it is? You should be sleeping. Our final test is tomorrow. Just think, Bethany. One more test, and if we pass it, we are both going to be diviners."

Bethany struggled to shift her focus from the things she had been reading. She caught some of his words, something about the hour being late. She stabbed at the pages of one of the books. "I've realized something. It was just a thought at first, but now I know for certain. For all the fuss, the diviners don't really know what they're doing... You see it, don't you? There's a lack of true understanding. What exactly is the path of stars? What are its limits? All we know is what the Korandians told us, and they told it to us over six hundred years ago."

Xander frowned at the books. "Anything else is lost to time. Come on, Bethany—"

"That's exactly my point," she persisted. "If something seems lost to time, we can't just give up on learning about it. Does anyone try to find out who the Eidar were? Where they went? When gateways fail, we can't repair them, we have to find an alternative gateway and build new roads. The fact is, there's so much we don't know. And our lack of knowledge leads to real danger."

He winced, as if her words had hurt him. "I understand, Bethany. That is something we know too well. But that doesn't mean that this is the time—"

"Think about it. What do we know about gateways? A gateway is a collection of nodes that warps the tapestry. It's always heavy, or massive in some way." She stared into the distance. "How do we build a gateway? What is the least amount of weight a gateway needs to warp the tapestry? Is it even about weight, or is it something else?" She let out a breath. "Aren't you frustrated?"

Xander's brown eyes became warm, gentle, and worried. "Yes I am. I feel bad as well. And I miss her too. But you need your sleep. And so do I. Please?"

Bethany knew there were spots of color on her cheeks. Resentment made her want to sweep all the books from the table onto the ground, but instead she began to fold them closed, one by one.

"Remember," he said. "Our final test is tomorrow." He helped her with the books, obviously relieved. "It isn't going to be easy, but we are going to do this, together. Nothing can stop us. You and I, together, Bethany. We are both going to become diviners."

✦

Bethany stood outside the door, summoning her nerve as she finally knocked. It was morning, yet despite the previous late night, she felt anything but tired. Her heart was already racing as she waited.

A crisp voice came from the other side. "Enter."

Recognizing the voice only made her more anxious. She opened the door to find herself in a study, where Diviner Gallow sat at an ornamental desk, a surprisingly beautiful item of furniture given his cold, authoritarian manner. Books filled shelves that stretched from floor to ceiling. Despite the summer heat, the window was closed, making the air feel still and stifling. The desk had nothing on it other than some colorful paper cards.

"Bethany, please sit," Gallow said, nodding at the vacant chair on the other side of the desk. He looked the same as ever as he watched and waited, with his bald crown, face full of sharp angles, and dark, calculating eyes.

After she sat in the chair, there was nothing to look at other than the cards on the desk's surface. There were six red cards, rectangles the size of her hand, and behind them, another two blue cards, all neatly laid out. She guessed that the cards were face down, with something on the other side—something related to her final examination, the test she would have to pass in order to graduate from the School of Divination.

Gallow cleared his throat. "As you are well aware, this is your final test. At other stages, we have offered you a chance to withdraw, to give up, to go home and recover from your training as you choose another path from than that of a diviner." He stared directly into her eyes. "Today, you are not going to be given that chance. You have come too far. You know too much. You will either graduate or you will fail. And failure might mean not just your death, but that of someone else."

Bethany tensed in her chair. She wouldn't just be risking herself. She was going to have someone traveling with her.

"For this test you are going to be traveling with your first ward. As a diviner, people will be trusting you, in your care, with their lives completely in your hands. You have to prove yourself worthy of that trust."

When he paused, she sensed that she should speak. "I understand."

"I hope that you do. Now, outside of desperate circumstances or war, you know the standard guidelines. A diviner must always rest in between travels. And a diviner must open no more than three gateways in a single day. These guidelines are there for a reason, to protect you and those who travel with you."

She nodded.

"Today is different," he said curtly. "For this, your final test, we are completely dispensing with the usual guidelines. Today, you will travel again, and again, and again."

If her heart rate was fast before, now her chest was truly hammering.

Gallow gestured to the red cards with his pale long-fingered hand. "The gateways will be the red cards here. Just like you, I do not know which six cards we have. Their order, which is the order you will visit them, is also random. Shall we see?" He touched the first of the red cards, on Bethany's left. "Turn the card over."

Bethany reached out to tentatively turn the first red card over. She read the crisp, cursive writing.

"The Temple of Darsh in Ganouda," Gallow said. "A difficult first gateway. From there, you will go directly to…" As he pointed, Bethany turned the next red card. "Read it out loud."

"The Arch of the Pilgrim."

"Next…"

Bethany turned another card. "The Wheel of Klare."

"Next…"

Her head was spinning as she discovered her next gateway. "Torvil Temple."

Gallow again nodded down at the surface of the desk. "Next."

"The Hexagon at Sedgeford."

"And finally…"

She turned over the last card. "The Statues of Malange."

"And last of all – it shouldn't need to be said, but just to be clear – you return back here to the Crystal Dome."

Bethany scanned the cards, taking in the locations. From Ganouda to Malange. One temperature extreme to the other. The two blue cards had yet to be turned over. "What about the other cards?"

"This is your final test. There will be no others. It is not supposed to be easy."

"What are they?" she insisted.

He rested his fingers on the two blue cards. "When you first started, we asked you for two names—the two people we might be able to contact if you were in trouble and needed help. Or just someone to take you home in the event that you were no longer pursuing your studies."

Bethany remembered. Her two names belonged to her mother and Charlton.

"Two names," Gallow said. "Two cards. One of them is going to be your ward today. Please. Turn a card over."

Bethany paled. She wasn't just going to be risking her own life, but also the life of one of the two people she cared about most. Gallow continued to watch her with his penetrating eyes. She tried not to show any emotion as she reached forward, picking up the edge of a card, and then quickly turned it over.

The name jumped out at her.

Maryam Sylvana.

She stared at the card. "But she's—"

"Blind and in poor health. It makes no difference. As a diviner, you may be required to guide someone injured or decrepit or even a babe for that matter. Humans, animals—everyone and everything might travel the gateways under your direction."

Stunned, she fell back into her chair.

"You and your fellow students will be departing at staggered intervals. I suggest you meditate, in addition to preparing for your travels. You may take the six cards with you. Please make your way to the Crystal Dome at exactly eight-thirty this morning."

Chapter Forty-Two

BETHANY WAITED UNDER the Crystal Dome's immense lattice. Ahead of her, Xander prepared to open a gateway, with his older brother Jordan just behind him. Jordan looked terrified. He had to place all of his trust in his youngest brother. Xander wasn't expecting to fail, but tragic accidents were all too common.

Xander raised his staff into the air and then brought it down hard, to slam the base on the ground. A dull clank resounded through the area contained by the dome. Xander wove his staff from side to side, picking up pace, and then sliced at the air. His portal opened and he reshaped it to form a tall rectangular doorway. Xander and his brother stepped through the opening. The gateway closed behind them.

After Xander, Bethany waited for the next student, Hesta. The time passed in a trickle as Hesta spent a long time with her eyes closed to prepare herself, and Bethany used the opportunity to remind herself about the properties of each gateway she had to visit.

She turned her head when she heard her mother's voice.

"I trust you, Betani. You can do this."

Maryam rested some of her slight weight on her ebony cane, and if she were apprehensive, she didn't show it on her face. There was a lot more gray in her long copper hair, even compared with when Bethany had last seen her. Her brown eyes were open, but she wasn't seeing what was taking place in the Crystal Dome, and she was still enough that her dangling earrings, like acorns on metal thread, didn't flick from side to side.

"Don't worry about me." Maryam grinned, dimples coming to her cheeks. "I've swallowed enough medicine to make my steps as light as a feather."

Bethany didn't know how to react. "Are you sure that's safe?"

Her mother snorted. "I know what I am doing. Don't forget, I've been taking it for a long time now."

After Hesta disappeared through her gateway, Bethany's heart rate picked up tempo; it was now her turn. She spoke in a clear but low voice. "Come with me. We're about to leave."

Maryam held Bethany's left elbow as they walked together, with Bethany's staff in her right hand. Keeping careful track of the time, Bethany moved slowly until she was nearly under the dome's highest point. Still a short distance from where she needed to be, she stopped.

"Wait here. I need some space to work."

"I am yours to command. You just do what you need to do."

Leaving her mother, Bethany stepped forward, checking over her shoulder to confirm she had created enough distance. She reached a point directly beneath the Crystal Dome, in the center of the vast area.

It was time.

She readied her orb, making sure it was facing the correct way, just as she had been taught. The orb made a subtle click.

Taking a deep breath, she prepared herself. This was her final test. Her mother was with her, and would be with her until the end. She had come so far. She couldn't fail now.

She raised her staff high into the air. *Focus. You can do this.*

She let out the breath she was holding as she slammed the staff down onto the ground. The now familiar stench of tar reached her nostrils as she inhaled.

Her head started to spin.

The world began to hum around her. She allowed herself to feel the tapestry resonating, pulsing like the skin of a drum in the moment after striking. Finding the rhythm, matching it with her staff, she swept the pole back and forth until the staff and the tapestry were in accord.

She sliced the staff down. A flash of light accompanied the motion. A tearing sound reached her ears. The fabric of the universe split and she peeled it open, maneuvering her staff, widening the hole, reframing it as a black mirrored surface, a tall rectangle. A doorway.

A gateway.

Heart hammering, she lowered the staff and turned back toward her mother. Usually a ward would be able to enter on their own, but her mother couldn't see.

"Mother?"

"It is open, isn't it?"

"Yes."

"I'm so proud of you."

Bethany's heart swelled; her mother's words were the last thing she expected to hear. For a moment her vision blurred with tears.

"Now I will walk forward," her mother said, "and you stop me if I'm doing something wrong."

Maryam took one tentative step, then another, until Bethany helped and her mother was able to again take her by the elbow. Bethany guided her to the gateway, until they were both facing it.

"Here we go. Stay with me."

Together, Bethany and her mother stepped through to the other side.

✦

Bethany was in the path of stars, approaching the end of a long, grueling day. In between her travels, she had found herself needing to rest for longer and longer intervals. The Weaver's Breath was taking a heavy toll, and she had already emptied the contents of her stomach until there was nothing left to eject.

But she couldn't rest for too long. She had a deadline to meet. All of her travels had to be completed by sunset in Everlast.

She and her mother had gone from soggy heat in the jungles of Ganouda, to the windswept plains of Klare, and onward to icy cold in the frozen city of Malange. In and out of gateways, Bethany had struck the ground with her staff again and again.

Her mother gave her strength. She wasn't a burden at all, and in fact Bethany was now sure that she couldn't have done this without her. Her mother's voice called her back to reality when they reached Torvil Temple and Bethany fell down to her knees, unable even to speak. Her mother had cradled her head as she laid on her back at the Hexagon of Sedgeford, trying to regain her sense of who she was and where she was and to stop the world from spinning. At Malange, fighting the shivering cold, they had held each other tight as she recovered.

Now, in the path of stars, she looked over at her mother. Maryam's face was blank, like the face of someone sleeping. In this place, she would follow any instruction Bethany gave her. As she walked, Maryam held onto the fabric of Bethany's dress to free Bethany's hands to work with her staff and navigate back to Everlast.

Bethany found the snake constellation. She moved the heavens, sweeping her staff from left to right. The leaf constellation came into focus. Her arms were tired. Her body ached.

"How are you feeling?" Bethany softly asked.

"Tired," Maryam replied. She spoke woodenly, like someone struggling to wake from a deep slumber. In here, there was no dissembling, no hiding the truth. In addition to following Bethany's instructions, she would answer any questions with brutal honestly. "I have a headache. My stomach hurts. My jaw is sore from clenching it. My legs are shaking. I want to sit down."

Bethany blinked away tears. "This is the last one, I promise. It will all be over soon."

Maneuvering her staff, she couldn't let her focus slip, now that she was here, at the end. But by the stars, it was hard. The pain in her head was pounding along with her heartbeat. Her churning stomach meant she had barely enough energy to keep moving.

A star grew bigger, and she pulled it closer still.

Wait. It wasn't her star.

Realizing her mistake, she rotated the heavens again. She couldn't think about how costly the error might have been. If she tried to open a gateway in the wrong place, she wouldn't live to tell the tale.

Her mother. She had to do this for her mother. Maryam had suffered. She had been witness to her own failing health and the one person she needed, her daughter, hadn't been there in her time of need. Instead, Bethany had been at the Observatory, at the School of Divination. Bethany had given so much. This was her one opportunity. She couldn't fail now.

The path of stars pulsed with the same vibration that quivered in her mind. Her chest convulsed and she swallowed, again tasting bile at the back of her throat.

There. A golden star, enlarging to a sun, revealed sparkling dots that grew to become the nearest planets to her own world, Kaspar. She continued to work her staff, making the heavens appear as they would from Everlast a short time before sunset.

This was the last time today she would have to do this. Her test was nearly complete.

She pulled the tunnel's end toward her. With heavy arms, she raised her staff high and cut a diagonal line across her vision. Her limbs were heavy, and she had to try again. Her second attempt was just as feeble. Panic began to set in.

For some reason, the voice in her mind belonged to Xander. *You can do this.*

She sucked in a deep breath, focusing on the long exhalation. She summoned the last of her strength to bring the staff high above her head and slash it down with force.

Relief flooded through her. The air split apart as the gateway peeled open.

"Follow me," she told her mother. "We are about to arrive. Hold my elbow. Now take a long step."

With a tingle all over her skin, Bethany stepped back into the familiar world, careful to bring her mother with her. A familiar texture in the air greeted her. After emerging from the gateway, she immediately recognized the Crystal Dome.

But this time, things were different.

The space under the dome was filled with diviners, men and women, of all ages, colorfully dressed in fine clothing but all wearing matching gray cloaks. All heads were turned Bethany's way; all eyes were on her as she arrived.

She twisted her staff to close her gateway.

Diviner Trask stood just in front of the platform. Along with Trask, there were the teachers of all her classes, from meditation to divination, logic to symmetry, orientation to travel, and finally delirium. Diviner Gallow stood with some colleagues, silently regarding her. Diviner Mei smiled at her; Bethany hadn't seen Mei since their exhilarating synchronized staff work, resulting in Carina accidentally striking Gregor, and she was reminded: neither Carina nor Gregor made it to the end.

And there, up on the platform, was a face she hadn't seen since her very first day at the school. Looking out at her from his high position was an old, stately man with a lustrous white beard, a stooped posture, and an immense star partly visible on his cloak.

High Diviner Garl Azren walked to a gong. Taking the striker, he sounded the gong, and as the crashing sound made reverberations that grew fainter and fainter, he called out.

"Your tokens?"

Bethany reached into a pocket and closed her hand around her tokens. These were the items she had been tasked to collect as evidence, picked up from each of her six gateways. As she held her diviner's staff in her right hand, with her left, she pulled out the tokens and opened her hand to display them. Diviner Trask walked over. He looked down at her open hand, and then turned to nod at the platform.

"Your tokens have been verified," High Diviner Azren said in an ancient but clear voice. He bowed at Bethany, and along with him, all of the other diviners bowed also. "The staff you hold now is yours to keep…"

Stunned, Bethany stared at the staff in her right hand. The staff was straight and smooth, beautifully carved with curling patterns, crowned with an intricate orb of shining metal. It wasn't just any staff. It was hers.

"Congratulations, Bethany Sylvana. You are now a diviner."

Chapter Forty-Three

BETHANY COULDN'T TAKE her eyes off the paper on the desk in front of Diviner Trask.

Written on the piece of paper was her first assignment. She might start by taking people to and from the Nexus, or work for a group of traders needing travel between their outposts. The empire was vast. Officials came and went from the capital constantly.

Diviner Trask rested his fingertips on the paper, and then looked at her seriously. "I can see you want to know." He hesitated, and still didn't lift the paper. "We are aware that your mother is unwell."

She looked at him quickly.

"The cause is in her brain. She is in pain. You must buy her expensive medicine."

A frown tightened her forehead. Why was he mentioning her mother? He was simply stating what surely everyone knew by now.

Trask glanced down at the paper. "This commission is well paid. I was surprised, I must say, to see it. Orders from above. You have performed well in your studies, some would say extremely well..."

"What is it?"

Trask picked up the paper, turning it over and placing it in front of her. There were words and numbers on the paper: position titles, duties, earnings... but it was his next words that seized her attention.

"You have been offered a place in the household of the Conways of Esk."

She couldn't hide her surprise. *A house diviner?*

"Esk?" she asked, confused.

"It is near the sea, in the region of Umber."

"I know where Esk is." The implications began to sink in. "I assumed I would be based here, in the capital."

"You know our adages. One must never make assumptions. Diviner Sylvana, this is your assignment."

"My mother—"

"The pay is generous. There is no scope for change. You have your assignment."

"I don't understand," she persisted. "Why Esk?"

"Clearly, the lord and lady are in need of a house diviner." After a long pause, he continued, "You do realize who the lord of Esk is?" He waited, but she didn't reply. "You have not heard of Kendrick Conway?"

The name was familiar. "Wasn't he involved in a battle...?"

Trask's shaggy black eyebrows came together. "Not just any battle. Kendrick Conway is the hero of the siege of Curran Castle. We hold him in high esteem, here at the Observatory. After all, what he did involved shielding one of us, a diviner, in the face of terrible odds."

She still remained blank-faced.

Trask let out a breath. "If you are going to be the Conways new house diviner, I should remind you of the tale. Curran Castle is built around a gateway, but the diviner was singled out and murdered, and under siege, the people inside were starving. The barbarians relentlessly bombarded the castle, but there were few soldiers inside, it was mainly common folk. There were women there with babes. Young children shaking at night to the sound of crashing boulders. Little boys and girls with stomachs shrunken, wasting away to shadows, uncomprehending why there was nothing at all to eat. Sir Kendrick – he was a knight at the time – gathered some men to break through the siege and get a diviner inside. Half of his force was wiped out but he saved countless people, among them our future emperor, Rigel Regus." He stared directly at her. "And you are going to be his new house diviner."

Even as Trask spoke, she was still struggling to make sense of her assignment.

"Lord Conway will soon be hosting a fielding. It is a momentous event, and will result in the reformation of the Armies of the West. Tens of thousands will gather at the Conways' estate. Knights will be proving themselves. Mercenaries will come looking for work. Lords and ladies of note will be there, all the way up to the crown prince and the emperor himself. Lord Conway has important business. His previous diviner has retired. You have now been chosen. It is a remarkable honor, to be house diviner to a great family."

House diviner...

Trask rapped his fingers on the desk and frowned. "Do you accept the commission, Diviner Sylvana?" He emphasized her new title, which still sounded strange in her ears.

"The Conways... will they have business here in the capital? I assume they will need to come here sometimes?"

"They may or they may not. It is not for me to say what they will need your services for." He leaned forward. "Do you accept? The pay is sixteen silver crowns per week."

The money was enough to change her and her mother's lives. She now belonged to the corpus; she wasn't being given a choice.

She took a deep breath. "I accept."

As soon as she spoke, the realization came: she would now be leaving the School of Divination, packing up her possessions, and departing the Observatory, the Corpus, and Everlast altogether. All of a sudden, Trask became an important ally.

"What else can you tell me about the Conways?"

"Good question. I was about to come to that. You will be representing the corpus, and we can't have the outside world think poorly of our diviners. Lord Kendrick Conway is married to Lady Anthea Conway. They have three children, two boys and a girl. The eldest child is Troy Conway, aged twenty-one. Next is Caden Conway, nearly two years younger. The youngest is Isabelle Conway, aged thirteen. The Esk estate is sizable, to say the least. Perhaps eighty-thousand farmers, craftsmen, and merchants, across six towns and many villages and homesteads. You will be busy." Trask paused, allowing her some time to process what he had said. "You will want to spend some time in the library. The corpus's clerks know everything you could wish to know about the various noble houses."

Bethany was relieved; she had been worried that this would be her one chance to learn about her new role.

"Lord Conway's sons both seek to become knights. Lady Conway is an influential custodian. When she hosts a banquet, powerful people attend and listen to what she has to say. As I said, you will want to conduct your own research prior to your arrival. First impressions are important. You have your assignment. Congratulations, Diviner Sylvana. And good luck."

As Trask climbed to his feet, Bethany stood also; she knew when she was being dismissed. "Thank you."

She took the piece of paper as she left Trask's study. After she closed the door, she stared down at the words and numbers, the position title, list of duties, and the name of the place where she would be living and working: Fernley Manor.

And then a warm feeling welled up from deep in her body, a thrill of excitement and apprehension like nothing she had felt before, not even on her first day at the School of Divination.

Her entire life was about to change.

✦

"The Conways?" Xander asked incredulously. "You're going to be be house diviner to Kendrick Conway? He's famous. You do realize that, don't you?"

"I assumed I would work here in Everlast."

As they sat side by side on a bench, they were the only people in the atrium; the other graduates were all packing up in their quarters. Bethany drank in the familiar sight of the great oak tree, the draping plants on the balconies, the fountain in the shape of a hand. She would have little reason to visit the School of Divination. Would she ever come to this place again?

"You'll be given your own quarters," Xander continued. "If no one travels for a week, you'll be free to study or ride horses." He ventured a smile. "Or meet handsome visiting noblemen."

He said the last words in a strange way. She quickly turned toward him, but he was just the same Xander, mocking her as he liked to do.

"I thought I hadn't done too badly, but for you to be house diviner... by the stars..." He shook his head. "While I'm engaged to the corpus, taking clerics and confessors from place to place, you'll be eating fine food, with servants to change your linen and wash your clothes."

"At least you'll get to see your family."

"Ha." He snorted. "When my brother talks to me again."

"You both made it through, didn't you?"

"Let's just say he didn't enjoy the experience. And not just for the travel sickness. I told him to bring a warm coat but he said he was fine. Then, when we were in the middle of a blizzard and I needed to rest, he kept pushing me to leave before I was ready. Jordan's always been able to tell me what to do, but not this time."

Bethany smiled. But then time passed, and the growing silence began to feel awkward. "Your family must be proud of you."

"They don't say it like that..."

She grinned. "But they are."

He shrugged, and then he actually blushed. "My mother's making me a special meal tonight. I'm just glad I'll be able to help with the debts. Ten crowns a week... it's going to make a big difference."

"It wasn't easy, but we did it together. Like you always said we would."

She didn't mention Carina, but she knew they were both thinking about her.

The silence began to grow again. Xander glanced at her and then looked away, as if he wanted to say something but kept changing his mind.

"When do you leave?" he finally asked. "I have to go within the hour."

"I'm already packed up. I'll be visiting home and staying tonight, and then tomorrow I'll be on my way to the Star Temple at Esk."

"We will still see each other," he said. It sounded like a statement, but there was an inflection at the end.

"Of course."

He moved a little closer to her on the bench. Facing her, taller than she was, he opened his mouth and closed it. Now, she thought he might be summoning his courage to ask her whatever was on his mind.

All of a sudden, she remembered something she had spent a long time trying not to think about. When she had first started at the school, she had been taking the place of his best friend. What would he think, if he knew that her father had done something, probably something terrible, to bring about her change in circumstance?

They both spoke on top of each other, at the same time.

"Bethany, I—"

"You've been a good friend, Xander."

He flinched like she had slapped him in the face. "Friend?"

A new voice interrupted them. "Diviner Sylvana?"

Bethany turned. A stocky woman with a round face, dressed in a gray tunic and trousers, was wringing her hands as she approached.

"Yes?"

"Diviner Sylvana, it's your mother. You need to come right away."

Chapter Forty-Four

BETHANY STARED DOWN into the tea, spoon still held in her fingers although her hand wasn't moving at all. The rippling liquid caught the low light of the dormus's few lamps and showed her something else altogether. In the reflection, there was her mother, crying out as she tripped, unable to stop herself falling, making a clatter as she tumbled down the stairs of Compound 12C. The ebony cane went flying, before bouncing from one stone step to another. The final thud her mother made was gut-wrenching. Maryam ended up sprawled out on the landing, her cheek pressed against the stone. Meanwhile her cane stopped two flights down.

But her mother had been lucky, and other than some sore parts, she wasn't hurt at all. Bethany was now making two teas, one for herself and the other for her mother, who was seated in her usual armchair with her head faced in Bethany's direction.

Forcing herself to move, Bethany took the pair of mugs and carried them back across the living room.

"All I can say is, the sound must have scared the wits out of the neighbors. I wasn't hurt though. I don't know why they told you to come running. Nothing bad happened."

"I'm not going to pretend that nothing happened," Bethany said, unable to keep a sharp spike out of her voice.

She set the mugs down on the low table between the armchairs, before taking a seat opposite her mother. She gently took her mother's hand and showed her where the mug's handle was. "Here. Careful, it's hot."

"It was just a fright. Sometimes I don't think to take the rail. Believe me, I won't be making that mistake again."

"You can't say this was something small—"

"I can and I will. These things happen." Maryam squeezed Bethany's hand and then smiled. "I'm stronger than you think, my love."

Bethany stared anxiously into her mother's face. Maryam was now thin, rather than spry. Her unfocused gentle brown eyes had lost some of their twinkle, but when she smiled, it still creased the corners of her mouth. She kept her graying red hair cut shorter, easier for her to fashion.

Bethany's mother sipped her tea, blowing on the mug's surface, and the little acorn earrings she wore gave off their familiar tinkle. "Now, we have just this one night before you're off to Esk, and we have more exciting things to talk about than my adventures with some stairs—"

"Mother, you need to take this seriously—"

"And I am. Enough, Betani."

Bethany pressed her lips together. Her mother hadn't been hurt in the tumble. But what if she had been? Here Bethany was, accepting the role of house diviner somewhere far away. She was desperate to be here, where she was needed.

At the same time, her new position was the very reason she had been able to buy more medicine, and could firmly give a long list of instructions to Dahlia, her mother's carer. Bethany would visit, as much as she possibly could.

"Now, tomorrow we'll be able to go and collect your new dresses from the shop on Needle Street. I hope you're as excited as I am... their dressmakers are good at what they do. Remember, it's not just the cloak and the staff that will give you respect, as important as they are. Your hair, clothing... it all forms part of the impression you are going to make..."

Bethany turned her head, feeling a lightening of her spirits to see her diviner's cloak hanging from a hook on the back of the dormus's front door, together with the staff that leaned in the corner. Her future now

314

awaited her.

"House Diviner to the lord and lady of Esk," Maryam said, shaking her head. She nodded to indicate the dormus, although she couldn't see it herself. "You don't need me to tell you how proud I am. This must all seem quite small now."

Bethany finally allowed the conversation to move on from her mother's fall. "It isn't about being big or small. This is our home." She reached out to clasp her mother's hand. "Dormus twenty-seven. Level four of Compound 12C. I remember you teaching me when I was little."

"And now you will be living in a manor," Maryam said in awe. "Not just any manor, the manor of a great house, one of the most powerful houses in the realm. By the stars, after the fielding, they will all know who you are. Are you nervous?"

Bethany sipped her tea. "Nervous? I'm terrified. What if I say the wrong thing? I haven't spent any time around people like that."

"You will do just fine," Maryam soothed. "Remember, you are there as a diviner, not as a courtier. All you need to know is that it is not 'm'lord', it is 'My Lord'. The same thing goes for the lady. You will call the children 'miss' or 'master' followed by their first name." Her face became worried. "Oh. I just realized something. The fielding. Your father is going to be there."

"I know. But it's unlikely that I would see him up close."

"One can only hope." Maryam paused for a moment, and then changed the topic. "It's a shame you missed Charlton. He's the one who said there was no harm done in the fall, and you know you can believe what he says."

"How is he?"

"The same as ever. He is a good man. He still visits, at least once a week. The Weaver blessed you the day you met him. He is going to love seeing you before you go. Now, tell me more about Xander."

"Why him?" By now, Xander would have already gone. They had never even said a proper goodbye.

"Because when you told me about the other students, you said his name differently." Maryam gave an impish grin. "Go on. Say it."

"No..." Bethany protested.

"Go on!"

"Xander."

"See!"

Bethany laughed, and she pulled her armchair a little closer to her mother's.

✦

Bethany had washed with hot, soapy water and brushed her long copper hair until it fell shining straight down her back. She was well-rested, and her brown eyes were clear and sparkling. The gray cloak that decorated her shoulders was fresh and new, with the soft luxuriant feel of expensive material. Under her cloak, she wore a brand-new emerald-green dress, decorated in silver stars, snug at the hips and bodice. She had her staff in hand, wooden pole polished, orb gleaming, as she entered the House of Healing on Dyer Street.

Heads turned her way, as the city folk waiting on benches caught sight of her. Mouths dropped open. She tried to ignore them, to instead focus on the door that led to the rooms in the rear section of the building.

Charlton walked out, side by side with a coarsely dressed laborer whose bandaged arm was in a sling. Charlton looked much the same as ever, with his unruly graying hair, worried-looking face, and eyes as blue as the summer sky. He was in the middle of one of his instructional speeches.

"...and keep the wound clean. Come and see me if you see any redness or swelling or you get any fevers. Understood?"

The injured man nodded.

"Listen to me well," Charlton continued, staring into the man's eyes. "You will need to let some of your friends and family help you for a while. Just let them. It is better for everyone that you heal and heal well."

"Yes, Charlton. And thank you."

"It's what I do. Now, then, off you go." Charlton gave the man a squeeze on his shoulder to send him on his way.

Bethany shook her head, smiling as she stood in place. After all her time in the Observatory, it was now even more unusual, to hear a cleric addressed by his first name.

Charlton then turned. He rested his gaze on her.

His eyes gradually widened and his entire face changed. She saw herself as he saw her. There was no mistaking it. She was a diviner, dressed the same as any other diviner, with the staff and cloak to prove it. If anything, her clothes were brand new, and combined with her youth and shining copper hair, made her appearance even more striking.

Charlton just stared at her. He didn't approach. She was trying hard not to, but she knew that if he didn't stop, she would blush. She was conscious of all the sick and injured people on the benches looking her way.

A smile began to creep up on Charlton's face. With all his creases, it was a smile that transformed him completely. She would do anything to make him smile like this.

She found her voice. "What?"

"Bethany." He opened his arms. He was beaming as he came toward her, and then he was hugging her so tightly she almost winced. "I always knew you could do it," he whispered.

She hugged him back, and for a long time they both ignored all the onlookers. Bethany's eyes were moist, but she had them pressed up against the fabric of his white cleric's uniform. Charlton was breathing strangely, tremulously. When he pushed her away, his eyes were wet, but he wasn't self-conscious at all as he wiped them on the material of his collar.

"How was it? Was it hard?" He shook his head. "I have no doubt that it was."

She cleared her throat. "Yes." Even though she was here, acknowledged by a man she loved and respected, wearing the cloak of a diviner, she was still coming to terms with it all.

"You're a part of the corpus now. Like me. By the stars..." He appraised her again. "Look at you." He smiled in his way that made it impossible for her not to smile along.

"Only seven of us made it in the end."

"And one of them was you." He squeezed her shoulders. "What is your first assignment?"

"House diviner."

"Oh!" he exclaimed. "For which house?"

"The Conways of Esk."

"Hold on." Charlton tilted his head. "House diviner to the Conways of Esk?" When she nodded, he stared at her in amazement. "Oh, Bethany." He pulled her in for another tight hug, squeezing her for a long moment. "You will never know how proud I am."

"I won't be able to visit Everlast very often."

"I only know the Conways by reputation. Lady Anthea studied at the University. Lord Kendrick could have been powerful in the assembly but prefers the quiet life. From all accounts, they are good people. You will do well with them."

"I'm leaving in just a few hours. I'm going to miss you."

"You know that I will miss you too. But you always know where you can find me."

"Charlton!" a matronly voice called from the doorway at the back.

"I'm so sorry, my dear, but unfortunately I have to go. I know you will do well. Come and see me again, the next time you're in Everlast. I promise you I will keep a close eye on your mother."

"Charlton!" the woman called again.

Before she could say something meaningful, he hurried away. Bethany stood staring at the closed door he had just vanished through.

"Thank you," she whispered, but only she could hear it.

✦

Bethany planned to fetch her possessions and say a last goodbye to her mother, and then it would be time to go.

It was now afternoon and an angled sun shone down on the crowded buildings of the Fabric District. As she walked, many people around her trudged with bowed shoulders as they reached the end of a working day that had begun before dawn. Loud wooden clatters came from market stalls as they collapsed into sleeping positions. An old man carried a heavy garment bag over his shoulder. A plump woman, evidently a dyer, knelt at a bucket and tried to wash the stains from her hands. A cart rattled past, the bed at the back filled with bundles upon bundles of linen.

Bethany stopped to look back at the House of Healing. Once, she had stood just there, at the side of the road, waiting for Charlton, afraid to go

318

to Speaker's Corner alone. So much had happened since. She hadn't known about her mother's illness. She hadn't met Xander. She hadn't seen her father for years. Back then, she had never met Julian, her half-brother and the heir to the empire, face to face. She was just a young woman working in a seamstress's shop.

Facing forward once more, she lifted her chin and straightened her shoulders. She walked with purpose, and soon she was turning corner after corner, following the familiar streets until her compound appeared up ahead. The people around her might be at the end of their working day, but her work was only just beginning. Before the sun began to fall, she would be meeting the Conways of Esk, in another part of the empire altogether.

She was lost in thoughts of the future as she passed a hooded man with his head bowed as he waited for something at the side of the street. His brown cloak was plain and he looked to be of middle age, with a crisp beard and half a dozen pockmarks on his face. She barely gave him any notice until he lifted his head and reached out a hand to stop her.

"Bethany Sylvana?" he asked. In contrast with his blemished skin and plain clothing, his accent was rounded in the way of the wealthy. He quickly appraised her, from her copper skin and auburn hair to the diviner's cloak and staff. "You have been summoned."

Her heart sank. There was only one conclusion to draw. "I have somewhere to be—"

"That fact is known. Come. This will not take long at all."

Chapter Forty-Five

BETHANY WOULD NEVER have guessed that the innocuous alleyway led straight to a little door, embedded in the towering walls of the Nexus. The pockmarked man in the hooded cloak checked that they were alone, before rattling a key in the lock. The metal door, three inches thick, creaked open, revealing a dark corridor.

"This way," he said, nodding into the passage. "Please. Keep moving."

The corridor was more of a tunnel, with stone above and below. She wrinkled her nose at the wet smell in the air, even as she bent her shoulders to accommodate the low ceiling, and although the tunnel plowed a straight path straight through the wall, it felt like it continued for far too long.

The man with the pockmarked face always kept her moving, and she wondered if he knew who she was, and why she had been summoned.

At last they reached another metal door, and again an iron key opened the lock. The pockmarked man opened it wide to reveal a surprising vista: green fields, manicured hedges, rose gardens, and fountains. He indicated for her to exit and she emerged, blinking in the bright sunlight; she was somewhere in the Nexus gardens. The Imperial Palace rose above the trees in the distance. In the other direction, the spire of the Cathedral of the Hidden Source climbed the sky.

"Come. This way."

The pockmarked man led her along a path between the hedges. Soon, standing within the embrace of a stone wall in the shape of a crescent, an older man came into view.

The tall but slightly stooped man by the wall was her father. He was with a white-robed cleric, a pretty young woman with a heart-shaped face and flowing long blonde hair. The cleric issued some kind of instruction, watching him sip from a goblet before taking the goblet with her as she left him standing alone. Rigel rubbed at his chest, grimacing, but then turned toward Bethany as she approached.

"Ah, there you are." He nodded toward the man with her. "Leave us." He waited until the pockmarked man had gone, before appraising her for a moment, taking in her full appearance, along with her cloak and staff. "Well, well, Bethany. Look at you. It is good to see you. I must say, this clothing suits you well."

He paused, and she had to say something. "Father."

He wore a simple but elegant tunic, and his thinning white hair was neatly combed back from his forehead. There was something about him, though, that was different from when she had last seen him. He was pale. His eyes were usually penetrating, but today they were red-rimmed, with heavy shadows underneath.

"I believe congratulations are in order. I knew you would do well. You are my daughter, after all." He looked at her some more, along the length of his patrician nose, before clearing his throat. "And how is your mother?"

"Well enough—"

He showed her his palm, turning as a racking cough came out of his mouth. The fit of coughing went on and on, and he reached out for the nearby wall to support himself, but waved her away when she came forward. He spluttered and closed his eyes, until at last the bout of coughing subsided.

"Do you need help?" she asked. "You don't sound well at all."

"Age takes its toll on us all." He pulled a white cloth from a pocket and wiped his mouth. "Just a lingering case of congestion."

She paused to allow him to gather himself. "Why am I here?"

"Straight to the point, eh? You remind me of myself. Very well then. You are here to learn the true purpose of your new assignment."

He saw the change in her face, her eyes widening.

"Yes, yes," he said. "I was involved. I thought you would have guessed."

A feeling of dread sank into her chest. She had done it all herself—the studying, the physical work, the emotional exposure, the focus. No one had made her a diviner but her. She had assumed that her new position was also something she had brought about.

But no. He had made it happen.

"Now, listen to me, and listen carefully," Rigel said. "Kendrick Conway has a wife, Anthea. And Lady Anthea has a brother, Declan Quinn, Lord of Graystone, who is on a quest to see my son fall from grace." He paused for a moment. "I suppose I should tell you the full story."

She stared into his eyes. "You arranged the assignment."

He continued without bothering to respond, "I am sure you know of my son's wife, Samara. Many speak of her beauty, and it is fair to do so, but she is a spirited woman who has had an... interesting life. The daughter of Declan Quinn, from all reports, she was something of a rebellious child, and in particular she had a terrible rivalry with her younger brother Bryan. It is said that there was physical contact involved. Hitting. Although I do not know how true the stories are. Be that as it may, her parents decided she needed discipline and put her into a convent school. From which she duly escaped."

Bethany frowned; as her father spoke, despite herself, she was caught up in the story about someone so well known.

"Samara Quinn, eldest daughter of the lord of Graystone, was not seen again until she appeared back in Everlast, years later, after having made something of herself as a dealer in precious gemstones. How she made her wealth, as a single but beautiful woman... well that is the subject of much speculation. Her industry made her many friends here in the capital, and she captured my son's heart—despite my own misgivings, for nothing I said would deter him. Julian and Samara were married. With Samara now a princess, she threw a lavish birthday feast.

And then her brother, Bryan, turned up, having not seen his older sister since she left the family home."

From the grim tone in Rigel's voice, there was more to come.

"Bryan Quinn said many things about his sister, none of them good. And so Julian asked him to the lawn outside and did something very foolish. He challenged young Bryan to a duel. Now, there are different versions of what happened next. Most of them say that Bryan was drunk. Some that Bryan drew his sword, others that it was only Julian. You may not know this, but Julian is a skilled swordsman, which he does not need me to tell him. I believe Julian when he says he only wanted to draw blood and teach the man a lesson. Unfortunately, however, the wound was enough to cause young Bryan to linger for two days before he died at home with his parents."

Bethany gave an involuntary gasp.

"As a result, as I said, Declan Quinn wants my son to suffer. I love my son, and as much as there are elements to his character I question, I wish him a good life. At the same time, Julian has a tendency to stir up trouble, no doubt assisted by his headstrong wife. The Conways will soon be hosting the fielding, as you know, and this fielding is of particular importance. I need you, Bethany, to be my eyes and ears. If any trouble is brewing, I want to know it. From either Declan or my son. You will be close to everything. I simply wish to avoid any kind of crisis." He met her eyes. "Do you understand me, daughter?"

She remembered their last conversation. If she had thought he might forget, she was wrong. He wanted her to spy for him. In his mind, she wasn't her own person; she was his diviner. Not his daughter, or at least, he didn't give her any sign of affection. No. She was his diviner, to use in any way that he pleased.

There was also the conclusion she had drawn that day. He wouldn't live forever. And Julian didn't know who she was. She would eventually be free. In the meantime, she would be making her own allies and building something for herself, her own future, completely separate from her father and his furtive games.

"This man... Declan Quinn... how am I supposed to find out what he is planning?"

"You will be with the family constantly. Kendrick and Anthea will discuss Anthea's brother. The children will talk about their uncle. You may even get a chance to guide Declan as your ward, in which case you could interrogate him while he is in a dream state."

The potential for questioning someone while on the path of stars had never occurred to her. The thought was worse than distasteful.

"As for Julian, his role in the fielding should be a minor one. I want it to stay that way. Remember. You are a diviner because of my influence."

She spoke before she knew what she was saying. "I did it all by myself."

He drew back, surprised. "I am a powerful man, Bethany. Do not displease me."

As they locked eyes, she remained silent. He nodded to himself, as if she had acknowledged his superior status.

"Now, find out what you can, and we will talk very soon."

"And if I don't learn anything?"

"You will."

"What if I learn something but can't get to you in time?"

"Find a way. I am depending on you." He jerked his chin back the way she had come. "Congratulations, Daughter. Now go."

Chapter Forty-Six

BETHANY STOPPED AT the beginning of the sloping path. Knapsack on her shoulder, staff in hand, she took a moment to look over the heads of the people in the crowd in front of her.

The Argent Arch filled her vision, looming from atop its hill, big enough to make her gaze rise higher and higher. The arch was massive and weighty, with a span wide enough to accommodate fifty men standing side by side. Made of granite and veinous white marble, its silver glow lent it an aura of awe-inspiring grandeur as it shone in the afternoon sun. Ancient symbols decorated its surface, some worn to the point of obfuscation, providing a constant reminder that the people who called the empire home didn't build the Argent Arch; it was already here when the first Dymantines came from across the sea. The gateways were made by the Eidar, and who the Eidar were, and why they vanished, was entirely shrouded in mystery.

Everlast's main gateway was always busy, and many of the people around Bethany were joining the queue that climbed the slope. She turned to look back behind her, to where the path widened to become Imperial Avenue, a street broad enough to house an entire army if need be. The Nexus's great gates stood wide open at the end of Imperial Avenue, connecting the palace and the Marble Court to the wider empire. From somewhere within the Nexus's walls, the spire of the Cathedral of the Hidden Source, the tallest point in Everlast, pointed up at the clear blue sky.

After a final frown in the direction of her father's residence, she faced forward once more. Her innate sense of time told her she had come at the exact moment she had chosen, matched to the appointed hour.

Even as she had the thought, bells began to peal in unison.

No matter where they were in Everlast, the bells were perfectly synchronized, whether from the lofty heights of cathedrals or from village temples in the city's outer fringes. There was something strangely comforting about the fact that the entire city of eleven million inhabitants all heard the bells together. Some people would scowl at the sound, others would worry, but most wouldn't react at all. Up ahead, within the span of the mighty arch, a sharp crackle indicated that someone was using the gateway in perfect accordance with the bells all striking the hour. After all, to a diviner, time was everything.

The bells reminded Bethany to keep moving. Staff in hand, cloak on her shoulders, she passed alongside the queue to climb the path toward the Argent Arch. All manner of folk occupied a place in the line: merchants, craftsmen, nobles, and farmers, most of them stoic as they waited their turn. A bearded diviner stood with a lord and lady and a handful of servants dressed in livery. Wagon after wagon waited one behind the other, horses snorting, their drivers hands poised on their fastened brakes, ready to nudge their cargos forward another few paces. A snarl made her focus snap to the side; a bear in a cage was staring at her, kept by a traveling troupe, complete with two pretty women in rainbow-colored dresses with balls that they juggled back and forth.

A paved area surrounded the arch like a stage, where on the hill's flat top, a diviner coordinated the comings and goings. He was perhaps in his fifties, with a long, kind face, green eyes, and a well-trimmed white beard. His name was Diviner Brooks, and although Bethany had never spoken to him, she had seen him many times; given his role, his name was known everywhere in the city. She headed over to announce herself so he could assign a time for her departure.

Holding a board pinned with a number of sheets of paper, Diviner Brooks waved the next diviner forward: a middle-aged woman in a silver star-spotted dress. The woman gathered her two wards, a pair of well-dressed boys, to head straight over to the arch. The people in the queue had little else to occupy their attention, and watched as she opened her portal. Meanwhile Diviner Brooks paused as Bethany approached.

"Diviner Brooks? My name is—"

Diviner Brooks raised an eyebrow. "Ah, look who it is. I know who you are, Diviner Bethany Sylvana, the new house diviner to the Conways of Esk." His green eyes twinkled, lightening his face, even as he waved the next group forward to use the arch. "I have you right here." He pointed to his sheets of paper as he leveled her with his gaze. "Truth be told, I've been eager to meet you in person. As you can probably guess, given the chaos here, I don't get to spend as much time at the Observatory as I might like. There is quite a delay today, but never fear, when I saw you on the list I placed your name right at the front."

Bethany turned toward the queue, which stretched all the way down to Imperial Boulevard. She tilted her head. "Thank you… But surely these people all have important business…?"

Dimples creased the edges of Diviner Brooks's mouth. "I know what I am about, Diviner Sylvana. Everyone's business is important. These are just the usual traders and visitors. The Conways of Esk, on the other hand, are in dire need of your talents. They are hosting the fielding, directly involved with building an army to carry the banner of our great empire." He waved another diviner onward toward the gateway, even as his eyes took on a faraway look. "Ah, the fielding. If only I could go, just to see it unfold. You, Diviner Sylvana, will be in charge of Esk's primary gateway, and when anyone comes or goes, your face will be the first they see. The most important people in the realm are all going to know who you are."

Unbidden, Bethany's father's stern face appeared in her mind's eyes. *Remember, you are a diviner because of my influence.* And she remembered her own reply. *I did it all myself.*

Diviner Brooks cleared his throat. He was strangely hesitant; he had something more to say. "I must confess to something. I was one of the diviners who reviewed the assignments before recommending you to the Conways. I take my work seriously, and I spoke to your teachers myself."

Her breath caught, but then his next words surprised her.

"The Conways are lucky to have you." He lowered his tone. "And what you need to know, and why I bring this up, is that without my recommendation, you would not be in your position, no matter what the palace says or does. Divination is our business, not theirs. Our important work can never be subject to undue influence. Our reputation is at stake."

She couldn't prevent her mouth dropping open. Meanwhile Diviner Brooks glanced at the gateway, and held up a warding hand to the next group, instructing them to wait.

"Now, I believe it is your turn next. Good luck in your new role. You will do well, Diviner Sylvana. We all expect great things from you. Now, go on. Let's not keep everyone waiting."

After his nod, she took her staff in hand, lifting her chin as she strode up to the Argent Arch. She had a multitude of people watching her: lords and ladies, diviners and clerics, people of wealth and influence. She knew enough about the narrow confirmation vote to know that some would be Julian's supporters, while others would be his enemies. Both kinds would be attending the fielding.

She stopped when she was standing directly under the arch, keenly aware of its weight, its size, and more than anything else, its ancient mystery.

Could she keep her two worlds separate? Her father's world, of empire, nobles, and power... and the world of divination, of Xander, stars, and gateways? Her intuition told her no. Her two worlds were going to collide.

She cast her mind back to the demonstration she had witnessed as a girl. Only the most skilled diviners could make light sizzle around a gateway, meaning that the act of opening was something akin to perfect.

Up on a hill, alone, all eyes were now on her. She readied her orb, and then raised her staff high, dramatically over her head. After a steadying breath, she slammed the metal base on the ground. She began to whirl her staff. The time was now upon her.

The crowd behind her gasped, as a rainbow of light, a flame as thin as thread, coiled around the arch, sizzling as it traveled from one end to the other and back again.

She opened her gateway, and with a black mirrored surface in front of her, she stepped inside.

* * *

The Second Book Is Coming!

Wrath and Ruin (The Gateway Saga, Book 2) is out **29 April 2025.**

As the fielding begins, Bethany's new role as house diviner to the Conways brings her into collision with the secrets of her past. Meanwhile, with Queen Zhuana losing patience at the border, will the empire's new army be ready to face her down?

Pre-order on Amazon Today!

Acknowledgements

This novel has been a long time in the making and there is one person without whom I don't believe it would be here—thank you Alicia, my wife and strongest supporter.

And to Mark and Peta: your feedback has been invaluable, and your faith and friendship even more so. Thank you!

Thank you Marcus for the strength and wisdom of your input.

I am extremely grateful to my readers Amy and Amanda, and my wonderful editors Amina and Niki.

A huge shout out to Marc for putting in so much effort and love to create a beautiful fantasy map.

Finally, to my amazing readers: there would be no books without you. Thank you for your support over the years, for your warmth and feedback and for taking the time to leave reviews of my books. We are all growing... we are all learning... we are in this journey together.

Printed in Great Britain
by Amazon

60127042R00201